SLAUGHTER ON THE WESTERN FRONT

. . . It was only after the chaotic skirmish had persisted for ten to fifteen minutes that the officers in charge of the convoy attempted an organized surrender which, after some residual firing, was successful. The SS troopers attempted to induce the Americans to remove those vehicles of their convoy still capable of movement from the road but received no cooperation. The prisoners, variously estimated from eighty to two hundred . . . were herded into an enclosed field along the road . . .

At least eighty-six American prisoners were killed, most, apparently, by machine-gun fire . . .

HITLER'S GUARD

D0752838

HITLER'S GUARD

Inside the Führer's Personal SS Force

James J. Weingartner

BERKLEY BOOKS, NEW YORK

This Berkley book contains the complete text
of the original hardcover edition. It has been
completely reset in a typeface designed for easy
reading and was printed from new film.

HITLER'S GUARD

A Berkley Book / published by arrangement with
Battery Press, Inc.

PRINTING HISTORY
Battery Press edition published 1974
Berkley edition / October 1990

ISBN: 0-425-12305-7

A BERKLEY BOOK® TM 757,375
Berkley Books are published by The Berkley Publishing Group,
200 Madison Avenue, New York, New York 10016.
The name ''Berkley'' and the ''B'' logo
are trademarks belonging to Berkley Publishing Corporation.

PRINTED IN THE UNITED STATES OF AMERICA

10 9 8 7 6 5 4 3 2 1

CONTENTS

.

PREFACE

Hitler's Third Reich presented to the casual observer an awe-inspiring image of monolithic unity. Nowhere was this impression more effectively conveyed than at the annual Nuremberg Party rallies of 1933–39. Who can forget the scenes, still routinely pictured today in freshman history textbooks, of perfectly disciplined masses of men and women marching before their Führer under the swastika banner with a docility and precision which seemed to be the visual expression, par excellence, of a totalitarian society? Always prominent in these pageants were the black-uniformed formations of the SS (Schutzstaffeln), who appeared to march with significantly greater precision and purpose. Their favored position vis-à-vis the sacred person of Hitler was reflected in the body of SS men who accompanied him to Nuremberg (and virtually everywhere else) and in the annual ritual conducted at Nuremberg of consecrating the standards of new party units by sacramentally touching them with the banner carried by the Nazis in the abortive Beer Hall Putsch of November 1923, the so-called Blood Flag, which was always borne by an SS man, Jakob Grimminger.

Yet, the monolithic aspect of the Third Reich was largely illusory. Hitler's Germany was not a rigidly centralized system in which the Führer exercised a monopoly of power but an agglomeration of quasi-independent and often competing power centers presided over by persons bound in ties of personal loyalty to their superiors and standing in what can be best described as a lord-vassal relationship to them. The authority wielded by the vassal was legitimized by Hitler and revocable by him, but the practical result was a fragmented power system which was the antithesis of the popularly held notion of the Third Reich as a monistic political entity. Hitler openly conceded this fact in a speech delivered barely two months after his appointment as German chancellor. "When our opponents say, 'It is easy for you, you are dictator,' we answer them, 'No, gentlemen, you are wrong; there is no single dictator but ten thousand, each in his own place.' "[1]

A combination of three factors offers the best explanation for this situation: first, Hitler's own undisciplined nature and aversion, except in times of crisis, toward the kind of regularized work habits which would have been required by a true system of personal dictatorship; second, the very real advantages offered by minutely fragmented and competing authority which, if it exacted a high price in terms of efficiency, also rendered less likely the rise of organized opposition to Hitler within the Nazi hierarchy; third, the romantic cult of the heroic leader, the glorification of the individual willing and able to take decisive action and willing, too, to accept responsibility for his deeds, rather than the mechanical, uncreative (and often unidentifiable) bureaucrat safely hidden in a cranny within a hopelessly complex power-flow chart.[2]

What was true of the Third Reich as a whole was also true of its elite of violence, the SS. There was, in fact, no single SS (a fact tacitly recognized in the frequent use of the plural *Schutzstaffeln*) but several distinct functional elements (police, concentration camp system, militarized Verfügungstruppe-Waffen-SS as well as the unspecialized General SS) under the suzerainty of Heinrich Himmler, linked together by a vague ideological commitment but each possessing an inner dynamic and following a direction largely its own. This was a phenomenon which was most pronounced within the military wing of the SS, which occupied an ambiguous dual position within the Nazi party and within the German state as part of its defense system.

It may be asked whether such a loose structure is compatible with the concept of totalitarianism. The answer must be "yes." The force which legitimized authority at all levels was Hitler's charisma which could be revoked or redirected at any time with consequences ranging from a simple loss of influence (although the outward trappings of power might remain) to death.

The subject of this book, the Leibstandarte SS Adolf Hitler, is a case study in Nazi feudalism. Leibstandarte was organized on the personal order of Adolf Hitler as a "household" guard with direct links and access to his person (the German word *Leibstandarte* means, literally, "body regiment") through its commander, Sepp Dietrich, who was frequently referred to in terms evocative of medieval imagery ("the Führer's paladin," "knight without fear and without reproach"). In practical terms, Leibstandarte represented an instrument which Hitler could use at any time to reassert his direct authority within the feudal structure beneath him and forcefully revoke his charismatic legitimation as actually took place in the Blood Purge of June–July 1934. Although Leibstandarte remained a part of the SS and, therefore, technically subject to Himmler's authority, in effect it operated outside his effective control.

Leibstandarte played a significant and, in some respects, unique role in World War II. On the purely military level, it evolved into one of the crack armored divisions which formed the backbone of the German blitzkrieg and was usually to be found on the most crucial sectors of the fighting front. Much of this book will be devoted to a careful consideration of its combat role and the leadership qualities of Sepp Dietrich. At the same time, however, Leibstandarte acted as the tangible and militarily highly effective representation of Hitler on the battlefield, a surrogate of the feudal war lord who in medieval times would have led his knights and levies personally against the enemy.

This book has been written largely on the basis of research in captured records both of the German Army and of the Waffen-SS. The author recognizes the dangers of relying on the records of an organization in attempting to write its history but has made a diligent effort to evaluate these sources critically in order to identify and counteract self-serving bias.

Throughout the process of writing this book, the author has remained conscious of the fact that the Leibstandarte SS Adolf Hitler, for all its unique qualities, remained a part of the SS, the organization which willingly carried out the major element of Nazi atrocities, most notably the attempted extermination of the Jewish population of Europe. To recount that barbaric record would be redundant and impractical, although close attention will be given to those atrocities in which Leibstandarte was directly implicated. At the same time, it must be conceded that the members of Leibstandarte fought as brave and skillful soldiers, although that recognition must not be interpreted as approval of the criminal cause in which they fought.

JAMES J. WEINGARTNER

ACKNOWLEDGMENTS

Many are deserving of thanks for their support and assistance in the making of this book. Robert L. Koehl of the University of Wisconsin provided invaluable guidance made possible by his unrivaled knowledge of the SS, while Robert Wolfe of the U.S. National Archives, as well as the staffs of the Bundesarchiv, Koblenz and the Bundesarchiv/Militärarchiv, Freiburg im Breisgau, gave unstintingly of their time in locating vital source materials.

I should also like to gratefully acknowledge permission to quote from the following books: Joachim Fest, *The Face of the Third Reich*, translated by Michael Bullock, copyright 1970 by Weidenfeld and Nicholson Limited, reprinted by permission of Pantheon Books/A Division of Random House, Inc.; Helmut Heiber, ed., *Hitlers Lagebesprechungen: Die Protokollfragmente seiner militärischen Konferenzen, 1942–1945*, Deutsche Verlags-Anstalt; Heinz Höhne, *Der Orden unter dem Totenkopf. Die Geschichte der SS*, Verlagsgruppe Bertelsmann GmbH and Martin Secker and Warburg, Ltd.; Erich Kern, *Die letzte Schlacht–Ungarn 1944-45*, Verlag K.W. Schütz KG; Ernst-Günther Krätschmer, *Die Ritterkreuzträger der Waffen-SS*, Verlag K.W. Schütz KG; Klemens von Klemperer, *Germany's New Conservatism: Its History and Dilemma in the Twentieth Century*, copyright 1957 by Princeton University Press, reprinted by permission of Princeton University Press; Fritz Nova, *The National Socialist Fuehrerprinzip and Its Background in German Thought*, Ph.D. dissertation, University of Pennsylvania, 1943.

Unless otherwise noted, translations from the German are the author's.

Finally, I must record a particular debt of gratitude to my wife, Jane Vahle Weingartner, for her encouragement and assistance at all stages of the project.

I
"Your Honor Is Loyalty"

Violence was an integral part of the Nazi movement, not only as a vehicle for achieving power and preserving discipline, but as a fundamental and, perhaps, the central element of the Nazi *Weltanschauung*. It was the threatened violence of the marching SA Sturm; the psychopathic brutality of the Potempa murder; the glorification of the ancient Germanic warrior, the *Landsknecht*, the Prussian guardsman; and the technically refined violence of the panzer division and of Auschwitz.

While violence permeated the Nazi movement at all levels from the Führer who viewed existence as the successive triumphs of the strong and vigorous over the weak and passive to the SA-Mann who smashed Jewish shop windows, it was the SS which by 1934 came to constitute the Nazi instrument of force par excellence. Unlike the brown-shirted SA, which it succeeded in the summer of 1934 as the chief Nazi paramilitary organization, the black-uniformed SS was relatively small, carefully selected, and highly disciplined. It had originated in 1925 when a chastened Hitler, newly released from Landsberg fortress where he had been imprisoned for his leadership of the abortive Putsch of November 1923, concluded that he required a bodyguard "which even though small, would be unconditionally loyal to me, and would march even against their own brothers. Better only twenty men from a city—under the condition that one can depend upon them absolutely—than an unreliable mass."[1]

So was born the SS (Schutzstaffel). For the first four years of its existence under three inconsequential leaders, it remained small and inconspicuous but distinguishable from the masses of the SA brown-shirts by its members' black breeches, ties, and ski caps from whose crown grinned the skull and crossbones. Its duties had been modest: protecting Hitler and other party dignitaries and, incongruously, selling subscriptions to party periodicals.[2] The great turning point in the early history of the SS came in January 1929 with Hitler's selection for the office of Reichsführer-SS of Heinrich Himmler, heretofore minor party functionary and since 1927 deputy leader of the SS.[3] At the time, the appointment could scarcely have been considered a major one, involving as it did the command of 280 men scattered throughout Germany and subordination to the vastly larger SA.[4] With Hitler's encouragement Himmler completely altered the character of the SS and in the space of four years not only effectively detached it from the SA but transformed it into a second "party army," numbering in excess of fifty thousand men. The SS now began to assume obvious police functions within the Nazi movement and, foreshadowing its assumption of police functions within the German state after January 30, 1933, undertook the surveillance of rival political parties as well.[5] The new SS proved its worth in assisting to suppress the Stennes Putsch of early 1931, in the aftermath of which Hitler delivered to the SS the accolade, "SS man, your honor is loyalty," words soon to be preserved on the belt buckle of every SS man.[6] Concurrently, Himmler began to define for the SS its role as a racial elite within the Nazi movement, a role which was not fully developed and formalized until well after the Nazi seizure of power.[7]

In its functional development and numerical growth since January 1929, the SS lost its original character as a compact security force for the protection of Hitler and other party leaders. The need for such a force had not vanished, however, and became even more critical with Hitler's appointment to the chancellorship of Germany on January 30, 1933. Hence, on March 17, 1933, Hitler ordered the organization of a special SS guard for the Reich Chancellery, an act which may be viewed as a setting aside of a small element of the SS for a return to first principles.[8] More than seven years later, Himmler was to recall that the new guard had been selected from among the reliable "old fighters" of the SS, a category intended to exclude the personally ambitious and opportunistic who began to flood its ranks after the Nazi seizure of power.[9] Such a man was the commander of the new Chancellery guard, SS-Gruppenführer Josef (Sepp) Dietrich.

Even among an elite not notable for its imposing social antecedents or academic and professional attainments, Dietrich's background was remarkably humble. He had been born in 1892 into a peasant family of the Swabian village of Hawangen (an illegitimate birth which seems to have been later legitimized) and, after having completed eight years at the *Volksschule*, had abandoned the agrarian life for a series of menial hotel jobs throughout Europe, evincing thereby if not any remarkable talent then at least a reluctance to be swallowed by the dull repetitiveness of a backwoods society. In 1911 Dietrich enlisted in a cavalry regiment of the Bavarian Army.

As for millions of other Germans, World War I was a pivotal experience in Dietrich's life. In service with the Bavarian Army he displayed an unmistakable capacity for soldiering, which in a less rigidly structured military community might have earned him a commission. Much decorated for bravery while serving in the elite Second and Fifth Bavarian Storm Battalions, Dietrich finished the war, portentously, a sergeant in the thirteenth Bavarian tank formation.[10]

Only the spottiest information is available on the next decade of Dietrich's life. He appears to have served for a time in the Bavarian state police and was definitely a member of the Bund Oberland Free Corps, participating in the fighting against Polish annexationists in Upper Silesia. His first contact with the infant Nazi movement probably occurred in the late summer and fall of 1923 when Bund Oberland, allied with Hitler in the Deutscher Kampfbund, took part in the abortive plot to seize power in Bavaria and overthrow the Weimar government. Like his future superior, Heinrich Himmler, he was present for the debacle of November 9, being placed by later Nazi propagandists "in the front ranks."[11] Unlike Himmler, he did not remain active in the now apparently moribund Nazi movement. Not until May 1928 did Sepp Dietrich join the Nazi party and simultaneously the infant SS, initially combining his official duties with employment as a shipper in the offices of the Nazi publisher, Franz Eher.[12]

Promotions came quickly to Dietrich, particularly following Himmler's assumption of the leadership of the SS. By that time he had already attained the rank of Sturmbannführer (major) and was in command of the SS in Munich, a particularly prestigious and advantageous position in that the Bavarian capital was the headquarters of the Nazi party and its paramilitary adjunct, the SS. The late summer of 1929 saw Dietrich's promotion to SS-Standartenführer (colonel) and his assumption of the command of the Brigade Bayern. Less than a year later, he had risen to SS-Oberführer (senior colonel) and the command of SS Group South, the administrative district embracing Bavaria.[13]

Nineteen thirty was a notable year in Dietrich's career, as it was for the Nazi party. He was placed on the party's slate of candidates for the September Reichstag elections and rode into the legislative body on the first great wave of Nazi electoral success. Never a politician and even less an orator, the stocky, balding and jug-eared Dietrich maintained a mute presence in the chaotic Reichstag, expressing himself only to include his vote within the monolithic anonymity of Nazi bloc politics.[14] The presence in the national legislature of a specialist in violence such as Dietrich was eloquent testimony to Nazi contempt for the democratic institutions of the Weimar Republic.

The SS remained Dietrich's proper milieu, and what must be considered the crucial turning point in his career came in October 1932 when he was appointed simultaneously chief of SS Group North (headquarters Hamburg) and Hitler's personal bodyguard.[15] By that time Dietrich was well known to Hitler both as the successful organizer of the SS in South Germany and as one of the SS leaders who had aided in suppressing the Stennes Putsch two years earlier. During the period between October 1932 and the end of January 1933, Hitler was further impressed by Dietrich's coolness and courage in encounters with toughs of the German Communist party.[16]

Three days after Hitler had ordered the formation of an SS Chancellery guard, initially designated Stabswache or Staff Guard, Dietrich was relieved of his broader administrative duties within the SS in order to devote full attention to his new assignment. The 120 SS men who formed the core of the Staff Guard were drawn largely from Dietrich's former command, the SS of Munich, and were initially housed in Berlin's Alexander Barracks near the Friedrichstrasse Railway Station, less than a mile from the Reich Chancellery.[17]

As an element of the Nazi party armed and trained for the protection of the German chief of government, the Staff Guard occupied an anomalous position and represented one of the early instances of the progressive acquisition of governmental functions by party organs, as Dietrich's SS men gradually assumed complete responsibility for the security of the Reich Chancellery and certain other governmental buildings.[18] It was not the first example, however, of this ominous blurring of functional lines between party and state. Hermann Goering, as Prussian Minister of the Interior, had earlier begun utilizing large numbers of SA, SS, and Stahlhelm personnel as auxiliary police for the purposes of organized terrorization of real and imagined adversaries of Nazism.[19]

An important part of Goering's police organization was sheltered in Berlin's Lichterfelde Barracks. In Imperial times the stark, walled complex of brick buildings had housed Germany's most prestigious military academy, the so-called *Hauptkadettenanstalt*. After World War I, Lichterfelde had been converted into a police barracks, which purpose it continued to serve immediately following the Nazi seizure of power as the base of operations for a heavily armed state police unit under the command of police major (later colonel) Walter Wecke as well as auxiliary police formations controlled by him.[20] It was Wecke's police group which was to be used as a cover for the expansion of the Staff Guard into a sizable party-based military force, one of the nuclei of the wartime Waffen-SS.

In April 1933 Goering lent to the Staff Guard the status of an auxiliary police unit and subordinated it, nominally, to Major Wecke.[21] The advantages of such an arrangement were obvious. The Staff Guard, while remaining under the effective control of Dietrich, Himmler, and Hitler, could now draw upon the resources of Prussia for equipment and training and enjoy the legitimation of its acts conferred by its status as state police officials. Shortly thereafter, the Staff Guard was redesignated with purposeful vagueness and redundancy Sonderkommando Berlin zur besonderen Verwendung (special command Berlin for special purposes), reflecting Goering's obscure definition in April of the Staff Guard's function as "protection of the Chancellor" and "other assignments."[22]

In the spring of 1933 the Sonderkommando Berlin could scarcely have been considered a formidable organization. At the beginning of June, however, two additional Sonderkommandos were formed, Sonderkommando Zossen and Sonderkommando Jüterbog, both place names referring to army training installations in the vicinity of Berlin. To these camps came SS and SA men detached from other units for service with the Sonderkommandos, and there they were given three months of military training under the tutelage of Reichsheer personnel aided by police officials and SS instructors.[23] The acquisition of new personnel took place with great rapidity during the early summer of 1933, not without friction between the Sonderkommandos and the commanders of two other units, many of whom resented Dietrich's high-handed recruiting methods.[24] By the midsummer of 1933 the Berlin-area Sonderkommandos contained some eight hundred men, most of whom remained at the training camps while the core group of Sonderkommando Berlin had joined Wecke's state police unit at Lichterfelde.[25]

In view of the threat which the Nazi paramilitary organizations posed to the traditional role of the German army, the cooperation of the latter in providing instructors and training facilities for the SS seems anomalous. It was contemporaneous, however, with a still greater anomaly. By early July the army had completed a three-month training program for the SA which, considering its greater size and the ambitions of its chief of staff, Ernst Roehm, was seemingly a much more potent threat.[26] The army did, indeed, fear the SA, but during the early months of Nazi hegemony, the possibility of a preventive war launched by Germany's neighbors, particularly Poland, was considerably more unnerving. The army was therefore anxious to construct a reservoir of trained manpower which, while circumventing the restrictions of the Versailles Treaty, could be thrown into the breach in a military emergency.[27] The training program in which the Sonderkommandos participated during the summer and early fall would appear to have been an extension of this program to part of the SS, and while the Sonderkommandos were the only SS units present in the training camps as *units*, individual members of the other SS units were temporarily attached to the Sonderkommandos for training purposes.[28] Much of the training received by the Sonderkommandos was administered by the Eighth and Ninth Prussian Infantry Regiments under the jurisdiction of Wehrkreis III, commanded by General Werner von Fritsch.[29]

The later Waffen-SS thus was born in the training camps of the army in 1933. Certainly, the training received there hardly constituted the Sonderkommandos as professional threats to the army. Their training was superficial, and the equipment at their disposal, the most murderous of which was a few machine guns, fitted them for little more than a brave show and the possible liquidation of unarmed political adversaries.[30] Although technically dependent upon the Prussian Ministry of the Interior through Wecke for supplies, Sonderkommando Berlin soon began to break free of its reliance upon the Prussian police and, hence, from Goering. By the middle of August, Prussia was being reimbursed by the Reich government for expenses occasioned by Sonderkommando Berlin, an important step in the gradual transformation of the SS from a purely party organ to one which shared executive state functions with the army.[31] In this respect Sonderkommando Berlin was well in advance of its provincial counterparts, the Politische Bereitschaften (political alert units), which discharged quasi-official police functions in the other German Länder but which received no support from the central government.[32] The transitional stage was short-lived, for on October 1, 1933, an agreement between the Prussian government and the Reich placed Dietrich's men on the payroll of the national government on the same pay scale as Reichswehr members.[33] The penetration of the German state by Himmler's SS had clearly begun.

While the intrusion of Dietrich's SS units into the German state was a momentous triumph for Heinrich Himmler, it was not without its awkward aspects. As early as September 1933 the Sonderkommandos had been amalgamated at Lichterfelde Barracks under Dietrich's command, and to the eight-hundred-man, armed unit was given the designation Adolf

Hitler Standarte (Adolf Hitler regiment).[34] The title expressed something that had been implicit in the development of the unit since March: namely, that it possessed a unique bond to the person of the Führer and Reich Chancellor through its commander, Sepp Dietrich. While Himmler discharged his dual function as Reichsführer-SS and Police President of Munich in the Bavarian capital, Dietrich had offices in the Reich Chancellery at the right hand of Adolf Hitler.[35] Berliners seemed to assume with some justification that the Adolf Hitler Standarte was a reincarnation of the guards regiments of the kings of Prussia, while Dietrich himself, by virtue of the arrangement of October 1, tended to regard himself as the functionally independent commander of the Führer's guard and only nominally subordinate to Himmler.[36] The impression of the existence of a special relationship between Dietrich's organization and Hitler was reinforced in a ceremony held in Munich on the night of November 9, 1933, the tenth anniversary of Hitler's abortive putsch. By torchlight at midnight drawn up in front of the Feldherrnhalle, Dietrich's guardsmen, renamed collectively Leibstandarte Adolf Hitler, swore an oath of allegiance before the Führer. It was the same oath which was to bind all SS men: ''We swear to you, Adolf Hitler, loyalty and bravery. We pledge to you, and to the superiors appointed by you, obedience unto death—so help us God.'' The oath was spoken personally by all Leibstandarte members to Hitler, while the remainder of the SS was merely represented by SS district and group leaders.[37]

Dietrich had overtly defied Himmler's authority five days prior to the Munich ceremony when he openly declared the Leibstandarte to be an independent organization.[38] As was frequently his practice in jurisdictional disputes among his underlings, Hitler did not interfere in what must be termed Dietrich's rebellion. Himmler proceeded slowly and with some subtlety—in part because he was preoccupied with other important matters, namely, the acquisition of control over the political police of the German Länder. On November 24 Himmler named Dietrich commander of Oberabschnitt Ost (Superior Section East), the SS administrative district roughly equivalent to the old Mark of Brandenburg and encompassing Berlin. Significantly, the appointment was made retroactive to October 1, the day which Dietrich had regarded as marking his emancipation from the Reichsführer's authority.[39] The purpose of the appointment was to return Dietrich to a clearly defined position within the SS hierarchy subordinate to Himmler; and by making the appointment, Himmler was, in effect, conceding Dietrich's point. The wily Dietrich, however, sought to evade the significance of the appointment by refusing to recognize the subordination of the Leibstandarte to Oberabschnitt Ost; that is, Dietrich as commander of the Leibstandarte refused to recognize Dietrich as commander of Oberabschnitt Ost as his superior, hence refused to concede the subordination of the Leibstandarte to Himmler.[40] Here the matter rested until the following spring.

In the meantime the Leibstandarte Adolf Hitler continued to grow. By March 1934 it numbered approximately one thousand men, distributed among four rifle companies, a machine gun company, a motorized company and a reconnaissance company as well as support units.[41] Most of the Leibstandarte's recruits were prior SS and SA members, although police and army veterans supplied a valuable leavening.[42] These men were carefully selected for their imposing physiques, membership in the Leibstandarte being contingent upon a minimum height of 1.80 meters (5′11″), a requirement which, however, had been waived in the case of the barrel-chested, squat Dietrich.[43]

The typical candidate for membership in the early days was young—between the ages of nineteen and twenty-two—with roots in the working or lower middle class. He had joined the Nazi party only recently and, in many cases, had belonged to the Hitler Youth before having graduated to the SS. This initial layer of membership was not significantly removed in the background and attitude from the SS and SA in general whose depredations were generating considerable apprehension among the "respectable" elements of German society during the early months of Nazi supremacy. Affrays with the civilian populace and with other SS men were common occurrences. The officers recruited by Dietrich were of a caliber ill-suited to curb the disquieting propensities of their charges. One Sturmbann (battalion) commander, for example, had been arrested on numerous occasions for assault prior to January 1933 and had served a jail sentence for pimping, to boot. Dietrich's future adjutant had a police record for burglary and theft, some of it of a political nature, that is, supplying party paramilitary organizations with stolen army goods. An instructor at Zossen accused another officer, who was destined for prominence in World War II, of inciting men to insubordination with assertions that Dietrich encouraged "irregularities." If so, the worthy in question was, himself, thus encouraged, for he was nearly expelled from the SS and party for swindling and sexual excess. Significantly, he was taken under the wing of Dietrich's deputy after having given assurances of self-reform.[44]

As yet, this menacing company had discharged in addition to their duties of guarding the Reich Chancellery, Hitler's retreat at Obersalzberg and some public buildings in Berlin, only minor ceremonial functions.[45] Indeed, the external picture of the Leibstandarte presented to the German public in the prewar years was usually one of tall, black-uniformed young men resplendent in polished white leather accouterments posting guard at the Chancellery or marching with admirable precision in public parades. The Leibstandarte's first-class military band under the direction of Hermann Müller-John became a much sought-after attraction at Nazi party functions throughout Germany.[46]

April 1934 saw the establishment of a *modus vivendi* between Heinrich Himmler and Sepp Dietrich. Through the acknowledgment of the subordination of the Leibstandarte to Oberabschnitt Ost, Dietrich formally acknowledged his personal subordination to Himmler.[47] Earlier in the same month, the Reichsführer had placed the capstone on his program of establishing personal control over the German political police systems through his appointment as deputy chief and effective commander of the Prussian secret state police (Gestapo).[48] This appointment may, indeed, have given Himmler the leverage and confidence he needed to bring Dietrich to heel. Nevertheless, the arrangement brought with it important advantages for Dietrich. The Leibstandarte was to be expanded to a level of approximately fifteen hundred men and was given carte blanche to recruit throughout Germany, a significant privilege in that local SS leaders were jealous of authority within their own bailiwicks and anxious to secure the best youths for their own units.[49]

Dietrich's recognition of the Leibstandarte's administrative subordination to Himmler carried with it far-reaching implications for the SS. The SS had secured thereby a militarily trained and equipped unit soon to grow to regimental strength. Further, as an organization which owed much of its effectiveness to the instruction which it had received from the army, the Leibstandarte had set a precedent for future cooperation between the SS and the Wehrmacht on a larger scale.

During the first eighteen months after the Nazi seizure of power, the SA remained the primary instrument of internal terror and control while the German army, operating basically outside the Nazi movement but on the whole amenable to its aims, remained the primary potential instrument of external aggression. Himmler, having acquired control of the German political police and having established the first SS-run concentration camps, had by the spring of 1934 laid the groundwork for a vastly more efficient system of internal control.[50] The crucial significance of the formation of the Leibstandarte and its integration into the SS structure, however, lies in the fact of its potential versatility. Initially organized as an armed unit for the personal protection of Hitler and for ceremonial purposes, it could also be used as an instrument of counterrevolution as well as a portal to encroachment on the monopoly of the army.

The Waffen-SS divisions of World War II, whose roots lay with Dietrich's Sonderkommandos on the training fields of Jüterbog and Zossen, were still far in the future. In the spring of 1934 the function of the Leibstandarte was purely internal and growing in importance, as is indicated by the installation of direct telephone connections between the Gestapo and Dietrich's headquarters.[51] The Leibstandarte was to demonstrate its worth, however, not in the persecution of demoralized Social Democrats and Communists but in the destruction as a significant force within the Nazi movements of the organization with which the SS had long been associated—the Brown Shirts of Ernst Roehm's SA.

2
Execution and Expansion

Ernst Roehm, Chief of Staff of the SA, was a man of far-reaching ambitions, but there is no evidence that he seriously intended to lead a coup against Adolf Hitler. Nevertheless, the random acts of terror performed by his Brown Shirts and Roehm's open desire to submerge the army in the much larger numbers of the SA made him an acute embarrassment to Hitler. The acceptance of the Nazi movement by "respectable" elements of German society and the cooperation of the army were critical for a completion of Hitler's victory of January 1933 and for the pursuit of an energetic foreign policy.[1]

After much vacillation, Hitler, urged on by Himmler and Goering, made the decision to remove Roehm and much of the SA leadership and thus destroy the SA as a threat to the stabilization of the Nazi revolution.[2] Simple expulsion from the party would not have been sufficient and might well have added to the danger. Roehm's charismatic influence over the SA was too great to have been broken by so feeble an expedient. A trial based on trumped-up evidence of treason was also a possibility that may have been rejected as impractical. Even were the desired verdict handed down, the trial would have been necessarily protracted and would have involved the exposure of the many scandals the party had hidden. Roehm and his companions were therefore to be murdered in a carefully planned and suddenly executed blow.[3] The task was to be carried out by the SS.

Himmler, Reinhard Heydrich, and Hermann Goering prepared lists of those to be liquidated. Others had lists too, and

many besides Roehm and his associates were to fall, the victims of personal grudges. Heydrich, chief of the Prussian
Secret State Police Office and head of the Security Service
(SD) of the SS, forged documents attesting to Roehm's trea-
sonous intent, and this "evidence" was brought to the attention of the army leadership, assuring its acquiescence and
cooperation.[4]

As the best-equipped and best-trained element of the SS,
Leibstandarte was designated to carry the brunt of the murderous strike. Perhaps in order to lull the SA leadership into
a sense of false security, Leibstandarte was sent on leave for
part of the month of June. On the twenty-third a practice alert
was ordered for June 25. The same day, conferences between
the SS regional commanders and Himmler began in Berlin.[5]
Two days later Dietrich visited the Reichswehr Ministry and
requested supplemental arms for a "secret and very important assignment" ordered by Hitler.[6] On the following day
all companies were required to submit the addresses and telephone numbers of officers and men still on leave. On the
twenty-ninth all leaves were cancelled. Leibstandarte was
placed on alert late that night, by which time Dietrich had
already joined Hitler for further instructions at Bad Godes-
berg. Shortly thereafter, two companies of Leibstandarte left
Berlin by train for Kaufering, west of Munich, there to ren-
dezvous with their commander.[7]

Dietrich and his forces had been expected to join Hitler for
a surprise descent on Bad Wiesee, the resort where Roehm
and his associates were spending a holiday. Due to wet and
slippery roads and the necessity of refueling along the way,
Dietrich's convoy was delayed.[8] In the meantime, Hitler and
a small party proceeded by Junkers 52 from Bonn to Munich's Oberwiesenfeld airfield and by automobile to Bad
Wiesee, arriving there at around 6:30 on the morning of June
30.[9] The move, unsupported by Leibstandarte, was a rash
one, for Hitler and his party narrowly avoided a confrontation
with Roehm's bodyguard. Nevertheless, Roehm and his associates were successfully seized and brought to Munich's
Stadelheim Prison.[10]

Dietrich presented himself before Hitler shortly after noon
at the Brown House. Around five o'clock in the afternoon,
the Führer ordered him to select a firing party from among

his men and to proceed with them to Stadelheim Prison, there to liquidate six SA leaders whose names made up a list given him by Martin Bormann, Chief of Staff to Rudolf Hess. Dietrich chose "six good shots" and departed.[11] He was not comfortable with his assignment—some of the victims were well known to him as comrades of the *Kampfzeit*—but he dutifully overcame his pangs of conscience. Early in the evening, the six fell before a Leibstandarte firing squad in the courtyard of the prison; Roehm himself was murdered in his cell on the following day by Theodor Eicke, Commandant of Dachau concentration camp, and his aide, Michael Lippert.[12] Most of the Leibstandarte Adolf Hitler had remained behind in Berlin, but these men had not been idle. Hermann Goering oversaw the murders in Prussia, and the carnage there seems to have been much greater than in Bavaria. Dietrich had left SS-Sturmbannführer Martin Kohlroser in command of the units in Lichterfelde, and he had assembled special temporary units, some probably as execution squads, others, perhaps, as defenses against possible SA countermeasures. One of these, a machine-gun unit, was placed at the disposal of the Gestapo while another, composed of two light machine guns and their crews plus six riflemen, was given to Heydrich's SD.[13] According to the official list of victims, fourteen were shot in Lichterfelde Barracks, including the Berlin SA leader, Karl Ernst. Shootings continued in the barracks courtyard until the predawn hours of July 2, at which time Hitler ordered the killing halted.[14]

It is impossible to determine the precise number of Leibstandarte members that actually participated in the killings of June 30–July 2. On July 5, however, twenty-five men including Dietrich, who was promoted personally by Hitler to Obergruppenführer (lieutenant general), received advancements in rank for "distinguished service" during the purge and later were presented commemorative daggers by Himmler. All members were ordered to remain silent concerning the murders and were threatened with harsh punishments for breaches of secrecy.[15]

The purge was not the only event to capture headlines in July 1934. On the twenty-fifth, the Austrian chancellor, Engelbert Dollfuss, was assassinated by a band of Austrian SS men in an ill-planned attempt to execute a Nazi *coup d'état*.[16]

Hitler officially denied the complicity of his regime in the plot although his sympathy with the aims of the affair is difficult to doubt. If Hitler was not aware of what was being planned, others in the regime, including Himmler, certainly knew.[17] Austrian SS men, including members of the Standarte 89 who murdered Dollfuss, had been given training in Germany since the summer of 1933.[18] Leibstandarte was also given a role in the abortive coup. At the time of the assassination, a small unit of thirty-two men under the command of an Austrian citizen, SS-Obertruppführer Fritz Zechmeister of the Leibstandarte's Third Company, was being held in readiness at Dachau.[19] Under the temporary authority of SS-Brigadeführer (brigadier general) Alfred Rodenbücher, who had been occupied in training the Austrian SS since the previous summer, Zechmeister's detachment was made up of communications, machine-gun, and transport specialists. These men were to have been sent into Austria, apparently in the event of the success of the initial stages of the coup, and probably were intended to act as technical advisors to the Austrian SS.[20] That they remained at Dachau was due to the swift and effective measures taken against the conspirators by the Austrian authorities.

The events of June and July 1934 marked another turning point in Leibstandarte's course of development. Roehm was replaced as chief of staff of the SA by Viktor Lutze, a weak personality who owed his new position entirely to Hitler.[21] The last bonds linking the SS to the SA were now severed, and Himmler's black-uniformed army emerged as the primary party instrument of violence, responsible directly to Hitler; Leibstandarte's role in the purge had clearly demonstrated to Himmler and Hitler the value of a militarily armed and trained branch of the SS. The Reichswehr, too, had reason to be grateful to the SS. Roehm and his dangerous ambitions had been the Army's chief concern, and the purge had been brought about with only minimal involvement of the army. It must have regarded the training given Leibstandarte, in retrospect, as an excellent investment. Concurrently, Dietrich and the Leibstandarte had become irrevocable parts of a criminal organization whose later deeds were to make the murders at Stadelheim and Lichterfelde fade into near insignificance. The teleological relationship between the purge and the genocidal acts of World War II was recognized by Himmler nine years later in a speech on the SS role in the war delivered to high SS leaders at Posen: "We did not hesitate on June 30, 1934, to do the duty we were bidden and stand comrades who had lapsed up against the wall and shoot them. . . . We have never discussed it among ourselves. . . . It appalled everyone, and yet everyone was certain that if it is necessary and such orders are issued, he will do it again."[22]

By the end of July normal activity was restored to Lichterfelde. In preparation for the earlier-planned expansion, members were urged to encourage young SA, SS, or senior Hitler Youth members to apply for membership.[23] As yet, no formal racial standards were imposed for admission, although by 1935 all aspiring SS men would be required to undergo rigorous racial examinations and submit elaborate ancestral charts.[24] Prior to the purge, plans for spending another summer in training with the army at Jüterbog had been made and were only temporarily interrupted by the events of late June and early July. New recruits departed for Jüterbog during the last week in July and remained there until mid-October.[25]

The growth of Leibstandarte was part of a broader expansion of the armed elements of the SS. As the early history of Leibstandarte had indicated, the army was not opposed in principle to a militarily armed and trained party organization as long as it remained relatively modest in size and the army's primacy as weapons bearers of the nation remained unaffected. On July 5, 1934, with the destruction of the SA as a threat to this primacy still fresh in mind, the malleable defense minister Werner von Blomberg offered the SS a quantity of arms sufficient to equip a division;[26] and in the early fall an agreement formalizing the status of the militarized SS was concluded among Hitler, Himmler, and von Blomberg. The resulting document placed emphasis on the militarized SS (now designated SS-Verfügungstruppe or "disposal troops" in the sense of their being at the disposal of the regime) as an instrument for the preservation of internal order, although the possibility of its commitment on the battlefield in wartime was also envisioned. The decision as to the Verfügungstruppe's wartime sphere of employment was reserved to the Defense Ministry.[27] This appeared to be a substantial concession to the army but would become meaningless when in

February 1938 the Defense Ministry was abolished and its functions assumed by the OKW (Oberkommando der Wehrmacht) under the servile Keitel. Two new militarized SS units of roughly regimental strength, later to be designated *Germania* and *Deutschland*, and a communications detachment were planned.[28] These formations were manned by members of the General SS, Politische Bereitschaften, and state police veterans, and they, together with Leibstandarte, were to constitute the Verfügungstruppe; but it was clear from the outset that Leibstandarte was to occupy a favored position. Only Dietrich's unit was to be permitted a staff organization to coordinate its three infantry battalions, while the other two units were at first so loosely organized as to be regiments in name and numbers only. Only Leibstandarte was permitted to recruit throughout Germany, while the new units were limited in this respect to their own army corps area.[29] The army, however, was to govern the flow of recruits into the Verfügungstruppe, sell to the SS the arms necessary to equip it, and provide it with training directives. As had long been the arrangement with Leibstandarte, Verfügungstruppe personnel were to be paid by the Reich Ministry of the Interior.[30]

In one important respect the SS struck out on its own. In place of the haphazard training programs for officers which Leibstandarte had previously conducted, formal officer academies were now to be established, first at Bad Tölz and shortly thereafter at Braunschweig.[31] Even though the Defense Ministry claimed the right to approve the budgets of these so-called *Junkerschulen*, the schools, at least during the prewar period, not only trained officer candidates for the Verfügungstruppe but for the General SS, the police and security service, and the Totenkopfverbände (concentration camp guards units) as well.[32]

Perhaps the most significant feature of the agreement was that Dietrich's subordination to Himmler was now formalized in an arrangement to which Himmler, von Blomberg, and Hitler were parties. The Defense Ministry was to deal only with Himmler's staff in matters relating to the Verfügungstruppe, and it was Himmler's staff that ordered equipment from the Defense Ministry and therefore controlled its flow to subordinate units.[33] This is not to say that Dietrich was rendered a docile tool in the hands of Himmler; he was to remain throughout his career the *enfant terrible* of the SS leadership—an elemental force with which Himmler never seemed quite comfortable.

If the fall of 1934 had brought new restrictions and a more rigidly structured *modus operandi* to the Leibstandarte, it also saw the departure of Goering's police from Lichterfelde Barracks. Lichterfelde, Dietrich, and the Leibstandarte now came to symbolize the rugged but wholesome life of the National Socialist soldier. Memories of the firing squads in Lichterfelde's courtyard and the miserable wretches who had trembled in its coal cellar awaiting their turns at the wall were masked if not eradicated by picture spreads in illustrated magazines depicting blond-haired and apple-cheeked young men cheerfully going about the barracks routine.

In Sepp Dietrich, Leibstandarte had a colorful personality in contrast to the relatively unknown, if technically more competent Felix Steiner and Karl Maria Demelhuber, who were to emerge in 1935 as the commanders of the Deutschland and Germania regiments, or the reserved and pinch-faced Prussian, Paul Hausser, former army staff officer and major general, first commandant of Junkerschule Braunschweig and in October 1936, Inspector of the SS-Verfügungstruppe.[34] Dietrich had a passion for hunting and auto racing and was sought after by the Daimler-Benz and Auto Union motor companies as a driver for their cars in road races.[35] As a result of his experience with the primitive tanks of World War I, he fancied himself an expert on mechanized warfare and occasionally offered ill-appreciated advice to the army in these matters. He frequently accompanied Hitler on maneuvers and on inspections of military installations, remaining throughout the prewar years a member of Hitler's entourage.[36]

Sepp Dietrich's *Landsknecht* personality, combined with a rough intelligence and a sense of intense loyalty to Hitler, explains his rise to a moderately lofty status in the Nazi hierarchy. At the same time, he was able to develop and maintain the loyalty of his subordinates with a degree of success which characterizes him as a first-class leader of men. A visitor to Lichterfelde Barracks once described a tour of the compound in Dietrich's company and emphasized the affection with which the men greeted their commander and the concern which he, in return, evinced for their personal welfare. When the visitor remarked on the glow in the men's eyes when they saw their commander, Dietrich replied simply, "Well, yes, it makes them happy when they see me."[37] He often dined in the enlisted men's mess hall, and when a rebellious recruit on one occasion threw his rifle at a noncommissioned officer and the latter hurried off to file a report on the incident, Dietrich disciplined the noncom for cowardice while permitting the recruit to go unpunished.[38]

Lichterfelde Barracks was developed by Dietrich, with Hitler's encouragement, into something of a military showplace, the home of "a spirited example of a National Socialist *Kampfgemeinschaft* [combat association]."[39] One entered the barracks from a pleasant, tree-lined street. Flanking the main gate were two heroic-sized statues of German soldiers in overcoats and coal-scuttle helmets, standing at parade rest. The buildings which made up the Lichterfelde complex were constructed within a huge, walled rectangle. At each corner of the rectangle were the large dormitory blocks which housed the men, these having been designated "Adolf Hitler," "Horst Wessel," "Hermann Goering," and "Hindenburg." The interior of the rectangle was dominated by a large building containing classrooms and other instructional facilities; south of it was the barracks chapel to which the civilian population of the Berlin suburb of Lichterfelde-West was admitted for Sunday and holiday services.[40]

The two kitchens and the cavernous mess hall could feed seventeen hundred men at a sitting. Here, enlisted men dined surrounded by walls on which were hung paintings depicting the history of the Nazi movement. The heart of the barracks, however, was the *Führerheim* (officers' home). Dietrich's offices were located here, and here too his officers dined and held their revels. The dining hall was appropriately dominated by an enormous oil portrait of Hitler which had been set into the wall and topped by a handwrought metal flying eagle. The reception hall was the aesthetic center of the barracks. It was furnished with pieces beautifully fashioned of natural oak, and one section of the wall was covered with Nordic runes inlaid in silver along with their translations. Other areas were hung with photographs of Leibstandarte officers as well as those of leaders of the party and state, including identically sized portraits of von Blomberg and Himmler. A huge fresco depicted the deeds of German arms from Hermann the Cheruscan through Frederick the Great, von Moltke to—presumptuously and prematurely—the Leibstandarte SS Adolf Hitler.[41]

In addition, Lichterfelde Barracks contained riding stables, spacious exercise fields, an indoor swimming pool, a two hundred meter underground shooting range and a mammoth garage provided with the most modern equipment. While enlisted men lived in the barracks, two hundred modern apartments were constructed nearby on the Teltower Strasse for married officers and noncommissioned officers.[42]

Lichterfelde Barracks acquired an international reputation as the last word in modern military installations. A Chinese mission to Europe pointedly requested permission to visit the barracks during their stay in Germany; and Himmler, as host to an Italo-German conference on police affairs in 1935, held an elaborate banquet at Lichterfelde Barracks ''in order to give the guests the best impression of the SS.''[43]

During the period between the summer of 1934 and the outbreak of war in September 1939, Leibstandarte settled into an essentially passive routine. The primary responsibility of Dietrich's unit remained the protection of Hitler's person, and elements of Leibstandarte were always on duty at the Reich Chancellery and at Hitler's retreat at Obersalzberg where, clad in white vests and black trousers, they also waited on the Führer's table.[44] Appointment to guard duty at the Chancellery rotated frequently among the constituent units of Leibstandarte, while companies were exchanged between Berlin and Obersalzberg at intervals of about two months.[45] Facilities for housing the guard at Obersalzberg were at first meager, for part of it was quartered at the inn *Zum Türken* in the town. Later, however, commodious barracks were constructed within the compound.[46] A sizable body of the Leibstandarte usually accompanied Hitler on his travels. Before the Führer departed for Bayreuth on a ten-day visit with Winifred Wagner during the Wagner Festival of July 1936, for example, Sepp Dietrich preceded him in order to ascertain the accommodations and provisions for dining planned by Frau Wagner, and when Hitler arrived, he was accompanied

by a guard of sixty men and nine commissioned and noncommissioned officers.[47]

Included on Leibstandarte's roster were Hitler's chauffeurs,
Julius Schreck and Eric Kempka, and his personal pilot,
Flight Captain (and SS-Standartenführer) Hans Bauer.[48]
Kempka, later the author of a sensational account of Hitler's
last days, joined Hitler's entourage as a reserve chauffeur,
although he was also included for a time on the roll of Leibstandarte's 2nd Company, and became primary chauffeur
upon the death of Julius Schreck in 1936.[49]

Only rarely in the long interim between July 1934 and September 1939 did Leibstandarte perform duties other than those
of a palace guard in both the decorative and functional sense.
For a brief period following the Roehm purge, Dietrich's men
guarded the infamous Columbia Haus detention center in Berlin and later aided the Gestapo in the destruction of gathering
places for homosexuals in the Berlin area.[50] Since Leibstandarte members frequently served as orderlies at state recep-
tions and banquets, they were well situated to eavesdrop on
the conversations of guests and were instructed to attempt to
gather information in this fashion.[51]

Yet, the original purpose of Leibstandarte as an instrument
of violence at Hitler's personal disposal was not forgotten.
The conspirators who plotted to overthrow Hitler in the fall
of 1938 identified the Leibstandarte SS Adolf Hitler as a major obstacle to be overcome and assigned to General Eric
Hoepner's First Light Division the task of blocking Leibstandarte's access to Berlin.[52] Foreshadowing the role which it
was to play in Hitler's war of aggression, Leibstandarte had
been the first German unit to enter the Saar district in March
1935 following the plebiscite conducted by the League of
Nations[53] and later with other elements of the SS-
Verfügungstruppe took part in the occupation of Austria, the
Sudetenland, and Bohemia-Moravia. Masked by the ostenta-
tious public display of the prewar years, however, was a process of intensive technical and ideological preparation which
laid the groundwork for Leibstandarte's spectacular career in
World War II.

3
Definition and Indoctrination

The functional vagueness clouding the image of the Leib-standarte in the prewar years was shared by the other formations of the SS-Verfügungstruppe. Between 1934 and 1935 several efforts were made to define the purpose of these units, but all of them left considerable room for political maneuvering. It is likely that Hitler and Himmler purposely avoided a strict definition which would have limited the Nazi leadership's flexibility in employing the Verfügungstruppe. No less crucial a consideration was that of reassuring the army that there did not lurk in the SS a threat to it more potent than that which had been destroyed in June–July 1934.

Hitler issued a secret order on February 2, 1935, "in order to remove the existing doubt concerning the organization of the SS-Verfügungstruppe":

1. The SS-Verfügungstruppe is to be made up of three SS Standarten [regiments] including the Leibstandarte SS Adolf Hitler, one engineer battalion and one communications battalion.

2. Each of the three Standarten is to have a reconnaissance platoon of two medium and four light armored cars for the purpose of combatting internal disturbances.

3. The formation of artillery units and a reconnaissance detachment remains in abeyance.

4. The organizational unification of the units of the Verfügungstruppe is foreseen.

5. Directives for the material outfitting and recruitment for
the SS-Verfügungstruppe will be issued by the Reichswehr
Minister.

In time of war:

1. The SS-Verfügungstruppe will be incorporated into the
army. They are then subordinated to military laws which
also apply to matters of recruitment.

2. The Verfügungstruppe is to constitute a division. The
army will supply artillery, staffs and other special formations which are lacking in peacetime. The preparation of
the Verfügungstruppe for employment in war will proceed
even in peacetime under the responsibility of the Reichswehr Minister to whom they are subordinate in this respect.

Adolf Hitler[1]

The decree suggests an organization whose purpose is to act
as an armed reserve for the defense of the regime in time of
peace while preparing itself for combat employment in wartime. It is envisioned that the Verfügungstruppe will be removed from the "home front" at the very moment when
internal unrest might seem most likely—and certainly most
dangerous—when the state is at war. In a totalitarian system,
there may be no time when rebellion is less likely, but this
was far from clear to the Nazis and to Himmler himself who
appears to have been hagridden by visions of another "stab
in the back" in the fashion of 1918.[2] However, Hitler had
dealt with this difficulty in an earlier pronouncement which
had provided for a special twenty-five-thousand-man SS "police reinforcement" to be effected upon the outbreak of war
for purposes of maintaining internal security.[3]

By stressing the police functions of the Verfügungstruppe
in peacetime and their subordination to the army in time of
war, Hitler may have been simply seeking to insure the cooperation of the army in the training and outfitting of this
nucleus of a party army. A commitment to give the Verfü-

gungstruppe into the hands of the army in wartime could be readily and with impunity revoked under the stress of war, and Himmler clearly envisioned this possibility. The Reichsführer regarded, in fact, a blooding of the Verfügungstruppe at the front as essential to their efficacy as an internal security force in wartime, for only thus would they earn the respect requisite to protect the regime against a second *Dolchstoss*.[4] During the course of World War II, elements of Leibstandarte were always present in Berlin and Obersalzberg, and personnel were rotated between these home duty stations and the contingents fighting at the front. Quite probably, Hitler always intended to use the Verfügungstruppe, including his own Leibstandarte, in whatever way seemed to be suggested by the exigencies of the hour but did not declare his intentions openly until 1938 after the army had quietly submitted to the degradation of von Blomberg and von Fritsch, indicating that he had little to fear from that quarter. In August 1938 Hitler redefined the role of the Verfügungstruppe in wartime:

The employment of the SS-Verfügungstruppe in case of mobilization is twofold:

1. By the commander-in-chief of the army within the framework of the army. They then are subordinate exclusively to military laws and regulations but remain politically an arm of the Nazi party.

2. In time of internal emergencies according to my orders. They are then subordinate to the Reichsführer-SS and Chief of the German Police.

I reserve to myself the decision as to the time, strength, and form of the incorporation of the SS-Verfügungstruppe into the army at the time of mobilization, according to the then-existing internal political conditions.[5]

Whether in war or peacetime, it was only in the case of Leibstandarte that the identity of the Verfügungstruppe as an armed force at Hitler's personal disposal was fully developed. Sepp Dietrich requested training facilities for Leibstandarte, literally Hitler's palace guard, near Berlin in accordance with the ''will of the Führer,'' so that the unit could be ready for action at a moment's notice.[6] This physical proximity to Hitler and the personal ties which bound Dietrich and the Führer frequently permitted the head of Leibstandarte to ignore his formal subordination to Himmler's SS empire. The embarrassment which this situation caused the Reichsführer and his impotence to arrest it are eloquently conveyed in a plaintive letter written by Himmler to Dietrich in March 1938:

> Your officers are so gracious as to honor me personally, but otherwise the Leibstandarte SS Adolf Hitler is an undertaking for itself which does what it wants and which doesn't need to trouble itself about superior orders [and] which thinks about the SS leadership only when some debt or other, which one of its gentlemen has incurred, has to be paid or when someone who has fallen in the mud has to be pulled out of the mess.
>
> Please do not forget that what you do as first commander of the Leibstandarte SS Adolf Hitler will naturally be taken as right by the next twenty commanders. I do not believe that you have adequately considered that this would be the beginning of the end for the SS in future years.[7]

It would appear that Hitler actively encouraged Dietrich's spirit of independence. In July 1938 Himmler reproached Dietrich for admitting into the Leibstandarte youths who had not completed the six months of labor service which, since June 1935, had been required of all young German males. The commander of Leibstandarte, however, cited a directive issued by Hitler during the previous year and about which Himmler apparently knew nothing, which permitted Leibstandarte to ignore the labor service requirement in recruiting new members.[8] So pronounced was the degree of Dietrich's independence from the SS command structure that the Inspector of the SS-Verfügungstruppe, Brigadeführer Paul Hausser, threatened to resign his office and suggested to Himmler, no doubt maliciously, that Dietrich be made commander of the entire SS-Verfügungstruppe.[9]

The favored position of Leibstandarte was reflected in its course of development during the prewar years. By the fall of 1934, it had grown to roughly regimental strength with about 2500 men distributed among three battalions of three infantry companies and a machine gun company each.[10] The two additional Verfügungstruppe regiments which had been launched in the fall of 1934, approximately matched the strength of Leibstandarte by the end of 1935 and remained equal in manpower through most of 1936.[11] Leibstandarte then advanced rapidly until, by the fall of 1937, it fielded a strength of 3622 men compared to Deutschland's 3161 and Germania's 2621.[12] By the end of 1938 the disparity in numbers was even more pronounced. Leibstandarte essentially preserved its strength of the previous year, while Deutschland had fallen to 2850 and Germania to 2448.[13] The widening gap was due to the fact that Deutschland and Germania had contributed part of their strength to a fourth Verfügungstruppe regiment, Der Führer, which had been organized in the wake of the Anschluss and was made up largely of former Austrian citizens. Dietrich, apparently, had contributed very little of his unit, which was one of the reasons behind Hausser's threat of resignation. The strength of Der Führer by the end of 1938 was 2418 men.[14]

The wartime relationship of Leibstandarte to the rest of the Verfügungstruppe remained unclear throughout the prewar years. In February 1938 Hitler had again declared that Leibstandarte, Deutschland, and Germania would form an SS division along with a communications battalion and an engineer battalion.[15] Already, however, Leibstandarte had been marked out for motorization and moved far ahead of Deutschland and Germania in this respect during the prewar years.[16] Hitler himself had forbidden the numerical amalgamation of Leibstandarte as "Regiment 1" of the envisioned three-regiment SS division. Deutschland was designated "SS-Regiment 1," Germania, "SS-Regiment 2," and later Der Führer, "SS Regiment 3," but Dietrich's regiment remained simply "Leibstandarte SS Adolf Hitler."[17] Nevertheless, the intention to include Leibstandarte within the SS division was regularly restated until three months prior to the outbreak of World War II.[18]

While Leibstandarte was able to provide its recruits with the rudiments of military training by the mid-1930s, for more sophisticated instruction it, along with the rest of the Verfügungstruppe, remained dependent upon the army. This is where the most basic weakness of the Verfügungstruppe lay, for in acquiring the techniques of modern warfare, its personnel were essentially forced to puzzle through the technical literature provided for them by the Wehrmacht and hope that points of confusion would be resolved during their occasional and brief training sessions under army tutelage. It appears that most of the instruction given to the Leibstandarte by the army took the form of the detailing of individuals or, at most, small groups to army training centers. These men were then expected to return to Lichterfelde and to act as instructors for the rest of the regiment.[19] Joint exercises and maneuvers with army units were rare and on a vary small scale. Leibstandarte briefly participated in field exercises with army contingents in Berlin's Grünewald Park until these were cancelled due to damage of turf and foliage.[20]

A serious shortcoming in the training establishment of the Verfügungstruppe was the lack of formal facilities for the continuing education of officers. Even though it had been originally envisioned that SS officers would be seconded to army units for long periods of training and for the acquisition of command and tactical experience, this, in fact, occurred very infrequently if at all.[21] By 1935, however, something approximating a correspondence school for Verfügungstruppe officers was in operation under the supervision of the SS Main Office. Officers worked out monthly map exercises and submitted them to the Main Office, while battalion, company, and platoon commanders regularly gathered for sessions of Kriegsspiel.[22]

In the same year, the Verfügungstruppe began to construct a technical training complex of its own. By 1938 this included a motorized transport school, an engineers' school, and an armorers' course operated at the Dachau installation. This, however, was but a foretaste of the very extensive training establishment which the Waffen-SS was to construct in the course of World War II.[23]

While the prewar Verfügungstruppe was occasionally made an object of derision by the army rank and file and was certainly not equal in quality to the best army units, it had developed into an organization of substantial military value by the eve of World War II. Felix Steiner's Standarte Deutschland performed brilliantly before Hitler in maneuvers in May 1939, a demonstration which was instrumental in securing

for the Verfügungstruppe its own artillery regiment.[24] While
the former inspector of the SS-Verfügungstruppe, Paul Hausser, notes with perhaps a hint of scorn that Leibstandarte
placed unusual emphasis on parade-ground drill due to the
ceremonial functions required of it as Hitler's guards regiment, the consequences were not of disastrous proportions,
for in April 1939 an inquiry was made by the Wehrmacht as
to whether Leibstandarte members who had completed four-
year terms of service as enlisted men would be interested in
joining the army as noncommissioned officers.[25] In a sense,
the wheel had turned full circle.

It was not in the area of military and technical training that
the Verfügungstruppe most clearly distinguished itself from
the army. The SS was defined by Himmler as an order of
"political soldiery," and that definition was more appropriate
to the Verfügungstruppe than to the part-time and poorly
trained General SS.[26] By "politics" was understood unquestioning adherence to the ideological underpinnings of National Socialism and a commitment to the actualization of the
aims of Nazism in the name of Adolf Hitler. The task of
rendering the SS politically reliable in this sense during most
of the prewar years was the responsibility of the SS Race and
Settlement Main Office, which in the course of 1934 constructed an indoctrination system which was intended to per-
meate the SS at all levels.[27] Into each SS unit was introduced
an "education leader" whose chief duties included ideological indoctrination and the supervision of the preparation by
SS members of the elaborate racial credentials which by that
time were being required for final acceptance into the SS.[28]

Leibstandarte received its chief education leader in April
1934.[29] This worthy, in later describing his indoctrination
program, declared that

> its main point is so to influence the Leibstandarte that it
> can at any time be the shock troops of the regime in ideo-
> logical struggles. That is to say, it must recognize no
> other ties than to the Führer and his orders. . . . We must
> and can so use the time . . . to weld the units of the Leib-
> standarte together and make them into a stout tool in the
> hand of the Führer.[30]

The effort to render the Leibstandarte "a stout tool in the hand of the Führer" was to be achieved through weekly indoctrination sessions conducted by the education leaders.[31] These sessions, by 1935 standardized for the entire SS through the introduction of indoctrination journals (*SS-Leithefte*), concentrated upon a small number of stock ideological themes: the danger posed to the German *Volk* by the Jews and by the ideologies linked in the minds of the Nazis to Jewishness—Freemasonry, socialism, communism and liberal democracy; the corrosive effect of Christianity (particularly Roman Catholicism), internationalism, pacifism upon the German *Volk* spirit; conversely, the glorification of the German *Volk* and the Nordic race, the rooted agrarian life, military virtues and fecundity.[32] The character of this material is best conveyed by a few excerpts from the *Leithefte*.

The *Leithefte* instructed SS men that "one had better not speak at all about a feeling of honor among Jews," and that "within our nation they may have under no circumstances a voice in any matter."[33] An article on "The Spiritual Roots of Monastic Immorality" explained that "it was considered necessary in the ninth century to ask a new bishop whether he had had sexual relations with men or animals, married women or nuns." The article implied that similar suspicions were well founded in the subsequent eleven-hundred-year history of the Church.[34] Explaining the importance for SS men of knowledge concerning Freemasonry and Bolshevism, a *Leiheft* of May 1935 declared that "Freemasonry and Bolshevism are only to be understood in the context of Jewry and its striving after world domination."[35]

Himmler hoped to create in the SS an organization of militant ideologues analogous to the crusading orders of the Middle Ages and the Society of Jesus in the Counter-Reformation.[36] Yet, it would be a mistake to assume that all who joined the SS were fanatical Nazis or that the *Leithefte* were successful in converting all skeptics. Many individuals joined the SS not out of a desire to range themselves in the foremost ranks of the ideological struggles but in the hope of more rapid advancement in civilian life, a desire for social prestige or the satisfaction of belonging to an exclusive organization or, on the lowest level, simply out of enthusiasm to wear the smart black uniform of the SS.[37] The incidence of extraideological reasons for joining the SS may have been more frequent in the Verfügungstruppe than in other branches because the function which the Verfügungstruppe appeared to serve seemed to be pragmatic and easily definable in traditional terms. Guards regiments in the service of an autocratic ruler were not novelties, and members of the Verfügungstruppe were trained as soldiers and were in frequent contact with members of the army. For many, service in the Verfügungstruppe became simply an alternative path toward a military career or the satisfaction of military obligations following the reintroduction of conscription in Germany in May 1935. Service in the Verfügungstruppe was equated with service in the army, navy, and air force, and Verfügungstruppe members were reimbursed on the same pay scale as that of the army, trained according to army regulations, and after 1935 for Leibstandarte and 1936 for other Verfügungstruppe units were issued field uniforms of army field gray.[38] A young German's attraction to the Verfügungstruppe instead of to one of the nonparty armed forces could be based on nonideological considerations: prestige, more glamorous and comfortable duty assignments, or the likelihood of more rapid advancement. Educational requirements for officer training were less stringent than those in the army, thereby luring men who relished careers as officers but for whom the door was closed in the traditional armed forces.[39]

Some of the nonideological factors were accentuated within the Leibstandarte. It remained by far the most glamorous unit within the Verfügungstruppe. Only Leibstandarte members, by Hitler's personal order, wore striking white leather accouterments with their black dress uniforms, and only they were permitted to wear the simple SS runes on their collar tabs, while other units had to supplement them with an identifying Standarte numeral.[40] Leibstandarte members were required to be significantly taller than applicants for other Verfügungstruppe units, thus introducing a young man's pride in his physique as a motive for joining.[41] The fact that the Leibstandarte was Adolf Hitler's personal regiment was not prima facie evidence that the recruit chose to identify himself with the ideology which the Führer represented; the prestige inherent in wearing the name of the head of state as a disembodied abstraction on the lower left sleeve of the uniform was motive enough.[42] The public image of Leibstandarte as a superelite military unit, though perhaps a distortion of reality during the prewar years, was widely propagated by the mass media and was doubtless an important factor in inducing young Germans to apply for membership. The Syndikat Film G.m.b.H., for instance, made a movie about the Leibstandarte in 1935 which was shown suggestively along with the spectacle on Frederick the Great, *Fridericus Rex*.[43]

Ideological fanaticism, to be sure, occasionally manifested itself, indicating that the indoctrination program was more than a formalistic exercise. A Catholic cleric was on one occasion beaten and relieved of his trousers on the barracks grounds; the barracks chapel was defaced on several occasions, and church-goers in Berchtesgaden were harassed.[44] Yet, complaints were voiced by enthusiastic Nazi members to the effect that military professionalism was threatening to neutralize ideological commitment, and it is clear that the Race and Settlement Main Office's indoctrination program was received with less than general enthusiasm by officers and men alike.[45] Nor was this phenomenon unique to Leibstandarte. Lack of interest in ideological questions and poor attendance at indoctrination sessions were generally bemoaned by Race and Settlement Main Office agents.[46]

In the final analysis, it is impossible to arrive at a valid assessment of the impact of ideology on Leibstandarte members in the prewar period. While admitting that it probably sharpened hatred of ''the enemy'' among the rank and file, most of whom were in their impressionable late teens and early twenties, the original indoctrination program operated by the Race and Settlement Main Office was apparently regarded by Himmler as a failure and was substantially modified. At the end of 1935, responsibility for indoctrination was placed in the hands of company commanders themselves who, nevertheless, were expected to be guided by Race and Settlement Main Office agents and to use the *Leithefte* as source materials.[47] According to Paul Hausser, indoctrination under these circumstances tended to be limited to general and military history although, as the following excerpt from educational material used by Leibstandarte indicates, that limitation could still embrace a great deal.

The well-known leadership of the Jews in international socialism must of necessity reveal itself most sharply in Soviet Russia because in old Russia the Jews were the bearers of the Revolutionary Idea. . . . The Comintern, like Soviet Russia, is led by Stalin and his Jewish clique. . . . The Soviet Union is not only a Jewish-led slave state, but at the same time the hearth of Jewish international communism for the entire world, the central bureau for the overthrow and revolutionizing of all states.[48]

Indifference to the program of ideological indoctrination must not be interpreted as resistance to or disagreement with its content. As was laconically noted by one education leader, "It is difficult to interest the simple SS man in historical questions."[49] The indoctrination program tended to be viewed by officers as an inconvenient intrusion upon the training and duty schedule; and if long hours of military training, in part in the company of army personnel, engendered no overt hostility to Nazi ideology among enlisted men, it did tend to crowd out the more abstract representations of the *Weltanschauung.*[50]

Far more relevant than tortured historical interpretations and racial mysticism was the glorification of war, violence, and simple activism. Regular "ceremonial hours" conducted within Leibstandarte seem to have been devoid of any clear ideological content other than perfunctory references to the history of the Nazi movement. The tone of these programs owed more to the spirit of Ernst Jünger than to Heinrich Himmler or Richard Walther Darré. One of these, for example, included a choral rendition of "Tomorrow We March in the Enemy's Land with Music," readings from *The War Letters of Fallen Students,* and the singing of *"Ich hatt' einen Kameraden"* and "Our Heaven is the Great War." The latter composition began:

> Our heaven
> Is the great war
> On Earth.
> We live in battle
> Our eternal life.[51]

A former member of the Leibstandarte has written retrospectively that Dietrich's unit in the prewar years was a world in which "The heart asked and was answered by other hearts. Youth found it magnificent, Sepp Dietrich and his Leibstandarte—that was stirring. The rules of Germanness were not read out; one learned them by leaps from ten meter towers, by thirty kilometer marches, and by the most severe training on the exercise grounds."[52]

It would thus be an attitudinal and ideological witches' brew which Leibstandarte would carry with it into battle, one that would undergo additional change under the pressures of war.

4
From Vienna to the Vistula

Leibstandarte's role as a vehicle of Nazi conquest began not in September 1939 but eighteen months earlier as a result of Hitler's sudden decision to solve the Austrian problem by drastic means. Hitler approved the operational plans for the invasion on the evening of March 10, 1938. According to these plans, units of the German army and the SS-Verfügungstruppe under the command of Colonel-General Fedor von Bock were to be sent into Austria "in order to establish constitutional conditions," Hitler's euphemism for a brutal *coup d'état*.[1]

Major-General Heinz Guderian, recently appointed commander of XVI Army Corps, was placed in charge of the motorized elements of the invasion force. He was informed by General Ludwig Beck, Chief of the Army General Staff, that his forces were to include his earlier command, 2nd Panzer Division, and the Leibstandarte SS Adolf Hitler, the inclusion of the latter having been a decision made by Hitler.[2] Shortly before midnight on the tenth, Guderian in Berlin communicated the news of the mobilization personally to Dietrich. Guderian took advantage of Dietrich's late evening appointment with Hitler to secure permission from the Führer to bedeck his tanks with green foliage as a sign to the Austrian populace of the invaders' peaceful intentions.[3]

The assembly area for XVI Corps was Passau at the confluence of the Danube and the Inn Rivers and just over the border from upper Austria. At 9:00 A.M. March 12, Guderian's columns began to flow across the frontier with Dietrich's

Leibstandarte bringing up the rear. By noon Guderian's corps had reached Linz and remained there for Hitler's triumphal entry early that evening into the city of his boyhood. Two days later XVI Corps was in Vienna where parading German and Austrian units celebrated the union of Austria with the German Reich.[4]

The invasion of Austria involved no combat and hence was a poor index of fighting potential. Nevertheless, Leibstandarte had performed its assignment well, having covered the approximately one thousand kilometers separating Berlin from Vienna in about forty-eight hours with no serious problems. This performance may have prompted the decision to completely motorize the remainder of the SS-Verfügungstruppe.[5]

By April Leibstandarte had returned to its quarters in Berlin.[6] Already Hitler was laying plans for the dismemberment of Czechoslovakia, although it was not until May 20 that the first directive for military operations against that country was drafted by the Oberkommando der Wehrmacht.[7] By the second week in July, Hitler had decided that the SS-Verfügungstruppe were to be committed with the initial elements of the Wehrmacht in the event of war, and Leibstandarte, as in the Austrian occupation, was to operate with motorized units of the army.[8]

As war with Czechoslovakia and perhaps a general European war seemed to grow imminent in the first week of autumn 1938, Leibstandarte, 1st Panzer Division, and the corps command of XVI Army Corps were engaged in intensive training exercises at the army's Grafenwöhr training installation.[9] Concurrently, the conspiratorial group including General Beck, Karl Goerdeler, General von Witzleben, and Ulrich von Hassel were planning the arrest of Hitler, the absence of Dietrich and Leibstandarte from Berlin being a key condition.[10] Mussolini's peace initiative, which resulted in the Munich agreement, deprived Leibstandarte of both its baptism of fire in war and its reconfirmation as Hitler's scourge against counterrevolution. As an element of XVI Army Corps, Leibstandarte again enjoyed an operation which was little more than a parade, as German forces occupied and incorporated the Sudetenland into the Reich and participated six months later in the occupation of Bohemia and Moravia which marked the temporary destruction of the Czechoslovakian state.[11]

Leibstandarte returned to the Berlin area during the second week in April 1939 and by the middle of June had received orders under the code name *Sommerübung* (summer exercise) to be prepared for combat by August 1, 1939.[12] Later in the month Dietrich's regiment was tentatively assigned to General Johannes Blaskowitz's 8th Army, actual absorption to take place on receipt of the code words "it is to be promptly proposed."[13] A month later Dietrich received marching orders from the Army High Command, which erased any remaining doubt that an attack on Poland was imminent.[14]

The SS-Verfügungstruppe, while equipped with trench mortars and light antitank weapons, entered its last peacetime year with no artillery arm of its own. By the beginning of June 1939, this critical weakness was being corrected at the army's Jüterbog training installation. There, under army supervision, as SS artillery regiment was organized and trained, approximately two thousand men having been contributed by Leibstandarte, Deutschland, and Germania.[15] By the middle of August, at which time final troop dispositions for the invasion of Poland had to be made, the SS Artillery Regiment was fit only for the simplest tasks; and although it was assigned to a mixed panzer division under the command of Lieutenant-General Kempf, composed of SS-Standarte Deutschland and SS support units as well as the army's 7th Armored Regiment and an engineer battalion, little was expected of it.[16] As a stop-gap measure, Leibstandarte was reinforced by II Battalion of the army's 46th Artillery Regiment.[17]

On August 25, 1939, Leibstandarte moved out of Lichterfelde Barracks, its home since 1933, never to return as a unit. Left behind were a reserve and training battalion and small elements to discharge Leibstandarte's security functions. Accompanied by Himmler's order of the day, "SS men, I expect you to do more than your duty," Dietrich's reinforced regiment began arriving in its assembly area around Hundsfeld-Kunersdorf north of Breslau on the evening of August 25.[18]

The overall assignment of Blaskowitz's 8th Army was to act as a shield to the left flank of General von Reichenau's powerful and highly mobile 10th Army as it thrust toward the Vistula in an effort to envelop and destroy Polish forces west of the river.[19] It was a potentially difficult task in that the 8th

Army was weak and slow-moving, being made up of only four infantry divisions in addition to Leibstandarte and, except for Leibstandarte, unmotorized.[20] Blaskowitz's orders for the first day of operations were to take the heights around Schildberg and if possible the crossings over the Prosna River in the Wieruzow-Grabow area.[21] The major objective was a crucial one—to reach the Warta River before the Polish army could set up organized defenses along it—and much of the tactical burden for the operation fell upon the motorized Leibstandarte which was expected to open the crossings over the Prosna and then leap ahead in order to seize Sieradz on the west bank of the Warta.[22]

The morning of September 1, 1939, held the promise of a warm day for the opening of the attack on Poland and offered an initial advantage to the attacker in that a ground fog covered the border area before 8th Army.[23] At 4:45 A.M. the Polish border was crossed according to plan. Although it had to traverse swampy terrain, Leibstandarte was approaching Boleslawiec on the Prosna by 6:30.[24] Shortly thereafter, Leibstandarte suffered its first casualties as an armored reconnaissance car struck a Polish mine. Boleslawiec was found to be stoutly defended, but shortly after ten o'clock Leibstandarte had taken the village after heavy fighting. By midafternoon the enemy was hurriedly withdrawing behind the Prosna, which Leibstandarte itself crossed later in the day. The price in men for the first day's combat was light—seven killed and twenty wounded.[25]

On September 2, Leibstandarte overcame light resistance northwest of Boleslawiec and linked up with 17th Infantry Division to which it was subordinated. The objective assigned for the following day was the Warta River in the vicinity of Burzenin.[26] Due to stiffening enemy resistance as well as sandy soil which was difficult for vehicles to negotiate, the Warta was not reached, an awkward situation because elements of 10th Army were already in the process of crossing the river.[27] In fact, it was not until late in the afternoon of September 4 that Leibstandarte, leading the way for 17th and 10th Infantry Divisions (with Leibstandarte, components of XIII Corps) effected a crossing in the face of heavy enemy resistance.[28] Casualties were now beginning to mount to the obvious detriment of morale and discipline. The commander of 17th Infantry Division, Major-General Loch, complained about wild shooting and burning of villages from which troops had supposedly received fire and criticized specifically the motorized units under his command, undoubtedly referring to Leibstandarte. Loch's reprimand was not intended as a negative moral judgement but was based on operational considerations. The burning of villages tended to obstruct the line of march and deprived the troops of necessary shelter.[29]

The crossing of the Warta was followed by a day of heavy combat during which Leibstandarte and the rest of the XIII Corps nevertheless succeeded in advancing approximately twelve miles to the north bank of the Widawka River.[30] The entire 8th Army was now ordered to pursue the enemy as fast as possible to the area around Lodz and the Bzura River. In cooperation with 10th Army, it was hoped that five or six Polish divisions of the "Posen Army" might be encircled and destroyed.[31]

Thirteenth Corps was assigned the task of closing the southern exit to the pocket. In pursuit of this aim, Dietrich was to thrust to Pabjanice and then advance to Rzgow in order to close off Lodz from the south.[32] This was the most crucial burden yet imposed upon Leibstandarte, and it was undertaken with something less than aplomb and expertise. The advance on Pabjanice began on the morning of September 7, and while initial progress was encouraging, it soon bogged down in the face of blown bridges at Grabia and Przygon. This necessitated a lengthy detour over sandy terrain in which Dietrich's vehicles made slow progress and obstructed the forward movement of the two infantry divisions which otherwise might have preserved the momentum of the advance.[33] Dietrich seems also to have been excessively concerned about the safety of his southern flank and reacted with unwarranted concern to the presence of a Polish regiment which had no intention of attacking.[34]

Consequently, the advance on Pabjanice did not resume in earnest until well into the afternoon, and when the town was finally reached, it was found to be stoutly defended. Twice Leibstandarte launched frontal attacks on the Polish defensive positions, and twice its attacks were repulsed. Not only were its efforts unsuccessful, but Leibstandarte soon found itself surrounded by the Polish defenders and was extricated from its awkward situation only by the intervention of Infantry Regiment 55 of 10th Division.[35]

Leibstandarte's failure produced no serious consequences. On September 8 the Poles abandoned Lodz and were funneled into a wider pocket west of Warsaw and the Vistula.[36] Nor was Leibstandarte alone the object of adverse criticism by the army. The same day saw the transmission of a proposal by 3rd Army to Army Group North suggesting that Kempf's composite SS-army division be dismantled because of deficiencies in training and that while the 7th Panzer Regiment should be given to 10th Panzer Division and thus remain in combat, the SS units should be relegated to Army Group Reserve.[37] This proposal was not implemented; Leibstandarte was, nevertheless, detached from 8th Army under somewhat strained circumstances and subordinated to Lieutenant-General Reinhardt's 4th Panzer Division, then operating with XVI Corps of von Reichenau's 10th Army west of Warsaw.[38]

Leibstandarte's new assignment was of mixed significance. As an element attached to a fast-moving armored division, it would not have the same opportunity to distinguish itself in combat, but neither would it be as likely to hurtle headlong into difficult circumstances as had happened at Pabjanice. On the other hand, as part of 10th Army, the major German striking force in the Polish campaign, it would be more likely to share in the credit for final victory.

Hitler himself may have been responsible for Dietrich's transfer to 10th Army.[39] If in peacetime Leibstandarte's association with the Führer and Reich Chancellor carried with it certain ceremonial and symbolic functions, in wartime this association had critical connotations. Hitler was acutely aware of the propaganda significance of such symbolism. The pocket battleship *Deutschland* was renamed *Lützow* shortly after the outbreak of war, apparently because of Hitler's fear of the negative impact which the sinking of a vessel bearing the name of the fatherland might exercise on public morale.[40] Similarly, his interest in a military formation bearing his own name was intense. During the Polish campaign Hitler had marked on a large map in the Reich Chancellery the simple notation, ''Sepp,'' to reveal to him at a glance the location of ''his'' Leibstandarte.[41] Later in the war Hitler declared that he always gave Dietrich ''the opportunity to intervene at sore spots''; these sore spots, of course, were the decisive areas where victories were to be won—victories which would re-dound to the credit of the Leibstandarte SS Adolf Hitler and, symbolically, to the Führer himself.[42]

Together with 4th Panzer Division, Leibstandarte was or-dered north to the Bzura River sector to prevent strong Polish forces, being driven southeast by Army Group North, from crossing the river and falling back on Warsaw.[43] Eighth and 10th Armies were to trap the retreating enemy in the trian-gular area west of Kutno where the Bzura approaches and finally joins the Vistula near Wysczogrod, approximately thirty miles west of the Polish capital. While the commander of 4th Panzer Division, Lieutenant-General Reinhardt, con-fidently declared that serious resistance was no longer to be expected from Polish forces in the Bzura sector, events proved his prediction to have been overly optimistic.[44]

Sixteenth Army Corps (Leibstandarte, 4th Panzer Divi-sion, and 31st Infantry Division) were committed on Septem-ber 11 in the area east of Blonie about fifteen miles east of the Bzura and only some twelve miles from Warsaw in order to block the western approaches to the city.[45] Fourth Panzer Division and Leibstandarte soon found themselves involved in stiff defensive action against strong enemy forces moving against them both from the Warsaw area and from the west. Here Leibstandarte acquitted itself well in beating off Polish attacks, although not without loss. During the night of Sep-tember 12–13, 6th Company of II Battalion was overrun and its commander, Hauptsturmführer (Captain) Seppel Lange, killed.[46]

Polish forces in the Bzura sector were stronger than antic-ipated, and on September 13 XVI Corps was shifted west-ward to the Bzura and placed under the temporary command of 8th Army, whose front was reeling under Polish attacks in the direction of Lodz.[47] The enemy between the Bzura and the Vistula was now to be destroyed by concentric attacks carried out by 8th and 10th Armies strongly supported by Air Fleet Four (General Alexander Löhr).[48] The commander of Army Group South, Colonel-General Gerd von Rundstedt, assumed personal control of the Bzura ''battle of annihila-tion'' in which XVI Corps with Leibstandarte played an im-portant role. On September 14 it was ordered to seal off the eastern exit from the Bzura pocket by attacking northward on both sides of the Bzura from Sachaczew to the Vistula, a goal which was reached on the morning of September 19.[49]

Leibstandarte had indeed participated in a great victory. In addition to enormous quantities of equipment, the Bzura battles yielded approximately 105,000 prisoners, of which 20,000 were claimed by 4th Panzer Division and Leibstandarte.[50] The only remaining centers of significant Polish resistance were now Warsaw itself and the fortress complex around Modlin, some fifteen miles to the northwest where the Narew joins the Vistula. The Vistula between Modlin and Warsaw was already held by German forces although the Poles maintained communications between the two cities. As the first step toward the reduction of both places, each was to be surrounded and isolated from the other.[51]

Leibstandarte was placed under XV Corps of 10th Army on September 21 for the purpose of invading Modlin from the south, while II Corps including Panzer Division Kempf was to prepare an assault from the north which was to be launched on September 25 after intensive air and artillery bombardment.[52] The role of Dietrich's unit was a static one, and 2nd Company, including Leibstandarte's commander, could be spared to greet Hitler when he visited 8th and 10th Armies on September 25.[53]

The assault on Modlin had scarcely begun on the morning of September 28 when its Polish defenders surrendered unconditionally, adding 31,000 men to the German bag of prisoners.[54] On the previous day Warsaw itself had surrendered, and except for a few isolated pockets of resistance which were subdued by the end of the first week in October, the Polish campaign was ended.[55]

Leibstandarte did not remain in Poland long enough to witness the conclusion of hostilities. During the Polish campaign, Dietrich's command had engaged in orthodox military operations under army control, although it had not always limited itself to orthodox military functions. The sometime director of Leibstandarte's band, for example, had been arrested by army authorities for his role in the shooting of "Jewish criminals."[56] With the termination of the siege of Modlin, Leibstandarte passed under the operational control of Himmler as its political function again manifested itself.[57]

At the beginning of October the entire unit was transported to the vicinity of Prague, probably as a result of anti-Nazi demonstrations in the city.[58] Following an enthusiastic welcome by the German elements of the population and a welcoming speech by Reich Protector Konstantin von Neurath, Leibstandarte operated briefly as a security force in the Czech capital, taking the place of SS Regiment Der Führer which had been sent to the West Wall fortifications at the opening of the Polish campaign. Leibstandarte performed routine duties consisting primarily of the guarding of public buildings, including the Hradcin Castle overlooking the city.[59]

The months between the victory in Poland and the opening of the campaign in the West was a period of reorganization and expansion for the entire Verfügungstruppe. Himmler now succeeded in securing permission to organize three SS field divisions. The first of these, the Verfügungs Division, was to be based upon the regiments Deutschland, Germania, and Der Führer. The Leibstandarte SS Adolf Hitler was not to be included in the new division.[60] Perhaps it was not deemed appropriate for the Führer's regiment to be absorbed into a larger unit; and, in any event, the Leibstandarte had already been envisioned in divisional strength.[61] Dietrich's unit did play an important role in the formation of the two other SS divisions which had been granted to Himmler. November and December saw the transfer of officers to the Totenkopf and Polizei Divisions, which were organized around former concentration camp guards and police personnel and which were in dire need of experienced officers.[62]

As these transfers were taking place, Leibstandarte had already departed from Prague and had taken up quarters in the Coblenz area. Here, it once again fell under the command of General Heinz Guderian, newly decorated with the Knight's Cross for the exploits of his XIX Army Corps in Poland.[63] It was generally assumed by Dietrich's officers that the regiment would soon be in action across Germany's western frontier.[64]

5
The West—1940

In its new quarters near Coblenz, Leibstandarte incorporated replacements and engaged in intensive training. Dietrich and his men enjoyed the signal honor of a visit by the Führer on Christmas Eve, evidence of a devotion reciprocated in Dietrich's New Year's order which declared that "We will always be his [Hitler's] most loyal soldiers."[1]

In a further display of favor toward Leibstandarte, Hitler personally ordered the formation of a motorized heavy infantry gun company, personnel for which was to be provided by the SS Verfügungs Division stationed at nearby Ems.[2] Dietrich's strength in heavy support weapons was vastly increased in April with the posting of an entire artillery battalion to his control.[3]

These augmentations of Leibstandarte's combat capability and the addition of a fourth infantry battalion in January 1940 might lead one to infer that its original role as a security force for Hitler and his regime was being abandoned; this is not correct.[4] Elements had remained at Berlin and Obersalzberg, personnel on occasion rotating between these security units and the front-line combat force. In January Hitler ordered that a special battalion be organized for security duties only. This battalion was to be equipped exclusively with small arms and was to be permanently garrisoned in Berlin. The high command of the Waffen-SS, as the SS-Verfügungstruppe had been redesignated, balked at setting up a battalion that was not fit for combat and urged Himmler to prevail upon Hitler to give it full combat equipment.[5] It is probable that Hitler purposely limited the combat effectiveness of this battalion in order to diminish the likelihood of its removal from Berlin to the front.

The substantial reinforcement of Leibstandarte prior to the opening of the campaign in the West was possible only because of the repeated postponement of the date of attack.[6] Had the initial operational plan been implemented, Leibstandarte, 2nd and 10th Panzer Divisions, 2nd Infantry Division (motorized), and the infantry regiment Gross Deutschland (motorized) would have been carrying out the initial phases of a wheeling movement to the southwest, essentially in repetition of the Schlieffen Plan of World War I.[7] In February 1940 the German plan of attack was fundamentally altered. A sweep through the Low Countries was now made a diversionary maneuver, while the attack through the Ardennes became the focus of the offensive.[8] The new plan, largely the work of General Erich von Manstein, Chief of Staff to von Rundstedt, had naturally won the enthusiastic support of Guderian whose XIX Panzer Corps along with General Reinhardt's XXXXI Panzer Corps would constitute the core of the main German offensive. Guderian's assignment involved the partial reorganization of his Corps, Leibstandarte, and 2nd Infantry Division being replaced by an additional panzer division.[9]

Dietrich's reinforced regiment was now removed from the area of von Rundstedt's Army Group A and shifted north to the secondary sector of Colonel-General Fedor von Bock's Army Group B. Initially subordinated to Hausser's SS-Verfügungs Division in the area of Lüdinghausen near Münster, Leibstandarte was attached to Major-General Frederick Zickwolff's 227th Infantry Division by March 1940 to form Schnelle Gruppe Nord (Mobile Group North) for the invasion of Holland.[10] On receipt of the code word "Danzig" this force was to break through the Dutch border defenses and thrust toward the line of the Yssel River.[11]

At dawn on May 10, 1940, the German war machine turned on the West. Bombers and fighters struck airfields in Holland, Belgium, and France while airborne troops seized crucial airfields, bridges, and fortifications. Leibstandarte surprised Dutch border guards opposite Gronau, and within five hours Kurt Meyer's motorcycle company had advanced forty-eight miles without meeting resistance.[12] Indeed, the provinces of Overyssel, Drente, Gronigen, and Friesland, comprising Dutch territory north and east of the Yssel, were garrisoned only by a few lightly armed battalions, and under these circumstances it was no remarkable feat of military prowess that Leibstandarte should have reached Zwolle on the Yssel by noon.[13] Although both bridges over the river had been destroyed by their defenders, Leibstandarte's III Battalion forced a crossing far to the south at Zutphen.[14] In spite of a thirty-six-mile advance beyond the Yssel by elements of Leibstandarte, on the evening of May 10 von Bock detached Dietrich's regiment from 227th Infantry Division, which continued westward toward Amersfoort.[15] Leibstandarte was dispatched to the southwest to link up with Lieutenant-General Alfred Hubicki's 9th Panzer Division which crossed the Maas on the morning of May 11 and hurtled westward toward Moerdijk and the southern approaches to Rotterdam via the bridges over the Holland Deep.[16] These bridges, one rail and one road, had been seized by German paratroopers on the initial day of the invasion and were being held in expectation of the arrival of powerful armored forces.[17] Ninth Panzer Division crossed the bridges on the evening of May 12, followed early in the morning of May 14 by Dietrich's reinforced regiment.[18] On the previous day 9th Panzer Division, 254th Infantry Division, Leibstandarte and the airborne forces in the vicinity had been drawn together by Lieutenant-General Rudolf Schmidt's XXXIX Corps headquarters for the assault on Rotterdam, which promised to be a difficult undertaking. Dutch forces had sealed off the bridgehead leading into Rotterdam, and artillery was positioned in the center of the city in order to pound and disrupt the impending attack.[19]

By the morning of May 14, events far to the south in the area of von Rundstedt's Army Group A were serving to impart added importance to the seizure of Rotterdam and the destruction of "fortress Holland." Guderian's panzer corps had achieved a breakthrough over the Meuse at Sedan, and 9th Panzer Division and Leibstandarte were now needed for its exploitation.[20] Hitler and Goering, therefore, decided to accelerate the fall of Rotterdam through the massive application of air power, a decision which resulted in the leveling of the center of the city and the killing of some nine hundred civilians.[21] The raid was carried out at three in the afternoon by Heinkel 111 bombers of Kampfgeschwader 54, and scarcely two hours later the commandant of the city surrendered Rotterdam to XXXIX Corps.[22]

Leibstandarte, which had received orders on the morning of May 14 to pass through or around Rotterdam to relieve airborne units surrounded between Rotterdam and Delft and then to strike on to The Hague, now had easy passage.[23] Although small-arms fire occasionally sounded in the streets, most of the Dutch garrison was in the process of marching to collection points to surrender their weapons as Dietrich's motorized units roared northward through the city. Suddenly, an element of Leibstandarte encountered an armed group of Dutch soldiers and, taking no chances, sprayed them with machine-gun fire. Casualties among the hapless Dutchmen are not known, but a stray bullet struck and seriously wounded Luftwaffe Lieutenant-General Kurt Student, Commander of 7th Air Division, as he stood at the window of his command post.[24] Student had jumped into the Rotterdam area with his paratroopers on May 10 and, having survived the fire of the enemy for four days, nearly succumbed, to Leibstandarte's case of combat nerves. Lieutenant-Colonel Dietrich von Choltitz, commander of the III Battalion of the 16th Infantry Regiment, which had been attached to Student's force, dashed from the building and herded the confused Dutchmen to safety in a nearby church as Dietrich's men raced on, having on that day taken over 3500 prisoners.[25]

Dietrich's haste proved unnecessary. Almost simultaneous with the wounding of Student, the Dutch commander-in-chief, General Winkelmann, ordered all Dutch forces under his command to cease hostilities, and the following morning the formal instrument of capitulation was signed in a small village between Rotterdam and Dordrecht.[26] Leibstandarte, which by this time had reached the vicinity of Leyden, and 9th Panzer Division were ordered to undertake a grand tour of the Netherlands to impress the Dutch populace with the power and discipline of the German Wehrmacht. Wearing clean uniforms and sitting at attention in their armored cars and trucks, Leibstandarte drove from Leyden through Haarlem, Amsterdam, Utrecht, to Arnheim, and through Nijmwegen, Venlo, and Roermond before crossing into northeastern

Belgium and reaching Tongeren on May 18.[27] The following day Dietrich's regiment joined Hausser's Verfügungs Division for a night march to the vicinity of Huy and proceeded on the twentieth to an assembly area south and southeast of Dinant.[28]

At Dinant near the intersection of the Meuse and the Franco-Belgian frontier, Leibstandarte was far behind the most advanced point of the German thrust through northern France. On the evening of May 20 2nd Panzer Division of Guderian's XIX Corps had reached the Channel coast at Abbeville, thus driving a wedge between French, Belgian, and British forces in Belgium and the bulk of the French army south of the Somme.[29] North of this wedge there remained some forty Allied divisions whose only hope of survival seemed to lie in breaking through German forces to the south and linking up with the French army south of the Somme, which if accomplished would also have cut off and exposed to mortal danger the tip of the German spearhead on the Channel coast. A combined British-French thrust southward in the vicinity of Arras on May 21 struck the right flank of Brigadier General Erwin Rommel's 7th Panzer Division and SS-Gruppenführer (Major-General) Theodor Eicke's newly committed, motorized SS Totenkopf Division, causing momentary consternation but, due to the weakness of the attack and the absence of a synchronized northward attack by French forces south of the Somme, produced no amelioration of the Allies' critical situation.[30] Leibstandarte found itself involved in an aftershock of the abortive offensive on May 22, successfully repulsing weak French attacks directed southward in the vicinity of Valenciennes. Nevertheless, the threat of a French breakout in this sector of the front remained, and Leibstandarte stood in defensive in positions east and southeast of the town until the evening of May 23.[31]

In the meantime, the German encirclement of Allied forces north of the Somme continued. Guderian's XIX Panzer Corps forced its way into Boulogne on the afternoon of May 22 while Reinhardt's XXXXI Panzer Corps, advancing on Guderian's right flank, captured St. Omer on the twenty-third.[32] On the evening of that day, Leibstandarte's positions around Valenciennes were assumed by 1st Infantry Division while

Leibstandarte in a night march hurried westward to join Guderian's Corps, now bearing down on the port of Dunkirk.[33]

By May 24, the day on which Leibstandarte joined Guderian, XIX Panzer Corps had reached the Aa Canal, which
runs in a southeasterly direction from a point on the Channel
Coast near Gravelines, and had established several bridgeheads on the far side, approaching to within fifteen miles of
Dunkirk at the nearest point.[34] Dietrich's reinforced regiment
went into the line between Holques and St. Momelin, where
the canal had not yet been crossed, and prepared to add its
motorized strength to the further constriction of the Channel
pocket.[35]

On the evening of the twenty-fourth, the German High
Command issued its notorious and controversial order halting
the advance on Dunkirk at the line of the Aa Canal and leaving to the Luftwaffe the task of destroying Allied forces within
the Dunkirk perimeter.[36] Dietrich was certainly apprised of
the order but chose to ignore or at least to modify it. On the
morning of May 25, the commander of the Leibstandarte ordered his III Battalion to cross the canal and seize Watten on
the far side.[37] Dietrich's breach of the halt order was sound
tactical decision displaying an intelligent sense of initiative.
As Dietrich explained to Guderian, the 230-foot heights at
Watten dominated the surrounding marshy plain and permitted its defenders to "look down the throats" of Leibstandarte
as it lay on the west bank of the canal.[38]

The remainder of the twenty-fifth and the following day
were utilized in consolidating Leibstandarte's newly won
bridgehead. It was also a time for reasserting soldierly discipline and bearing, which seem to have broken down in the
course of the victorious advance of the previous two weeks.
The men were ordered to cease wearing civilian business
suits, which some had apparently "liberated," and to banish
dogs, dolls, and stuffed animals from their vehicles, which in
Dietrich's words had taken on a "gypsylike appearance."[39]

Leibstandarte's thoroughness in mopping up the area behind its sector of the front also seems to have been less than
adequate, a shortcoming which proved nearly fatal for Dietrich. On the twenty-sixth, as he and his adjutant were driving
toward the front, their car came under machine-gun fire from
an isolated house, which unbeknown to the Germans, had

been occupied by British troops. The automobile's fuel tank caught fire, and its flaming contents pursued Dietrich and his subordinate as they fled to the shelter of a roadside ditch and then into a culvert passing beneath the road. Although providing protection from enemy bullets, the culvert was not proof against the heat of the blazing gasoline, forcing the two men to smear themselves with wet mud, which to their good fortune was present in abundance. Fortunately too, Dietrich's plight was observed by one of Leibstandarte's radio units which alerted Guderian's headquarters, precipitating a gallop to the rescue by a tank regiment of the 2nd Panzer Division, whose men in due course deposited the dripping Dietrich before an amused audience at XIX Panzer Corps headquarters.[40]

Shortly before noon on the day of Dietrich's discomfiture, Hitler permitted a resumption of the advance on Dunkirk.[41] As part of the revived undertaking, a powerful and highly mobile striking force was assembled in Leibstandarte's bridgehead around Watten, including 20th Infantry Division (motorized), Dietrich's reinforced regiment, the Army's elite reinforced motorized infantry regiment Grossdeutschland, and substantial quantities of medium and heavy artillery.[42] On May 27 this force was to launch an attack in a northeasterly direction from the Watten bridgehead on Wormhoudt, about ten miles south of Dunkirk, which, if seized quickly enough, would cut the avenue of retreat to the Channel coast for large numbers of Allied troops. The attack began as scheduled and moved forward against opposition which inflicted only light casualties. Wormhoudt itself, defended by the 2nd Warwickshire Regiment, had fallen by the evening of May 28, yielding to Leibstandarte approximately 750 British prisoners.[43]

However, the evacuation of the British Expeditionary Force and large numbers of French troops from the beaches and quays around Dunkirk was operating in top gear, and the German High Command was growing increasingly pessimistic about the chances of penetrating to Dunkirk before the evacuation had been substantially completed, a realistic assessment of the situation in view of the tenacity of the Allied defense and the swampy and canalized terrain which was totally unfit for mechanized operations. At the end of May 1940, the seizure of Dunkirk could be regarded as a problem of secondary importance in view of the fact that the bulk of the

French army was still largely intact south of the Somme.[44] On May 29, therefore, Guderian's XIX Panzer Corps was relieved by von Wietersheim's XIV Corps, the former to move south of the Somme and Aisne Rivers for operations intended to penetrate deep into the enemy's rear, preventing an orderly retirement and the construction of new defensive positions. Leibstandarte was initially subordinated to XIV Corps and, although ordered to prepare for an attack on Dunkirk on May 30, was removed from Wietersheim's command on the following day and sent into quarters south of Calais.[45] Although the French commander-in-chief, General Maxime Weygand, could dispose of approximately seventy-one divisions or their equivalents, his troops were outnumbered by almost two to one, and his disadvantage was even greater in terms of armor and airpower. Weygand's hope that the Somme line might be held until June 15 was indeed a pathetic one.[46]

The new stage of the offensive, Operation Red, commenced at dawn on June 5 with a general attack by von Bock's Army Group B directed toward the Seine on both sides of Paris, followed four days later by a second attack between Bock's left flank and the Franco-German border by von Rundstedt's Army Group A.[47] Leibstandarte began its operations alongside Hausser's Verfügungs Division as part of Kleist's Panzergruppe, the major element of von Reichenau's 6th Army in the center of the front of Army Group B.[48]

Following initial combat around Marquion northwest of Cambrai, Leibstandarte had crossed the Somme at Pérone on the seventh and advanced south to Roye on the Avre River in the wake of XVI Corps' armor.[49] The French 47th Division had established itself south of the river around Crapeaumesnil, a move which was interpreted by XVI Corps headquarters as part of an effort to build a new front behind the Oise.[50] The progress of Kleist's Gruppe had been much slower than expected and at considerable cost to its armored strength. On the right of 6th Army, von Kluge's 4th Army, led by Hoth's XV Panzer Corps, stormed irresistibly ahead toward the Seine west of Paris, while to the east of Kleist's forces the Aisne had been reached both by the infantry of Reichenau's easternmost corps (XXXXIV) and by elements of 9th Army east of Soissons.[51] In this sector it appeared that a rapid advance to the Marne was possible.

Sixteenth Corps planned a two-pronged attack for the morning of June 8 which was to punch through French positions around Crapeaumesnil with Leibstandarte on the right flank leading the way under cover of artificial smoke for the SS Verfügungs and 3rd Panzer Division.[52] At the last moment, however, the attack was cancelled and the participating units withdrawn into defensive positions. The sudden cancellation was the result of von Bock's decision, made on the same morning, to withdraw Kleist's Panzergruppe from the center of Army Group B's front and to recommit it further to the east where the going had proven considerably easier.[53] Early in the evening Leibstandarte was detached from XVI Corps and subordinated on the ninth to Lieutenant-General Ferdinand Koch's XXXXIV Corps.[54] On the morning of the tenth, Koch's Corps launched an attack directed toward the heights west and southwest of Chateau-Thierry in preparation for a crossing of the Marne. For this attack Leibstandarte's forces were divided with the bulk of the regiment attacking on the right with 72nd Infantry Division and a reinforced battalion on the left attached to 1st Mountain Division.[55] Enemy resistance was stiff, and in spite of the fact that Leibstandarte and 72nd Infantry Division took five hundred prisoners in the course of heavy fighting on June 11, the Marne was not crossed until the morning of the twelfth with Leibstandarte's II Battalion securing a bridgehead at St. Aulde.[56]

Von Bock had already ordered Kleist's Panzergruppe up to exploit the Marne crossings, and the latter's two corps (XVI and XIV), much delayed by colossal traffic jams on the Aisne and Marne bridges, were arriving on the Marne front by June 12.[57] On the thirteenth, Leibstandarte was reassimilated into Kleist's Gruppe as its mobile reserve, and on the following day the Panzergruppe, now transferred to von Rundstedt's Army Group A, thrust toward the Seine southeast of Paris, the same day on which the French capital was entered by elements of the 8th, 9th, and 28th Divisions and the Maginot Line was penetrated by 1st Army south of Saarbrücken.[58] The Allied cause in France was now clearly hopeless, and the German advance assumed the aspect of a French rout.

Kleist's Panzergruppe was in substantial measure an SS striking force, for in addition to four army panzer divisions

(3rd, 4th, 9th, and 10th) and a motorized infantry division
(the 13th), it included the SS Totenkopf Division, SS Verfügungs Division and Leibstandarte.[59] The two SS divisions
plodded along behind the fast-moving panzer divisions, dealing with isolated pockets of resistance and rounding up prisoners, until on June 20 both were reassigned with XIV Corps
to von Bock's Army Group B for the uneventful securing of
the French coast to the Spanish frontier.[60]

In the meantime, Leibstandarte acted as a fast reconnaissance
force for Kleist's Panzergruppe, racing deep into east-central
France. Often the regiment did not pause to take prisoners
but simply diverted the demoralized French soldiery to the
rear without guard.[61] Occasionally, Leibstandarte encountered determined resistance. On June 20 near Riom Leibstandarte's 6th Company came under heavy French machine-gun
and mortar fire, which was quickly suppressed by direct fire
from the 12th battery of the regiment's artillery detachment.[62]
By June 21, Leibstandarte, with headquarters in Vichy, had
assumed security duties in the Riom-Vichy-Clermont-Ferrand
area west of the Loire, an assignment which included the
guarding of part of the vast cache of prisoners and booty
taken by the XVI Corps.[63]

While enemy resistance had virtually ceased west of the
Loire, farther to the east in the mountainous Franco-Italian
border region between Mont Blanc and the Mediterranean
coast strong French forces were ensconced and successfully
resisting the feeble offensive begun by Mussolini on June 21.[64]
The opportunity existed for XVI Corps to strike eastward and
take the small French army of the Alps in the rear, thus opening the road into southeastern France for their Italian allies.
As Italian claims to a share in the French booty were likely
to be linked to the depth of their military penetration, this
opportunity was not seized with enthusiasm by the Germans.[65] On the morning of June 23, XVI Corps began a cau-
tious advance up the valley of the Isère against tough
opposition offered by French mountain troops but had not yet
reached Grenoble when, at 1:35 on the morning of June 25,
all combat operations ceased. In this, the last offensive of
Operation Red, Leibstandarte took and secured St. Étienne
as the anchor of the Corps' right flank.[66]

The conclusion of the campaign in the West was an occasion for celebration and euphoric self-assessment. Unlike its hesitant and awkward performance in the Polish operations nine months earlier, Leibstandarte's conduct in the West demonstrated self-assurance and aplomb which the army was reluctant to acknowledge.[67] Dietrich, however, exulted in what he considered to be the almost flawless performance of his regiment and expressed pride in having led "the only unit in the *army* [italics mine] to bear the Führer's name."[68] This remarkable statement demonstrated a sense of identification with the regular army which was to become progressively stronger in the mind of the former sergeant of World War I. Hitler's satisfaction with Leibstandarte's performance was demonstrated in the awarding to Dietrich of the Knight's Cross of the Iron Cross, specifically for his seizure of the Watten bridgehead, even though that had been accomplished in defiance of others. A short time later, Hitler declared to Leibstandarte that, "It will be an honor for you, who bear my name, to lead every German attack."[69]

Leibstandarte was denied the satisfaction of marching through Paris before its Führer when Hitler, with unusual restraint, contented himself with a guided tour of the city in place of a triumphal military procession.[70] Dietrich's regiment was ordered to Metz for further training and refitting. There, it was briefly caught up in the confused and vacillating preparations for the amphibious invasion of England. Waterborne exercises were carried out on the nearby Moselle, and the men of Leibstandarte acquainted themselves with the use of British maps and, no doubt disturbingly, the use of life jackets as well.[71]

Of greater significance to the future combat role of Leibstandarte was the substantial expansion undertaken during the interlude at Metz. On August 12, Himmler informed the army high command that Hitler had ordered his Leibstandarte enlarged from a reinforced regiment to a "strong brigade."[72] This reinforcement was ultimately to entail the addition of an engineer battalion, a heavy weapons battalion, and the expansion of the artillery battalion to regimental strength.[73] The manpower available to the Waffen-SS was still severely limited by the army, and the growth of Leibstandarte, therefore, was not primarily a matter of inductions and training of fresh recruits but of robbing Peter to pay Paul. Many of the men

required to effect the expansion were taken from the Verfügungs and Totenkopf Divisions.[74]

By the beginning of 1941, the restructuring and reinforcement of Leibstandarte had been largely completed. The
expansion of the unit to brigade strength was correctly interpreted by its members as a portent of its imminent commitment to a new theater of operations, and one of the most
common topics of barracks scuttlebutt was its future destination.[75] Rumors proliferated when on the morning of January 14 an advance element entrained at Metz for a "secret"
destination, but the departure of the mass of the unit, seemingly scheduled for the end of January or beginning of February, was suddenly cancelled on Hitler's orders.[76] At last, in
the first days of March, Leibstandarte departed Metz and
headed eastward.[77]

6
Marita

Mussolini's attack on Greece in October 1940, which began almost immediately to stumble toward disaster, and the right obtained by Great Britain to land military forces in that country presented Germany with an awkward situation, particularly in view of Hitler's determination, expressed in Directive No. 21 of December 18, 1940, to seek a military decision with the Soviet Union in the spring of the following year. Five days earlier in Directive No. 20, Hitler had ordered the planning of a limited operation in the Balkans to eliminate the protracted danger of a second front in that area (Operation Marita). At first Marita involved only an invasion of Greece to be carried out by 12th Army under the command of Field Marshal Wilhelm List.[1] The newly refurbished Leibstandarte was immediately allotted to List's army, which was to strike south from Bulgaria, a signatory of the Tri-Partite Pact, across the Greek frontier toward Salonica.[2] Dietrich's unit traveled from Metz across Southern Germany, Bohemia, and Hungary into Rumania, with assembly in an area west of Bucharest, where an effort seems to have been made to mask it as part of a German training mission. By March 23 Leibstandarte was moving south to its staging area in Bulgaria.[3]

The overthrow of the pliable Yugoslav government on March 27, less than two days after it had signed the Tri-Partite Pact, put that country, too, on the list of Hitler's victims, necessitating the hasty revision of operational plans and the postponement of the attack on the Soviet Union for at least a month. Twelfth Army was now ordered to thrust west across the Yugoslav-Bulgarian border toward Skoplje and then swing south into Greece. Second Army was to attack southward from the Klagenfurt area toward Zagreb while XXXXVI Panzer Corps, attacking from southwestern Hungary, and Kleist's Panzergruppe, thrusting across the Yugoslav-Bulgarian frontier north of Sofia, were to advance on Belgrade from the north and south respectively. The fact that Marita could be so substantially revised without the necessity of postponing the attack indicates the high quality of German organization and staff work.[4]

Early on the morning of April 6, XXXX Corps (9th Panzer Division, 73rd Infantry Division, and Leibstandarte) launched an attack from the area west of Kyustendil toward the Yugoslavian frontier. Leibstandarte was to remain on Bulgarian soil in the opening stages of the offensive, preparing to follow 9th Panzer Division as a mobile reserve.[5] Temporary inactivity did not, however, prevent casualties, for a Yugoslavian air strike on the opening day of the offensive, ironically carried out by German aircraft earlier sold to Yugoslavia, seriously wounded the commander of II Battalion and the chief of the second battery of Leibstandarte's artillery regiment.[6]

A motorcycle company of the Leibstandarte following advanced elements of 9th Panzer Division reached an area northwest of Kratovo by early afternoon on the seventh, and a few hours later Skoplje was in German hands.[7] The bulk of Leibstandarte now crossed the Yugoslavian frontier and, skirting Skoplje on the southeast, thrust due south leading 9th Panzer Division toward the Greek frontier. In the early morning of April 9, Leibstandarte reached Prilep almost fifty miles south of Skoplje without having encountered enemy resistance. Dietrich now ordered his reconnaissance detachment to move forward to the area Bitola-Monastir and to reconnoitre across the Greek frontier in the direction of Florina and Veve. Here, significant resistance was encountered for the first time, Bitola being taken by late afternoon only after stiff house-to-house combat. The entire operation was an impressive victory for the Leibstandarte, netting some six hundred prisoners and large quantities of equipment for a cost of two men killed and five wounded.[8]

Far more significant than the destruction of two confused and demoralized Yugoslavian battalions, however, was the fact that Leibstandarte, in preparing to strike through the Monastir Gap toward Florina and Veve, threatened the left flank of the hastily fashioned defensive line of British Lieutenant-General Sir Henry Wilson. Should the Germans penetrate the Klidi Pass southwest of Veve, not only would Wilson's line from Veve to the Gulf of Salonika become untenable, but the tenuous link with the Greek front in Albania would be severed.[9]

By the early evening of April 9, the Leibstandarte's motorcycleborne riflemen had crossed the Greek frontier and penetrated to Florina, a few miles west-northwest of Veve. Florina was found to be free of the enemy, and the cyclists continued in darkness toward Veve itself, passing through motorized British forces being assembled for the defense of the vital pass. Wilson's men were obviously unprepared for the sudden arrival of Dietrich's forward element, for the town was entered at about ten o'clock against light opposition. Almost immediately, however, the cyclists came under heavy artillery and small-arms fire from strong enemy positions on the heights south and east of town. The lightly armed reconnaissance force thereupon withdrew to the railroad station west of Veve to await the arrival of reinforcements.[10]

The Leibstandarte's reconnaissance detachment, which had been sweeping the area to the west of Monastir, made contact with the left wing of the Italians' Albanian front on the afternoon of April 11. British fighters and light bombers along with small British combat groups sent north to harass the Germans disrupted the Leibstandarte's main line of advance from Bitola southward toward Veve.[11] The delay was of vital importance to Wilson's forces, for the decision had already been made to abandon the northern defense line and fall back on new positions south of the Aliakmon River. To block the British retreat, which had been anticipated by the Germans, XXXX Corps headquarters ordered Leibstandarte to strike through the Klidi Pass and on to Kozani.[12] Wilson considered it crucial that the pass be held by the British at least until the night of April 12–13 to give his forces adequate opportunity to regroup.[13]

The way through Klidi Pass was led by a battlegroup under the command of Sturmbannführer Fritz Witt, one of the original members of the Leibstandarte SS Adolf Hitler. Battlegroup Witt, composed of one battalion of infantry supported by field howitzers and 37 and 88 mm. antiaircraft guns, set out on the morning of April 10, struggling painfully forward over the most difficult terrain and under constant fire from machine-gun nests situated in the rocky heights, their task further complicated by blown bridges, mines, occasional air attacks, and a sudden fall of snow.[14] Finally, on the morning of the twelfth, Witt's group stood before Height 997, the key to the defense of the pass, held by Wilson's rear guard, from which the men of the Australian 6th Division had been able to observe the battlegroup's every move. Supported by a mass of artillery, including guns sent forward by XXXX Corps, Leibstandarte's 1st Company, led by Obersturmführer (First Lieutenant) Gert Pleiss, stormed the height and took it in hand-to-hand combat.[15]

Progress southward now continued at a faster pace as Witt was able to use the captured height to direct machine-gun and 37 mm. antitank gunfire against remaining enemy strongpoints. By late afternoon the village of Klidi and the southern exit of the pass were reached as the defenders fell back toward Ptolemais, although Witt's group continued to receive fire from rear guards throughout the evening.[16]

On the morning of the thirteenth, Witt's battlegroup stood at the crossroads west of Soter, about ten miles north of Ptolemais. A dozen British tanks, probably of the 1st Armored Brigade Group, appeared on the heights southeast of the north-south road around 6:30 and brought the leading elements of the battlegroup, including Witt's combat headquarters, under machine-gun and cannon fire. A 37 mm. antitank gun, which was quickly brought forward, had no discernible effect on the British tanks, which rolled slowly forward. Two hours later Leibstandarte's 88 mm. flak battery took the British armor under fire and, according to German records, destroyed eight tanks and forced the remainder to retire.[17]

Witt's battlegroup was relieved by 9th Panzer Division, moving southward through the newly opened pass and taking over the pursuit of the retreating enemy. The three-day action in the Klidi Pass had cost Witt thirty-seven officers and men killed and ninety-five wounded. On the other side of the ledger, the battlegroup had taken 520 prisoners and captured or destroyed much heavy equipment.[18] Its most significant achievement was the opening of the pass itself, which led into the heart of Greece. For this action Gert Pleiss was to receive the Knight's Cross, and fourteen other members of Battlegroup Witt the Iron Cross First Class.[19]

If the army had earlier been reluctant to recognize the achievements of the Waffen-SS, it could not readily ignore the Leibstandarte's success. In an order of the day, the commander of XXXX Corps, General of Cavalry Stumme, expressed to the Leibstandarte his

> thanks and fullest recognition for the opening of the Klidi Pass, which resulted from the same unshakeable offensive spirit which the Leibstandarte constantly displays.
>
> The present victory signifies for the Leibstandarte a new and imperishable page of honor in its history. Forward for Führer, Volk and Reich![20]

The mountainous Greek terrain forced the invaders to operate in relatively small, self-sufficient units. As was illustrated by Witt's thrust through the Klidi Pass, the Leibstandarte performed well under these conditions. The advance of the Leibstandarte's reconnaissance detachment under the command of the flamboyant Sturmbannführer Kurt Meyer southwest from the Klidi area through the Klissura Pass to Lake Kastoria, then being used by the Greek Albanian army as a pivot in its withdrawal from Albania, further demonstrated Leibstandarte's competence in this type of fighting.

Meyer's attack, which began in the mid-afternoon of April 13, encountered problems similar to those faced by Witt a few days earlier. The defenders, this time Greek, occupied strong positions, some of them on rocky promontories towering almost five thousand feet above sea level.[21] Supported by a battery of 150 mm. howitzers, the attack proceeded initially without great difficulty. By the morning of the fourteenth, Meyer's force encountered the enemy well entrenched in the village of Werjes and on the heights on either side. Organized in three assault groups, one led personally by Meyer, an attack was launched at dawn and had broken through the outer defenses by eleven o'clock. By afternoon, Meyer had captured over six hundred officers and men of the Greek 20th Infantry Division for a loss of one officer and six men killed and one officer and seventeen men wounded.[22] In the course of the following day Meyer's reconnaissance detachment swung south of Lake Kastoria and, advancing north along the western shore, took the town of Kastoria from the south by early evening. The booty was impressive, including over twelve thousand prisoners and untold quantities of equipment and supplies.[23] For this and subsequent actions in the Greek campaign, Meyer, too, was to receive the Knight's Cross.[24]

The Greek army in its retreat south from Albania was now being funneled into Epirus between the Pindus Mountains and the Ionian Sea. Fortieth Corps was given the opportunity to sweep in a southeasterly direction and fall upon the new British defense line behind the Aliakmon River in the flank and rear, a particularly attractive prospect since probing frontal attacks on the line in the Servia area on the night of April 14–15 had been roughly handled.[25] On April 16, Leibstandarte was ordered to undertake such a flanking maneuver by striking south from Kastoria toward Elasson, south-southwest of Mt. Olympus.[26]

General Wilson, having already perceived the mortal danger to his expeditionary force, had initiated a retirement to the Thermopylae positions far to the south preparatory to a possible general evacuation of the Greek Peninsula.[27] By April 18 the retreat was well under way with the bulk of XXXX Corps in pursuit. Leibstandarte, however, was now swung back to a southeasterly direction and advanced through the Pindus Mountains to prevent the continued retreat of the now thoroughly demoralized Greek Army in Epirus and to thrust into its flank and rear.[28]

Shortly after nine o'clock on the morning of April 20, the leading elements of the Leibstandarte's II Battalion stood in the Katarra Pass, the sole entrance to Epirus through the Pindus range. After a brief fire-fight, a motorcycle carrying a white flag appeared in the pass followed by two automobiles containing Greek staff officers. A Greek lieutenant speaking in halting German informed a flabbergasted German platoon leader that the entire Greek Army in Epirus, totalling sixteen divisions, was prepared to surrender to the Leibstandarte. The following message was immediately relayed to Dietrich:

The point of Battlegroup Horstmann reached the Katarra Pass at 8:15. After a brief preliminary engagement . . . , a Greek delegate under a flag of truce offered the surrender of the entire Greek army (General Tsolakoglou). The reinforced II Battalion is detaining the delegation, keeping the army under surveillance, and requests that the Obergruppenführer come forward. . . .

Dietrich at once set out for II Battalion but due to heavy traffic on the mountain road did not reach the area until almost four in the afternoon. Second Battalion had already erected a swastika banner which fluttered over the road as Dietrich arrived to the enthusiastic cheers of his victorious troopers. The Leibstandarte's commander was in understandably high spirits as he stepped from his car, delivered a ''well done'' to the men of II Battalion, and set out through the Greek lines for a personal interview with Tsolakoglou.[29]

Dietrich had not informed his superiors of the impending capitulation but was justified in seizing the opportunity offered him, as prior to the opening of the campaign Hitler had ordered that every enemy offer of surrender be accepted on the spot by the local commander.[30] The instrument drafted by Dietrich and Tsolakoglou was chivalrous, even anachronistic in the context of World War II. Officers were allowed to retain their weapons, and enlisted men, after having surrendered their arms, were permitted to retire to their homes. The two principals returned to the pass for the actual signing of the capitulation which took place under both national flags.[31] It was Hitler's fifty-second birthday.

Not until noon of the following day did Dietrich meet the commander of 12th Army, Field Marshal List, on the airfield at Larrissa and inform him personally of the previous day's events. Hitler, too, had been told of the capitulation and initially agreed to its terms. Mussolini, however, when informed of the surrender, flew into a rage at its lenient terms and its having been concluded without the knowledge and participation of the Italians.[32] On April 21, therefore, a second surrender agreement was signed by Tsolakoglou and Lieutenant-General Hans von Greiffenberg, List's chief of staff, and formally adhered to by Italy on April 23. This harsher document provided for the temporary detainment of Greek soldiers in prison camps although Greek officers were still permitted to retain their side arms. Hitler, somewhat unfairly, chided Dietrich for the strain imposed on the Rome-Berlin Axis by his excursion into the sphere of high diplomacy. "You are a good, brave soldier, but no diplomat, and still less a politician. You forgot that we still have a friend called Mussolini, and he is angry."[33]

Greek and German soldiers shared a strong admiration for each other's fighting qualities and contempt for the ineptitude of the Italian army. As the Leibstandarte advanced through Greek lines following the surrender of the Epirus Army, its members were greeted by applause and shouts of "Heil Hitler" and "Heil Germania," which Leibstandarte's II Battalion, detached from the brigade in order to effect a linkup with Italian forces in southern Albania, actively protected the withdrawing Greek forces from pursuit by the long-frustrated and overzealous Italians.[34]

Operation Marita, to all intents, had ended for Dietrich and the Leibstandarte with the surrender of the Epirus Army. The surrender of that army had also made hopeless the position of the British Expeditionary Force in the Thermopylae defenses, and the decision to begin the evacuation from Greece had been made early on the morning of April 21.[35] Embarkation began on the twenty-fourth and continued until the night of April 28–29. As at Dunkirk almost a year earlier, most of the surviving personnel of the British Expeditionary Force but little equipment was rescued, the tenacity of the defense at the points of embarkation and the unsuitability of the terrain for armored units robbing the Germans of an annihilating victory.[36]

It was not until April 26 that Leibstandarte (minus II Battalion) began moving south from the Jannina area toward the main embarkation ports on the Peloponnese.[37] By the twenty-seventh, after a daring amphibious raid by Meyer's detachment, Leibstandarte had been ferried across the Gulf of Corinth and had taken the port of Patras preparatory to sweeping down the west coast of the Peloponnese to Pirgos. On the eastern side of the peninsula 5th Panzer Division had moved into the Peloponnese on the twenty-eighth and had swept south and west to Kalamata by evening. By that time, however, the bulk of the British Expeditionary Force had been successfully evacuated, and the lightning thrusts by both units netted few prisoners.[38]

The SS derived intense satisfaction from the spectacular performance of Dietrich and his unit. SS-Obergruppenführer Kurt Daleuge, with Dietrich an *alter Kämpfer* and veteran of the formative stages of the SS, wrote to his old comrade of "the great joy that you are able to prove here [in Berlin] once again what one as an *alter Kämpfer* is able to perform without general staff training. Once again, proof for the Wehrmacht that they must change their opinions once and for all!"[39]

During a brief refit near Brno Leibstandarte was given an additional motorized infantry battalion and was now officially designated SS Division "Leibstandarte SS Adolf Hitler."[40] The directives surrounding this reinforcement are important in revealing the élite character which the Leibstandarte still possessed. Again the necessary personnel were to be taken from preexistent Waffen-SS units but the men selected were to be the best, of the proper height and, most significantly, Reich Germans.[41] The growing Waffen-SS was already drawing heavily on *Volksdeutsche*, persons of German ancestry residing outside Germany's frontiers, and upon non-German "Nordics" to fill its ranks. The decision to incorporate these persons into the Waffen-SS could be justified ideologically but was taken largely because of the slim allotments of Reich German recruits permitted the Waffen-SS by the Wehrmacht.[42] It is clear that the Leibstandarte was being preserved as a purely German unit, even under the pressure of the exigencies of combat, undoubtedly because it was assumed that Dietrich and his men would return to their original role as a security force for the Nazi regime after the war, in the fulfillment of which their ties to the Führer would have to remain undiluted by exterior loyalties. Indeed, in the fall of 1941 grandiose plans were afoot for the quartering of the Leibstandarte upon its return to Germany, presumably upon the conclusion of the war, which at that time was almost momentarily expected. It was proposed, for example, that an enormous barracks complex be constructed in Berlin large enough to house the entire eighteen-thousand-man division which the Leibstandarte was shortly to become.[43] The barracks were never constructed, but even at one of the most critical stages of the war, the potential role of the Leibstandarte as an internal security force was not forgotten. Goebbels predicted in March 1943 that ''in case there were ever an attempt at revolt in Berlin by foreign workers, the Fuehrer would send his Leibstandarte to the capital; it would make an example of them all that would make every lover of such excesses lose all itch for them.''[44]

Goebbels's conjecture was contemporary with the achievement by Dietrich and the Leibstandarte of the apex of their prestige and their attainment, in Hitler's mind at least, of a reputation as a military force of almost superhuman qualities. This image, suggested by the operations in the West in 1940 and much advanced by the spectacular coups in Greece of the following April, was matured in the cataclysmic campaigns on the Russian front.

7
Barbarossa

The German invasion of the Soviet Union (Operation Barbarossa), unleashed in the predawn hours of June 22, 1941, took place along a front over nine hundred miles in length, stretching from the Baltic in the north to the Black Sea in the south. For the initial assault, 139 divisions were distributed among forty-four corps, twelve armies and armored groups, and three army groups.[1]

Leibstandarte was assigned to Rundstedt's Army Group South, and although directly subordinated to Colonel-General Ewald von Kleist's Panzergruppe 1, Rundstedt's primary mobile striking force, it did not enter the Ukraine until June 30. The one-week delay was due to the extensive refitting program undertaken in the aftermath of the Balkan campaign.[2]

The overall aim of the German offensive was to effect deep penetrations into the mass of enemy forces north and south of the Pripet Marshes, then to surround and annihilate the detached masses of the Russian armies.[3] Army Group South's general objective was the destruction of Russian forces between the Pripet Marshes and the Carpathians and the securing of bridgeheads over the Dnieper at and below Kiev, after which the army group was to strike for the heavily industrialized Donetz Basin.[4]

Unlike Army Groups North and Center, Army Group South faced bitter resistance in the opening days of the offensive. Although Kleist's group optimistically reported on June 22 that "tactical surprise" had been achieved and that some enemy units were retreating "helter-skelter," Rundstedt was forced to admit on the twenty-eighth that Army Group South was facing a "most determined adversary."[5] Indeed, Leibstandarte entered combat on July 1 in the vicinity of the Luck bridgehead over the Styr River in the face of vigorous Russian counterattacks from the northwest.[6] By July 4 the Russians were slowly withdrawing toward their fortified line (part of the so-called Stalin Line) behind the Sluch River with Kleist's group in pursuit. Leibstandarte, attached to General Eberhard von Mackensen's III Corps, had orders to protect and reconnoiter along the corps' lengthening northern flank. On July 7 the Stalin Line was breached at Hulsk and a bridgehead established on the east bank of the Sluch.[7] The breakthrough was expanded to the southeast with the taking of Berdichev on the same day; to secure the town Leibstandarte was briefly subordinated to Kempf's XXXXVIII Corps.[8] Early on July 9 Leibstandarte was reassigned to III Corps for a descent on Zhitomir which was taken later in the day after light combat. Kiev now seemed to be within reach, and 13th Panzer Division reached the inner defense line to the southwest of the city early on July 10.[9]

But the enemy's powers of resistance were far from broken. Poorly coordinated but vigorous Russian attacks struck both flanks of the German spearhead, the most dangerous being launched southward from the Pripet Marshes by the Russian 5th Army.[10] Until July 16 Leibstandarte was involved in furious defensive battles west of Zhitomir along the Kiev Road, defending without reserves a front of some eighteen miles but taking on July 14 some six hundred prisoners. Dietrich's division, having been relieved by 6th Army's infantry following slowly behind Kleist's mobile forces, now sped eastward to lend its strength to the defensive efforts of 73rd Panzer Division, facing attacks from three directions on both sides of and along the Kiev Road.[11] By the time the situation had been stabilized and the general advance to the southeast resumed on July 20, Leibstandarte had suffered substantial losses, numbering 683 men killed and wounded and more than one hundred vehicles rendered unserviceable.[12]

With Kleist's northern flank secured and its defense assumed by a newly arrived infantry division, the prerequisite for a devastating offensive stroke by his armored group had been achieved. South of the Kiev Road and west of the Dnieper, numerous Soviet divisions had been bypassed and were now being enclosed in a great pocket formed by the infantry divisions of von Reichenau's 6th Army to the north, von Stulpnagel's 17th Army advancing east on the Lemberg-Viniza Road to the south and von Kleist's armored group sweeping southeast from the Zhitomir-Berdichev area.[13]

To Mackensen's regret, Leibstandarte was removed from the control of III Corps and given to Kempf's XXXXVIII Armored Corps on July 24. While Mackensen's corps secured Kleist's left flank along the west bank of the Dnieper, the remainder of Kleist's force drove toward the juncture with the infantry divisions of 17th Army which would trap some twenty Soviet divisions in the Uman area.[14] By August 1 Kleist had broken through the Russian defenses at Novo Archangelsk and on the following day sealed the Uman pocket at Pervomaysk.[15] Leibstandarte's performance in the action was lauded by the commander of XXXXVIII Corps as follows:

> Since 24/7, the Leibstandarte SS Adolf Hitler has taken the most glorious part in the encirclement of the enemy around Uman. Committed at the focus of the battle for the seizure of the key enemy position at Archangelsk, the Leibstandarte SS Adolf Hitler, with incomparable dash, took the city and the heights to the south. In the spirit of the most devoted brotherhood of arms, they intervened on their own initiative in the arduous struggle of the 16th Infantry Division (motorized) on their left flank and routed the enemy, destroying numerous tanks.
>
> Today at the conclusion of the battle of annihilation around Uman, I want to recognize and express my special thanks to the Leibstandarte SS Adolf Hitler for their exemplary effort and incomparable bravery.
>
> The battles around Archangelsk will be recorded indelibly and forever in the war history of the Leibstandarte SS Adolf Hitler.[16]

Of the 103,000 prisoners and vast quantities of equipment captured or destroyed in the Uman operations, Leibstandarte had taken 2200 officers and men and destroyed sixty-four tanks.[17]

Army Group South was now free to move up to the west

bank of the Dnieper within the great bend of the river from Kiev south to the Black Sea. While Mackensen's III Corps drove on Dnepropetrovsk, Leibstandarte with 16th Panzer Division took Nikolayev on the Southern Bug and then proceeded independently to Kherson near the mouth of the Dnieper, taking the city on August 19.[18] Here, Dietrich's division wreaked considerable havoc upon Russian river shipping with its 50 mm. antitank and 88 mm. antiaircraft weapons.[19]

Having been in continuous combat for over seven weeks, Leibstandarte's exhausted men and battered vehicles were in dire need of respite, and on August 22 the unit was ordered to a quiet area south of Kirovograd for refitting. The much-needed refit was only partially successful since the required equipment had not reached the rest area; 674 replacement troops were received, indicating the relatively severe losses which the division had sustained in the actions of the previous weeks.[20]

In the meantime, a fateful decision had been made concerning the future conduct of Barbarossa. To the dismay of the army high command, Hitler on August 21 ordered that Moscow be abandoned as the immediate and overriding objective of the German offensive. Instead, two major efforts were now to be made on both flanks of the Russian front with Leningrad and the Crimea and Donetz Basin as their objectives, these, particularly the latter, having come to represent in Hitler's mind decisive economic targets which far outweighed the merely "geographical idea" of the Russian capital. Involved in Hitler's order of August 21 was another factor which constituted both an attractive end in itself and a prerequisite to the flank solution. Concentrated east of the Dnieper in the Kiev area were the one million men of Marshal Semyon Budenny's Southwest Front, which seemed to offer itself enticingly to a double envelopment by the mobile forces of Army Groups Center and South. Furthermore, the advance of Army Group South toward the Crimea and the Donetz could not well be undertaken with so powerful a force menacing its left flank.[21]

Guderian's Panzergruppe 2 was diverted south from its line of advance on Moscow and crossed the Desna by the beginning of September.[22] On September 12 a spearhead of Guderian's Group reached Lokhvista and there awaited the arrival of Kleist's Panzergruppe 1, which on the previous day had begun to cross the Dnieper southeast of Kiev at Kremenchug. On September 15 the two panzer groups closed the ring encircling Budenny's armies. The subsequent liquidation of the human and material contents of the great pocket yielded 665,000 prisoners and vast quantities of equipment and supplies.[23]

Although Kempf's XXXXVIII Corps had played a major role in the battle of Kiev, having alone taken more than 109,000 prisoners, Leibstandarte did not share in the triumph. On September 3 Dietrich's division was assigned to 11th Army, then under the command of Colonel-General Ritter von Schobert but soon to be given to General Erich von Manstein following Schobert's death in an airplane crash. To 11th Army on the extreme right flank of Army Group South fell the task of leading Army Group South's drive toward the Crimea and the Donetz.[24]

By the time Leibstandarte had joined it, 11th Army had already established a bridgehead on the east bank of the Dnieper opposite Berislav. Meyer's reconnaissance detachment led Leibstandarte across the pontoon bridge at Berislav on September 11, and the division burst through the Russian defenses attempting to contain the bridgehead, reaching the Black Sea west of Perekop on the thirteenth. Manstein hoped to effect a rapid seizure of the Crimea, to which the Perekop Isthmus was the key, but his army, containing not a single tank unit, was inadequate for the task. Leibstandarte with its armored scout cars and half-tracked personnel carriers was 11th Army's ersatz panzer division, and much of the burden of effecting a breakthrough fell to Dietrich's understrength division. In fierce fighting from September 24 to September 26 Leibstandarte, operating side by side with the 46th and 73rd Infantry Divisions, succeeded in achieving a partial penetration of the stout Russian defenses, in the course of which its Engineer Battalion distinguished itself in the seizure of the key strong point of Preobrashenka.[25]

Eleventh Army faced other difficulties to the north and east, on the bleak plains of the Nogay Steppe fronting on the Sea of Azov. A weak fraction of Manstein's force, General von Salmuth's XXX Corps, supported by the ill-equipped and

poorly trained Rumanian 3rd Army, faced the powerful 9th
and 18th Russian Armies east of Melitopol. The Russians
produced an extremely awkward and hazardous situation for
11th Army on the evening of September 23–24 by launching
an attack which succeeded in tearing a wide gap in the
German-Rumanian front at the juncture point between the
Rumanian 3rd Army and von Salmuth's corps.[26] Manstein
was forced temporarily to abandon the Crimean undertaking
and throw all available support behind his eastern front which,
according to an assessment by 11th Army's intelligence, was
being assaulted by nine divisions and one armored brigade
backed by strong aerial support. Forty-ninth Corps and Leibstandarte were directed north and east to the Melitopol sector, leaving only the much weakened LIV Corps as a holding
force on the Perekop Isthmus. The highly mobile Leibstandarte, by now having achieved the reputation as a military
"fire brigade," was committed by Manstein on September
30 at the crucial joint where the 170th Rumanian Infantry
Division met the left flank of XXX Corps and where a new
Russian breakthrough threatened. Having repulsed a Russian
night attack, Dietrich restored the German-Rumanian front
in a successful counterattack.[27]

Already, however, powerful assistance was on the way
which would convert Manstein's dangerous predicament into
another colossal German victory. By the end of September
Kleist's Panzergruppe (soon to be redesignated "1st Panzer
Army") was freed of its duties in the Kiev sector and was
advancing in a southeasterly direction in order to participate
in the thrust along the north coast of the Sea of Azov toward
Rostov-on-Don.[28] The inner flanks of 11th Army and Kleist's
group met on October 6 in the Orechov sector and the outer
flanks around Berdyansk on the Sea of Azov the following
day. It was Dietrich's fast-moving division that closed the
pocket around a substantial Russian force, numbering on this
occasion between six and seven divisions of the Russian 9th
and 18th Armies. In addition to Berdyansk, Leibstandarte netted over two thousand Russian prisoners as well as two batteries of artillery, while on the previous day much of the staff
of the Russian 9th Army had been captured at Romorovka.[29]

The battle on the northern shores of the Sea of Azov, which
by its conclusion on October 10 had gained for Kleist and

Manstein some one hundred thousand prisoners and much equipment, permitted a resumption both of Army Group South's drive eastward and a renewed attempt to conquer the Crimea. This time, however, the entirety of Manstein's 11th Army would be committed to the Crimean undertaking which, nevertheless, would not be completed until July of the following year.[30]

Hitler had already determined that Dietrich's division was not to return to the Crimea but was rather to be reincorporated into Kleist's 1st Panzer Army for the pursuit of the remnants of the Russian 9th Army and the advance toward the lower Don.[31] To Mackensen's satisfaction, Leibstandarte was again assigned to his III Corps on October 7 and formed the spearhead of its thrust eastward, again proving its worth by seizing the port of Mariupol the following day, capturing three ships anchored in the harbor, and sinking a three thousand ton tanker with fire from its 88 mm. dual-purpose guns. Not until the morning of October 10 did the II Corps' 13th Panzer Division catch up to the Dietrich at Mariupol, relieving Leibstandarte for an advance to the lower Mius, the last natural obstacle before Rostov.[32]

Leibstandarte's progress, as usual, was being closely watched by Adolf Hitler. Already he envisioned "his" division on the far side of the Don and solicitously warned Dietrich of the danger which might be posed to the Don bridge south of Rostov by Russian gunboats operating on the river, advising him to site his 100 mm. batteries well north and south of the bridge as the best means of defending it.[33] Dietrich had not crossed the Mius, much less the Don, and it was not until the evening of October 12 that Fritz Witt's I Battalion was able to secure a foothold on the east bank north of Taganrog.[34]

The headlong advance of III Corps led by Leibstandarte now ground to a temporary halt in the face of heavy rain and stiffening Russian resistance.[35] On the evening of October 14 Leibstandarte encountered a Russian police battalion operating from Taganrog which raided the bridgehead at Koschkin and effected isolated although temporary penetrations.[36] By the morning of October 17 III Corps was ready for a general attack out of the Mius bridgehead. While 13th Panzer Division struck east across the Ssambek, Leibstandarte thrust south to Taganrog, finding the port city partially destroyed by the fleeing Russians and once again exercising its 88 mm. guns against numerous targets in the harbor.[37]

The latest triumph of III Corps was followed by ominous signs. Fuel shortages were general throughout Kleist's army and rendered impossible the immediate resumption of the eastward advance on Rostov. Heavy rains and resulting mud were accompanied by cold winds sweeping off the Sea of Azov, heralding the approach of winter for which neither Leibstandarte nor its army comrades were adequately clothed or equipped. Leibstandarte had not received adequate replacements for vehicles lost in combat or worn out through normal usage in spite of the occasional opportunity to incorporate captured Russian equipment.[38] Dietrich had already signaled Himmler to this effect, explaining that "the Leibstandarte SS Adolf Hitler was in most cases put forward for assignments in which the distance which needed to be traveled was far greater than for other units."[39]

On October 20 Mackensen's corps resumed its movement toward the lower Don under circumstances which rendered its ability to overcome determined Russian resistance, much less a major counterattack, extremely problematical. In the course of the following week, elements of the corps successfully beat off local Russian attacks, but by the end of the month the condition of III Corps was little short of disastrous.[40] As a result of disease (particularly dysentery) and combat attrition, 13th Panzer Division and Leibstandarte were reduced to roughly half their normal combat strength, while continued shortages of fuel had immobilized most of the combat vehicles of both divisions.[41] Mackensen frankly informed von Kleist that his corps might be able to carry out a raid of about 150 miles but only if it did not involve heavy combat.[42] In practical terms this meant that Rostov might be taken but probably could not be held against a major Russian counterattack.

On the left flank of Mackensen's Corps, XIV Panzer Corps had already knifed deep into the Donetz industrial area, having taken Stalino on October 20, and had penetrated to the upper Mius by the end of the month.[43] Fourteenth Corps was well situated to turn southward and fall upon Rostov from the north, and at the beginning of November most of the fuel and ammunition available to Kleist's army was funneled to this corps for that purpose. Fourteenth Corps was about to strike on November 7 when renewed heavy rain and resultant mud rendered its southward movement impossible.[44]

In the meantime Leibstandarte had succeeded in pushing northeast to the Tusloff River, about fifteen miles north of the city. Initially, Dietrich's division was ordered to swing to the south and open the way to Rostov for XIV Corps, but this assignment lapsed with the cancellation of the attack.[45] November 13 brought a sharp drop in temperature which, although subjecting the inadequately clothed troops to terrible sufferings and threatening to immobilize the remaining vehicles due to a shortage of antifreeze, restored the road surfaces to a passable state. Dietrich's progress had placed III Corps in the more advantageous position for a renewed assault on Rostov, and the corps was ordered to take the city in a lightning stroke.[46]

Leibstandarte, to which a reinforced panzer regiment of 13th Panzer Division had been subordinated, led the assault on November 17, quickly breaking through the Russian defensive positions south of the Tusloff. Progress was slower on the following day, but on the nineteenth Leibstandarte took the sprawling and heavily fortified village of Ssultan Ssaly while 14th Panzer Division penetrated to the northern suburbs of Rostov. The twentieth saw Leibstandarte and 14th Panzer Division break into the city and sweep through to the Don, their momentum being sufficient to secure two bridgeheads on the far side.[47] Following street fighting, some of it extraordinarily savage, which lasted into the afternoon of November 21, Rostov seemed firmly in German hands, although areas of the city were brought under heavy Russian artillery fire.[48]

On November 22 III Corps released a statement officially announcing the fall of Rostov and declaring that "thereby an important commercial and traffic center has fallen into our hands which is of *decisive importance* [italics mine] for the further prosecution of the war." Referring to the italicized words, someone on III Corps' staff penciled on the copy surviving in the corps' files the words, *"Das war unvorsichtig!"* (That was careless!).[49] Indeed, it was careless, for, since November 18, powerful Russian forces had been exerting increasing pressure against the northern wall of the German bulge around Rostov. On the same day that III Corps issued its triumphant pronouncement, Kleist ordered a gradual withdrawal from the Rostov bulge to winter positions behind the Mius.[50]

By the following morning the situation on the northern front of the bulge had seemingly been stabilized through a withdrawal to defensive positions south of the Tusloff. Kleist now recovered his nerve, cancelled the order of the previous day and even dared to think of renewed offensive operations.[51] On November 25, however, powerful Russian attacks were renewed not only against the northern wall of the bulge but to the south along the Don as well. Some of the heaviest of these attacks fell upon the suburb of Gnilowskaya, held by the Leibstandarte's reconnaissance detachment, then commanded by Hauptsturmführer Hugo Kraas in the absence of Meyer, ill with dysentery. On the morning of November 25 Kraas's men had succeeded in beating off an assault by elements of the 31st and 343rd Russian Divisions, killing 310 men and capturing 400 for a loss of two killed and seven wounded. Kleist seized upon this spectacular, although local defensive victory as a demonstration of the supposed fact "that a bold and self-assured unit will be master of the strongest mass attack."[52] It was, indeed, on the quality of *Draufgängertum* (dash), alluded to by Mackensen on this occasion, that Dietrich and the Leibstandarte were building their military reputation, but it was to be of little avail against the massive Russian superiority around Rostov. A rumor to the effect that Stalin had personally ordered the taking of the city by December 1 was current among the troops of III Corps, and given the numerical disparity between the opposing forces, it was clear that Rostov could not be held much longer. By November 27 Mackensen's corps was attempting to hold a seventy-mile front with three understrength divisions against what was estimated to be at least seven Russian infantry divisions and three cavalry divisions, an estimate later revised upward to fifteen divisions and several armored brigades.[53] Leibstandarte continued to be subjected to particularly heavy pressure which began in the predawn hours with heavy attacks by three Russian divisions supported by artillery and rocket fire and continued into the evening hours. Dietrich's division held that day, but by the early afternoon of November 28 Russian forces had penetrated to the industrial suburbs southwest of Rostov and were being engaged there. Simultaneously, heavy attacks strongly supported by armor were occurring all along the front, and early that evening Kleist ordered a general withdrawal from the Rostov sector.[54]

The abandonment of Rostov, the first major German setback on the eastern front, came as a rude shock to the Wehrmacht and to Hitler himself. The Führer seems to have accepted the idea of a partial withdrawal from the Rostov bulge, and, in fact, an effort was made to hold intermediate lines first behind the Temernik and then the Tschaltyr. Continued Russian pressure, however, made it imperative that Kleist's entire front be withdrawn to the shortest possible defensive line in preparation for the approaching winter, and on the afternoon of November 30 Kleist's Panzer Army began a final withdrawal to a line behind the Mius and Ssambek Rivers, some fifty miles west of Rostov.[55]

Hitler was enraged, and while Kleist escaped with an accusation of cowardice, von Rundstedt's command of Army Group South was given to Field Marshal Walther von Reichenau in the hope that the dashing and politically "reliable" former commander of 6th Army might restore the situation.[56] Here, Dietrich's personal friendship with the Führer assumed substantial tactical significance, for on the afternoon of December 1 Dietrich reported to von Reichenau that there was no chance of holding a line east of the Mius-Ssambek positions and requested that this evaluation be transmitted to Hitler. Later in the day, Dietrich sent a report directly to Hitler in which he frankly revealed the perilous condition of the Leibstandarte; its combat strength had now been reduced to 4713 officers and men and only 15 percent of its vehicles were still operative.[57]

In a remarkable demonstration of confidence in his comrade from the Kampfzeit, the Führer boarded a plane early in December and flew to Mariupol in order to learn directly from Dietrich the truth about the situation in the right flank of Army Group South. The Leibstandarte's commander succeeded in persuading him that the withdrawal from Rostov had not been due to deficiencies in leadership within Army Group South. On his return flight Hitler visited von Rundstedt and assured the latter of his continued confidence in him, although this rapprochement did not result at that time in a new command for the field marshal.[58]

Hitler's recourse to Dietrich for "the truth" was indicative of his growing estrangement from the leadership of the German army. Rundstedt's removal from command of Army Group South was only the first stage of a general shake-up of personnel within the higher command levels which occurred in the wake of the setbacks on the eastern front imposed by weather and the still-unbroken offensive strength of the Red Army. While Field Marshal Walther von Brauchitsch was relieved of his post as commander-in-chief of the army, an office now formally assumed by Hitler himself, and wholesale dismissals were taking place down to the corps level, Dietrich was being lionized by his supreme commander.[59] On December 31 Hitler awarded Dietrich the Oak Leaves to his Knight's Cross, an event which was celebrated a few days later in an article published in *Das Schwarze Korps*, the official SS journal.

> Always the same in the most difficult battles, in the bleakest hours [is] SS-Obergruppenführer Sepp Dietrich. Dietrich the commander, as the father of his men, as the model for his unit commanders, a hard soldier with a strange tender heart for his comrades. Ruthless in combat, demanding the ultimate in the attack, blessed with an ever-renewed and well-deserved soldier's luck, always the same old National Socialist, always the same old vassal of Adolf Hitler, simple and faithful in word and deed.
>
> The high decoration for Sepp Dietrich is recognition for a life spent in Adolf Hitler's battle for the Reich. . . .
>
> . . . In each hour of this hard life, he remained always the same, as a knight without fear and without reproach: the National Socialist soldier.[60]

The article in *Das Schwarze Korps* was paralleled in less inflated prose by Hitler:

> The role of Sepp Dietrich is unique. I've always given him opportunity to intervene at sore spots. He's a man who's simultaneously cunning, energetic and brutal. Under his

swashbuckling appearance, Dietrich is a serious, conscientious, scrupulous character. . . . For the German people, Sepp Dietrich is a national institution. For me personally there's always the fact that he is one of my oldest companions in the struggle.[61]

Hitler was shortly to give tangible expression to his affection in the form of a commission to Reich Minister Albert Speer to secure for Dietrich an elegant new residence in Berlin.

Implicit in Nazism and an outgrowth of its neo-Romantic roots was a deep-seated suspicion and even a hostility toward the application of closely reasoned and methodically prepared solutions to complex problems, be they political, social, diplomatic, or military. With the failure of the military technicians of the caliber of von Brauchitsch, von Rundstedt, and von Bock to achieve the aims mapped out by him, the Führer was inclined to turn with increasing frequency and desperation to figures who seemed to be guided by irrational qualities such as intuition, loyalty, and fanaticism. This development was a facet of his own progressive retreat from reality which assumed such bizarre proportions following the winter of 1942–43. Sepp Dietrich, with his minimal degree of formal education, his apparent lack of some of the elementary skills prerequisite to military command (according to one contemporary, he was unable to read a battle map), and his record of political reliability and absolute loyalty to Hitler, could scarcely have represented a more decisive alternative to the pedantic and elitist members of the German officer caste. The undeniable success of the Leibstandarte in the campaigns of the previous eighteen months lent additional weight to the Führer's conviction that charismatic qualities could overcome material and numerical obstacles to victory.

Other leading figures in the Nazi hierarchy were quick to emulate Hitler's recognition of Dietrich's unorthodox genius. Ulrich von Hassel asserts that at Goering's birthday party on January 12, 1942, the Reich marshal seized Dietrich and presented him to the company as the "pillar of the eastern front."[62] Goebbels reports that, in the course of a conversation on January 27, Dietrich described to him "in detail how the bourgeois generals on the southern front lost their nerve and how this weakness of character naturally communicated itself to the troops.''[63] Goebbels's statement, probably a distortion reflecting the propaganda minister's contempt for the ''bourgeois generals,'' may have been stimulated by unsettling rumors then current in SS circles of a supposed failure by army formations to have adequately supported Dietrich in the Rostov operations. A countersuspicion was current in army circles that Dietrich had played a decisive role in the fall of von Brauchitsch and von Rundstedt into official disfavor. This, however, was without foundation.[64]

Hitler's enthusiasm for the Leibstandarte's past performance and his confidence in its potential manifested themselves in a further strengthening of the division. Near the end of January 1942 Hitler personally ordered the formation of an armored detachment for the Leibstandarte to consist of three companies equipped principally with the 75 mm. gun-armed Mark IV tank. Training was to take place under the supervision of army instructors at the Wildflecken training installation.[65] At least some of the personnel for the armored detachment was probably drawn from a group of 480 boys whom the leadership of the Hitler Youth generously ''offered'' to the Leibstandarte, all of whom were of the required height and ''at least seventeen years old.''[66] In February Hitler ordered a further reinforcement of the division especially with artillery and antitank guns and forbade any reorganization of the Leibstandarte save on his personal command. The actual incorporation of the new units into the Leibstandarte remained in abeyance until the spring of 1942.[67]

While Sepp Dietrich, the ''national institution,'' was being feted in Berlin and, later, touring construction sites and delivering propaganda speeches to workers in the company of Albert Speer, his division was bearing the heavy burdens of defensive war in the savage eastern winter.[68] By the middle of December Leibstandarte had taken up positions on the right flank of III Corps along a short stretch of the coast of the Sea of Azov west of Taganrog and along a north-south line behind the Ssambek River for a distance of about six miles north of Taganrog. Along this line, the division was subjected to frequent harassment from Russian artillery and occasional probing infantry attacks although these did not

produce heavy casualties.[69] Far more dangerous was the nu-
tritional state of officers and men which had been deteriorating at an alarming rate since November and was due largely
to the overburdening of the German supply system during the
winter defensive campaigns. Leibstandarte had, however,
been the beneficiary in December 1941 of a large shipment
of winter clothing of unsavory provenance, drawn from SS
stocks in the Polish General Government.[70]

Toward the end of January von Mackensen was relieved of
his command of III Corps and sent north to assume control
of a composite group with headquarters at Stalino in order to
deal with a dangerous Russian thrust across the Donetz in the
area of Izyum.[71] Leibstandarte, along with the remaining
components of III Corps, remained on the Mius-Ssambek
line under the command of XIV Corps until the end of May.
Then the division removed by stages to an assembly area near
Stalino for a sorely needed refit and for the incorporation of
those new units ordered by Hitler during the previous winter.
Leibstandarte's combat strength had been partially restored
to around 5800 men, most of whom had not been granted
leave for more than two years.[72]

Also joining the division after its withdrawal from the
Mius-Ssambek line was a fifth infantry battalion. This battalion was apparently the Guard Battalion which Hitler had
ordered for "permanent" quartering in Berlin in January
1940. Its former role as a guard and security detachment was
filled by a new skeleton battalion designated "Guard Battalion Berlin" by the end of the year and "SS-Guard-Battalion
1, Berlin" by December 1943. This unit remained in the
Berlin area until the end of the war and participated in the
last-ditch defense of the capital in April–May 1945.[73]

Fifth Battalion had been removed from Lichterfelde
Barracks on February 22, 1942, and flown by a Luftwaffe
bomber group to the Leningrad sector of the front, where it
fought initially as part of a battlegroup commanded by the
brutal Higher SS and Police Leader "Ostland," SS-
Obergruppenführer Friedrich Jeckeln, although later removed
from Jeckeln's authority by Hitler's order.[74] Russian military
intelligence was quick to discover the presence of an element
of Hitler's personal guard and harassed the battalion over

loudspeakers with "We greet the Leibstandarte. Think about Rostov! We'll smash you here just as we did in the south."[75] Although this had been its first experience in combat, V Battalion acquitted itself well and was highly praised by L Corps before entraining in the second week of June for the trip south to the parent division.[76]

The army's general staff had intended to use the rebuilt and reinforced Leibstandarte in the renewed offensive operations of the summer of 1942 and, in fact, thought it of considerable importance to the success of 1st Panzer Army's thrust toward the lower Don.[77] Hitler, however, was convinced of the imminence of a descent by British forces on the Atlantic coast to provide relief for the hard-pressed Russian armies and refused to release Dietrich's division for the eastern offensive. By July 9 Hitler had decided to send Leibstandarte to the West, and on July 11 the division began to entrain for transfer to the Paris area.[78]

Following unloading and assembly at Fontainbleau, Dietrich's division was given the opportunity, denied it two years earlier, of marching through the French capital. The division's triumphal procession down the Champs Elysees on July 29 was witnessed by the new commander-in-chief West, Field Marshal von Rundstedt, the circumstances surrounding whose departure from Army Group South some eight months earlier were still fresh in Dietrich's mind.[79]

Hitler's sudden transfer of Dietrich's "fire brigade" to France illustrates the Führer's confidence in the Leibstandarte's unique potency on the battlefield as a result of the ideological commitment of its membership and the fanatical loyalty and charismatic qualities of its commander. Dietrich had written earlier to Himmler: "If our losses have not been exactly light, we have borne them proudly for our Führer and our homeland. Wherever we've fought we've successfully passed the test of strength. . . . And be assured, we'll continue to endure. . . . You can depend on us." He stressed to his subordinates in October 1942 the importance of indoctrinating the troops "in the National Socialist sense" and pointed out that when Hitler spoke of "the last battalion in the field" (presumably either in victory or defeat) he meant by his own statement the Leibstandarte SS Adolf Hitler.[80] The entire Waffen-SS claimed to possess this superior ideological commitment as is reflected in the following verses of an SS marching song:

> Comrade, and when the Führer speaks,
> SS springs at that bell.
> The Führer's word our duty is;
> Who quails at death and hell!
>
> The world to our step hearkens, for
> It knows from whence we came.
> We carry right and freedom—
> SS in Führer's name![81]

Three other SS divisions, Das Reich, Totenkopf, and Wiking, had reached a developmental stage equal to that of Leibstandarte and had, in fact, achieved the status of full division much earlier than Dietrich's unit. Two of these divisions, too, were transferred to France, Das Reich in July and Totenkopf in October 1942. It had already been planned at the end of May that the three SS divisions would constitute the components of an SS corps, but although the staff for such a corps was organized in June 1942 at the Bergen-Belsen training camp under the command of SS-Obergruppenführer Paul Hausser and transferred to France in July, Leibstandarte was not subordinated to it until January 1943.[82]

The five-month sojourn of Leibstandarte in France was relatively uneventful and served as a valuable rehabilitative period following the difficult fighting of the previous fall and winter. At the same time the division was unable to familiarize itself with terrain which would be the scene of bitter fighting two years later. As part of von Rundstedt's reserve Leibstandarte was alerted on the morning of August 19 and remained on alert for twenty-four hours as a British and Canadian reconnaissance force landed at Dieppe, but was not required to deal with the incursion.[83] Another charge of excitement passed through the division in the middle of September when intelligence sources suggested that a British landing was imminent on the Channel coast north of Le Havre and at an undefined point in Holland. By October 9 Hitler, according to von Rundstedt, was convinced that an assault on

Normandy was imminent and ordered that Leibstandarte be moved to Normandy to meet it. It was probably Hitler's certainty that Leibstandarte would be required for operations in France that prevented the division's transfer to North Africa during the same month.[84]

Hitler's increasing reliance on the elite Waffen-SS divisions led to the further strengthening of Leibstandarte during the fall of 1942. In October the division's armored detachment was increased to regimental strength and placed under the command of SS-Sturmbannführer Fritz Schönberger, while Das Reich and Totenkopf were comparably reinforced.[85] Hitler now ordered that all SS motorized divisions, which included Leibstandarte, Das Reich, Totenkopf, and Wiking Divisions, be redesignated ''SS-Panzer-Grenadier'' divisions, and Leibstandarte was to bear this designation until October 1943. In November Leibstandarte was allocated a company of super-heavy tanks (Tigers) which joined the new panzer regiment at its assembly area near Evreaux. The fact that these sixty-ton monsters had only entered service in September and were in very short supply is eloquent testimony of the favor in which the elite Waffen-SS divisions were now held. The heavy tank company was apparently almost immediately expanded to battalion strength and placed under the command of SS-Sturmbannführer Joachim Peiper.[86]

During the fall of 1942 the fortunes of the German war machine reached their apex, trembled at the summit for a brief instant, and then began a steady although not immediately precipitous decline. Since the beginning of November, Rommel had been falling back in good order from El Alamein, and on November 8, American and British forces landed in strength in French North Africa. Although surprised by the Allied *coup de main*, Hitler reacted quickly and vigorously, ordering an occupation of Vichy France in which operation Leibstandarte, Das Reich, and Totenkopf participated. Dietrich's division seized the harbor of Toulon on November 26.[87]

Four days earlier the mighty arms of a Soviet pincers had met at Kalatsch on the Don, surrounding the 6th Army at Stalingrad and cutting it off from Army Group B.[88] An effort to relieve the beleaguered garrison in December failed, in part owing to a new and massive Russian offensive on the middle Don. Here was a challenge worthy of the SS *corps d'élite*, and on December 30 Hitler ordered Leibstandarte, Das Reich, and Totenkopf, as components of Generalkommando SS-Panzer Korps, to prepare themselves for recommitment in the East.[89]

8
Kharkov and Kursk

At the beginning of 1943 the situation on the army southern sector of the eastern front was critical. Paulus's 6th Army, surrounded at Stalingrad, was beyond earthly salvation, while Manstein's Army Group Don, having failed to rescue Paulus, was itself threatened by Russian envelopment from north of the Donetz and south of the great bend of the Don.[1] Should Manstein's forces be destroyed or forced into a hasty withdrawal to escape destruction, von Kleist's Army Group A in the Caucasus would be hopelessly cut off. A threat to Rostov and hence to Kleist's exit from the Caucasus was staved off, but farther to the north around Voronezh, the Russians had opened a gap 175 miles wide and by the end of January had crossed the Donetz to the southeast of Kharkov.[2]

By that time Generalkommando SS Panzer Korps had taken up headquarters at Kharkov. At first, the operational strength of the corps included only Leibstandarte and Das Reich, Totenkopf having remained on coastal defense duty in France until the end of January.[3] Hitler expected the SS Panzer Corps to vigorously counterattack toward the southeast against the Russian breakthrough, although the confused and everywhere critical situation in the Kharkov area encouraged the piecemeal commitment of elements of the corps for meeting local crises. The Russians, retaining the initiative, forced the SS Panzer Corps into a defensive role from which it was unable to extricate itself.[4] Although ordered by Hitler to defend Kharkov to the last man, Hausser wisely withdrew from the city, threatened with encirclement, moving his corps south-west to the area around Krasnograd on February 16.[5]

Hitler at first demanded the immediate recapture of Khar-kov. Hausser's withdrawal, however, conformed in general with Manstein's plan which called for the removal of German forces to shorter and more economically defensible lines to permit the concentration of an operational reserve, a plan to which Hitler had given his assent on February 6.[6] By the fourth week in February, Army Detachment Hollidt and 1st Panzer Army, recently extricated from the Caucasus, held strong positions behind the Mius River shielding Manstein's gathering forces. On the morning of February 19, SS Panzer Corps led by Das Reich had boldly thrust toward the south-east from Krasnograd across the front of the Russian advance and, much strengthened by the arrival of the Totenkopf, had linked up with the three panzer divisions of XXXXVIII Pan-zer Corps on February 22.[7]

The two armored corps, one army and one SS, as the com-ponents of 4th Panzer Army, now launched a concentrated attack with effective air support northward in the direction of Pavlograd and Losuvaya and by February 25 had cut off and virtually annihilated a Russian armored group commanded by General M. M. Popov.[8] Having regained the initiative, SS Panzer Corps pursued disorganized Russian forces to the north and northeast, not, however, without loss. On February 26 the commander of Totenkopf and ex-commandant of the con-centration camp system, SS-Obergruppenführer Theodor Eicke, was killed when his light communications aircraft was shot down by Russian ground fire.[9] By March 6 a substantial victory was won as SS Panzer Corps, XXXXVIII Panzer Corps and Army Detachment Kempf encircled and destroyed large Russian armored forces west of Krasnograd, accounting for 615 tanks and some 1000 artillery pieces.[10] Forty-eighth Corps now swung east toward the Donetz while SS Panzer Corps pressed north toward Kharkov, the Tigers of Leibstan-darte's heavy tank battalion reaching the western fringes of the city on March 8. Hausser issued orders on the evening of the following day for the assault on the city proper to be undertaken on March 10. The third battle of Kharkov was about to begin.[11]

Hausser planned a multipronged attack against the city.

Totenkopf and Leibstandarte swung to the north of Kharkov on March 10, and while the former shielded the city against a possible Russian thrust from that direction, Dietrich's division prepared to enter the city from the north and northeast. Das Reich detached forces to cover the southern approaches while assembling assault groups for a penetration of Kharkov from the west.[12]

Leibstandarte, claiming over 150 Russian tanks destroyed in the previous month's combat, had also suffered heavy losses in armored equipment. On March 11 when the initial penetrations of the city from the north were effected, Dietrich had only twenty-three battleworthy tanks and, apparently, not a single Tiger.[13] Inside Kharkov were not only large numbers of the redoubtable T-34 tanks but a formidable series of defensive lines crisscrossing the city with strong points located in massive apartment complexes. In bitter house-to-house fighting, Leibstandarte succeeded in establishing contact with the advanced elements of Das Reich in the northwest quadrant of Kharkov by the evening of March 12, but while claiming sixteen T-34s destroyed in tank battles within the city, Leibstandarte was reduced to a total armored strength of fourteen Mark IV and five Mark III tanks.[14] Dietrich's division, paying the heavy cost of house-to-house fighting, moved painfully southward until on the evening of March 14 the southern positions of the city were secured.[15]

The recapture of Kharkov and the seizure of Belgorod four days later by SS Panzer Corps restored the southern wing of the Russian Front and brought to a close the grave crisis which had existed in that sector since November 1942. SS Panzer Corps had paid a heavy price in blood—according to Hausser, over eleven thousand officers and men were killed, wounded, or missing during the period between the arrival of the corps in Russia and the conclusion of the Kharkov-Belgorod operations.[16]

As the first major German victory in many weeks and against the background of Stalingrad, the triumph at Kharkov produced jubilation at all levels with Dietrich and the Leibstandarte receiving the lion's share of adulation. Shortly before the fall of the city, an aspiring poet at SS Panzer Corps headquarters sent the following verse to Leibstandarte:

> Up, Leibstandarte heroes, do your duty,
> Capture Kharkov, list the booty,
> On the Leibstandarte's square,
> Now heap up the victor's share.[17]

Goebbels records Hitler's exultant response to the Kharkov victory:

> Late in the evening [March 15] the Führer called me to brief me on the overall situation. He was exceptionally happy about the way the SS-Leibstandarte was led by Sepp Dietrich. This man has personally performed real deeds of heroism and has proven himself a great strategist in conducting his operations.[18]

Dietrich received the Oak Leaves with Swords for his Knight's Cross from Hitler, and in reporting the event, the SS propaganda machine enthused:

> In Poland and in France, in Greece and above all in the endless expanses of the East the Leibstandarte has stood in battle, and the same men have committed themselves with arms for the National Socialist greater Germany, who, even before 1933, strove in the black Schutzstaffeln for the victory of the National Socialist movement. That their Obergruppenführer, the soldier of the World War, the fighter of November 9, 1923, the loyal companion of the Führer, the old SS-leader and present general of the Waffen-SS, who exactly ten years ago set up the Leibstandarte and commanded it as a regiment and now as a division in the field was today decorated with the Oak Leaves with Swords, is their greatest joy and greatest pride.[19]

Of the three divisions of SS Panzer Corps, Leibstandarte garnered the major share of the most prestigious decorations for its role in the winter operations of 1943—fourteen Knight's Crosses and higher orders thereof as compared to ten for Das Reich and five for Totenkopf.[20]

Dietrich's by now secure niche in Nazi mythology as the Führer's unconquered and unconquerable paladin in war and peace was accompanied by what was, according to Goebbels,

Hitler's "unlimited confidence" and a lionization by Goebbels's propaganda machine which exceeded that accorded Rommel.[21] If Dietrich was unique, as Hitler believed, then an obvious way to multiply his effectiveness was to increase the number of men commanded by this military wonder. Since January 1943, discussions concerning the formation of a new SS division to be made up largely of Hitler Youth members born in 1926 and had been in progress between the Reichsjugendführer (Reich youth leader) Arthur Axmann and the SS leadership, and the project had received Hitler's approval in February.[22] In combination with Leibstandarte, the SS-Panzer-Grenadier Division Hitler Jugend (later 12th SS-Panzer-Division Hitler Jugend) was to constitute the I SS-Panzer Korps. Leibstandarte (Hausser's corps was demoted to II SS-Panzer-Korps) under Dietrich's command. While the ranks of the new division were to be filled by senior Hitler Youth who had already received some military preparation in *Wehrertüchtigungslager* (military fitness camps), officers and senior noncommissioned officers were supplied by the Leibstandarte. The first commander of the new division, appointed in July 1943, was the sometime commander of Leibstandarte's 1st Panzergrenadier Regiment, SS-Standartenführer Fritz Witt, who along with SS-Obersturmbannführer (lieutenant colonel) Kurt Meyer (the division's second commander after Witt's death in action in June 1944) had been awarded the Oak Leaves to the Knight's Cross for his performance in the Kharkov operations.[23]

Himmler proposed to Hitler in June that Dietrich be promoted to the recently (April 1942) instituted rank of SS-Obergruppenführer (colonel-general) to which no Waffen-SS commander had yet been appointed. Hitler, however, demurred in fear of an adverse reaction from the army. Dietrich was, after all, still only a divisional commander for which the customary army rank was merely major-general (Generalleutnant), and Hitler advised that the promotion be deferred until Dietrich had actually received his corps.[24] Although I SS-Panzer-Korps Leibstandarte was officially activated at Berlin-Lichterfelde on July 27, 1943, it did not become truly operational until the spring of 1944, and Dietrich's promotion was deferred until the summer of that year although then made retroactive to April 20, 1942. Hitler honored Dietrich on June 23, 1943, with the unique rank of "SS-Obergruppenführer

und Panzergeneral der Waffen-SS'' in recognition of his status
as the senior active tank man at the front.[25]

Although the expansion of Dietrich's command responsibility to the corps level was largely based on the irrational
conviction that charismatic qualities and political reliability
could achieve miracles on the battlefield, Dietrich's limitations in the manipulation of large bodies of troops were implicitly recognized in the appointment of Colonel Fritz
Kraemer as the chief of staff of I SS-Panzer-Korps Leibstandarte. Kraemer had been a lieutenant in the Stettin and Berlin
municipal police and, as part of the clandestine process of
expanding the Versailles Army prior to the formal disavowal
of the disarmament provisions of the treaty, had been sent to
the Berlin War Academy in October 1934 for command training. In May 1935 he had been promoted to captain and simultaneously transferred to the army. By June 15, 1943,
Kraemer had attained the rank of colonel in the General Staff
Corps and was on that date detached to the Waffen-SS as chief
of staff of the future I SS-Panzer-Korps Leibstandarte, although his formal transfer to the Waffen-SS with the rank of
SS-Brigadeführer (brigadier general) did not take place until
August 1, 1944.[26] In Kraemer, Dietrich received an assistant
who effectively supplemented his own untutored leadership.

In the spring and early summer of 1943 the operational
reality of Dietrich's corps was more than a year in the future.
SS-Panzer Grenadier-Division Hitler Jugend began working
up at the Belgian training camp at Beverloo in July 1943, but
it was not to experience combat until June 1944.[27] In the
meantime, Leibstandarte remained never far from a focus of
Germany's crumbling military situation.

On March 27, SS Panzer Corps was withdrawn from combat for refitting and for the reconstruction of the defenses of
Kharkov. For the latter purpose, some 25,000 Russians, presumably both prisoners of war and conscripted civilians, were
employed.[28] Dietrich was flown to the Führer headquarters in
East Prussia to brief Hitler on the military situation in the
Kharkov sector and to receive personally from his supreme
commander the Swords and Oak Leaves to the Knight's
Cross.[29] Dietrich's treatment, it should be noted, was in sharp
contrast to that accorded the corps commander, SS-
Obergruppenführer Paul Hausser, who did not receive the

Oak Leaves to his Knight's Cross until four months after the Kharkov operations following additional bitter fighting.[30]

Leibstandarte, Das Reich, and Totenkopf were quickly brought up to full strength, Dietrich's division having clearly received preferential treatment in this respect.[31] Not all replacements were of the highest quality. Hausser complained that most were not fully trained, and, indeed, some were former Luftwaffe personnel whose infantry training was virtually nil. The exigencies of war were now diluting the elitist qualities of the Leibstandarte, and for the first time desertion became a problem of sufficient dimensions to warrant mention in divisional correspondence. To cope with the problem, company commanders were urged to carefully indoctrinate and mold these men in the "way of the SS."[32]

On April 24 the process of refitting was declared completed, Leibstandarte having been brought to a strength of over 21,000 men.[33] The rapid reconstruction of the SS Panzer Corps, one of the major striking forces on the eastern front, was a portent of imminent offensive operations. The enormous losses of the previous winter and the impending catastrophe in Tunisia precluded the resumption of a general offensive, but a tempting target for a limited undertaking was presented by the great westward bulge left in the German lines on either side of Kursk between Orel and Belgorod following the reestablishment of a stable front in March 1943. The pinching out of the Kursk salient through concentric attacks from north and south (Operation Citadel) promised the destruction of substantial Russian forces with a consequent disruption of enemy offensive plans and a valuable shortening of the front in this sector. That the Russian general staff would expect a German attack against the salient, which projected from the lines north of Kharkov like a huge boil, was to be assumed, but the attendant risks might be minimized by a quickly executed stroke.[34]

Planning for the attack began in March, but the date for commencing the operation was repeatedly postponed due to unfavorable weather, Hitler's uncertain attitude which vacillated between an inclination to abandon the gamble altogether and a desire to procrastinate until large numbers of the new Panther tanks and Ferdinand assault guns were available for support, and the uncertainties imposed on the overall military situation by the collapse of the Tunisian front. Finally, on June 16 Hitler ordered that the attack begin in early July. In the meantime, the Russians had been afforded the luxury of virtual certainty as to the object of the offensive and ample time to prepare countermeasures.[35]

The thrust against the northern flank of the Kursk salient was to be carried out by the seven infantry and eight panzer and panzer-grenadier divisions of Colonel-General Walter Model's 9th Army while that against the southern flank was made the responsibility of Colonel-General Hermann Hoth's 4th Panzer Army (XXXXVIII Panzer Corps and Hausser's II SS Panzer Corps) supported on the right by Army Detachment Kempf. Although strictly limited in its territorial objectives, Operation Citadel had called forth the greatest concentration of German armored strength yet seen on the eastern front—approximately three thousand tanks and assault guns, almost as many armored vehicles as had been available along the entire front at the opening of the Russian campaign in June 1941.[36]

Hitler hoped that Citadel would constitute a stunning victory which would regain for Germany the initiative in the East but at the same time would be an economical undertaking. Hausser informed the commanders of his SS divisions that it was the "will of the Führer" that they be sparing of men and that the operation be carried out with the smallest possible sacrifice of blood through the effective employment of heavy weapons.[37] The prospects of cheap victory were sharply diminished by the deep defensive lines and powerful mobile reserves established by the Russian defenders, which rendered the Kursk salient, according to XXXXVIII Panzer Corps' chief of staff, "the strongest fortress in the world."[38]

At 3:10 on the morning of July 5, following a brief but intense artillery preparation, Leibstandarte, with Das Reich on its right and 167th Infantry Division on its left, attacked northward from an area west of Belgorod in the direction of Bykovka. The weather was warm and clear, and with powerful air support Leibstandarte penetrated the first Russian line of defense by afternoon. Resistance by elements of the elite 6th Guards Army had been fierce, however, for the first day's combat had cost Leibstandarte 97 killed and 522 wounded as well as the loss of several heavy weapons.[39] The

following day saw a further advance northward, and by midday the II SS Panzer Corps as a whole had penetrated twenty
miles into the salient. It appeared that the front of the 6th
Guards Army had been torn open, but again losses were heavy
although somewhat lighter than those of the previous day—
84 killed and 384 wounded for Dietrich's division.[40]

For the next several days the good fortune of the bold
seemed to ride with Leibstandarte and II Panzer Corps as
they swept toward the Psel River, the last natural obstacle
before Kursk, thirty-seven miles beyond. On July 9 in the
Luchki area, Leibstandarte won an impressive defensive victory when a Russian effort to envelop its forward elements
was beaten off with the destruction of eighty-eight Russian
tanks, and on the following day to the left of Leibstandarte,
Totenkopf reached the Psel and prepared to cross.[41] Leibstandarte and Das Reich now sought to protect Totenkopf's right
flank as that division began bridging operations. At six
o'clock on the morning of July 10 after heavy artillery and
air preparation, Dietrich's division attacked in a northeasterly
direction along the Teterevino-Prokhorovka Road. Strong enemy resistance and periodic heavy rains, which turned por-
tions of the road into seas of mud, prevented the capture of
Prokhorovka although Leibstandarte claimed the destruction
of fifty-seven Russian tanks for a very modest cost in blood.[42]
The following day saw little additional progress, and on July
12 Leibstandarte was brought to a halt about two miles southwest of Prokhorovka and during the night was subjected to
violent counterattacks by an estimated three hundred tanks of
the Soviet 5th Guards Tank Army, part of one of the largest
tank battles of World War II.[43] Third Panzer Corps of Army
Detachment Kempf, which was to protect Hausser's right
flank, had gotten bogged down east of the Donetz and had
not arrived. Although Totenkopf had established a bridgehead
across the Psel, the continued pressure of Russian armor
against the right flank of the corps would soon render it untenable.[44]

Leibstandarte fought energetically, but neither it nor its
sister divisions could make further progress. Forty-eighth
Panzer Corps, on Hausser's left, virtually abandoned efforts
to advance northward on July 13. The attack against the
northern wall of the salient by Model's 9th Army had made

even less progress and was in serious danger from fierce Russian counterattacks in the Orel area by July 12. Russian losses had been heavy. According to Manstein, eighteen hundred Russian tanks had been destroyed in the southern sector alone, of which Leibstandarte had claimed over five hundred by July 14. German losses in armor had also been heavy, although in human terms total German casualties were moderate by the standards established on the eastern front.[45] Whether Citadel might have been profitably continued is open to question. Manstein believed that it might, but the decision to abandon Citadel was, uncharacteristically, Hitler's.[46] In the early hours of July 10 the American 11th and British 8th Armies had landed in Sicily, and later in the day British forces had taken Syracuse.[47] As early as the beginning of May, Hitler had given orders to OKH to be prepared to transfer powerful forces from the East to the Mediterranean area at short notice and had particularly specified the SS divisions of Hausser's corps, supposing that these ideologically "sound" and battle-proven units would have an energizing effect upon the Italian armed forces and populace.[48] On July 13 Hitler reached the decision to abandon Citadel and four days later ordered the withdrawal of Hausser's corps for transfer to Italy. Leibstandarte was ordered into reserve, but the Russian general staff was not inclined to play a cooperative role in Hitler's reshuffling of divisions. That same day, the Russian summer offensive struck in the Kuban, on the Mius, and in the Izyum sector, while Leibstandarte prepared to counterattack from the Slavyansk area south of Izyum. On July 24, however, Leibstandarte's action was cancelled, and on the morning of the twenty-seventh the division began to entrain at Stalino for Innsbruck, Austria.[49] Two days earlier, Mussolini had been overthrown, and so anxious was Hitler for the hasty arrival of Leibstandarte in Italy that the division was ordered to leave its armored equipment in Russia, arrangements having been made for the acquisition of replacements at the western terminus of the journey. Das Reich and Totenkopf remained in the East, although the staff and corps troops of Hausser's panzer corps (including Hausser) were transferred to Italy a few days later.[50]

The departure of Leibstandarte at the end of July 1943 marked a clearly defined stage in Dietrich's career. As noted above, I SS-Panzer-Korps Leibstandarte was officially activated on July 27 although almost half of the new SS corps, the Hitler Jugend Division, was many months distant from combat readiness. Nevertheless, Dietrich on that date formally assumed command of the nascent corps while command of the SS-Panzer-Grenadier Division Leibstandarte SS Adolf Hitler was given to a longtime member of the division's officer corps, SS-Brigadeführer Theodor (Teddy) Wisch.[51]

Dietrich's experiences in the East during the period February–July 1943 had had an intensely disillusioning effect upon him. Leibstandarte had fought well in the Kharkov sector and in the Kursk salient, and German forces had inflicted heavier losses than they had suffered; and yet, following the maximum German efforts in these areas, the Russians had been able to undertake massive counteroffensives with fresh and well-equipped troops. As an experienced front-line commander, Dietrich found it impossible to share Hitler's confidence in the ability of ideologically committed and energetically led troops to counterbalance material and numerical superiority of the magnitude which the Russian army had demonstrated in July 1943. It appears that shortly after his return from the East Dietrich acquitted himself of a quasi-public declaration to the effect that Germany could no longer hope to defeat the Russians. The statement was picked up by Alfred Rosenberg's *Ostministerium* and seems to have become something of a *cause celebre* in the rivalry for influence in the eastern territories between Himmler and Rosenberg. Late in August 1943 Himmler wrote to Dietrich expressing his confidence that Rosenberg had "misinterpreted" a statement made by Dietrich concerning the fighting qualities of the Russian army and had noised it abroad for his own purposes. The Reichsführer suggested that Dietrich correct Rosenberg's misinterpretation at the earliest possible opportunity and with his closing paragraph indicated the direction which the clarification should take: "I know better than anyone what you think about the war in Russia. It is clear to us that it is not easy. But it is just as much for us a certainty that the Russians can and will be beaten in the foreseeable future."[52] Whether or not Dietrich made the desired representations to Rosenberg is not known, but his ability and willingness to objectively judge Germany's deteriorating position would be further demonstrated in the future.

Leibstandarte's transfer to Italy and its commitment there for something in excess of three months involved little combat and served as a useful recuperative period. Hitler feared that a surrender by the Badoglio government would present the Allies with an opportunity to effect landings at Genoa and Leghorn and, perhaps in concert with Italian forces, to seize the Alpine passes leading into Central Europe.[53] By the second week in August Leibstandarte, soon to be reinforced by a detachment of Tiger tanks which had been working up at the Sennelager tank school for Dietrich's corps, had arrived in South Tirol and joined forces with 44th Infantry Division, the Mountain Group ''Feuerstein'' and the headquarters and corps troops of II SS Panzer Corps for the defense of the Brenner Pass.[54] The threat to the Alpine passes was not imaginary. According to an intelligence report of Army Group B dated August 25, Italian divisions were engaged in preparing some defensive measures against the north, including barbed-wire obstacles and tank traps. While it was clear to German observers that the Italians were war-weary, it was nevertheless recognized that the blowing up of an Alpine tunnel or pass could have serious consequences for German forces in Italy.[55]

Concurrently, Leibstandarte, as intended by Hitler, functioned as a tangible representation of German imperial power vis-à-vis the wavering Italian military leadership. On August 15 the last formal Italo-German military conference took place at Bologna. Host of the conference was General Mario Roatta, chief of the Italian general staff, who was to receive Field Marshal Rommel, commander of Army Group B, and Colonel-General Alfred Jodl, Chief of the OKW operations staff. Although Italy was still technically Germany's ally, the Italians were shocked to discover a company of the Leibstandarte drawn up at the airfield to receive the German guests. The presence of the company, it was learned, was due to a personal order from Hitler. SS men hovered menacingly over the Italian guards, and as the participants took their places in the meeting hall, two remarkably large SS men goose-stepped into position at either side of the entrance.[56]

On September 8 the surrender of the Badoglio government to the Allies (the terms had actually been signed five days earlier) was formally announced. German forces in Italy undertook the disarming of the Italian military, which with few exceptions took place with little resistance. Substantial numbers of the former membership of the Italian Royal Army were immediately formed by antifascist officers into guerrilla bands, which quickly aroused the concern of German military authorities. Initially, the focus of greatest activity was in the northeast border areas and was estimated to include as many as fifteen thousand men, some of these drawn from the late Torino and Isonzo Divisions.[57]

Elements of Leibstandarte took part in the initial stages of the German antiguerrilla campaign in Northern Italy, but this was a most transitory phenomenon. On October 20, 1943, Leibstandarte received word of its impending recommitment to the Russian front.[58]

9
Crisis on the Dnieper

In the months following Leibstandarte's departure from Russia in July, the southern flank of the German front had undergone a catastrophic deterioration. While Manstein's Army Group South found itself hard pressed to replace the losses suffered in Citadel, the Russians launched their first sustained summer offensive of the war in August with overwhelming strength which by the end of September had pushed to the east bank of the Dnieper.[1] Due largely to Hitler's fear that prepared defenses would act as a magnet encouraging the withdrawal of fighting forces, the Dnieper line had not been fortified to any significant degree and acted as only a very temporary hindrance to a further Russian advance. In fact, by the end of September the Russians had established two bridgeheads on the west bank of the river, one between Kremenchug and Dnepropetrovsk and another at Pereyeslav, south of Kiev.[2] Into the former the Russians funneled four armies of General Ivan Konev's Second Ukrainian Front, including over nine hundred tanks, which by the third week of October had succeeded in folding back the inner wings of the German 1st Panzer Army and the 8th Army, thus opening the path into the Dnieper bend and threatening to cut off 1st Panzer Army and Army Group A.[3] To counter this potential catastrophe, OKW had detached Leibstandarte, which on October 22 had been redesignated 1st SS Panzer Division Leibstandarte SS Adolf Hitler, and four other panzer divisions from other theaters and prepared to send them east.[4] The emergency on the Dnieper rudely interrupted the gestation of Dietrich's I SS-Panzer-Korps Leibstandarte. Several elements of corps troops, including two companies of the heavy tank detachment (Tigers) were sent east as reinforcements for 1st SS Panzer Division Leibstandarte SS Adolf Hitler. On November 11 Hitler ordered Dietrich to temporarily resume his old divisional command.[5] In the face of the Russian crisis, the revival of the previously potent combination of Sepp Dietrich and his division Leibstandarte took precedence over the bringing to combat readiness of his corps. In December 1943 the headquarters of I SS Panzer Corps Leibstandarte was established near Brussels. The corps included not only the remaining corps troops and the infant 12th SS Panzer Division Hitler Jugend but temporarily 9th SS Panzer Division Hohenstaufen (then also in its formative stages) as well. The latter division, too, would be tossed into the Russian caldron in March 1944.[6]

By November 7 the transfer of the 1st Panzer Division Leibstandarte SS Adolf Hitler to the Ukraine had been completed.[7] In the interim the situation on the west bank of the Dnieper had altered substantially. A sharp and brilliantly executed counterattack by XXXX Panzer Corps at the end of October had temporarily neutralized the threat of Konev's divisions' debouching from the bridgehead south of Kremenchug.[8] Manstein now thought to utilize this breathing space for the execution of a larger counterstroke on the lower Dnieper which would restore a German front west of the Nogay Steppe and preserve contact with 17th Army in the Crimea. In the latter stages of the operation the armored divisions which had been promised Manstein in October (now reduced to a total of three, including Leibstandarte) were to be employed.[9]

Before Manstein's attack could be launched, a fresh crisis broke on the left flank of Army Group South. Powerful elements of Lieutenant-General N. F. Vatutin's First Ukrainian Front, which since early October had been concentrating in two bridgeheads on the west bank of the Dnieper north of Kiev, burst through the defenses of 4th Panzer Army and by November had driven the German defenders out of Kiev.[10] As Vatutin's divisions began to sweep to the southwest against ineffective opposition by 4th Panzer Army, the danger arose of a vast envelopment of the entire southern wing of the Russian front between Kiev and the Black Sea. After some hesitation, Hitler, who was much taken with Manstein's planned attack on the lower Dnieper and reluctant to abandon it, consented to the employment of the three newly arrived panzer divisions for the containment of Vatutin's breakthrough.[11] This involved considerable delay and confusion, as elements of the three divisions had already unloaded in the Nikopol area and now had to be reassembled and rerouted to the north.[12]

During the second week in November Leibstandarte, along with 1st and 25th Panzer Divisions, was incorporated into General Hermann Balck's XXXXVIII Panzer Corps. Recently transferred from 1st Panzer Army, XXXXVIII Corps boasted an on-paper strength of seven divisions, although two of its panzer divisions were in a much-weakened condition, and was to form a *corps d'élite* within the 4th Panzer Army for a great counterattack against the southern wall of the Kiev salient.

The operations of XXXXVIII Panzer Corps against the Kiev salient between the middle of November and Christmas 1943 are detailed by the corps' chief of staff, Major General F. W. von Mellenthin.[13] Balck had planned to strike directly to the base of the salient at Kiev, thus paralyzing further Russian movement to the southwest, but was overruled by the commander of 4th Panzer Army, General Erhard Raus, who preferred a more orthodox attack against the tip of the salient and the important road junctions at Zhitomir.[14] The major thrust of Balck's counterattack, which opened on November 15, was launched by Leibstandarte and 1st Panzer Division into the left flank of Vatutin's spearhead. Complete surprise was achieved, and two days later Leibstandarte and 1st Panzer Division had reached the Kiev-Zhitomir railroad while the Russians were falling back to the east on Brussilov in some disarray. Zhitomir itself was taken by 1st and 7th Panzer Divisions on the evening of November 17–18, while a vigorous Russian reaction from the Brussilov area was beaten off by XXXXVIII Corps. Balck now decided to undertake an envelopment of this strong Russian force remaining in and around Brussilov, which included the 1st Guards Cavalry Corps and the 5th and 8th Guards Armored Corps. Leibstandarte was to launch a two-pronged attack against the western wall of the Brussilov concentration while 1st Panzer Division swept around its northern perimeter and then attacked south to link up with 19th Panzer Division. The operation, begun on November 20, was not an unqualified success. Leibstandarte was unable to penetrate the Brussilov pocket from the west ("the first time in the war that this famous division had launched an attack and failed to gain its objective")[15] while excessive caution on the part of 1st and 19th Panzer Divisions in closing the pocket permitted the escape of numerous enemy. Nevertheless, by November 24 the Brussilov pocket had netted XXXXVIII Corps three thousand Russians killed, a substantial number of prisoners, and much equipment abandoned on the battlefield.[16]

Still, XXXXVIII Corps was far from having achieved a decisive victory. A sudden rise in temperature on November 25 made roads virtually impassable, and while offensive operations came to a standstill, the Russians took up strong defensive positions east of Brussilov and north of the Zhitomir-Radomyshl Road, the former blocking the approaches to Kiev and the latter threatening the left flank of such an approach. It was wisely decided to neutralize the latter problem as soon as conditions permitted, and on November 30 XXXXVIII Corps was ordered to strike at the right flank of the Zhitomir-Radomyshl positions and attempt to roll up the entire front from west to east. Between December 6 and 9, Leibstandarte and 1st and 7th Panzer Divisions penetrated the Russian right and swept behind Russian lines to Malin and Radomyshl, completely disrupting what proved to be preparations by the Russian 16th Army for a major offensive.[17] During the next few days Leibstandarte and 1st Panzer Division succeeded in encircling and destroying three and one-half Russian divisions on the west bank of the Teterov River near Radomyshl, but XXXXVIII Panzer Corps was approaching the end of its run of good fortune. With well-disciplined and experienced divisions such as Leibstandarte and 1st and 7th Panzer Divisions controlled by a tactician of Balck's poise and skill, a much larger enemy force had been thrown off balance and its offensive operations temporarily disrupted. Yet, by the end of November Balck's superiors, Hoth and Manstein, had realized that with the forces at their disposal it was futile to think seriously of regaining the west bank of the Dnieper at Kiev.[18] Vatutin had been hurt but still had vast reserves at his disposal.

The limits of XXXXVIII Corps' offensive capabilities were reached in the period December 16–21. In the Meleni area north of the Irscha River approximately twenty-eight miles northwest of Radomyshl, Russian forces of undetermined strength were believed to be massing for a renewed thrust to the southwest toward Zhitomir.[19] Balck thought not only to launch a spoiling attack against this concentration but hoped to envelop and destroy it. Once again Leibstandarte and 1st and 7th Panzer Divisions were designated for an attack role. From the Malin bridgehead north of the Irscha and east of Meleni 7th Panzer Division was to attack the left flank of the Russian concentration while Leibstandarte and 1st Panzer, from an assembly area south of Korosten, were to strike at its right. The attack, begun on the morning of December 16, again achieved complete surprise. Leibstandarte, with the armor of 1st Panzer Division under its temporary control and supported by the massed fire of thirty artillery batteries and a mortar brigade, broke through the Russian defenses and with 1st Panzer Division advanced eastward roughly parallel to the Irscha River. Northwest of Malin, 7th Panzer Division, attacking in the opposite direction, also made initially encouraging progress, and by the evening of December 16 it appeared that the three divisions might succeed in cutting off and surrounding the enemy forces around Meleni. In the succeeding several days, however, Russian resistance stiffened, and although Leibstandarte alone destroyed forty-six tanks, the enveloping attacks made little additional progress. On December 21 massive counterattacks from within the Meleni pocket began, and XXXXVIII Panzer Corps was ordered by 4th Panzer Army to go on the defensive.[20] It was only now that the audacity of the corps' undertaking was realized, for around Meleni had been concentrated no fewer than three armored and four infantry corps![21]

Although the operations of XXXXVIII Panzer Corps since November 15 had been collectively a brilliantly executed spoiling attack on a very large scale, they were not of decisive significance. Vatutin had not been seriously injured and, in fact, had been able to muster overwhelming strength for a fresh offensive. This struck 4th Panzer Army on December

24 and within a few days reached the Kiev-Zhitomir Road along an eighteen mile front. By January 3, 1944, Vatutin had won back all the territory lost since the middle of November, had driven a wedge between Army Group South and Army Group Center, and threatened to sever the rearward lines of communication of Manstein's Army Group. Far to the south in the Kirovograd sector, Konev's Second Ukrainian Front struck at the hinge joining 6th and 8th Armies, thus raising the specter of a double envelopment exceeding the scale of Stalingrad a year earlier.[22]

At the beginning of January, Manstein had withdrawn 1st Panzer Army from the Dnieper bend and shifted it northwest to the sector of 4th Panzer Army, then hard pressed to resist Vatutin's massive assault.[23] Manstein elected to strike at the most dangerous head of Vatutin's hydra, that constituted by 1st Tank Army and 40th Army which was biting deep into the left flank of his army group. In mid-January Manstein began a series of attacks against both flanks of the Soviet spearhead which again succeeded in dealing Vatutin a stinging setback.[24]

Leibstandarte's fighting strength had been severely depleted by the heavy combat of the previous two months. Sturmbannführer Joachim Peiper's armored battlegroup, for example, had been reduced to a total armored strength of three tanks.[25] Nevertheless, the division was still regarded as one of the most potent striking forces within Army Group South and was selected to lead an attack by XXXXVI Panzer Corps into the right flank of the Russian 1st Tank Army. This limited operation, begun on the morning of January 24 from an area west of Vinnitsa, proved enormously successful, destroying some seven hundred Russian tanks and killing or capturing over thirteen thousand men of the Red Army by the end of the month.[26] Impressive though Manstein's counteroffensive was, given the numerical disparity between the opposing forces, it did not succeed in dissipating the atmosphere of perpetual crisis which hung over the front of Army Group South. On January 25, 45th Guards Army of Konev's Second Ukrainian Front burst through the lightly held positions of General Wilhelm Stemmermann's XI Corps northwest of Kirovograd and poured twelve infantry divisions into the gap. On the following day, about forty-five miles to the north, the

Russian 6th Tank and 27th Armies punched through the right wing of Lieutenant-General Theobald Lieb's XXXXII Corps and raced south. On the afternoon of the twenty-eighth the tips of the two spearheads met at Shpola, encircling six and one-half divisions of the two German corps (389th, 57th, 72nd, and 88th Infantry Divisions plus 5th SS Panzer Division Wiking and the Belgian SS Brigade Wallonien) totaling 56,000 men in a pocket west of Cherkassy and centered on Korsun.[27]

Manstein immediately undertook to open the Cherkassy-Korsun pocket, a task rendered more difficult by Hitler's initial refusal to permit a breakout attempt by the encircled divisions. The XXXXVII and III Panzer Corps, the latter reinforced by Leibstandarte, were to converge on the Cherkassy-Korsun pocket, and, following the limitations imposed by Hitler, their original objective was simply to restore contact with the trapped forces in the pocket. Manstein's relief attacks, stalled for twenty-four hours due to fog and deep mud produced by a sudden thaw, began to inch toward the perimeter on February 4. By February 6 it was clear that neither of the relieving corps would be able to make contact with the pocket, and that evening Hitler gave permission for a breakout to be undertaken. Again, Leibstandarte found itself at the focus of combat. On the evening of February 16–17 as the encircled forces began to cut their way through Russian defenses to the tip of III Panzer Corps southwest of Dzhurzhentsy, two battalions of Leibstandarte tried gallantly and at heavy cost to take the ice-covered slopes of Hills 239 and 222, key positions standing between the beleaguered divisions and their would-be rescuers, but to no avail. Nevertheless, some 30,000 men of the 56,000 originally caught in the Cherkassy-Korsun pocket managed to escape, although virtually all heavy equipment had to be abandoned.[28]

Leibstandarte's troopers had displayed heroism in the battles for the relief of the Cherkassy-Korsun pocket. Early on the morning of February 11, for example, II Battalion of 2nd Panzer-Grenadier Regiment was subject to massive Russian attacks against its position on Height 246.3 some two miles northwest of Tinowka. In the initial assaults most of 6th Company, protecting the battalion's open right flank, was wiped out. Four survivors then stood against sixty Russian infantrymen supported by three T-34s and quickly lost two of their number. The remaining two men, an SS-Rottenführer (corporal) and an SS-Sturmmann (private first class), held their ground, ultimately reduced to the use of their service pistols, until a battalion counterattack drove off the attacking Russians.[29]

Following the battles for the relief of the Cherkassy-Korsun pocket, the badly battered Leibstandarte was pulled back into the line northeast of Uman. It now appeared that Dietrich's exhausted troops, who had been in almost constant combat for three and one-half months, would be withdrawing for a needed rest and refit. For no very cogent reason save perhaps his own exhaustion in the wake of the seemingly endless series of crises of the previous months, Hitler believed that the Russians would not resume major offensive operations until spring and as an index of his confidence ordered Leibstandarte on February 27 to prepare for transfer to the West.[30] Yet, his division was to endure one more combat holocaust before enjoying a brief respite.

On the morning of March 4 First Ukrainian Front, now commanded by the dynamic Marshal Georgi Zhukov, struck Manstein's left flank as part of a general and massive Russian thrust toward the Carpathians. Army Group South's front north and east of Vinnitsa was badly fragmented. Leibstandarte was again subordinated to Balck's XXXXVIII Panzer Corps and along with 7th Panzer Division was thrust into the thirty-mile gap between Ternopol and Proskurov.[31] Both of these once splendidly equipped armored divisions had by now been reduced to little more than shadows of their former might. Seventh Panzer Division had no tanks while Leibstandarte reported to XXXXVIII Panzer Corps on the evening of March 6 that its armored strength consisted of five Panthers, one Tiger and three assault guns, and that its lone Tiger was then engaging thirty Russian T-34s.[32] Although Leibstandarte desperately attempted to build a continuous front, attacking westward toward the virtually immobilized 7th Panzer Division, it was unable to do so.[33] On March 21 two hundred tanks of the Russian 1st and 4th Tank Armies smashed through the Ternopol-Proskurov sector, sweeping the remnants of the two divisions before them into a pocket around Skala. This was occupied by Hube's 1st Panzer Army and formed by the southward rush of Zhukov's armor to meet the westward thrust of Second Ukrainian Front, which, also having opened its attack on March 4, had crossed the Dniester south of Mogilev-Podolskiy. Uncharacteristically, Hitler was quickly persuaded by Manstein to allow 1st Panzer Army to break out to the west and released to his command Hausser's new II SS Panzer Corps, now composed of 9th SS Panzer Division Hohenstaufen and 10th SS Panzer Division Frundsberg, to spearhead a supporting, eastward attack.[34] The operation was a brilliant success, and by April 10, 1st Panzer Army had again been fitted into a continuous front with 4th Panzer Army along the Strypa.[35]

Prior to the breakout from the Hube pocket, Hitler had effected two important command changes on the southern sector of the eastern front. On March 30, 1944, after awarding them the Swords to their Knight's Crosses, the Führer dismissed Field Marshals Manstein and von Kleist from their respective commands of Army Groups South and A. It is significant to note Hitler's justification of the dismissals. He observed that the time for operations in the grand manner had passed, that commanders were now required who were temperamentally suited to holding the line and who were to inspire in their subordinates a similar determination.[36] In brief, personal bravery, obedience, and stolidity had been elevated in Hitler's mind above tactical brilliance. These were qualities possessed in full measure by Manstein's successor, Field Marshal Walter Model, who, in addition to being a devoted Nazi, was indefatigable in defense and in a crisis was frequently present in the front lines. These were qualities, too, which had been demonstrated by Sepp Dietrich, and it was in the last year of World War II, during which the avoidance of the ultimate catastrophe rather than victory became the operative German aim, that Dietrich was to be catapulted through the command of an operational corps to that of a panzer army.

10
Invasion Front

Immediately upon its escape from the Hube pocket, the badly battered Leibstandarte was transported to Belgium and went into quarters formerly occupied by the now almost-battle-ready 12th SS Panzer Division Hitler Jugend at Tournhout adjacent to the Beverloo training installation. Leibstandarte had been largely burned out by the ferocious combat of the previous five months and, according to the chief of staff of I SS Panzer Corps Leibstandarte, had now to be almost completely reconstituted with fresh personnel and new equipment.[1] In view of the clearly impending Allied descent on the Atlantic coast of Europe, the refitting of Leibstandarte was a matter of considerable urgency, for the recent crisis in the East had temporarily denuded the West of all fully operational armored divisions with the possible exception of Hitler Jugend, which was without combat experience and at only 80 percent of established strength.[2]

Although Leibstandarte preserved a substantial core of well-trained and battle-hardened men around which an avalanche of replacements was poured, the division was far from combat readiness by the first week in May. Many replacements were poorly trained, heavy equipment was in short supply, and the rectification of both deficiencies was seriously hindered by frequent Allied air attacks. In spite of the mammoth task confronting the division, the importance of ideological indoctrination was not forgotten. As in peacetime, two one-hour indoctrination sessions were ordered held each week.[3]

June 6, 1944, found Leibstandarte at full strength in terms of personnel for its two motorized infantry regiments, armored regiment, and supporting units but not yet reequipped for combat as an armored division. Dietrich was in Brussels as the first waves of British and American troops stormed ashore from the Bay of the Seine. Hitler Jugend, in the vicinity of Evreaux some sixty miles in a direct line from the invasion front, was a part of OKW's armored reserve but, in spite of the urgent representations of Field Marshal von Rundstedt, Commander-in-Chief West, was not released to his operational control until 2:30 in the afternoon along with the powerful Panzer Lehr armored division, then in the Chartres area, and the command staff and corps troops of I SS Panzer Corps Leibstandarte. These divisions were subordinated to Rommel and Army Group B, which had a territorial responsibility extending from the Zuider Zee to the Loire, including the invasion sector. With the divisions went von Rundstedt's pointed observation that "In view of the known ability of the enemy to bite fast [*festbeissen*], the important thing is to annihilate the enemy as quickly as possible."[4]

This critical undertaking, rendered extraordinarily difficult by almost absolute Allied air supremacy and the long-ranging guns of British and American fire-support vessels, was assigned to Sepp Dietrich. Panzer Lehr and the already committed 21st Panzer Division were absorbed by I SS Panzer Corps Leibstandarte with headquarters now at Rouen. The 1st SS Panzer Division Leibstandarte SS Adolf Hitler was held back in Belgium, both because of its incomplete refit and because of Hitler's and von Rundstedt's conviction that the Allied operations were a diversionary maneuver preparatory to a main effort farther north.[5]

The force allotted Dietrich was an impressive one. Panzer Lehr with 192 tanks and 40 assault guns was the most powerful armored division in the Wehrmacht while Hitler Jugend was not far behind with 177 tanks and 28 assault guns.[6] Twenty-first Panzer, although it had already suffered some battle damage, was reasonably fresh and up to strength. Yet, it proved impossible to concentrate this formidable array of armor for a prompt counterthrust. By mid-morning on June 7, Hitler Jugend had gotten only as far as Villers-Bocage while Panzer Lehr had reached Thury Harcourt.[7] An attack which had been scheduled for dawn of that day and which was to throw Lieutenant-General Miles Dempsey's 2nd British Army from its lodgment north of Caen into the sea was, therefore, postponed until 4:00 P.M.[8] The reality fell far short of the intent: Panzer Lehr was stalled by the malevolent attentions of Allied fighter-bombers, and Dietrich was ordered by Rommel to attack without it; Twenty-first Panzer was forced onto the defensive by a British assault on Lebisey Wood while Hitler Jugend, represented only by a battlegroup commanded by the redoubtable Kurt Meyer, formed leader of Leibstandarte's reconnaissance detachment, was deflected by a Canadian thrust toward the Carpiquet airfield west of Caen.[9] No units were left for the main attack, and, as delicately noted by the military chronicler, the operation "later did not achieve its full effect."[10] By the following day 21st Panzer Division was still unavailable, Panzer Lehr had not yet arrived, and although Hitler Jugend was present in full strength, it was short of fuel. Dietrich was limited to directing Hitler Jugend against the Canadians on the Bayeaux-Caen Road at Putôt-en-Bessin and Bretteville, and limited local successes were quickly neutralized by Canadian counterattacks.[11]

The Caen sector of the invasion front was of crucial significance to the initial stage of the Allied operational plan. By exerting sustained pressure in that area, the commander of 21st Army Group, General Sir Bernard Montgomery hoped that British 2nd Army would attract the bulk of available German armor, thus permitting the American 1st Army to overrun the Cotentin Peninsula, capture the port of Cherbourg, and reassemble at the base of the peninsula for an eastward thrust toward the Seine. The Allied diversion was effective, for the threat to Caen was a thoroughly credible one; a penetration there would open the road to Argentan, Le Mans, and the Loire, thus flanking the entire German front south of the Seine.[12]

The threat to Caen appeared to require a more substantial and better-coordinated counterthrust than Dietrich had been able to deliver. Rundstedt ordered the commitment of 1st SS Panzer Division Leibstandarte SS Adolf Hitler and 2nd SS Panzer Division Das Reich for this purpose, but neither division was immediately available. Leibstandarte was still being held back in Belgium by OKW, and Das Reich was

involved in antiguerrilla operations in the Limoges area.[13]
General der Panzertruppen Geyr von Schweppenburg, commander of Panzergruppe West was therefore ordered to em-
ploy Dietrich's corps as well as elements of 7th and 15th
Armies in another major effort to drive the British 2nd Army
into the sea. Both Rundstedt and Rommel appear to have
entertained little confidence in Dietrich's tactical ability and
supposed that Geyr might achieve success where Dietrich had
failed. Geyr, however, was no better able to neutralize Allied
air supremacy than was the SS general, and an attack scheduled for the night of June 10–11 was cancelled at the last
moment due to Geyr's inability to assemble his forces and
"the further reinforcement of the enemy." At 8:30 on the
evening of the tenth, Geyr's poorly concealed headquarters at
La Caine was bombed by Allied aircraft with the result that
although Geyr survived, seventeen of his staff including his
chief of staff, Major-General von Dawans, were killed. Panzergruppe West now temporarily ceased to exist, and Dietrich's corps was subordinated to Colonel-General Friedrich
Dollman's 7th Army.[14]

Hitler still clung to the prospect of clearing the enemy from
its Norman lodgment but now recognized that a greater concentration of armor was necessary. On June 12 Rundstedt was
promised Hausser's II SS Panzer Corps (Divisions Hohenstaufen and Frundsberg) which, however, would be many days
in transit from the East; on the following day, Hitler ordered
1st SS Panzer Division Leibstandarte SS Adolf Hitler south
to join Dietrich's corps.[15] In the meantime, sharp and costly
local encounters between elements of 2nd British Army and
I SS Panzer Corps were testing the mettle of Dietrich's panzer
men.

Although Dempsey's 2nd Army had constructed a bridgehead twenty-two miles long and five to ten miles deep by the
evening of June 7, further progress was painfully slow and
costly. The rough *bocage* of Normandy with its dense hedge-
rows and sunken lanes favored the defense while the principal
German tanks, the Tiger, Panther, and even the latest version
of the elderly Mark IV were superior to the Churchills, Crom-
wells, and Shermans of the British armored divisions. Only
the Firefly, a Sherman fitted with the excellent seventeen
pounder (76 mm.) high-velocity gun, could be considered a

match for the least of the German models, and of these the British had few.[16]

The seizure of Caumont on the left flank of I SS Panzer Corps by the American V Corps on June 12 presented Dempsey with a seemingly splendid opportunity. Frontal attacks against the Tilly-sur-Seulles sector of the German line, held by Panzer Lehr, promised to yield no greater success than direct assaults on Caen, stoutly defended by Hitler Jugend.[17] The advance of the American V Corps, however, had opened a gap to the left of Panzer Lehr and into it was sent on June 12 the British 7th Armored Division in an effort to envelop the left flank of Panzer Lehr and, perhaps, to set the stage for the rolling up of the entire front of I SS Panzer Corps.[18] On the following morning the division's 22nd Armored Brigade, followed by motorized infantry, entered Villers-Bocage, well behind Panzer Lehr's positions around Tilly. Moving east on the Caen Road, the spearhead of the British division was intercepted by Tiger tanks of Dietrich's 501st SS Heavy Tank Battalion. Here occurred one of the most spectacular feats of arms of the entire war. SS-Obersturmführer Michael Wittmann, although detached from the panzer company which he commanded, opened the engagement by bursting out of woods along the road and sending shell after shell from his Tiger's 88-mm. gun against the orderly file of Shermans and Churchills. Within thirty minutes, twenty-one British tanks lay burning along the road. For his remarkable achievement, Wittmann received the nickname "Panzer Killer." Two companies of the SS battalion then engaged the balance of the British brigade west of Villers-Bocage and within the town itself. Although some British sources insist that the battle of Villers-Bocage was not a defeat for 7th Armored Division, the fact remains that the flanking effort of the division was abandoned on the afternoon of June 13.[19]

Nevertheless, I SS Panzer Corps remained under constant pressure from British thrusts in the Tilly sector as well as from fighter-bombers and the 15- and 16-inch guns of H.M.S. *Ramillies* and *Nelson* lying in the Bay of the Seine. The fire from these battleships, which could reach twenty miles inland, was particularly dangerous, for it struck without warning and with great accuracy. On June 14 a sudden naval bombardment killed SS-Brigadeführer Fritz Witt, first commander of 12th SS Panzer Division "Hitler Jugend" and one of the few survivors of the 120-man Staff Guard of March 1933, at his divisional headquarters southwest of Caen. Witt's role as divisional commander was immediately assumed by the flamboyant and effective SS-Oberführer Kurt Meyer.[20]

The war along the front of I SS Panzer Corps had become one of attrition, which in the long haul clearly favored the British 2nd Army, constantly supplied and reinforced from the sea. For Dietrich, as for all German commanders along the invasion front, reinforcement was meager, possible only during a few night hours and even then with attendant heavy losses. By June 13 it appears that Dietrich had virtually abandoned hope of smashing the developing invasion. In a report to von Rundstedt, he conceded that with two additional good panzer divisions and three infantry divisions it might still be possible to throw 2nd Army into the sea, but only if the operation were conducted in the immediate future and carried out with adequate air support.[21] First SS Panzer Division Leibstandarte SS Adolf Hitler and Hausser's II SS Panzer Corps, however, were not to arrive in the battle area for about a week, while Dietrich must have known that "adequate air support" was simply unavailable. Three days later, Dietrich reported to Rommel that he had committed the last of his reserves against a local breakthrough west of Tilly and had been able to close the gap only by throwing in engineers, communications personnel, truck drivers, and tank crews who had lost their vehicles.[22]

Nature briefly intervened on the German side. On June 19 the worst storm to strike the Norman coast in forty years swept the English Channel and the invasion beaches. Persisting for three days, the tempest inflicted such damage on the Allied supply system that the average daily tonnage deposited on the beaches on June 18 was not matched until the end of the month.[23] The elements thus seemed to favor another German effort to strike a decisive blow at the Allied lodgment. The subject had already been discussed by Hitler, von Rundstedt, and Rommel at a meeting on June 17 at Margival near Soissons, and a renewed counteroffensive was ordered by Hitler on June 20.[24] The Führer entertained high hopes for its success, his optimism based largely on the imminent availability of four more SS armored divisions, the 9th and 10th

A Leibstandarte Guard of Honor at the Reich's Party Day in Nurnberg.

Obergruppenführer Josef "Sepp" Dietrich (1892–1966)

A Guard of Honor in Munich in November 1935.

A formal parade for the Führer.

(Left to right) Rudolf Hess, Sepp Dietrich, Hitler, and Heinrich Himmler at a review of the Leibstandarte on Berlin's Wilhelmstrasse.

Standards of the SS

The motorcycle detachment of the Leibstandarte during the 1930s. One of the early views of the growing military role for the guard unit.

Sepp Dietrich escorts Hitler through the Leibstandarte Barracks in Berlin.

An early WWII photo of Hitler inspecting Leibstandarte personnel in field uniforms.

Engineer elements of the Leibstandarte carry assault rafts for crossing the Prince Albert Canal in May 1940.

Sepp Dietrich in conference with his unit commanders at Metz during the French campaign.

Accompanied by his staff, Sepp Dietrich arranges for the surrender of Greek forces during the 1941 invasion.

An antitank gun of the LSSAH engages Russian armor during the fall of 1941.

Units of the LSSAH parade in Paris during June 1942.

Panzer IVs approach the Arc de Triomphe during a parade in August 1942.

Sepp Dietrich in his command vehicle during the attack on Kharkov in February 1943.

Reconnaissance elements drive through heavy snow to reach assembly areas.

This photograph of LSSAH personnel illustrates the excellent equipment given to SS soldiers. Many of the Wehrmacht personnel did not have the winter clothing shown in this picture.

Tanks of SS Panzer Regiment 1 prepare for their attack against Russian forces at Kharkov.

Units of LSSAH experience better weather as the battles progress. Here tanks and infantrymen pause prior to resuming the offensive.

Sepp Dietrich in a winter command photograph.

SS infantrymen carry on an attack through a Russian village on the outskirts of Kharkov.

Reequipped LSSAH tank units move through French villages as they prepare to attack Allied forces in Normandy.

Dietrich on the Invasion front during the summer of 1944.

of Hausser's corps, the 2nd SS Panzer Division Das Reich, and the 1st SS Panzer Division Leibstandarte SS Adolf Hitler, which was to soon begin laboriously assembling by night marches over secondary roads in the area Dreux-Evreaux-Laigle.[25]

The initial plan of attack was ambitious. As outlined by Hitler, the major weight of the offensive was to be carried by 1st, 2nd, 9th and 10th SS Panzer Divisions and by the army's Panzer Lehr and 2nd Armored Divisions. These divisions were to strike at the hinge between the American 1st Army and the British 2nd Army at Balleroy driving through Bayeaux to the coast near Arromanches. As a prerequisite to this operation, however, a necessarily more limited but nevertheless substantial attack was to be launched against British 2nd Army east of Caen and the Orne by Panzer Lehr and 2nd Panzer Divisions, apparently to draw the enemy eastward from the main point of attack but also so to weaken the British in that sector as to permit the desired concentration of armor south of Balleroy. The staff of Geyr von Schweppenburg's Panzergruppe West, now rebuilt following the disaster of June 10, was to control the operation.[26]

Twelfth SS Panzer Division Hitler Jugend was by this time no longer fit for large-scale offensive operations. Having been at the combat focus around Caen since June 7, it had suffered extremely heavy casualties.[27] Although new to combat, this offshoot of the Leibstandarte had fought and would continue to fight with great steadfastness and ferocity, evoking from its adversaries awe liberally mixed with hatred. The hatred was rooted in something greater than the dangers attendant upon combat with a brave and determined enemy in difficult terrain. The thoroughly indoctrinated youth of the division frequently shot their prisoners, a practice which resulted in Kurt Meyer's trial and death sentence before a Canadian military court in 1945.[28] The cataclysmic atmosphere in which the division fought in the Caen sector is dramatically conveyed by a contemporary article in an SS periodical:

Thousands of aircraft, rolling barrages of the batteries, massed tank attacks hammered them in with bombs and shells. The earth heaved thunderously. An inferno was unleashed. But faith was the strongest support of courage.

Smeared with blood, covered with dust, gasping and fighting, doggedly dug into the earth, these youths brought the Anglo-Americans to a halt.[29]

The effort to organize the offensive encountered discouraging obstacles from the very beginning. Although Hausser visited Geyr's headquarters on June 22, his corps, which had been in transit for ten days, would not reach its assembly area around Alençon for another three days. First SS Panzer Division Leibstandarte SS Adolf Hitler was being forced by extensive bomb damage to the French rail network to approach the front by a circuitous route and finally had to unload in the Rheims-Chalons sur Marne area, over three hundred miles east of the fighting front.[30] Most inconvenient of all, the British 2nd Army launched a formidable offensive (Epsom) in the Caen sector on the morning of June 26, the aim of which was to sweep west and south of Caen across the rivers Odon and Orne and envelop the city. The inevitable result was that the hard-pressed Germans were forced to commit much of their attack reserve in order to hold the Caen front. The full weight of Epsom, carried out by the British XXX and VIII Corps (the latter fresh and at full strength), fell upon Dietrich's I SS Panzer Corps. This was now made up only of the much-weakened Hitler Jugend Division and a battlegroup of the Leibstandarte Division, Panzer Lehr and 21st Panzer Divisions having been given to XXXXVII Panzer Corps and LXXXVI Army Corps respectively. On June 28 Dietrich reported to Panzergruppe West that without the assistance of Hausser's II SS Panzer Corps, Caen would soon be lost.[31] The confusion and despair of that day were accentuated by the absence of von Rundstedt and Rommel, then on their way to Berchtesgaden for a conference with Hitler, and the sudden death by heart attack of the commander of 7th Army, Colonel-General Dollmann. The command structure on the fighting front was hastily revised with Hausser assuming command of 7th Army, including Geyr's Panzergruppe West, and SS-Gruppenführer Willi Bittrich, former commander of 9th SS Panzer Division Hohenstaufen, taking over II SS Panzer Corps. The latter corps was now temporarily made subordinate to Dietrich's I SS Panzer Corps.[32] The stature which the Waffen-SS had achieved by the fifth year of the war is no better demonstrated than in this assumption by senior SS officers of most of the responsibility for operations along the invasion front.

The subordination to Dietrich's command of II SS Panzer Corps, which was to have constituted the spearhead of the thrust to Bayeaux and Arromanches, effectively marked the abandonment of that offensive. Already, II SS Panzer Corps had formulated plans for a counterattack against the salient which the British had driven across the Odon. With heavy supporting fire from Nebelwerfer, 9th and 10th SS Panzer Divisions were to amputate the tip of the salient south of the Villers-Bocage-Caen Road. Dietrich was clearly uneasy over the prospects of success, for he urgently requested the support of Panzer Lehr on II SS Panzer Corps' left flank.[33]

Due to heavy enemy air and artillery bombardment and ground pressure against the left flank of 9th SS Panzer Division Hohenstaufen, the counteroffensive was not begun until 2:30 on the afternoon of June 29.[34] Tenth SS Panzer Division Frundsberg, on the right flank of the attack, made good initial progress, destroying eleven British tanks within the first ninety minutes in the Gavrus area, and twelve more soon after.[35] On the left flank, however, 9th SS Panzer Division Hohenstaufen was at first unable to advance due to heavy enemy artillery and naval support fire. Although by early evening the western flank of the salient had been pushed in to the line Rauray-Grainville-Gavrus (about one mile), with a total destruction of thirty-eight British tanks, this progress was nullified by British counterattacks supported by the big guns of *Ramillies* and *Nelson*.[36]

Efforts by II SS Panzer Corps to cut off the salient continued into the following day without much success. Dietrich, typifying his brand of leadership, was at the front while his chief of staff, Kraemer, followed the total situation at corps headquarters. By late afternoon on June 30, Kraemer was convinced that the offensive should be abandoned, for in spite of the fact that Gavrus had been retaken, Dietrich's forces remained under constant and ferocious enemy bombardment, suffering heavy losses.[37]

Hitler had been closely watching the abortive offensive, and the patent failure of his elite SS divisions to do more than dent the British salient had its effect upon him. He was now willing to concede the hopelessness of a major offensive in Normandy but did not draw the same conclusions from that assessment as did his commanders.[38] Second SS Panzer Corps was withdrawn to its start lines on the morning of July 1, but Rommel, who had returned to France, had decided that the entire front had become untenable, and in this Dietrich concurred.[39] The field marshal hoped to withdraw 7th Army from Normandy and with this army and the divisions then remaining elsewhere in France to establish a new front along the Seine. He gave permission for the evacuation of the Caen bridgehead to begin, but on the evening of July 1 this action was forbidden by Hitler who demanded that all positions be held and "that every breakthrough be prevented by stubborn defense or local counterattacks."[40]

In fact, Epsom and the German counteroffensive which it evoked had together produced an extraordinarily sanguinary stalemate. So fierce had been the combat in the Odon Valley that, according to reports, the small river had been dammed by knots of corpses.[41] But while the British had been unable to turn the corner behind Caen and had abandoned the effort by the end of June, they had, with the indispensable assistance of aerial supremacy and naval gunfire, foiled the German effort to amputate the Odon salient. More important, Epsom had rendered impossible the planned German offensive against the hinge of 1st U.S. and 2nd British Armies.

With the abandonment of Epsom, Dempsey (with great tenacity if not originality) returned to the simple but costly expedient of attempting to take Caen by direct assault, an undertaking anticipated by Panzergruppe West.[42] The assault opened on the morning of July 4 with a thrust by the Canadian 3rd Division toward Carpiquet, three miles west of Caen. By 6:30 that afternoon, Carpiquet had been secured with the assistance of an estimated forty to sixty tanks against which I SS Panzer Corps could accomplish little due to a shortage of artillery ammunition of all calibers.[43] While troops of 12th SS Panzer Division Hitler Jugend stoutly and successfully defended the airfield south of Carpiquet, Dietrich's corps began making preparations for combat within Caen itself, requesting permission on the morning of July 6 to evacuate the civilian population of the city. Although the evacuation was requested solely as a military and not as a humanitarian measure, it undoubtedly saved numerous civilian lives, for between nine and ten o'clock on the morning of July 7, heavy bombers of the Royal Air Force carpeted the city with 2500 tons of bombs.[44] The massive aerial assault was the prelude to a three-pronged converging thrust against Caen which was undertaken the following morning. While Hitler Jugend continued to stand fast, the poorly trained 16th Luftwaffe Field Division on its right, recently transferred from Holland, quickly found itself hard pressed by the onslaught of the British 3rd Division. Dietrich was called upon to support his crumbling neighbor with artillery and armor from Hitler Jugend, but this division, itself facing armored thrusts from the Buron area, could spare nothing. Although Rommel, following Hitler's directive, issued orders that Caen was to be held at all costs, Hitler Jugend found itself partly surrounded within the city on July 9 and was forced to fall back across the Orne into the suburb of Vaucelles.[45]

Caen was now in British hands, but a breakthrough had not been achieved. First SS Panzer Division Leibstandarte SS Adolf Hitler had been concentrated east of the Orne, and although Dempsey succeeded in penetrating the division's left wing in the Jumeaux area on July 10, the front was stabilized later in the day along the Venoix-Eterville Road. Leibstandarte, still at almost full strength, now assumed responsibility for the defense of the center of the Caen front from the exhausted division Hitler Jugend.[46]

Dietrich's I SS Panzer Corps had acquitted itself with magnificent *élan* in the savage battles of the previous month. Nevertheless, the corps and particularly 12th SS Panzer Division Hitler Jugend had been badly battered, the latter division having suffered five thousand casualties, the heaviest loss of any of the panzer divisions of Panzergruppe West. Under normal circumstances Hitler Jugend would have been withdrawn from combat for refitting, and the possibilities of this were discussed by Meyer and Field Marshal Günther von Kluge, since July 2, Commander-in-Chief West.[47] Nothing was available at that time to replace the division, however, and it remained in the line. Only a driblet of replacements for casualties was forthcoming from the SS-Führungshauptamt, totaling a mere one thousand men for the entire I SS Panzer Corps! In this as in most other respects, the SS was in as critical a condition as the army, and Dietrich warmly supported a representation to Hitler calling for the dissolution of all training establishments whose continued operation was not absolutely necessary. Dietrich's remarkably efficient tank-repair establishment, however, had performed wonders, having sent back into the field 137 damaged Tigers and Panthers within a space of four weeks.[48]

Meanwhile, Hausser's 7th Army had been giving a good account of itself in the Cotentin against Lieutenant-General Omar Bradley's 1st U.S. Army and with a much smaller concentration of armor.[49] With the failure of British 2nd Army to effect a decisive breakthrough around Caen, the danger now arose that von Kluge might divert powerful formations to the front of Bradley's army where the major breakthrough and exploitation to the Seine was to take place. Montgomery therefore ordered another major offensive in the Caen sector in order to achieve a breakthrough south of the Orne if possible but, above all, to keep the bulk of available German armor pinned down to the front of 2nd British Army. The overwhelming weight of the offensive (Goodwood) was to be carried by three armored divisions, which, sweeping out of a small bridgehead across the Orne northeast of Caen, would swing well south of the city and establish themselves on the ridgeline south of Bourguebus overlooking the road to Falaise.[50]

Two days before the onset of Goodwood, the weary 12th SS Panzer Division Hitler Jugend appeared likely to receive a long-overdue respite from combat. Still fearing a second major Allied landing north of the Normandy front, Hitler on July 16 ordered Meyer's division transferred north to join the 15th Army, which by that time had been largely denuded of its armored strength. The 272nd Infantry Division, recently arrived from southern France, was given to Dietrich in inadequate compensation for the loss of Hitler Jugend.[51]

Enfeebled though it was, Panzergruppe West enjoyed the advantage of virtual certainty of the impending British offensive, being able to observe visually the movement of armored forces in and around the Orne bridgehead. Dietrich needed only to place his ear to the ground in order to detect the rumbling of large numbers of vehicles transmitted through the limestone formations of the Caen plain. On the evening of July 16, 12 SS Panzer Division Hitler Jugend's prospects of enjoying a period of rest were dashed when it was ordered by Rommel into reserve in the area Lisieux-Pont Evêque.[52]

July 17 was a day of crisis for the Germans along the entire invasion front. Late in the afternoon Rommel, while driving to the battle headquarters of Panzergruppe West, was set upon by strafing British fighters near Vimoutiers and severely wounded.[53] At the same time, strong pressure by Bradley's 1st U.S. Army at St. Lô prompted Rommel's chief of staff, Lieutenant-General Hans Speidel, to suggest to von Kluge that 1st SS Panzer Division Leibstandarte SS Adolf Hitler be transferred to that sector. Kluge, however, refused, insisting that Leibstandarte must remain in the Caen area; he was already planning a major spoiling attack against British forces in the Caen sector in which I and II Panzer Corps were to be used.[54]

Kluge's plan was transformed into an academic exercise when on the morning of July 18 Goodwood was unleashed from the Orne bridgehead behind artillery drumfire and carpet bombing of unprecedented proportions. British armor quickly broke through the sector covered by the 16th Luftwaffe Field Division around Colombelles, and by 9:30 A.M. some fifty tanks had penetrated almost as far south as Cagny, about four miles from the offensive's start-lines.[55] This was a dire threat to the right flank of I SS Panzer Corps, and Dietrich reacted vigorously, dispatching the corps' Panther detachment to the Cagny area. These tanks took the leading element of the British 11th Armored Division under heavy fire, which, in combination with the support of 88-mm. guns sited to the south on Bourguebus Ridge, broke the momentum of the initial British effort. Small numbers of British tanks had broken through to the base of the ridge, but these were thwarted by Panthers of 1st SS Panzer Division Leibstandarte SS Adolf Hitler firing from hull-down positions on its crest. Subsequent counterattacks by Leibstandarte between Hubert Folié and Frenouville continued into the night but achieved little and Cagny fell to the Guards Armored Division. Nevertheless, an index of the efficiency of the German defense is offered by the fact that the spearhead of the British offensive, 11th Armored Division, had lost 126 tanks during the day, many of these having fallen victim to Dietrich's guns.[56]

In the course of the morning of July 19, Hitler Jugend moved into the line on the right of Leibstandarte. At the same time, bad weather restricted the application of Allied airpower. Nevertheless, enemy attacks toward the south continued, and by early afternoon the village of Bourguebus was taken by the British but quickly retaken by Leibstandarte.[57]

British and Canadian troops had cleared most of the northern slope of Bourguebus Ridge by July 20 but could not dislodge I SS Panzer Corps from its crest. Dietrich's corps was reinforced in the expectation of renewed major assaults against the ridge, but, in fact, the defensive battle had been won, albeit temporarily. On the night of July 20 the British armored divisions were withdrawn to lick their not-inconsiderable wounds. In fact, Goodwood had cost the British 2nd Army over four hundred tanks, although these could be quickly replaced.[58]

German tank losses, too, had been heavy. I SS Panzer Corps, by July 27, was reduced to a total strength of eighty Mark IVs and Panthers, and replacements were not forthcoming.[59] Yet the shortage of manpower remained the most critical problem faced by the Germans along the invasion front. Since June 6, German armies in the West had lost over 111,000 officers and men but had received as replacements slightly in excess of 10,000. First SS Panzer Division Leibstandarte SS Adolf Hitler had suffered approximately 40 percent casualties while those of 12th SS Panzer Division Hitler Jugend were in the vicinity of 60 percent. These casualties were comparable to those of army divisions fighting in the same sector.[60] Dietrich was badly shaken by the inability of the SS-Führungshauptamt to provide replacements in adequate numbers. The importance which the Commander-in-Chief West, Field Marshal von Kluge, assigned to the preservation of the combat effectiveness of the SS panzer divisions under his command was reflected in his request for permission to incorporate army personnel into these units.[61]

Dietrich's ability to inspire his weary SS troopers to magnificent feats of arms such as the defense of the Bourguebus Ridge was recognized by his superiors in the field. In the wake of those battles General Hans Eberbach, who had replaced Geyr as commander of Panzergruppe West early in July, observed that "Sepp Dietrich is something grand [*gross-*

zügig]."[62] Indeed, inspiration was all that Dietrich could offer his men in preparation for the even more difficult trials to come, and in this respect it must be conceded that he tried very hard. In an order of the day issued on July 24, he noted that:

> On 23.7.1944 the corps has reported the destruction of 1100 tanks, 110 aircraft and the capture of 70 officers and 1924 (enlisted) prisoners. These successes were achieved since the beginning of the battle on the Calvados Coast by units of the corps fighting at the points of crisis [*Brennpunkten*]. The difficult battles took place under great enemy material and air superiority. [But] in the hardest struggles, the enemy was denied his hoped-for breakthrough into the French interior. In spite of the most ruthless commitment of his men and materiel, the enemy has succeeded in making limited progress only at the price of high and bloody losses. The steadfastness of the German close-in fighter [*Nahkämpfer*] has again shown itself to be above praise.
>
> A new great struggle is impending. It will be particularly difficult because the enemy has concentrated his previously landed armored strength in order to force a breakthrough. The corps will stand in this battle, too, like a bronze wall. The heroism of the individual German fighter will counterbalance material superiority. The divisions, proven on the battlefields of Europe and welded into a sworn community [*Gemeinschaft*] will stand fast. In cooperation with all weapons and in loyal comradeship the German close-in fighter will again achieve victory over materiel.
>
> Each officer, noncommissioned officer, and man must be aware that this is a struggle for the fate of Germany. Each must be willing to fight at the most decisive sector of the front. We will prove ourselves worthy of our comrades who have fallen for the greatness of our *Volk*.
>
> Long live the Führer![63]

It is of interest to note that Dietrich's inspirational order made no reference to any unique burden to be borne in combat by SS men, nor indeed was the SS alluded to at any point.

Dietrich would have been most unpolitic to have done so, for at that point I SS Panzer Corps was evenly divided between SS divisions (1st, 9th, and 12th) and Army divisions (116th Panzer Division, 267th Infantry Division, and 272nd Infantry Division).[64] This is not to deny that Himmler encouraged SS combat units to view themselves as ideologically committed soldiers fighting as direct instruments of Hitler's will, but that had little perceptible relevance to the SS soldier in the field. His conception of eliteness tended to be of a more generalized and pragmatic nature, that of a sense of membership in a ruthless and fatalistic assault formation, and his personal loyalties were directed toward his comrades and charismatic commanders such as Kurt Meyer and Sepp Dietrich. In this context it might be noted that Leibstandarte division produced its own educational leaflet entitled simply, *Der Dietrich*.[65]

The degree to which the real functions of combat Waffen-SS units and the army had been fused by the experience of war is neatly illustrated by the events surrounding the attempt on Hitler's life of July 20, 1944. Leibstandarte, which had been formed in 1933 for the protection of the Führer and his regime, was then battling along the Bourguebus Ridge while the efforts of the conspirators in Berlin to seize power were nullified by army personnel under the command of Major Otto Remer. It has even been suggested that Dietrich and Hausser, the two senior Waffen-SS commanders, would have sided with the conspirators had the putsch seemed likely to succeed, although this is purely speculative.[66] No recorded utterance of Dietrich's bears on this episode beyond a vague statement made to Allied interrogators after the war to the effect that he and Hitler had drifted farther and farther apart due to his (Dietrich's) absence in the field.[67] It is most unlikely, however, that Dietrich, who owed to Hitler his lofty status in both the party and the military hierarchies, would have overtly turned against him.

On the morning of July 25 Dempsey's Canadians struck at the left wing of 1st SS Panzer Division Leibstandarte SS Adolf Hitler and achieved two penetrations in the vicinity of Tilly, advancing approximately two miles. This proved to be a purely local attack in limited strength, and by evening Dietrich's corps had regained all territory lost earlier in the day.[68]

The major event of the day took place not in the Caen sector of the invasion front but some thirty miles to the west at the base of the Cotentin Peninsula. The Canadian assault, beaten off by I SS Panzer Corps, had, in fact, been a diversionary move supporting Operation Cobra, a massive effort by 1st U.S. Army to pierce the lines of Hausser's 7th Army between St. Lô and Perier, laying the groundwork for a decisive breakout from Normandy by Patton's Third Army.[69] By July 30 VIII U.S. Corps had reached Avranches and on the following day turned the corner into Brittany. Kluge had foreseen the incalculable consequences of a breakthrough on Hausser's left wing but could do little to forestall it, for on the same day that Avranches had fallen, 2nd British Army had undertaken a major thrust toward Vire, the hinge between 7th Army and Panzergruppe West. As had been intended by Montgomery, this operation had pinned down the bulk of German armor and had effectively prevented its interference with the American breakout.[70]

With the German left barely preserving coherence and unable to prevent an avalanche of American armor from fanning out south of Avranches while the center and right remained under strong American and British pressure, reason might have dictated a general retirement to the Seine or even further east. Hitler, however, ordered on August 2 that the German front be restored by a major attack westward to the sea at Avranches which would not only reestablish the blocking position of Hausser's 7th Army at the base of the Cotentin but also cut off and destroy American armored strength pushing to the east, southeast, and south. Hitler believed that at least four armored divisions were necessary for the operation; but could they be found?[71]

Through a straightening of the front between Thury Harcourt and a point southwest of Vire and the arrival of two infantry divisions from 15th Army, an attack group was formed under Hausser's command. Leibstandarte was relieved by 89th Infantry Division along the Bourguebus Ridge and joined 116th Panzer Division, 2nd Panzer Division, and 2nd SS Panzer Division east of Mortain.[72] Hitler had hoped that Leibstandarte and Hitler Jugend could be committed together in the attack toward Avranches, but Meyer's division remained pinned in action south of Caen. In fact, with the departure of Leibstandarte to Mortain and the return of 9th SS Panzer Division to Bittrich's II SS Panzer Corps east of Vire, Dietrich was left with only the weak remnants of Hitler Jugend plus two infantry divisions to hold the Caen-Falaise Road against 1st Canadian Army.[73]

Leibstandarte's losses had been extremely heavy, particularly among its two panzer grenadier regiments, and by the beginning of August the division was able to muster only sixty tanks. As it happened, not even the whole of Leibstandarte could be employed in the Avaranches offensive. The continued threat to the crucial Vire hinge required that half of the division be employed there while only two weak battlegroups were made available for the attack, and these had not yet come up to the start lines by the evening of August 6 when the offensive was to begin. One armored battalion had been moving through a defile when an Allied fighter-bomber crashed full upon the leading tank, forcing the battalion to laboriously back out of the narrow thoroughfare. Hausser, who had decided to move on Avranches at 8:00 P.M., postponed the attack until shortly after midnight but then proceeded without Leibstandarte, planning to commit it as a second wave upon its arrival.[74]

Aided by darkness and then by a thick morning fog, the attacking divisions advanced about six miles toward Avranches (one-third the total distance) by noon on August 7. Leibstandarte, inserted in the center of the front at midmorning, had succeeded in taking Juvigny by storm. The protective layer of fog which had thus far shielded the panzer divisions from Allied air power lifted by afternoon, however, and swarms of rocket-firing fighter-bombers brought the first day's operations to a halt.[75]

Von Kluge, whose enthusiasm for the Avranches effort had been minimal from the beginning, was now prepared to abandon it but was overruled by Hitler.[76] The Führer insisted that the attack be pressed in greater strength, necessitating stripping the rest of the front of its remaining armor including the remnants of Hitler Jugend south of Caen. Hitler complained that the attack had been too weak, premature, and that Leibstandarte had been carelessly committed.[77] A second effort was to be made under the command of General Hans Eberbach whose 5th Panzer Army (as Panzergruppe West had been redesignated on August 5) now came under the temporary command of Sepp Dietrich, now SS-Oberstgruppenführer and as of August 6 holder of the Knight's Cross with Oak Leaves, Swords, and Diamonds.[78]

In the meantime, developments on both flanks of the German front threatened to render these plans academic. Late on the evening of August 7 First Canadian Army, behind the now customary multikiloton bomb carpet, struck again at the front of I SS Panzer Corps (now only one-third SS) in the oft-attempted effort to reach Falaise.[79] This attack was carried out in great strength by an estimated 600 tanks against which Hitler Jugend could throw only 45. The order to remove 12th SS Panzer Division (actually only two battlegroups remained) to the Mortain sector was cancelled by von Kluge shortly after midnight on August 8, and the incomparable tenacity of this division as well as the forceful personality of its commander had much to do with the preservation of the Caen front.[80] Shortly after the massive aerial bombardment which heralded Operation Totalize, Meyer, while personally reconnoitering behind the front discovered that

> Before me, making their way down the Caen-Falaise Road in a disorderly rabble, were the panic-stricken troops of 89th Infantry Division. I realized that something had to be done to send these men back into the line and fight. I lit a cigar, stood in the middle of the road and in a loud voice asked them if they were going to leave me alone to cope with the enemy. Hearing a divisional commander address them in this way, they stopped, hesitated and then returned to their positions.[81]

Fifth Panzer Army attempted to recover Leibstandarte from the Mortain sector, but this request was bluntly refused by von Kluge. By the evening of August 8 Hitler Jugend had sustained such heavy losses that it was no longer possible to assemble even one offensive battlegroup.[82]

Yet, the front before Falaise had been well provided by Dietrich with 75- and 88-mm. antitank guns, and these, in combination with the hesitancy of the enemy, prevented a clean breakthrough. The first twenty-four hours of Totalize had achieved a gain of only three miles, although it had also produced despondency at von Kluge's headquarters and near-panic at Eberbach's (at this time, still in command of 5th Panzer Army).[83] The Canadians pressed their attacks on the following day for an additional six miles as the Germans withdrew to new defensive positions, but Falaise was still seven miles distant. While British losses in armor had been appalling, they were not as great as those suffered during Goodwood. On the morning of August 10 Totalize was called off in spite of the fact that I SS Panzer Corps had been reduced to a total armored strength of thirty-five tanks.[84]

The limited defensive success of I SS Panzer Corps was mildly encouraging, but the front of 7th Army, from which the attack toward Avranches was to be resumed, was under heavy pressure. This had prevented von Kluge from sending to 5th Panzer Army any significant support and had, in fact, forced the abandonment of some of the meager gains made on August 7.[85] A far deadlier threat, however, was posed by the fact that XV Corps of the American 3rd Army had swept far to the south and east following the breakthrough at Avranches and had reached Le Mans on August 8. The Americans needed only to swing north in order to confront the entire German front in Normandy with the specter of double envelopment.

Eberbach had already decided to seek Hitler's approval of a postponement of the second phase of the Avranches attack until August 20 in order to assemble and partially reequip his forces and to take advantage of favorable moonlight and predicted inclement weather.[86] Such a postponement had as its prerequisite a long-term stabilization of the front on all sectors which, however, was not granted the Germans. The threat of double envelopment was made a reality when on August 10 the American XV Corps swung in a northerly direction from Le Mans toward Alençon.[87]

Clearly, the attack to Avranches was not feasible in the face of an impending encirclement of both German armies. On August 11, therefore, von Kluge abandoned temporarily the planned thrust to Avranches and ordered Eberbach to prepare a powerful armored attack to be hurled against XV Corps in the vicinity of Alençon.[88] In order to free a force adequate for the purpose, specified as 116 Panzer Division, 2nd Panzer

Division and 1st SS Panzer Division Leibstandarte SS Adolf Hitler, the Mortain salient had to be abandoned.

Eberbach intended to attack on August 14, but the progress of the U.S. XV Corps outstripped his plans. On August 12 XV Corps reached Alençon and pressed on toward Argentan at which point only twenty miles would separate it from the Canadians north of Falaise. Eberbach was therefore forced to commit his divisions to the defense of the town as they became available, 116th Panzer on August 12, Leibstandarte and 2nd Panzer on the following day. Three armored divisions seemed, on paper, more than adequate to cope with the two armored divisions of XV Corps, but these units were little more than weak battlegroups. Leibstandarte could field, at that time, a mere thirty tanks, and it was the strongest of the three divisions.[89]

Dietrich, as commander of 5th Panzer Army, was not directly involved in the trials of the western and southern sectors of the front but was feeling their effects. Operations there had sucked from his sector much of the available German armor, including his beloved Leibstandarte, in the face of continuing British pressure in the Caen area, and the progress of the American XV Corps had cut off the sources of supply of the 7th Army, making it dependent on 5th Panzer Army whose own logistical situation was critical.[90] Moreover, Dietrich was painfully conscious of holding the point where the British and American vice jaws, then north of Falaise and south of Argentan, were threatening to meet. With courage and foresight that surpassed those of his army colleagues, Dietrich noted on August 13 that

> if every effort is not made to move the forces toward the east and out of the threatened encirclement, the army group will have to write off both armies. Within a very short time resupplying the troops with ammunition and fuel will no longer be possible. Therefore, immediate measures are necessary to move to the east before such movement is definitely too late. It will soon be possible for the enemy to fire into the pocket with artillery from all sides.[91]

Similar representations were made to the headquarters of Army Group B on the evening of the same day in which

Dietrich specifically pleaded for the cancellation of Eberbach's attack, still scheduled for the following day.[92] Hitler, however, who had been won over by Eberbach's plan, was determined to proceed and had allocated an additional three armored divisions (9th and 10th SS and 21st Panzer) for the operation.[93] Sadly, Dietrich's courage failed him at the point where he might have had a real impact on the developing course of events—through personal intervention at Hitler's headquarters. In previous military crises, Dietrich had freely spoken his mind to the Führer, but those instances had antedated the assassination attempt of July 20, which had rendered criticism a much more dangerous undertaking. When urged to approach Hitler, Dietrich laconically remarked to the commander of the 272nd Infantry Division, "If I want to get shot, that's the way to do it."[94]

For reasons which need not detain us here, XV Corps, which had reached points on either side of Argentan on the evening of the thirteenth, advanced no farther northward.[95] Yet, Eberbach was not much benefited by this hesitancy, for the three divisions assembled for the counterstroke against the American XV Corps continued to suffer grievously from aerial bombardment and artillery fire. Moreover, on the morning of August 14 the Canadians struck once more at the German defenses north of Falaise (Tractable).[96] The full weight of the attack fell on the front of the much-debilitated I SS Panzer Corps and on the left flank of LXXXVI Corps to its right. Throughout the day, SS-Brigadeführer Fritz Kraemer, now exercising command of I SS Panzer Corps, prevented a clean breakthrough but was forced to gradually withdraw his front to the south. He despaired, however, of holding the Canadians from Falaise without substantial reinforcement, and Dietrich, who had arrived by afternoon at the front of I SS Panzer Corps, agreed, urgently requesting that 21st Panzer Division, then on its way to Eberbach, be brought up behind the corps' front. To this, von Kluge assented that evening.[97]

Twenty-first Panzer had not yet arrived by the following morning. Hitler Jugend, although reduced in strength to fifteen tanks and little more than five hundred men, managed to hold fast astride the Caen-Falaise Road but could not prevent enemy infiltration through its right flank where resistance was maintained only by isolated strong points. Kraemer desperately sought the support of the 88-mm. guns of III Flak Corps, but these were tied down in antiaircraft duties south of Falaise.[98] In an effort to close the widening space between I SS Panzer Corps and LXXXVI Corps, Dietrich ordered the latter corps south and east across the River Dives, but a breakthrough at St. Pierre sur Dives on the following morning opened a large gap which forced LXXXVI Corps to fight with a partially reversed front.[99] Hitler Jugend managed momentarily to seal off penetration of its sector in the vicinity of Falaise, but the front was rapidly disintegrating. On the evening of August 16, troops of the 2nd Canadian Division entered Falaise and took it house by house from a small contingent of 12th SS Panzer Division Hitler Jugend. In the *école superieure* sixty young SS troopers continued to resist for three days, and of these only four survived to be captured.[100]

With the loss of Falaise, the gap between the Canadian and American jaws had narrowed to twelve miles. On the southern flank of what can now be called the Argentan-Falaise pocket, Eberbach had been unable to launch his thrust against the American XV Corps. This had been due in some measure to the crisis on Dietrich's front which had taken from Eberbach part of the armor allotted to him, notably 21st Panzer Division, but also because of shortages of fuel and ammunition and the incessant attentions of Allied fighter-bombers. Eberbach could therefore do little but stand on the defensive while his already emaciated divisions were further whittled down.[101]

Although Hitler long resisted the abandonment of a major counterattack, the fall of Falaise in combination with a renewal of the American advance northward from Argentan effectively decided the issue. By late afternoon on August 17, 7th Army was streaming westward toward the narrowing exit which I SS Panzer Corps was desperately attempting to hold open north of Chambois. Allied fighter-bombers, constantly operating in the clear summer skies, poured rocket, cannon, and machine-gun fire into the disintegrating German formations. In the afternoon and evening of August 18, Canadians and Americans met in the vicinity of Trun, trapping 7th Army, Panzergruppe Eberbach (including Leibstandarte) and part of 5th Panzer Army including the remnant of Hitler Jugend.[102]

At nine o'clock that morning Field Marshal Walter Model, who had assumed command of the western theater and Army Group B from von Kluge on the previous day, had met with Dietrich and Eberbach to discuss means of dealing with their imminent encirclement. Model insisted that, above all, a coherent front must again be established but that the obvious prerequisite for this was an immediate evacuation of the pocket. At that time, a small gap still existed between Chambois and Trun which, it was hoped, could be held open by units outside the eastern perimeter of the closing pocket. These included, some elements of I SS Panzer Corps and II SS Panzer Corps, now composed of 2nd and 9th SS Panzer Divisions, which had earlier been detached from Eberbach's Gruppe to support Dietrich's 5th Panzer Army.[103]

The frightful carnage of the Falaise-Argentan pocket and the escape of an indeterminate fraction (probably less than 50 percent) of the encircled German troops have been too often described to warrant repetition here. War diaries of the German units involved, usually so meticulous in describing troop movements, have little to say concerning the breakout itself, indicating the desperation and wild confusion which largely characterized the operation. Remnants of Leibstandarte seem to have fought their way across the Dives in the St. Lambert-Chambois area early on the morning of August 20 followed by a bedraggled company of two hundred men led by Kurt Meyer of the 12th SS Panzer Division "Hitler Jugend" which eleven weeks earlier had been a splendidly equipped armored division.[104]

Those elements of Army Group B which had fought their way east across the Dives found salvation of only the most transitory nature. The American XV Corps had already reached the Seine northwest of Paris and was preparing to drive along the western bank of the river toward its mouth, thus threatening a wider encirclement of Army Group B.[105]

Model, on August 20, delegated to Dietrich command of the German front from the Channel coast to a line west and south of Paris.[106] This responsibility included authority over 7th Army, whose commander, SS-Obergruppenführer Paul Hausser, had been critically wounded during the breakout from the Argentan-Falaise pocket and had been borne to safety on the hull of a tank belonging to Leibstandarte.[107]

Seldom has a military leader inherited a command under bleaker circumstances. Hitler and Model hoped that a new front might be reestablished west of the Seine, but for this purpose Dietrich had only the fragments that had been extricated from the Falaise-Argentan catastrophe. Indicative of his resources is the fact that by August 21, 12th SS Panzer Division had been able to assemble a bare 300 men, 10 tanks and no artillery, while Leibstandarte was still too disorganized to make any report at all.[108] Other divisions allotted to Dietrich were in little better condition. With this rag-tag collection, it was impossible to hold a front of one hundred miles against simultaneous frontal pressure in the northwest by the British and Canadians and the American drive into its left flank in the southeast. The situation was rendered still more critical when, on August 21, elements of the American XV Corps established a bridgehead on the east bank of the Seine at Mantes.[109]

Hitler had already reluctantly accepted the likelihood that the front would have to be withdrawn behind the Seine, and on the evening of August 21 Dietrich's headquarters issued a directive ordering the movement in four stages.[110] But the prerequisite for an orderly withdrawal was an ability to prevent 5th Panzer Army's left flank from being rolled up by the northward pressure of the American XV and IX Corps, and this Dietrich with his meager resources found difficult to accomplish. Although the American 79th Infantry Division was successfully contained in the Mantes bridgehead for several days, American pressure along the west bank of the Seine was relentless. Splinter contingents, including remnants of Leibstandarte, fought fiercely under the command of SS-Standartenführer Wilhelm Mohnke but were steadily driven northward.[111] At around midday on August 23, Model ordered a concerted counterattack on both sides of Le Neubourg by the remnants of Leibstandarte, Hitler Jugend, and 2nd Panzer Division, subordinated to 116th Panzer Division. Dietrich was pessimistic concerning the outcome of the operation, reminding his superior that the four "divisions" to be employed were nothing more than a few weak battalions supported by at most thirty tanks.[112] The attack was launched late that afternoon but was almost immediately halted and driven back with the resultant loss of Le Neubourg. For the period of August 20–24, however, Mohnke's Kampfgruppe reported the destruction of forty-five enemy tanks as well as the killing of forty-one French guerrillas.[113]

The threat was grave that Dietrich's troops might be cut off from the Seine crossings and crushed between the American and British-Canadian forces advancing from the west. Substantial elements of 7th Army which had been considered unfit for combat had already been transported east of the river for refitting and for the preparation of defensive positions. In spite of the ceaseless air attacks, 5th Panzer Army was able to report that by the evening of August 24, large numbers of vehicles of all kinds had been taken across the Seine on ferries, small boats, and pontoon bridges.[114] By the morning of August 25, Elbeuf was entered by the Americans, and although the remnants of 2nd SS Panzer Division Das Reich retook the town, they were too weak to hold it and were withdrawn that afternoon. At the same time, British and Canadian forces were nearing the Seine, necessitating the immediate withdrawal of all remaining German forces to the east bank of the river; this was to be done on the evening of August 26–27 from two northward-jutting loops of the Seine, south of Rouen and Duclair, while battlegroups of 2nd and 9th SS Panzer Divisions and 21st and 116th Panzer Divisions acted as rearguards.[115]

The final stage of the withdrawal east of the Seine was only a limited success. Although many had to paddle across the river on homemade rafts and even to swim, the majority of troops were able to escape. Much heavy equipment, however, was abandoned on the west bank, and in this respect Dietrich later observed, "The Seine crossing was almost as great a disaster as the Falaise pocket."[116]

Although the war diary of 5th Panzer Army speaks as late as August 25 of the establishment of a new defensive line on the Seine,[117] such a stand was no longer feasible several days later. Not only had losses in equipment been very great, but the line of the Seine had already been made untenable by American crossings in strength on both sides of Paris. Fifth Panzer Army, whose combat strength on August 25 totaled 17,980 infantrymen, 314 artillery pieces, and 42 tanks and assault guns, seems to have had no alternative but to seek refuge in flight, particularly since thrusts by the American 1st

Army north and west of Meaux and Chateau-Thierry were interpreted (incorrectly) as an effort to swing behind and encircle both 5th Panzer Army and its neighbor on the left, 1st Army, between Flanders and the Seine.[118] A conference on August 28 among Model, Dietrich, Kraemer and the chiefs of staff of 7th and 15th Armies produced a decision for general retirement with a stand to be made on the so-called "Dieppe line" in order to grant additional time for the preparation of defenses along the Somme and the Marne.[119] This, too, was quickly rendered nugatory by rapid Allied progress which threatened to beat the Germans to the Somme-Marne line. On August 31 Amiens fell to the 2nd British Army. Dietrich was then in the vicinity of Amiens turning over the Somme sector to Eberbach, once again in command of a partially revived 7th Army, preparatory to moving his own headquarters far inland to Charleville and barely escaped capture by troops of the British 11th Armored Division. Eberbach, however, was not so fortunate. He and three members of his staff became prisoners of war and Dietrich, in consequence, reassumed control of 7th Army.[120]

The German front continued to fall back to the north and east. By September 8 Model was convinced that only along the permanent fortifications of the West Wall, extending from the German-Dutch frontier near Cleve to the Swiss border north of Basel, did the Germans have a chance of reestablishing a stable front. In general, Hitler was in agreement although for him a stable front was of importance simply as the prerequisite for renewed offensive operations.[121] The possibility of resuming the offensive was also dependent upon the reconstruction of a powerful armored reserve, and this process was furthered on September 4 when the remnants of 1st SS Panzer Division Leibstandarte SS Adolf Hitler, 2nd SS Panzer Division Das Reich, 12th SS Panzer Division Hitler Jugend, and four independent armored detachments were ordered to return to the Reich for complete refitting. On September 11 Dietrich was replaced in command of 5th Panzer Army by General Hasso von Manteuffel and ordered to report to Hitler for a new assignment.[122]

II
Ardennes

On September 13, 1944, Sepp Dietrich was charged by Hitler with the organization of a new army for use as an operational reserve in a future offensive stroke against the West. This army, designated 6th Panzer Army, was to come into being largely through the refurbishing of several worn-out SS armored divisions, then streaming westward from the battlefields of France, and later included army and Luftwaffe units.[1]

Initial progress in the building of 6th Panzer Army was slow, in large part because the western front remained fluid through the month of September, requiring the continued commitment of potential cadre personnel and attracting most available replacements and equipment.[2] During the fourth week in September, Dietrich activated an army staff at Bad Salzuflen near Cologne; troops were assigned to the army the following month. In October a coherent front had been re-established west of the Rhine, and although the western Allies retained the initiative, their advance was thereafter made haltingly and at considerable cost.[3]

Dietrich's success as the commander of Leibstandarte during the first four years of the war had been due in no small measure to the qualities of initiative and aggressiveness which he was able to transmit to the relatively compact and tightly knit body of fighting men, often personally selected by Dietrich. Hitler had observed in December 1942:

The battalions which Dietrich gets out there [Leibstandarte was then about to return from France to Russia] are all sort of preselected. He seeks out his people. . . . He has the right to pick out every single man, and he puts them in his replacement battalion for six to eight months because he says: "Otherwise he [the replacement] has no value; the marvelous kids will simply be shot to pieces."[4]

The *esprit de corps* and efficiency of the division unavoidably underwent dilution when in the spring of 1943 Leibstandarte began receiving poorly trained replacements, some of them ex-Luftwaffe personnel whose enthusiasm and capability for ground combat were minimal but who were immediately incorporated into combat formations as a result of the heavy losses suffered around Kharkov. The sense of cohesion within the division presumably also suffered with the promotion of Dietrich from the divisional command to control of I SS Panzer Corps Leibstandarte and the removal of experienced commissioned and noncommissioned officers to act as cadres for 12th SS Panzer Division Hitler Jugend. Two of Leibstandarte's most effective combat commanders, Fritz Witt and Kurt Meyer, departed from Leibstandarte to join Hitler Jugend and were lost to I SS Panzer Corps as well during the spring and summer of 1944. As already noted, Witt was killed near Caen in June and Meyer was taken prisoner on September 4 near Namur.[5] SS-Brigadführer Theodor Wisch, who had assumed command of Leibstandarte in July 1943, had been badly wounded in the flight from the Falaise-Argentan pocket and was replaced by SS-Oberführer Wilhelm Mohnke.[6] Leibstandarte, along with all of the elite Waffen-SS panzer divisions which had fought in France in the summer of 1944, had been decimated and had to be rebuilt from scratch in the fall of 1944 in an area southwest of Minden.[7] Replacements were funneled into the skeleton divisions with remarkable speed. Although still suffering serious shortages in equipment, Leibstandarte was reported to be at full strength in terms of personnel as early as mid-October 1944.[8] A minority (Kraemer later claimed 40 percent, which would seem too high) of replacements secured by Leibstandarte and Hitler Jugend divisions were veterans of the battles on the invasion front.[9] However, the ideal of Leibstandarte as an elite fighting order of German manhood was being eroded by manpower shortages as it was in the balance of the Waffen-SS, and Leibstandarte's admission standards were in sharp contrast to those of pre- and early-war years. Ethnic Germans from Rumania, Hungary, and Slovakia comprised a substantial percentage of total replacements, and some were in their forties and fifties. An admittedly extreme illustration of the nonelitist criteria now prevailing is offered in the person of Antonio B, an Italian citizen who was forty-eight years old at the time of his absorption into Leibstandarte's 2nd Panzer-Grenadier Regiment.[10]

The lack of inner cohesion within the frantically rebuilt Leibstandarte was regarded as a serious matter, and an effort was made to counteract it through indoctrination. Ideological instruction was still viewed as equal in importance to combat training, and both instruction and training were now pared to the bare essentials appropriate to the immediate problems with which Leibstandarte had to cope and the adversaries which it was likely to face. Simple appeals to the elitist ideals of the SS were combined with references to the heroic deeds of non-SS units which Leibstandarte, with its glorious combat tradition, must respect (and hopefully surpass). Thus, an article in a propaganda sheet distributed to Leibstandarte in November 1944 spoke at length and glowingly of the exploits of the 12th Volksgrenadier Division in combat with American troops around Aachen. The division had fought with great courage and tenacity in spite of being an improvised unit with no tradition, filled with overage personnel. But

> the Leibstandarte has, in over five years of war, pinned success upon success on its banners. And it has, along with these often decisive victories on all of the battlefields of Europe, brought the greatest sacrifices in blood and life, [and] always stands, by the will of the Führer, where things are going hardest. . . .
> . . . We want to be the best . . . , because one expects this performance from us and must expect it.[11]

It was not only by stressing the impressive combat record of Leibstandarte that fighting spirit was to be instilled in the hastily reconstructed division. The major adversary facing the Germans in the West, the American soldier, was both belittled and denigrated. Indoctrination material, while conceding that most American soldiers were racially similar to SS men, emphasized that they were not *political* soldiers like the Waffen-SS. Moreover, those materialistic "adventurers" engaged in acts of savagery against German civilians. At a farm near Trier, according to Leibstandarte's indoctrination sheet, American troops beat and raped the pregnant, thirty-two-year-old proprietress and beat her seven-year-old son as well when she attempted to prevent them from stealing cattle. In nearby Stolberg, the propaganda continued, black troops faced women and children to clear obstacles from streets while the town was still under artillery fire and compelled German women to polish their boots.[12]

Leibstandarte's new commander, SS-Standartenführer Wilhelm Mohnke,[13] encouraged frequent indoctrination sessions as the prerequisite for the production of "fanatical fighters" and probably as compensation for combat training which of necessity was hasty and incomplete. The stated goal in mid-October was to produce within four weeks a "useable" soldier able to fight within a reinforced battalion. During this brief period, infantrymen were to be instructed in attack and position warfare, reconnaissance and assault tactics, camouflage techniques, night and foul weather combat, the building of defensive positions and obstacles, and the use of the Panzerschreck and Panzerfaust short-range antitank weapons.[14] The problem of finding capable drivers for combat vehicles was particularly difficult and never really solved. During the battles on the invasion front, crews of disabled tanks had been pressed into service as infantrymen and in that capacity had suffered heavy casualties. Thorough training of replacements was virtually impossible in the fall of 1944 due to the general shortage of motor fuel, and many tank drivers were to enter combat in the Ardennes with but a few hours of driving experience behind them.[15] Training operations were suddenly interrupted when on November 9, 6th Panzer Army was ordered west of the Rhine to the Cologne-Bonn area for possible defensive operations in spite of the pleas of divisional commanders for another two to three weeks to pursue the rebuilding program. This movement was completed by November 20, however, and training resumed, continuing until early December.[16]

The battered German industrial complex, driven on by the

resourceful and energetic Albert Speer, was moderately successful in supplying Leibstandarte and the whole of Dietrich's panzer army with heavy equipment to replace that lost in the summer battles. As reconstruction had begun in mid-October, it had been intended that each of the SS armored divisions assigned to 6th Panzer Army (1st, 2nd, 9th, and 12th) would receive approximately 120 tanks.[17] This goal, however, was not achieved. By mid-December Leibstandarte, with the attached 501st SS Heavy Tank Battalion, disposed of a total of eighty-four tanks and twenty self-propelled assault guns, giving it a slight numerical superiority in tanks over its companion SS panzer divisions with the exception of 12th SS Panzer Division Hitler Jugend, which, although receiving more tanks and assault guns, had far fewer heavy Tigers.[18]

Hitler had never abandoned the intention to resume the offensive in the West, and this determination had been at the root of his decision to form 6th Panzer Army under Dietrich's command. On September 16, three days after the order to Dietrich had been issued, Hitler declared his determination to launch a major attack from the Ardennes with the port of Antwerp as the objective.[19] The operation was assigned the code name *Wacht am Rhein* (Watch on the Rhine) and was formalized by Hitler in a directive of November 10, 1944, which stated: "The goal of the operation is to effect a decisive change in the western campaign and thereby perhaps even in the entire war, through the annihilation of enemy forces north of a line Antwerp-Brussels-Luxembourg."[20] Under cover of bad weather (which was to determine X-Day), Army Group B (15th Army, 6th Panzer Army, 5th Panzer Army, and 7th Army) was to break through the front of 1st U.S. Army between Monschau and Wasserbillig (about sixty miles) and in a "bold and ruthless thrust" win the crossings over the Meuse between Lüttich (Liege) and Dinant. Then, through an advance to Antwerp and the west bank of the Scheldt mouth, the entire British expeditionary force and the northern wing of 1st U.S. Army were to be cut off and destroyed with the cooperation of Army Group H in the Netherlands.[21]

Dietrich's 6th Panzer Army was assigned the major role in the operation. With its mobile striking force of I SS Panzer Corps (1st SS Panzer Division Leibstandarte SS Adolf Hitler and 12th SS Panzer Division Hitler Jugend) and II SS Panzer

Corps (2nd SS Panzer Division Das Reich and 9th SS Panzer Division Hohenstaufen) supported by a number of Volksgrenadier and dismounted parachute divisions, Dietrich's army was to pierce the American front north of the Schnee-Eifel and, racing ahead without regard to its flanks, seize the Meuse crossings on both sides of Liege. The attached infantry divisions were then to establish a strong defensive front to the north and to fall under the command of 15th Army on Dietrich's right as the SS panzer divisions pressed on to Antwerp.[22]

On the left of 6th Panzer Army, General der Panzertruppen Hasso von Manteuffel's 5th Panzer Army was to thrust along the axis Bastogne-Namur and effect crossings of the Meuse north of Namur, to sweep on past Brussels, and then to swing up on Antwerp from the west and south. At the same time, Manteuffel's army was responsible for protecting 6th Panzer Army from possible threats to its rear from the southwest. Fifth Panzer Army's own left flank would be covered by the weak 7th Army. Preparation and assembly for the offensive was to be carried out with utmost secrecy under the cover designation ''defensive battle'' (Abwehrschlacht). All was to be in readiness by November 27.[23]

In spite of the secrecy which surrounded preparations for *Wacht am Rhein*, Mohnke and his staff had apparently long assumed that Leibstandarte would soon be involved in a major offensive. In October, map and sand-table exercises began to focus upon attacks through wooded terrain and the crossing of rivers under conditions similar to those which would be faced in renewed offensive operations. The enemy's advantages in equipment and air superiority would, hopefully, be partially nullified by movement in the hilly and wooded country assumed for the exercises and by the unfavorable flying weather of late autumn. Leibstandarte was described as being composed of recruits ''enthusiastic for battle'' (kampffreudig) although, in the main, inexperienced.[24]

After the war Dietrich stated to American interviewers that he had known nothing of the impending offensive until informed of it personally by Hitler on December 12.[25] This is a patent falsehood, growing most likely out of the effort of a man soon to be tried as a war criminal to appear as inconsequential as the credulity of his interlocutors would allow.

Lieutenant-General Gause, 6th Panzer Army's chief of staff prior to November 16, was sufficiently well informed of the plan to brief SS-Brigadeführer Fritz Kraemer, Dietrich's old chief of staff in I SS Panzer Corps, when the latter was appointed by Hitler to replace Gause, and it is difficult to believe that Dietrich was ignorant of impending events with which his two successive chiefs of staff were fully conversant![26] In fact, Dietrich was one of a group of high-ranking officers, including von Rundstedt, Model, and Manteuffel, who regarded *Wacht am Rhein* as beyond German capabilities and who attempted to persuade the Führer to undertake the much more limited objective of pinching off the Aachen salient.[27] Dietrich's minimal enthusiasm for the operation was again expressed to Hitler in the course of a conference at Bad Nauheim on the afternoon of December 12 attended by the Führer, Keitel, Jodl, von Rundstedt, Model, and the army and corps commanders involved in the forthcoming offensive. After hearing a classic Hitlerian monologue, each officer was permitted a few moments' conversation with the Führer. To Hitler's query. "Is your army ready?" Dietrich replied bluntly, "Not for an offensive," an assessment which was cavalierly pushed aside with "You are never satisfied."[28] Dietrich's pessimism was shared by the other commanders present but made no impression on Hitler. His only concession was to postpone the attack date, then fixed for December 15 (after several other postponements) to the morning of December 16, subject to further postponement only in the event of the much-dreaded good flying weather. During the few days separating the Bad Nauheim conference from X-Day, Dietrich sought an additional postponement to allow for more careful preparation but without result. He was later to condemn the Ardennes offensive as "the worst-prepared German offensive of this war."[29]

On the eve of the offensive, 6th Panzer Army's order of battle was composed of three corps of four SS panzer divisions, four Volksgrenadier divisions, one parachute division and supporting artillery and communications units. First SS Panzer Corps Leibstandarte, under the command of SS-Gruppenführer Hermann Priess, was the major striking force of Dietrich's army. Within this corps were reunited 1st SS Panzer Division Leibstandarte SS Adolf Hitler, under

Mohnke's leadership, and 12th SS Panzer Division Hitler Jugend, commanded by SS-Standartenführer Hugo Kraas. The two SS panzer divisions were supplemented by the 12th and 277th Volksgrenadier Divisions and the Luftwaffe's 3rd Fallschirmjäger Division. Second SS Panzer Corps was led by SS-Obergruppenführer Willi Bittrich and disposed of Bittrich's former command, 9th SS Panzer Division Hohenstaufen, now under SS-Oberführer Vestel Stadler, and 2nd SS Panzer Division Das Reich, commanded by SS-Brigadeführer Heinz Lammerding. The 246th and 326th Volksgrenadier Divisions made up LXVII Army corps under Major-General Otto Hitzfeld.[30]

Priess's I SS Panzer Corps Leibstandarte had the crucial task of reaching the Meuse and seizing crossings in the Liege-Huy sector. Although Dietrich had originally intended to use Leibstandarte to rip through the lightly held front of the U.S. V Corps covering the Losheim Gap, this decision had been overruled by Hitler five days before the opening of the offensive.[31] In order to preserve the armor of 6th Panzer Army for the long haul to the Meuse and Antwerp, the initial breach was to be made by infantry alone, armor to be employed only if the infantry became bogged down. Once an opening had been effected, a wedge of armor with Leibstandarte on the left and Hitler Jugend on the right was to push on to the Meuse and, if conditions permitted, to Antwerp. Second SS Panzer Corps was ordered to follow close on the heels of I SS Panzer Corps and either to drive with it to Antwerp or to proceed there alone while I SS Panzer Corps stood defensively on its right flank along the Albert Canal. The task of Hitzfeld's LXVII Corps was to clear the enemy from the Monschau area and to then turn north and west, establishing a front defending 6th Panzer Army's right flank along a line Simmerath-Eupen-Limburg-Liege, a line which would be extended further west by 12th Volksgrenadier and 3rd Fallschirmjäger Divisions after they had cleared the way for I SS Panzer Corps.[32]

The story of the Ardennes offensive has been told too well and too often to require detailed discussion here.[33] Neither Dietrich nor Manteuffel reached the Meuse, much less Antwerp, although the temporary confusion and panic produced by the offensive in the sector of 1st U.S. Army is beyond dispute. After the war Dietrich asserted that he had realized that the attack had failed by December 19 and attributed its failure to inadequate preparation, shortages of fuel and supplies, poor training, winter weather, and the ability of American forces to quickly regroup.[34]

In retrospect, Leibstandarte can be seen to have served as the weather vane reflecting the fortunes of 6th Panzer Army. That division made 6th Panzer Army's deepest penetration toward the Meuse, and its transfer to Manteuffel's 5th Panzer Army on December 26 marked the removal of the German *Schwerpunkt* from Dietrich's sector.[35] The battlefield conduct of Leibstandarte during the Ardennes offensive is also central to the much-discussed topic of Waffen-SS criminality.

Sixth Panzer Army's dash to the Meuse was to be led by an armored battlegroup, essentially Leibstandarte's 1st Panzer Regiment commanded by SS-Obersturmbannführer Joachim (Jochen) Peiper. Peiper, still a youthful twenty-nine-year-old, was a career SS officer, having spent the entirety of his adult life in the Schutzstaffel. He had graduated from the ten-month officer-training course at Junkerschule Braunschweig in 1935 and was posted to Leibstandarte the following year as an Untersturmführer (second lieutenant) in 11th Company, III Battalion. Peiper's association with the prewar Leibstandarte was brief, for the handsome and well-educated young Berliner was soon appointed to the staff of the Reichsführer-SS as adjutant but rejoined the unit upon the outbreak of war. In Russia Peiper earned a reputation as a cool and capable commander of armor and was awarded the Knight's Cross for energetic leadership during the critical days of February 1943.[36]

It is generally true in war that the line between energy and brutality is an indistinct one, and that distinction is further blurred and the inclination to give vent to bestial drives encouraged in situations where the identity of the "enemy" is imprecise or where he is defined as incarnate evil. Not only was the Leibstandarte frequently employed as a shock unit in combat roles, which demanded shooting first and asking questions later, but its members as SS men were subject to indoctrination of the most pernicious variety. Thus, the Russian was a subhuman subject of a "Jewish-led slave state" who at the same time was a masterful practitioner of guerrilla warfare. In the Soviet Union, therefore, the enemy was everywhere both in a military and ideological sense. Peiper has been implicated in two incidents which were duplicated innumerable times in the cataclysmic collision of two totalitarian powers which was the war on the eastern front. His battalion supposedly acquired the nickname "blowtorch battalion" for the burning of two Russian villages and the killing of all their inhabitants. He may have been involved in a similar massacre during Leibstandarte's Italian interlude in the summer and fall of 1943.[37]

Both the Russian and the Italian incidents associated with Peiper's name are vague and largely unsupported by documentation. Allegations of atrocious conduct on the part of Peiper's battlegroup in its drive toward the Meuse, however, rest on much firmer ground.

Peiper's task was to seize the Meuse crossings at Huy as quickly as possible, hopefully within the first twenty-four hours of the offensive. The first inkling of his assignment came to Peiper approximately five days before the attack began when Kraemer asked him how long it would take an armored regiment to travel forty-eight miles (the approximately distance from Leibstandarte's starting positions to Huy) and what he thought of the possibilities of offensive operations in the Eifel region. Peiper leaped into one of his own regiment's Panther tanks and made a practice run of the prescribed distance at night behind German lines. He was less than sanguine about the chances of duplicating this performance on the route to Huy assigned to his regiment, a poor quality track running north of the Ambleve River through Ligneuville, then south of the river to Stavelot where several routes were possible to lead the Kampfgruppe across the Salme at Trois Ponts. At the preattack conference on the morning of December 14, Peiper complained that the route assigned to him and the remainder of Leibstandarte which was to follow was "fit for bicycles," but his protest was parried with the observation that it had been chosen by Hitler himself and could not be changed. The only ray of light seemed to be the fact that west of Trois Ponts the terrain was more favorable for the rapid movement of armor through Werbemont, across the Ourthe and on to Huy.[38]

Instead of immediately beginning its thrust toward the

Meuse, Kampfgruppe Peiper spent most of December 16 milling about behind the front. Twelfth Volksgrenadier Division failed to dislodge the U.S. 99th Infantry Division from the Losheim sector into which Peiper's armor was to be inserted, while two blown bridges along Peiper's line of march promised further delay. During the evening of the sixteenth, the Kampfgruppe detoured westward to Lanzerath, hoping to find that 3rd Fallschirmjäger Division had opened a suitable gap, but encountered disappointment here too. In rage and desperation, Peiper "borrowed" a battalion of paratroopers, put two of his Panthers in the van, and with surprising ease penetrated three miles to Honsfeld.[39] Peiper asserts that he turned over to the paratroopers of 3rd Fallschirmjäger Division the responsibility for "mopping up" the town, and it may have been these men who were responsible for the deaths of nineteen American prisoners allegedly shot in Honsfeld that day.[40]

Peiper's orders now called for the taking of Schoppen, some five miles to the west. Finding the direct route virtually impassable due to mud, the Kampfgruppe detoured northward on the paved route to Büllingen, lured in part by reports that gasoline was to be found there. Easily overcoming the small American garrison in the town, the Kampfgruppe helped itself to 50,000 gallons of fuel, forcing fifty American prisoners to fill the tanks of its vehicles. Fifty prisoners were later reported to have been killed in Büllingen, perhaps the same men who replenished Peiper's fuel tanks.[41]

Peiper's Kampfgruppe swung southwest from Büllingen and resumed its westward march, passing through Moderscheid and Schoppen before noon. Sometime between noon and 1:00 P.M. near the Engelsdorf Road intersection several miles southeast of Malmedy, Battery B of the U.S. 285th Artillery Observation Battalion, on its way south to the Bastogne area in motor convoy, blundered into the point of Peiper's force. The SS troopers immediately opened fire while the Americans, who were without combat experience, scattered in wild confusion, some returning fire, others attempting to surrender, still others fleeing into the woods along the road.[42] Peiper, driving at the head of his column, raced on westward through the chaotic scene while the following armored detachment, later claimed to have been commanded by SS-

Sturmbannführer (Werner?) Poetschke who did not survive the war, was left to deal with the Americans.[43] It was only after the chaotic skirmish had persisted for ten to fifteen minutes that the officers in charge of the convoy attempted an organized surrender which, after some residual firing, was successful. The SS troopers attempted to induce the Americans to remove those vehicles of their convoy still capable of movement from the road but received no cooperation. The prisoners, variously estimated to number from eighty to two hundred (including, perhaps, prisoners which Kampfgruppe Peiper had taken elsewhere), were herded into an enclosed field along the road.[44]

That a mass killing of prisoners then took place is not a matter of dispute. At least eighty-six American prisoners were killed, most, apparently, by machine-gun fire, and for these killings seventy-four members of Leibstandarte, including Peiper, Dietrich, Priess, and Kraemer, were tried by an American military court at Dachau in 1946, and seventy-three were convicted.[45] On the basis of testimony taken from survivors, the prosecution maintained, in essence, that the massacre was the deliberate and cold-blooded killing of unresisting prisoners of war. SS-Rottenführer (corporal) Georg Fleps was asserted to have fired a pistol into the assembled mass of prisoners which seemed to serve as a signal for a general opening of fire.[46] Nor, according to the prosecution, were these killings simply the product of brutal initiative by a local commander but were encouraged and even required by orders issued by Hitler which Dietrich, Priess, and Kraemer willingly transmitted.[47]

In defense of the perpetrators of the Malmedy killings, it has been claimed that the shootings took place during an effort by the prisoners, or at least by a part of them, to escape from the roadside enclosure and that the incident, while regrettable, was an excusable tragedy of war. This, however, is in direct contradiction to the testimony of survivors who insist that no escape attempt was undertaken.[48] No copy of the supposed order to kill prisoners has been found, but Dietrich may justifiably be accused of ambiguity on this point. At a conference held on December 14 by Dietrich with his commanders (including Peiper), the question as to the disposition of prisoners was raised. "Prisoners?" Dietrich is reported to have replied, "You know what to do with them." At the Dachau trials, Dietrich asserted that he had simply meant that the provisions of the Hague Conventions relating to the treatment of prisoners were to be respected, although an army colonel who had been present at the conference later opined, "Addressed to the generals and senior officers of the Waffen-SS and in the atmosphere of the time, a phrase of this nature could mean only one thing: get rid of the prisoners."[49] This may be correct but is scarcely a conclusive piece of evidence. Further complicating the picture is the fact that in other instances Peiper's Kampfgruppe took and held prisoners of war and there is no evidence of deliberate killings of prisoners by other units engaged in the offensive.[50]

The seventy-three members of Leibstandarte were also accused and found guilty of murdering American prisoners and a large number of Belgian civilians at other points along Kampfgruppe Peiper's line of march. At Stavelot, the site of the worst of the alleged atrocities against civilians, ninety-three men, women, and children were killed by small-arms fire.[51]

None of the forty-three death sentences handed down at Dachau was carried out, in part as a result of irregularities in the investigative procedures prior to the trial. Certain of the allegations made against the defendants were challenged by seemingly reliable witnesses. It is possible that some of the "civilians" killed were actually guerrilla fighters. Nevertheless, it seems reasonable to conclude that Kampfgruppe Peiper operated during the Ardennes offensive with unusual ruthlessness.[52]

The Ardennes offensive was not the first instance giving rise to suspicions implicating Leibstandarte in questionable battlefield contact, as it was not the first for Peiper. When in October 1941 Leibstandarte captured the port city of Taganrog, it was discovered that six members of the division, captured earlier in the campaign, had been brutally murdered and mutilated in the local headquarters of the political police. In reprisal, Dietrich is supposed to have ordered that all Russian prisoners taken in the course of the next three days be shot, an order which allegedly resulted in the death of some 4000 men.[53]

The Dachau trials were not Sepp Dietrich's first experience

as a defendant in a war-crimes trial. Following the liberation of Kharkov in August 1943, the Soviet Union conducted the first war-crimes trial of the war. For the murder of 20,000 Soviet citizens in and around Kharkov following the reconquest of the city by Hausser's SS Panzer Corps in March 1943, Dietrich and five other individuals, including the commander of 3rd SS Panzer Division Totenkopf, SS-Gruppenführer Max Simon, were condemned to death *in absentia.*[54] Nothing is known in the West of the evidence which produced the convictions, but it is true that SS Panzer Corps utilized 25,000 Russians in forced labor for the construction of defensive positions in the city, and in these circumstances many may have died.[55]

Much of the evidence pointing to the criminality of Leibstandarte's conduct is of doubtful value, but the brutal and supralegal treatment of the enemy may be said to have been an element of the unit's tradition dating to the purge of June–July 1934. As an element of the Waffen-SS, its membership was steeped in the glorification of combat *à outrance* in the name of the Führer or simply in the name of primitive activism. This is of greater significance than Nazi racial ideology which, although much stressed during the prewar years, received less attention in combat Waffen-SS units during the war.[56] It is also of greater value in helping to explain why Leibstandarte members could murder Slavs and Americans, the latter their "racial equals," with an evenhanded facility.

White it is probably true that ideological preparation and a tradition of unquestioning service to a totalitarian leader must bear some responsibility for atrocious conduct in the field, these acts must also be considered within the context of a war whose overall conduct was a moral abomination and in which *raison de guerre* triumphed over all other considerations on both sides. And they must be viewed in the context of the role assigned to Leibstandarte as an elite assault unit to whom the attainment of the military objective ranked supreme.

By December 18 Peiper had lost the vital element of surprise, and on the following day further progress was blocked by serious fuel shortages and the presence of the U.S. 119th Infantry Division in the Stoumont-La Gleize area, still twenty miles in a direct line from the Meuse at Huy. Peiper's rate of advance had not been matched by the remainder of Leibstandarte, which was to follow close behind, or by 12th SS Panzer Division Hitler Jugend, whose assignment had been to follow a parallel route on Leibstandarte's right. In consequence, the U.S. 30th Infantry Division, sent dashing south from the Roer sector, had succeeded in seizing Stavelot on December 18 from a light holding-force which Peiper had left behind. The Kampfgruppe was now severed from its parent division. Efforts to supply it by air met with little success, and relief attacks by Leibstandarte failed to reestablish contact. On December 23 Peiper was ordered to attempt a breakout to the east and succeeded, though wounded, in leading 770 of his men (minus most heavy equipment) to safety Christmas morning behind Leibstandarte's line south of Stavelot.[57]

The withdrawal of Kampfgruppe Peiper marked the termination of 6th Panzer Army's preeminent role in the Ardennes offensive. To the south of Dietrich's sector, Manteuffel's 5th Panzer Army had made greater progress, elements of 2nd Panzer Division having driven within a few miles of the Meuse near Dinant on the twenty-fourth.[58] Hitler, with reluctance, transferred the *Schwerpunkt* of the offensive to Manteuffel's sector, forcing Dietrich to give up 12th SS Panzer Division Hitler Jugend and elements of 1st SS Panzer Division Leibstandarte SS Adolf Hitler to 5th Panzer Army on December 25 and 26 respectively. The survivors of Kampfgruppe Peiper, however, remained a component of 6th Panzer Army while an effort was made to reequip them as an armored reserve.[59]

Although Dietrich undertook local attacks with his remaining armored corps (II SS Panzer Corps), 6th Panzer Army was forced onto the defensive by December 28.[60] Hitler, however, had not abandoned hope of reaching the Meuse, but that responsibility was now to be borne by Manteuffel alone. The Führer insisted first, however, that Bastogne and its vital road hub, whose unbroken possession by the U.S. 101st Airborne Division had been a grave obstacle to the development of 5th Panzer Army's thrust, be taken. This was an objective now increased greatly in difficulty as the result of the success of Patton's U.S. 3rd Army in having driven a corridor through the German 7th Army to reach the beleaguered town on December 26.[61] Elements of Leibstandarte, primarily the 1st and

2nd Panzergrenadier Regiments, began to enter combat east of Bastogne on December 28. These units attempted to knife through the eastern flank of the Bastogne corridor but made little progress and suffered heavy losses at the hands of Patton's armor and the ubiquitous fighter-bombers. By January 5 the effort to take Bastogne had been abandoned, and 12th SS Panzer Division Hitler Jugend and the fragments of Leibstandarte given to Manteuffel were returned to Dietrich's command.[62] The abandonment of the Ardennes offensive was formalized on January 8 when Hitler ordered 6th Panzer Army withdrawn for use as an operational reserve in the event of a major Allied counterattack in the West.[63] In the course of the succeeding ten days, Dietrich's army fell back slowly and in good order toward the Belgian-German frontier; by January 18 the army headquarters was again established on German soil at Prüm.[64]

The operations of December 1944–January 1945 had been costly for 6th Panzer Army. Dietrich estimated that he had lost 37,000 men killed, wounded, and frost-bitten, and 350 to 400 tanks, although a considerably lower figure is given by his chief of staff, Fritz Kraemer. Leibstandarte, not surprisingly in view of the division's central role in the Ardennes offensive, suffered significantly heavier losses than the other three SS panzer divisions committed with 6th Panzer Army.[65]

Dietrich's reputation as a commander has not been enhanced by the unsuccessful Ardennes offensive. Historians of that undertaking tend to imply a causative link between the offensive's dismal failure and Dietrich's presumed lack of competence and experience at the army command level.[66] This line of analysis is doubtless encouraged by the resentment and scorn expressed by prominent members of the army's officer corps toward the plebeian and "uncouth" upstart who achieved fame and prominence as a military commander outside normal channels.[67] As Hitler's personal friend, Dietrich has also suffered from the inclination of apologists for the German army to place the blame for defeat on the supposed military idiocy of Hitler. Thus, a favorite of Hitler must, by definition, have been an incompetent (superficially tenable only if one conveniently ignores the likes of Rommel), particularly if a member of the Waffen-SS.

In fact, the nature of the offensive in 6th Panzer Army's

sector insured from the beginning that Dietrich's power to influence its outcome would be virtually nil. He had nothing to do with the formation of the operational plans (which he opposed), plans which assigned his army, much of which was deficient in training, to an area poorly provided with metaled roads and at a season quite unsuited to the massive deployment of armor. Nor could he produce nonexistent fuel for his armored assault groups or overcast weather to protect them from the consequences of Allied air supremacy. That 5th Panzer Army made significantly greater progress was more likely a product of better terrain than superior generalship on the part of Manteuffel, whose experience at the higher command echelons was no greater than Dietrich's.[68] The disappointing performance of 6th Panzer Army did not diminish Hitler's confidence in his friend and collaborator of over fifteen years. With a degree of charity seldom demonstrated to subordinates, the Führer seems to have been willing to attribute Dietrich's poor showing to exterior forces over which he had had no control.[69]

Neither Hitler nor Dietrich was granted the luxury of time to brood over their failure in the Ardennes. On January 12 as 6th Panzer Army was being extracted from the Bulge, the Russian winter offensive of 1945 set the eastern front in flames.[70]

12
The Last Act

At the beginning of January 1945, German faced Russian along a 750-mile front stretching south from the Bay of Courland on the Baltic to the eastern outskirts of Warsaw, then turning west to skirt the southern Slovakian frontier. Here, 160 German units of division or brigade size faced 414 Russian units of equivalent strength with more than that number in reserve. In terms of tanks, artillery, and aircraft Russian superiority was far greater.[1] On January 9 Colonel-General Heinz Guderian, then chief of the general staff, bluntly likened the eastern front in Hitler's presence to "a house of cards."[2] Guderian's evaluation proved catastrophically accurate, for within a few days after the opening of the Russian winter offensive, T-34 and Stalin tanks were racing toward the Oder.

It was, perhaps, inevitable that Dietrich's army (officially redesignated 6th SS Panzer Army) now being withdrawn into reserve, would be assigned to buttress the crumbling eastern defenses of the Reich. Hitler appears to have made this decision on January 16, although orders for the transfer of I SS Panzer Corps were not issued until the evening of January 20 and those for the remainder of the army two days later.[3] Much to Guderian's disappointment, the Führer declared his intention to commit Dietrich to southwestern Hungary for the defense of the last major sources of petroleum remaining to the German war machine southwest of Lake Balaton rather than to the support of the Oder line.[4]

Movement of the army from west to east was a painfully

slow operation under the conditions of January 1945. Due to heavy snows, fuel shortages, and Allied fighter-bombers, 6th SS Panzer Army did not complete its trek to the rail embarkation points at Wiesbaden, Coblenz, Cologne, and Bonn for almost two weeks. No time was granted for a refitting program worthy of the name, although Dietrich received some new vehicles and 22,000 replacements, far fewer than necessary to compensate for his losses in the Ardennes offensive.[5]

The route of Dietrich's Panzer Army to the Danubian plain passed through Berlin. Hitler and Dietrich saw and spoke to one another for the last time while the few surviving veterans of the prewar Leibstandarte had a fleeting opportunity to refresh old memories.[6] In the latter category was Leibstandarte's current commander, SS-Oberführer Wilhelm Mohnke, a member of Leibstandarte's officer corps since the summer of 1933. Mohnke remained in Berlin to play an important role in the cataclysmic defense of the capital and command of Leibstandarte passed to the division's fourth and last commander, SS-Brigadeführer Otto Kumm. A charter member of the officer corps of the prewar SS-Standarte Der Führer, Kumm came to Leibstandarte from the command of 7th SS Volunteer Mountain Division Prinz Eugen.[7]

Priess's I SS Panzer Corps, with Leibstandarte and Hitler Jugend, was the first component of 6th SS Panzer Army to reenter combat in the East. General der Infanterie Otto Woehler, to whose Army Group South 6th SS Panzer Army was assigned, secured permission from Hitler to use the two SS panzer divisions to eliminate the Russian bridgeheads across the Hron (Gran) River west of Esztergom.[8] The attack was begun on February 17 by the 44th, 46th, and 211th Infantry Divisions and joined by I SS Panzer Corps on the following day.[9] This operation may be justly regarded as the last victory in which Leibstandarte participated. By February 25 the bridgehead had been eliminated although this had been made possible, in part, by the fact that most Russian armor in that sector had been taken out of the line for refitting. The operation cost I SS Panzer Corps almost 3000 officers and men killed, wounded, and missing.[10]

Woehler's sharp but limited stroke against the Hron bridgeheads was but the prelude to the major offensive in

Hungary for which Hitler had envisioned 6th SS Panzer Army as the core. Code-named *Frühlingserwachen* (awakening of spring), the operation was aimed at destroying the Third Ukrainian Front of Russian Marshal Polkovnik Tolbukhin west of the Danube and establishing a strong barrier east of the Nagykanisza oil fields.[11]

Sixth SS Panzer Army, which had been assembling in the neck of land separating Lakes Balaton and Velencze camouflaged as an engineer army (Dietrich's cover designation was "Higher Engineer Leader, Army Group South"), constituted the largest force, in terms of subordinated divisions if not actual strength, yet commanded by Sepp Dietrich. In addition to 1st SS Panzer Division Leibstandarte SS Adolf Hitler, 12th SS Panzer Division Hitler Jugend, 2nd SS Panzer Division Das Reich, and 9th SS Panzer Division Hohenstaufen, the army included 1st, 3rd, 6th, and 23rd Panzer Divisions as well as three infantry and two cavalry divisions.[12] All of these divisions, however, were much below established strength.

The attack began on the morning of March 6 in less than satisfactory weather for armored operations. First and Second SS Panzer Corps deployed in heavy wet snow on both sides of the Sarviz Canal, some twenty to thirty miles west of the Danube and parallel to it, preparatory to driving south into the flank and rear of Tolbukhin's front. The roads over which the attack was carried were in deplorable condition, and supplies could only be brought forward in meager quantities by armored car and half-track.[13] Yet, Leibstandarte still displayed some of its old dash and energy after over five years of a war which was now clearly lost. While II SS Panzer Corps quickly bogged down east of the canal, Leibstandarte, setting the pace for I SS Panzer Corps, made fair progress along its western bank, thrusting almost twenty miles to Simontornya by March 12. By then, however, Tolbukhin had recovered his balance and on March 13 launched a sustained counterattack which brought I SS Panzer Corps to a halt.[14]

At the same time, Tolbukhin and his neighbor to the north, Marshal Rodion Malinovskiy, commander of Second Ukrainian Front, were preparing to harshly interrupt whatever momentary sense of euphoria 6th SS Panzer Army's advance had produced. Attacking west on March 10 from the right angle described by the Danube north of Budapest, the Russians cut across the rear of 6th SS Panzer Army and threatened to trap it east of Lake Balaton. Woehler's initial impulse was to turn Dietrich's army 180 degrees to strike into the southern flank of the Russian spearhead, but Hitler's permission for the maneuver came too late for it to be practically undertaken.[15] Sixth SS Panzer Army escaped in considerable disorder from the developing pocket via its attack route between Lakes Balaton and Velencze and was then swung northward by Woehler in an effort to reestablish a coherent front in company with Balck's 6th Army south of the Danube. By March 25 6th SS Panzer Army was holding a tenuous front from Papa north to the Danube at Komarno with, however, a gap of some ten miles separating its right flank from the left of 6th Army south of Papa. Through this yawning orifice, the Russian Sixth Guards Tank Army struck toward the Austrian frontier while both German armies fell back in the same direction.[16]

Hitler's disappointment over the failure of *Frühlingser-wachen* and the precipitate retreat to the Austrian frontier was profound. He had expected great things of Dietrich and had followed the performance of Leibstandarte with paternal concern as of old. During a situation conference on the evening of March 23, Hitler had declared: "I now demand one thing: that Leibstandarte, moreover the entire 6th Panzer Army be sent the last man available anywhere. I mean immediately! Sepp Dietrich must be informed instantly. Immediately!"[17]

The miracle demanded by Hitler had not come to pass. The demoralization and sense of hopelessness reported by Woehler to have become rife among the men of Army Group South had infected Dietrich's SS troopers as well, and 6th SS Panzer Army had fallen back contrary to Hitler's orders that the offensive be continued. According to an eyewitness, Hitler flew into a fury of rage and disappointment when apprised of this "treachery." The Führer ordered Guderian to descend upon 6th SS Panzer Army headquarters with an order that members of Dietrich's four SS divisions, including Leibstandarte, surrender both the Nazi eagle worn by each Waffen-SS man on the upper sleeve of his field tunic and the prized stripe *(Ärmelstreifel)* bearing the unit name worn on the lower left sleeve. Guderian demurred, suggesting that the mission was more appropriate for Himmler. Ultimately, a radio message was sent to Dietrich's headquarters on March 27 which, in addition to the required mutilations of the SS uniforms, notified the SS divisions that all promotions scheduled to be announced on Hitler's birthday were cancelled.[18]

Hitler's order was, of course, without practical significance. According to one colorful account, Dietrich on receipt of the order drank himself into a stupor (the bottle had never been a stranger to the lusty Bavarian), slept for three hours, then assembled the commanders of his SS divisions. Displaying the order, he snarled contemptuously, "There's your reward for all you've done these past five years."[19] Dietrich refused to transmit the order to his troops, although its contents seem to have become generally known to the lower ranks. A former Waffen-SS officer has provided the following fictionalized account of the atmosphere of despair into which the insulting command fell:

"Hungary! Hungary!" parried the Sturmbannführer nervously. "Now it's a matter of a lot more than that. There is no doubt that Tolbukhin and Malinovskiy are heading for Vienna. Beyond that," the Sturmbannführer looked uncertainly at the little knot of officers which had assembled, "if we fall back further, we're finished with Adolf."

No one answered him.

"We are, of course," declared the Sturmbannführer, "utterly despised in the Führer's headquarters. The army received the order that all SS divisions are to remove their sleeve stripes because of their failure."

"What was that?" asked the Oberjunker [senior officer cadet] sharply.

"It's just as I've said," affirmed the Sturmbannführer irritably. "Only," he smiled, "our Obersepp has not passed on the order."

"Isn't there anyone," asked Holmes desperately, "who can report the actual situation to those people up there?"

The Sturmbannführer shrugged his shoulders. He departed quickly and drove the motorcycle, by which he had come, to the rear.[20]

Hitler chose not to pursue the matter, and the fact that no effort was made to relieve Dietrich of his command (as Woehler was relieved on April 3 after having balked at Hitler's demand for a counterattack) suggests that the order was nothing more than the product of pique on the part of an increasingly desperate and irrational man.

On March 31, Russian forces crossed the Hungarian frontier into Austria west of Ödenburg.[21] Tolbukhin and Malinovskiy prepared to move on Vienna, a thrust which the badly fragmented front of Army Group South would find impossible to contain. Hitler demanded that Vienna be held and on April 4 ordered Dietrich to attack toward Ödenburg in order to close the gap in Army Group South's front which stood open west of that point.[22] This attack was not carried out; and although the gap between 6th Army and 6th SS Panzer Army was narrowed and finally closed on April 8, the Russians entered Vienna on the following day; after heavy street fighting, the city fell on April 13.[23]

All hope of serious long-term resistance on the part of 6th SS Panzer Army now seemed illusory, for the total strength of the army was far below that of a single armored division. First SS Panzer Division Leibstandarte SS Adolf Hitler, the most powerful "division" in Dietrich's army, had been reduced by April 7 to fewer than 1600 officers and men and 16 tanks.[24]

By the middle of April, pressure along most of the front of Army Group South eased, as the major weight of the Russian offensive moved north of the Danube. The army group was able to reestablish a coherent front south of the Danube along a line running west of St. Pölten to the Drava east of Varadin. This line was successfully held until near the end of April when, with the seizure of Passau by the U.S. 3rd Army, the danger of a thrust into its rear materialized.[25] Second SS Panzer Division Das Reich was swung around and directed toward Passau to intercept the American threat but was diverted north by Hitler to the crumbling front of Army Group Center in Czechoslovakia. Elements of the division, however, did go into action against 3rd U.S. Army near Passau.[26]

While Leibstandarte was sharing the death agonies of Army Group South in Austria, other SS men who bore the simple "Adolf Hitler" on their sleeves were discharging one of the functions for which Leiberstandarte had been originally organized in March 1933—the defense of the Führer's person. During the prewar period, responsibility for the immediate physical protection of Hitler had been progressively assumed by a "Reich Security Service" under the command of SS-Brigadeführer (by 1944) Hans Rattenhuber while Leibstandarte had evolved into a field unit for counterrevolutionary and orthodox military purposes, although Leibstandarte personnel were always present at the Chancellery and Führerhauptquartier.[27] In the suicidal resistance of Wilhelm Mohnke and his subordinates in Berlin, part of Leibstandarte would experience a reversion to first principles.

Large numbers of Waffen-SS men participated in the savage combat within the German capital which began on April 23.[28] Most of these, including the remnants of 11th SS Freiwilligen-Panzergrenadier-Division Nordland and 23rd SS Freiwilligen-Panzergrenadier-Division Nederland, were subordinate to General der Artillerie Helmuth Weidling's LVI Panzer Corps.[29] Several thousand SS men, including Leibstandarte's SS Wach-Bataillon 1, were organized as a battlegroup under Mohnke's command for the defense of the governmental quarter of the city, with headquarters in the bunker beneath the new Reich Chancellery. General Vasili Chuikov, commander of the Russian Eighth Guards Army, has recalled the tenacity with which Mohnke's battlegroup defended the approaches to the Chancellery.[30] Few of these SS men survived the fall of Berlin, although Mohnke himself successfully escaped from the city on the evening of May 1 after having set fire to the now-deserted Führerbunker.[31] By that time, Leibstandarte had lost its *raison d'être*, for Hitler had committed suicide on the previous day.

In contrast, the war terminated for the bulk of Leibstandarte in an anticlimactic fashion. Clamped between the U.S. 3rd and 7th Armies to the West and the Russian Second and Third Ukrainian Fronts to the East and with no hope of extrication, Army Group South ceased hostilities early on May 7. During the night of May 6–7, the army group successfully disengaged its eastern front and marched westward toward the American lines and into captivity near Steyr.[32]

13
Toward a Historical Perspective

It has become a commonplace that World War I introduced to the twentieth century the concept of war as a struggle of moral absolutes. The enormous casualties on the fighting front and the misery and suffering imposed on civilian populations required transcendental justification. The "enemy" became the faceless, dehumanized embodiment of evil with whom no compromise was possible; evil had to be annihilated so that good might triumph. This definition of war as a struggle between moral absolutes found greater acceptance among civilians, to whom the enemy was necessarily distant and abstract, than among soldiers on the fighting front, in whose eyes the enemy might be misguided but, nevertheless, a tangible human being suffering with them the discomforts and dangers of the trenches. Yet, its contribution to the barbarization of armed conflict is undeniable.

The sanguinary stalemate on the western front also gave birth to new weapons and tactics. Most important of these was the tank, a mobile fortress able to face with impunity the rifle and machine gun which had largely produced the hecatombs of the 1914–1918 war and, thus, restore mobility to the fighting front. While the western Allies were in the forefront of tank development in World War I, Germany, too, in a less dramatic fashion made an important contribution toward restoring the primacy of the offensive to the battlefield. This was the "storm" or "shock" troop, relatively small units of picked and battle-hardened soldiers armed with carbines, pistols, and hand grenades, pampered behind the lines but trained to lead in the assault by infiltrating the enemy's front lines and identifying weak spots for the following masses of infantry while spreading fear and confusion in the adversary's ranks. Youthful, self-confident, glorying in battle, and utterly ruthless, the storm troops were commanded by officers whose leadership was based less on formal authority than on personal example and charismatic attraction.[1]

In spite of some brilliant tactical successes by the German storm troops, most notably in the spring offensives of 1918, Germany went down to defeat at the hands of the Allies, in part because of the latter's employment of masses of tanks. Germany's near-victory and the final victory of the Allies had been partly achieved by the employment of two categories of elites, one psychological and one mechanical, which would find union a quarter century later in the armored divisions of the Waffen-SS.

As a veteran of the 2nd and 5th Bavarian Storm Battalions and the Thirteenth Bavarian Tank Formation, Sepp Dietrich was a product of both of these battlefield innovations. But the impact of World War I far transcended the sphere of military tactics and technology. Everywhere, the war produced a sizeable number of young men estranged from civilian society and unwilling or psychologically unable to reintegrate themselves into it. For much of the German ''front generation'' the war with its opportunities for the release of primitive passions and its stimulation of the fierce comradeship of the battlefield had been an intensely satisfying spiritual experience against the background of a prewar society which, to many, had seemed superficial, materialistic, atomized, or boring. This was a phenomenon which was understandably most pronounced among the veterans of the elite storm troops who had known combat in its purest and most concentrated form. They had become addicted to a potent drug for which there seemed to be no substitute in the fragmented society of postwar Weimar Germany, much of which seemed to repudiate the military glories which had given the lives of the front veterans a profound significance.

Ernst Juenger, the erstwhile commander of an assault unit, emerged in the postwar years as the most articulate spokesman of the storm-troop mentality. In a series of books and essays whose titles alone are highly revealing (among them, *In the Storm of Steel, Fire and Blood, Combat as Inner Experience*) battle is portrayed as "a magic delight. It is a 'magnificent show of destruction' and a splendid miracle: a transformation of the bourgeois into the adventurer. It is the birth hour of a new 'type'—the 'warrior,' who overcomes the meaninglessness of yesterday by a rediscovery of cosmic values. . . ."[2] Thus was formalized a concept of military elitism essentially divorced from either political or ideological loyalties, existing only for itself and devoid of inherent moral restraints.

Many Germans who had internalized the spirit of combat for combat's sake, and not all of them were war veterans, found their way into the Free Corps, volunteer units called into being by the Weimar Republic as a defense against radical Socialist and Communist revolution and for the protection of Germany's threatened eastern frontier. The Free Corps responded to the challenge with notable savagery, less, however, as the result of political commitment than from the primitive joy of conflict and destruction. Loathing for the Republic itself, undeniably present within the Free Corps and manifested in their participation in right-wing efforts to overthrow it, is best understood as blind rage against a political system striving to establish order and stability, the antithesis of the chaotic violence at the center of the Free Corps mentality.

It was only with great difficulty that the Republic succeeded in dissolving the Free Corps as it sought to place internal and external defense on a more stable foundation. Yet, the Free Corps movement, as a state of mind, was not dissolved. The intellectually purest exponents of the chaotic warrior spirit, such as Juenger and Ernst von Salomon, remained aloof from political attachments. But for others the glorification of struggle for its own sake found expression in subordination to aggressive and dynamic political movements, less, again, from a sense of political conviction than from a desire for community, leadership, and naked power. That the Nazi party became the primary beneficiary of this phenomenon is hardly surprising. Hitler himself was a former front-line soldier who viewed human existence—indeed, the whole of nature—as ceaseless struggle, who rejected the conventions of bourgeois morality, and who proclaimed his mission to free the German community from the malevolent forces of communism and Jewry, in effect the injection of the wartime collision of moral absolutes into domestic politics. Large numbers of former Free Corpsmen plus the down-and-out who internalized the freebooter spirit for want of an existential alternative swelled the ranks of the major party paramilitary organization, the SA (significantly, an abbreviation for *Sturm Abteilungen* or "assault detachments").

The SA, true to its ancestry, never developed a clearcut ideology and saw itself, to a considerable degree, detached from the purely political work of the party. Thus, an SA pronouncement of 1926 declared:

> The SA man is the sacred freedom fighter. The Party comrade is the instructor and skilled agitator. Political propaganda seeks to enlighten the adversary, to dispute with him, to understand his viewpoint, to go into his ideas, up to a certain point to agree with him—but when the SA appear on the scene, this stops. They are out for all or nothing. They know only the motto, "Strike dead! You or me!"[3]

The chaotic, combative spirit of the front fighter was of great value to the Nazi movement during its struggle for recognition and political supremacy. It was used to intimidate political adversaries and lent to Hitler's party an image of youthful dynamism and vigor which was in sharp contrast to the stodgy bourgeois political parties. But, by its very nature, it was difficult to control and became a political liability following Hitler's appointment as German chancellor in January 1933. Hitler still needed an instrument of terror, but one that could be controlled as a precision tool with the least possible disruption of those elements of German society which were to be preserved. Such an instrument already existed, in theory, in the SS, formed in 1925 as a small party security force and, since January 1929, enormously expanded by its fourth and last commander, Heinrich Himmler, a weak and dependent personality utterly devoted to Adolf Hitler. In seeking to define the role of the SS within the Nazi movement, Himmler seized hold of the deep-rooted imagery of military elitism: "The SA is the rank and file, the SS is the guard. There has always been a guard, with the Persians, the Greeks, Caesar, Napoleon, Frederick the Great, right up until the World War, and the guard of the New Germany will be the SS."[4]

Himmler's brief historical excursion may have suggested the joy of combat, but it also implied discipline, selection, and obedience to authority. Yet, the developmental thrust of the SS carried it far beyond the narrow image suggested by Heinrich Himmler. By January 1933 it numbered in excess of fifty thousand men, and its ranks were to be swelled by waves of opportunists who sought membership as an avenue to enhanced social and economic status. Although the loyalty of the SS to Hitler was never in serious doubt, its initial definition as a compact and select defensive and executive instrument at the disposal of the Führer was being undermined for, in addition to expansion in terms of sheer numbers, it was developing a vast bureaucratic infrastructure and functional elements with inner dynamics of their own.

Hitler's order to Sepp Dietrich of March 17, 1933, which resulted in the creation of the Leibstandarte SS Adolf Hitler, was motivated by a desire to reestablish an elite instrument of force immediately responsive to his will, comparable in some respects to the domestic functions discharged by the elite guards regiments of the monarchs of old. But the totalitarian dictatorships of the twentieth century were not recreations of preparliamentary monarchical systems. The object of service was not the dynastic ruler and the territorial interests of his house but, at least in theory, an all-embracing ideological framework (extremely vague in the case of Nazism and Italian fascism) embodied in and fully understood only by the dictator who, in the fullness of his understanding of the laws governing human existence, was essentially infallible and could not permit his infallibility to be challenged by dissident elements.

Yet even a revolutionary movement cannot construct a new world out of whole cloth. To some degree, if only during a transitional period, it must make use of preexisting institutions and their personnel to perform those functions which are necessary to any society. At the same time it can be of value for a totalitarian dictatorship to link itself to national tradition, a matter of particular importance to the Nazis who had based much of their popular appeal on intentionally evoked associations with the much-lamented pre-1918 German past.

The evolution of Leibstandarte reflected both the needs of the developing totalitarian dictatorship and the limitations imposed upon it by its milieu. On one level the formation of Leibstandarte in March 1933 represented an effort to harness the chaotic spirit of the World War I front fighter, embodied in Sepp Dietrich, the storm troop and Free Corps veteran, by linking it in bonds of personal loyalty to Adolf Hitler and at the same time to present it to the German people in a form easily understood and acceptable in traditional terms. Hence, the distinctive dress uniforms, impeccable drill, incessant parading, and concerts of military music which constituted such a large component of the Leibstandarte's public image in the prewar years. In practice, this association with centuries-old military pageantry constituted a useful bridge over the chasm separating Prussian monarchical tradition and Nazi totalitarianism, for while many Germans might experience uneasiness at rumors of supralegal SS activities—arrests in the middle of the night and inhuman treatment of prisoners in concentration camps—they could alternatively be reassured by the sight of other SS men marching along the Charlottenburger Chaussee to the tune of "Fridericus Rex" as snappily as the kaiser's Alexander Regiment had done.

The camouflage was partially lifted at the end of June 1934 when the Leibstandarte along with other SS men liquidated much of the upper leadership of the SA and thus destroyed, for all practical purposes, an organization in which the spirit of primitive activism had been most imperfectly tamed and which, therefore, had become an acute embarrassment to Hitler, no longer the rabble-rousing politician seeking power in the streets but the chancellor of the German Reich. The Leibstandarte's role in the Blood Purge represented the chaotic combat spirit deflected toward counterrevolution and stabilization.

The importance of the freebooter spirit can be overemphasized. In the early period of Leibstandarte's history, the brutal adventurer personality was dominant, as is evidenced by numerous affrays between Leibstandarte members and the police, army, civilians, and even members of other SS units. With the formalization of Leibstandarte within the SS-Verfügungstruppe as an internal security force and its quasi incorporation within the German defense system, it sought out and attracted types more amenable to discipline, particularly young men fresh from the Hitler Youth who relished the opportunity to fulfill their military obligations in the elite guards regiment of the "New Germany." By 1936 the products of the SS-Junkerschulen were flowing into the junior levels of its officer corps. While some of these men were fanatical Nazis, many were simply military careerists, and all had served at least one year in the ranks and had been selected for officer training on the basis of criteria established by Paul Hausser, the former general staff officer and a disciplinarian of the old school. During World War II, and particularly by 1943, Leibstandarte was receiving replacements who were not significantly different from those received by normal German line divisions. Yet, the influence of the freebooter spirit remained strong, primarily because of the charismatic, swashbuckling leadership offered by Sepp Dietrich and other remnants of the earliest stratum of membership such as Kurt Meyer, Fritz Witt, and Wilhelm Mohnke, which was present until the end of the war either within the division Leibstandarte or the I SS Panzer Corps Leibstandarte.

Another attitudinal influence played upon Leibstandarte: Himmler's aim of rendering not only Leibstandarte but the whole of the SS a body of ideologically committed crusaders against the worldwide "Jewish-Communist conspiracy." As an effort to generate enthusiasm for racial pseudoscience, neopaganism, and perverted history, it was a failure and was largely abandoned in 1938, although it undoubtedly served to stereotype and thus dehumanize the potential enemy. As politics had become war in the totalitarian state, so war was to become Armageddon. The SS Education Office by the beginning of World War II, however, had recognized the greater pragmatic value of reinforcing the spirit of combat *à outrance*. Thus, an article in an *SS-Leitheft* of 1943, entitled

"Artist and Soldier," declared that the experiences of the soldier and artist at the most intense moment of combat and in the moment of creative insight are essentially identical. In words strongly reminiscent of the aesthetes of violence produced by World War I, the article continued,

> It is as though a husk, in which one was enclosed, was suddenly burst asunder. One leaps out and feels like a god or a child. There is no more hesitation or reflection, no doubts or looking back. One moves free and true and knows everything that has to be known in that instant.[5]

This, albeit in excessively rarefied terms, approximates the ideology which permeated Leibstandarte and the whole of the Waffen-SS much more closely than the rural-racial twaddle of Himmler and Darré.

Leibstandarte earned for itself a well-deserved reputation as a body of dedicated and ruthless fighters during World War II. That reputation was built on the Aa Canal, in the Klidi Pass, at Kharkov, at Korsun-Cherkassy, in Normandy, in the Ardennes, and on the Hungarian plain. It was built, too, on heaps of the brutally slaughtered enemy in the Ukraine (in the month of February 1943, for example, Leibstandarte reported killing six hundred Russians while taking *five* prisoners) and at Malmedy. Leibstandarte was not a unit of "soldiers like any others," but neither was it an order of fanatical Nazi warriors which sought to annihilate its enemies as a quasi-sacramental act. Rather, it can be best conceptualized as an elite military until which, infused with the freebooter spirit which recognized no moral limitations, acted as an immediate executor of the Führer's will, a will that demanded extremes both of self-sacrifice and of ferocity. That was the essence of its elitism. But it was an elitism which could exercise only a secondary impact on a war in which the mass—of men, aircraft, artillery, armor—was the decisive factor.

In 1946 Sepp Dietrich was tried and sentenced to life imprisonment (reduced to twenty-five years in 1951) for his responsibility in the Malmedy killings. Released on parole in 1955, he was tried in 1956–57 by the Munich Landgericht and sentenced to eighteen months' confinement for his part in the Purge of June–July 1934. Dietrich thus suffered the consequences of his role as organizer and commander of the armed force whose fundamental purpose was to unhesitatingly strike down those within and beyond the frontiers of Germany defined as enemies by the totalitarian dictator. Revered by the well-organized Waffen-SS veterans association (HIAG), he died, somewhat incongruously, of a heart attack in 1966 at the age of seventy-four.

NOTES

References to U.S. National Archives Microfilm Publications are cited by microcopy number/roll number/frame number. Complete titles are given in the bibliography and are arranged by microcopy number. References to the Berlin Document Center, Dietrich File, are cited as BDC/frame number. References to the U.S. National Archives Foreign Military Studies Collection are cited as NAMS, followed by the manuscript number. Complete titles are given in the bibliography and are arranged by manuscript number.

PREFACE

1. Fritz Nova, "The National Socialist Fuehrerprinzip and Its Background in German Thought" (Ph.D. diss., University of Pennsylvania, 1943), p. 4, cited in Robert Koehl, "Feudal Aspects of National Socialism." *The American Political Science Review* 54(1960),925n15.

2. See Koehl, "Feudal Aspects," passim. Cf. Edward N. Peterson, *The Limits of Hitler's Power* (Princeton: Princeton University Press, 1969), passim. On Hitler's work habits, see Walter C. Langer, *The Mind of Adolf Hitler: The Secret Wartime Report* (New York: Basic Books, 1972), pp. 70 ff.

1 "YOUR HONOR IS LOYALTY"

1. Heinz Höhne, *Der Orden unter dem Totenkopf*, p. 27.

2. On the origins of the SS, see Hans Buchheim, "Die SS in der Verfassung des Dritten Reiches," *Vierteljahrshefte für Zeitgeschichte* 3 (April 1955), 128–29.

3. Höhne, *Der Orden*, p. 51.

4. George Stein, *The Waffen SS*, p. xxvi.

5. Hans Buchheim, "Die SS—das Herrschaftsinstrument," in *Anatomie des SS Staates*, ed. Buchheim, et al., 1: 32–33.

6. Ibid.

7. See, for example, "Der Reichsführer-SS, Rasse und Siedlungsamt, an die Herren Mitarbeiter," 12 Scheiding [September], 1933, U.S. National Archives Microfilm Publication, "Miscellaneous SS Records," T-354/366/4070792.

8. Dietrich's adjutant to adjutant, Chief of the SS-Hauptamt, September 19, 1935, T-354/201/3861842.

9. "Ansprache des Reichsführers SS aus Anlass der Übergabe der Führerstandarte an die Leibstandarte Adolf Hitler," September 7, 1940, U.S. National Archives Microfilm Publication, "Records of the Reich Leader of the SS and Chief of the German Police," T-175/90/2612647–51.

10. *Das Archiv* (July 1934), p. 487; *Der Freiwillige* 12 (May/June 1966), 3.

11. Baldur von Schirach, *Die Pioniere des Dritten Reiches* (Essen: Zentralstelle für der deutschen Freiheitskampf, n.d.), pp. 33–34.

12. "Lebenslauf des SS–Oberst-Gruppenführers und Panzer–Generalobersten der Waffen–SS Sepp Dietrich," BDC/12. Details given here on Dietrich's early military career disagree in minor respects with the sources cited above.

13. "Dienstlaufbahn," BDC/9.

14. See *Verhandlungen des Reichstags, V. Wahlperiode (stenographische Bericht)*, Berlin, *Bände* 444–47, passim.

156. BDC/1.

16. For a hostile view of Dietrich during this period, see Kurt Lüdecke, *I Knew Hitler* (London: Jarrolds, 1938), pp. 523, 529, 632.

17. K. G. Klietmann, *Die Waffen-SS, eine Dokumentation*, p. 51.

18. Stein, *Waffen-SS*, p. 5; T-354/199/3859164, 3859439.

19. Hans Buchheim, "SA-Hilfspolizei, SA-Feldpolizei und Feldjägerkorps und die beamtenrechtliche Stellung ihrer Angehörigen," *Gutachten des Instituts für Zeitgeschichte* (Munich: Institut für Zeitgeschichte, 1958), pp. 335–38.

20. On Lichterfelde, see unpublished manuscript of a newspaper article on Leibstandarte in T-354/210/3874673.

21. Goering memorandum (received by Wecke), April [date unclear] 1933, T-354/199/3859784.

22. Ibid.

23. T-354/195/3854104; 209/3873150; 225/3893744; Klietmann, *Die Waffen-SS*, p. 54.

24. T-354/199/3859338, 3859421, 3859870; 225/3893165–66, 3893203, 3893218, 3893754.

25. T-354/196/3854976; 225/3893730–31, 3893744.

26. Heinrich Bennecke, *Die Reichswehr und der Röhm Putsch* (Munich/Vienna: Günter Olzog Verlag, 1964), pp. 26–27.

27. Robert J. O'Neill, *The German Army and the Nazi Party, 1933–1939*, p. 34.

28. Adolf Hitler Standarte to 28th SS-Standarte, September 28, 1933, T-354/199/3859405.

29. See 14th Company, 9th Infantry Regiment to Adolf Hitler Standarte, September 25, 1933, T-354/196/3854979.

30. See reference to the "mangelhafte Ausbildung" at Jüterbog in T-354/225/3893168.

31. Memorandum of Chief of Staff (Police) von Oven of August 17, 1933, T-354/199/3859848.

32. Later, the Politische Bereitschaften, too, would be so financed. See Klietmann, *Die Waffen-SS*, pp. 53–54.

33. Dietrich to NSDAP Verbindungsstab, October 12, 1933, T-354/194/3853318.

34. "Die Adolf Hitler Standarte, führer, SS-Sonderkommando . . ." in a routine document dated September 27, 1933, T-354/199/3859381.

35. "Ein Tag in der Reichskanzlei," *Illustrierter Beobachter* 8 (February 18, 1933); "Der Führer an der Arbeit," *Illustrierter Beobachter*, Sondernummer, 1. Auflage; Ernst Hanfstaengl, *Hitler—The Missing Years* (London: Eyre & Spottiswoode, 1957), pp. 211, 218, 220, 243.

36. Ortsgruppe Wünsdorf to Sonderkommando Zossen, June 12, 1933, T-354/225/3893728; Dietrich to NSDAP Verbindungsstab, October 12, 1933, T-354/194/3853318.

37. Heinrich Himmler, "Die Aufgaben der SS," *F.M. Zeitschrift, Monatsschrift der Reichführung-SS für Fördernde Mitglieder* 4 (April 1, 1934), p. 1, T-354/211/3875796.

38. Dietrich to RFSS-Verwaltungsamt, Nov. 4, 1933, T-354/195/3854670.

39. "SS-Befehl Nr. 10," November 24, 1933, p. 14, U.S. National Archives Microfilm Publication, "Non-Biographic

Material Filmed at the Berlin Document Center by the University of Nebraska,'' T-611/3/Folder 429.

40. Dietrich to RFSS, January 9, 1934, T-354/195/3854660.

41. Leibstandarte Adolf Hilter to RFSS, March 6, 1934, T-354/195/3854619. See also T-354/194/3852165.

42. Former membership in right-wing veterans' associations and Free Corps was not uncommon. See, for example, T-354/225/3893622, 3893625.

43. The height requirement was later reduced to 1.78 meters, although this was still much in excess of Dietrich's officially claimed 1.70 meter physique. See BDC/1.

44. SD dossier, T-175/245/2735956–62; Bavarian Political Police dossier, T-175/242/2732295–305; T-354/225/3893604, 3893648, 3893652–55.

45. See, for example, ''Die alten Fahnen werden feierlich eingeholt,'' *Illustrierter Beobachter* 8 (March 31, 1933).

46. And to pass judgement on marches written by Himmler's elder brother, Gebhard. See Himmler to Leibstandarte Adolf Hitler, January 2, 1934, T-354/195/3854659.

47. ''Bataillon Tagesbefehl Nr. 157,'' April 26, 1934, T-354/197/3856245.

48. Buchheim, ''Herrschaftsinstrument,'' *Anatomie des SS Staates*, pp. 42–43.

49. Chef des SS-Amtes to SS-Oberabschnitte, May 26, 1934, T-354/195/3854526.

50. Martin Broszat, ''Nationalsozialistische Konzentrationslager 1933–1945,'' in *Anatomie des SS Staates*, ed. Buchheim, et al., 2: 15 ff.

51. And the occasional seizure of suspects. ''Bataillon Tagesbefehl Nr. 154,'' April 23, 1934, T-354/197/3856248; ''Bataillon Tagesbefehl Nr. 196,'' T-354/197/3856200. See also T-354/196/3855196

2 EXECUTION AND EXPANSION

1. Hermann Mau, ''Die 'Zweite Revolution'—Der 30. Juni 1934,'' *Vierteljahrshefte für Zeitgeschichte 2 (1953)*, 130.

2. Roger Manvell and Heinrich Fraenkel, *Himmler*, p. 42.

3. See Heinz Höhne, *Der Orden unter dem Totenkopf*, pp. 94–95.

4. Robert J. O'Neill, *The German Army and the Nazi Party*, p. 46; Höhne, *Der Orden*, p. 102.

5. "Betr. Dienstplanänderung für den 25 Juni, 1934," June 23, 1934, T-354/215/3881156; Cf. Alan Bullock, *Hitler, A Study in Tyranny*, p. 301.

6. Höhne, *Der Orden*, p. 101.

7. T-354/197/3856186; Höhne, *Der Orden* p. 106.

8. Höhne's account of the Roehm Purge, based largely on the records of the trial of Dietrich and Michael Lippert before the Munich *Landgericht*, is the best to have yet appeared. See Höhne, *Der Orden*, p. 111.

9. Ibid., p. 108.

10. Ibid., p. 109.

11. Ibid., p. 112.

12. John Dornberg, *Schizophrenic Germany* (New York: Macmillan, 1961), pp. 36–37.

13. I. Bataillon to Leibstandarte SS Adolf Hitler, T-354/220/3886702; "Bataillon Tagesbefehl Nr. 218," July 11, 1934, T-354/197/3856175; "Bataillon Tagesbefehl Nr. 221," July 14, 1934, T-354/197/3856171.

14. Höhne, *Der Orden*, p. 121.

15. "Bataillon Tagesbefehl Nr. 213," July 5, 1934, T-354/197/3856181. Other officers who were promoted one rank included: Bernhard Siebken, Albin Freiherr von Reitzenstein, Martin Kohlroser, Jürgen Wagner, Otto Reich, Herbert Samulewitz and Alfred Holstein (ibid.).

16. Höhne, *Der Orden*, p. 121.

17. Bullock, *Hitler*, p. 328.

18. Höhne, *Der Orden*, p. 247.

19. Obertruppführer Fritz Zechmeister to Leibstandarte, July 29, 1934, T-354/220/3886650. Zechmeister retained his Austrian citizenship for some time thereafter. See Der Gerichsführer LSSAH to Sturmbannführer Ernst Deutsch, January 11, 1935, T-354/220/3887166–67.

20. Zechmeister to Leibstandarte, T-354/220/3886650; Höhne, *Der Orden* p. 247.

21. Bullock, *Hitler*, p. 307.

22. George Stein, *The Waffen-SS*, p. 7.

23. See "Bataillon Befehl Nr. 202," June 23, 1934, T-354/197/3856192.

24. See, for example, "Musterung für die SS—V.T.," 23 Heuert [July], 1935, T-354/408/4124089.

25. Colonel Moser, Commandant Jüterbog, to Obersturmbannführer Otto Reich, June 22, 1934, T-354/196/3854963. See also 197/3856156, 3856159–60, 3857124.

26. Paul Hausser, *Soldaten wie andere auch*, p. 13; Hans Buchheim, *SS und Polizei im NS-Staat* (Bonn: Selbstverlag der Studien für Zeitprobleme, 1964), p. 166.

27. "Der Reichsverteidigungsminister, Nr. 1139/34, g.k. L IIa," September 24, 1934, Section I (Aufgaben und Gliederung der SS), Article 4, subsection b, National Archives Microfilm Publication, "Records of Headquarters, German Army High Command," T-78/427/6397243–48.

28. Ibid. 1/2/a.

29. Ibid., II/10.

30. Ibid., II/1, III/1, II/9, II/10.

31. Ibid., II/8.

32. See, for example, "Auf den SS-Führerschulen Tölz und Braunschweig ausgebildete SS-Führer" in *Dienstaltersliste der Schutzstaffel der NSDAP, Stand vom 1. Dezember 1936*, T-175/204/2674095–98.

33. "Der Reichsverteidigungsminister, Nr. 1139/34," II/9.

34. Höhne, *Der Orden*, pp. 408–10.

35. T-354/201/3861804–6.

36. *Illustrierter Beobachter*, 10/29 (July 18, 1935); ibid., 10/41 (October 10, 1935). Dietrich was asked to intercede in high places for a rocket project on the grounds that he was "unprejudiced toward innovations" and that he was free "von allen ministeriellen und ähnlichen Hemmungen." Fritz Michael Endres, Politischer Referent des Präsidenten im Centralverband des Kohlenhändler Deutschlands e.V., February 7, 1935, T-354/201/3861909–10. See also T-354/196/3854810–11.

37. Unpublished article by a correspondent for the *Kieler Neueste Nachrichten* entitled, "Ein Besuch bei Obergruppenführer Dietrich," p. 3, T-354/210/3874673–78.

38. This information is included in a generally critical statement seemingly made by a malcontent to a low-grade Gestapo official who passed it on to the RFSS. See T-175/88/2611449.

39. "Ein Besuch," p. 1, T-354/210/387463–78.

40. K. G. Klietmann, *Die Waffen-SS, eine Dokumentation*, photograph opposite p. 224; map of barracks, T-354/195/3854482.

41. "Ein Besuch," pp. 2–3, T-354/210/3874673–78; Brigadeführer Karl Wolff to Leibstandarte, March 22, 1935, T-354/210/3874122.

42. "Ein Besuch," T-354/210/3874673–78, p. 4. The apartments were built in cooperation with the German Labor Front. See Leibstandarte to Staatskommissar der Stadt Berlin, April 21, 1936, T-354/211/3875229.

43. NSDAP politisches Amt to Leibstandarte, November 21, 1935, T-354/201/3862168. See also T-354/195/3854155.

44. George Stein, *The Waffen-SS*, p. 5.

45. Wolff over SS-Hauptamt to Leibstandarte, February 1, 1937, T-354/220/3886980.

46. Albert Speer, *Inside the Third Reich*, p. 84; see photograph of SS-Kaserne "Obersalzberg" in Klietmann, *Die Waffen-SS*, opposite p. 160.

47. T-354/210/3874235, 3874321.

48. "Personalbefehl Nr. 13," May 4, 1934, p. 5, T-611/3/Folder 429; "Führerlist der LSSAH," November 20, 1936, T-354/201/3861602–5.

49. Erich Kempka, *Ich habe Adolf Hitler verbrannt* (Munich: Kryburg, n.d.), p. 18.

50. In matters of managing Columbia Haus, Leibstandarte was in communication with Theodor Eicke, after July 4, 1934, Inspekteur der Konzentrationslager und SS-Wachverbände, T-354/195/3854438; report of Obersturmführer Carl Marks, March 11, 1935, T-354/220/3886407.

51. Der Reichsführer-SS, Chef-Adjutant, to Leibstandarte, November 26, 1935, T-354/201/3862028.

52. Joachim Kramarz, *Stauffenberg*, p. 70.

53. "Ansprache des Reichsführers SS," September 7, 1940, T-175/90/2612648–49.

3 DEFINITION AND INDOCTRINATION

1. "Der Führer und Reichskanzler, 15/35 g. Kdo. S.," February 2, 1935, T-78/427/6397237–38.

2. George Stein, *The Waffen-SS*, pp. 15–16; Gerald Reit-

linger, *The SS: Alibi of a Nation, 1922–1945* (New York: Viking Press, 1957), p. 74.

3. "Der Reichsverteidigungsminister, Nr. 1139/34 g.K. L IIa," September 24, 1934, T-78/427/6397243.

4. Stein, *Waffen-SS*, pp. 16–17.

5. "Der Führer und Reichskanzler, Geheime Kommandosache," August 17, 1938, reproduced in K. G. Klietmann, *Die Waffen-SS, eine Dokumentation*, pp. 29–30.

6. Dietrich to RFSS, May 7, 1935, T-175/147/2674369.

7. Himmler to Dietrich, March 5, 1938, T-175/33/2542516–17.

8. Himmler to Dietrich, July 27, 1938, T-175/33/2542485; Dietrich to Himmler, July 29, 1938, ibid.

9. Hausser to Himmler, May 10, 1938, BDC/82–83.

10. T-354/192/3850106; 201/3861619 ff.; 209/3873009; 218/3884532.

11. *Statistisches Jahrbuch der Schutzstaffel der NSDAP, 1937*, P. 47, T-175/205/4042264.

12. Ibid.

13. *Statistisches Jahrbuch er Schutzstaffel der NSDAP, 1938*, p. 73, T-175/205/4042332.

14. Ibid.

15. "Der Führer und Reichskanzler, 15/35 g. Kdos.," February 2, 1935, reproduced in Klietmann, *Die Waffen-SS*, p. 20.

16. Not until after the Anschluss with Austria in March 1938 was full motorization ordered for all of the Verfügungstruppe. See Paul Hausser, *Soldaten wie andere auch*, p. 21.

17. Otto Weidinger, *Division Das Reich*, 1: 19.

18. "Der Führer und Reichskanzler, Geheime Kommandosache," May 18, 1939, reproduced in Klietmann, *Die Waffen-SS*, p. 32.

19. See, for example, Kommando der Panzertruppen to Leibstandarte Adolf Hitler, August 26, 1936, T-354/196/3854792; Chef des SS-Hauptamtes, September 24, 1935, T-175/147/2674108.

20. Oberbürgermeister Berlin to Leibstandarte Adolf Hitler, July 18, 1937, T-354/205/3867106–7.

21. Paul Hausser, *Waffen-SS im Einsatz*, p. 13; "Tagesbefehl Nr. 115," June2, 1939, T-354/199/3859993.

22. Chef des SS-Hauptamtes, October 14, 1935, T-175/147/2674066.

23. T-175/147/2674145; T-354/200/3860666, 213/3877007.

24. Stein, *Waffen-SS*, pp. 25–26.

25. Hausser, *Soldaten*, p. 41; "Tagesbefehl Nr. 83," April 14, 1939, T-354/199/3860044.

26. See Hans Buchheim, "Befehl und Gehorsam," in *Anatomie des SS-Staates*, ed. Buchheim, et al., 1: 221.

27. "Dienstliches Verhältnis des Rasse und Siedlungsamtes SS zu den SS Einheiten," October 15, 1934, T-354/194/3853000–3003.

28. Ibid.

29. Obertruppführer Georg Weibgen to Schulungsleiter of Leibstandarte, April 21, 1934, T-354/220/3886769.

30. Activity Report of Abteilung Schulung, February 4, 1935, p. 1, T-354/218/3884526.

31. See, for example, "Jahresplan für die Weltanschauliche Schulung in der Leibstandarte Adolf Hitler," T-354/218/3884562–63.

32. Ibid. A selection of *SS-Leithefte* is available in T-611, Rolls 43, 44, 45.

33. "Was der Judenfreund sagt," *Leitheft 4, 3. Jahrgang*, pp. 34, 36, T-611/43.

34. "Die seelischen Wurzeln klösterlicher Sittenlosigkeit," p. 56, T-611/43.

35. "Warum über Freimaurerei und Bolshewismus geschult," *Leitheft 4, 2.* Jahrgang, May 29, 1936, p. 6, T-611/44.

36. Roger Manvell and Heinrich Fraenkel, *Himmler*, p. 48.

37. Georg Weibgen, Leibstandarte's chief education leader, recalled that the answer which he most frequently received to the question, "Why did I become an SS man?" was, "Because the black uniform, especially that of the Leibstandarte, looks the nicest." Activity Report of Abteilung Schulung, February 4, 1935, p. 8, T-354/218/3884533.

38. Chef des SS-Hauptamtes, May 9, 1935, T-175/96/2616417; Chef des SS-Hauptamtes, August 21, 1935, T-175/147/2674151; T-354/192/3850357, 3850427.

39. Stein, *Waffen-SS*, p. 13.

40. Weidinger, *Division das Reich*, 1: 19.

41. In 1936 the minimum height for membership in Leib-standarte was reduced to 1.78 meters although this standard remained significantly greater than the minimum height for acceptance by other Verfügungstruppe units (1.74 meters). See "Merkblatt für die Einstellung bei den SS-Verfügungstruppe und SS-Totenkopfverbänden," T-175/96/2616699.

42. When asked by his education leader whom he would support in a clash between Hitler and the papacy, one Roman Catholic member replied, "Naturally, the Pope!" Activity Report of Abteilung Schulung, February 4, 1935, p. 1, T-354/218/3884526.

43. T-354/210/3875172–73.

44. A member of the Standarte was punished for having talked too freely of the incident. See T-354/195/3854414, 3854416. The harassment of Catholics in Berchtesgaden was something of a cause célèbre. See Hess to Himmler, January 31, 1936, T-354/220/3887079–80.

45. "Weltanschauliche Schulung in der Leibstandarte SS Adolf Hitler," T-354/218/3884560–61.

46. See, for example: "Arbeitsbericht des 1. Viertel-jahres, 1935" (SS-Motorsturm 7/2), March 30, 1935, T-354/408/4124350–51; Schulungsleiter, 2. SS-Standarte to Rasse-referent, SS-Oberabschnitt Rhein, 16 Heumond (July) 1935, T-354/407/4122573–74.

47. Himmler's order of November 30, 1935, T-354/366/4070504.

48. Hausser, *Soldaten*, p. 41; "Bolshewismus" (XIV) Blatt 1, T-354/217/3883321–22.

49. T-354/408/4124350–51.

50. This is a point stressed by veterans and apologists for the later Waffen-SS. See Hausser, *Soldaten*, p. 41.

51. T-354/218/3883885–86, 3883896.

52. Ernst Günther Krätschmer, *Ritterkreuzträger der Waffen-SS* (Göttingen: Plesse Verlag, 1955), pp. 10–11.

4 FROM VIENNA TO THE VISTULA

1. Alan Bullock, *Hitler*, p. 428; Paul Hausser, *Soldaten wie andere auch*, p. 21.

2. Heinz Guderian. *Erinnerungen eines Soldaten*, p. 42.

3. Ibid., p. 43.

4. Ibid., pp. 43–45.

5. Hausser, *Soldaten*, p. 21; Guderian, *Erinnerungen*, p. 46.

6. Guderian, *Erinnerungen*, p. 49.

7. Robert J. O'Neill, *The German Army and the Nazi Party*, p. 49; Bullock, *Hitler*, p. 446.

8. "Mobilmachung der SS-Verfügungstruppe," July 9, 1938, p. 1, T-354/612/000539.

9. See T-354/612/000250 ff.

10. Joachim Kramarz, *Stauffenberg*, p. 70.

11. See order of 1. Panzer-Division (to which Leibstandarte was attached), September 30, 1938, T-354/612/000247. "Bataillonsbefehl für den 1. April 1939," T-354/612/000351.

12. "Leibstandarte SS-Adolf Hitler, Nr. 59/39 g. Kdos.," June 12, 1939, T-354/612/000498.

13. AOK 8, *Feldzug Polen*, entry of June 21, 1939, U. S. National Archives Microfilm Publication, "Records of German Field Commands—Armies," T-312/37/7545816–18.

14. Ibid., entry of July 20, 1939, T-312/37/7545834.

15. Otto Weidinger, *Division Das Reich*, 1:114.

16. "Id Nr. 196/39 g. Kdos.," August 16, 1939, *Anlagenheft 5 zum KTB, H Gr. Nord*, U. S. National Archives Microfilm Publication, "Records of German Field Commands—Army Groups," T-311/200/001563.

17. "Regimentsbefehl," August 25, 1939, T-354/609/000145–47.

18. "SS-Befehl," August 24, 1939, T-354/609/000116; AOK 8, *Feldzug Polen*, entry of August 25, 1939, T-312/37/7545884.

19. *Die Armee Blaskowitz im Polenfeldzug*, p. 1, T-312/37/7545293.

20. A detachment of Panzer-Regiment 23 was also subordinated to 8th Army. . . . *seit heute wird zurückgeschossen! Der Polenfeldzug der 8. Armee*, T-312/37/7545210.

21. Ibid., 7545211.

22. Ibid.

23. Ibid., 7545215.

24. Ibid.

25. Ibid., 7545217; "Gesamtverlust-Liste für das I.R. A.H.," T-354/609/001128.

26. *Die 17. Division in Polen*, pp. 1–2, T-312/37/7545551–52.

27. . . . *seit heute wird zurückgeschossen!*, T-312/37/7545224.

28. AOK 8, *Felzug Polen*, entry of September 4, 1939, T-312/37/7545940.

29. "Divisions-Befehl für das Verhalten der Truppe im Operationsgebiet." September 4, 1939, T-354/609/000109–10.

30. . . . *seit heute wird zurückgeschossen!*, T-312/37/7545236.

31. "Armeebefehl Ia Nr. 15/39" in AOK 8, *Felzug Polen*, T-312/37/7545953.

32. "Korpsbefehl für 7.9," September 6, 1939, T-354/609/000105–7.

33. *Die 17. Division in Polen*, p. 5, T-312/37/7545555.

34. AOK 8, *Feldzug Polen*, entry for September 7, 1939, T-312/37/7545957.

35. *Die 17. Division in Polen*, p. 5, T-312/37/7545555.

36. AOK 8, *Feldzug Polen*, entry for September 8, 1939, T-312/37/7545961.

37. AOK 3 to H Gr. Nord, September 8, 1939, T-311/200/001385.

38. AOK 8, *Feldzug Polen*, entry for September 8, 1939, T-312/37/7545967.

39. Leibstandarte had earned a bad name for itself with XIII Corps. See "Abschrift der Anlage 1 zu Korpskommando XIII," October 7, 1939, U. S. National Archives Microfilm Publication, "Records of German Field Commands—Corps," T-314/509/000007-10.

40. William L. Shirer, *The Rise and Fall of the Third Reich* (New York: Crest, 1963), p. 926.

41. Otto Dietrich, *Auf den Strassen des Sieges—Erlebnisse mit dem Führer in Polen* (Munich: Zentralverlag der NSDAP, 1939), p. 21.

42. *Hitler's Secret Conversations, 1941—1944*, p. 178.

43. Division Reinhardt, "Befehl für die Erweiterung der Sperrstellung am 10.9.39," T-354/609/000088-89.

44. Ibid.

45. AOK 8, "Abt. Ia Nr. 20/39, Armeebefehl," September 11, 1939, T-312/37/7545746.

46. Division Reinhardt, "Divisionsbefehl Nr. 15," September 12, 1939. T-354/609/000084-87; Kurt Meyter, *Grenadiere*, p. 12.

47. AOK 8, "Armeebefehl," September 13, 1939, T-312/37/7546443-45; Nikolaus von Vormann, *Der Feldzug 1939 in Polen*, p. 131.

48. Vormann, *Feldzug 1939*, p. 133.

49. AOK 8, *Feldzug Polen*, entry for September 14, 1939, T-312/37/7546019; Meyer, *Grenadiere*, p. 13.

50. Vormann, *Feldzug 1939*, p. 137; 4. Panzer Division, "Divisionstagesbefehl," September 20, 1939, T-354/609/000063.

51. Heeresgruppe Süd to AOK 8 and 10, September 21, 1939, T-312/37/7546360-61.

52. Ibid; Korpskommando XV A.K. to Leibstandarte, September 21, 1939, T-354/609/000061.

53. "Anwesenheit des Führers am 25.9 bei 8. u. 10. Armee," T-354/609/000227.

54. *KTB, H. Gr. Nord*, "Einnahme von Modlin," T-311/200/000181-87; ibid., 000136-41; Weidinger, *Division Das Reich*, 1: 257.

55. AOK 8, "Armeebefehl," September 27, 1939, T-312/37/7545781.

56. Undated message of Hauptsturmführer Hermann Müller-John to Dietrich, T-354/609/000937-38.

57. Fernspruch, OKH to AOK 8 and 10, October 1, 1939, T-312/37/7546700.

58. Ibid. See also Radomir Luza, *The Transfer of the Sudeten Germans: A Study of Czech-German Relations* (New York: New York University Press, 1964), pp. 205 f.; "Les Allies et la Resistance Tchecoslovaque" in *European Resistance Movements 1939-1945* (New York: Macmillan, 1964), p. 230.

59. "Bataillonstagesbefehl Nr. 21," October 11, 1939, T-354/613/001072; Meyer, *Grenadiere*, pp. 14-15.

60. George Stein, *The Waffen-SS*, p. 32.

61. Hausser, *Soldaten*, p. 63.

62. T-354/205/3867271 ff.

63. Meyer, *Grenadiere*, p. 16.

64. Ibid.

5 THE WEST—1940

1. Kurt Meyer, *Grenadiere*, p. 16; "Neujahrsbefehl," December 12, 1939, T-354/613/000898.

2. "Oberkommando des Heeres, AHA/la IV Nr. 1481/40 geh.," January 21, 1940, T-175/106/2629789.

3. "Inspekteur (E) der SS-Verfügungstruppe, Tgb. Nr. 434/40 geh.," April 17, 1940, T-175/104/2626417.

4. "Inspektion (E) der SS-Verfügungstruppe, II b E/Az. Abgabe 7/1/40 z/geh.," January 13, 1940, T-354/193/3851298.

5. "Adjutantur der Wehrmacht beim Führer und Reichskanzler an das OKW," January 13, 1940, T-175/106/2629736; Kommando der Waffen-SS, June 3, 1940, T-175/106/2629735.

6. Eddy Bauer, *Der Panzerkrieg*, 1: 48.

7. Heinz Guderian, *Erinnerungen eines Soldaten*, p. 79. In the fall of 1939, Hitler considered using XIX Panzer Corps in a lightning thrust through the Ardennes for the seizure of a bridgehead over the Meuse at Sedan. See Bauer, *Panzerkrieg*, 1: 48.

8. Telford Taylor, *The March of Conquest*, p. 173.

9. Guderian, *Erinnerungen*, pp. 80–81.

10. "Divisions-Befehl," February 29, 1940, T-354/610/000016; "AOK 18, Abt. Ia Nr. 2400/40 geh.," ibid., 000017; "Schnelle Gruppe Nord, IIa Tgb. Nr. 49/40 g. Kdos.," April 8, 1940, T-354/614/000116–19.

11. T-354/614/000116.

12. Meyer, *Grenadiere*, p. 20.

13. Taylor, *March of Conquest*, p. 195; Meyer, *Grenadiere*, p. 22.

14. Meyer, *Grenadiere*, p. 22.

15. "Tagebuchaufzeichnungen des Oberbefehlshabers der Heeresgruppe B, Gen. Oberst Fedor von Bock," entry for May 11, 1940 in Hans-Adolf Jacobsen, ed., *Dokumente zum Westfeldzug 1940*, p. 15. Meyer, *Grenadiere*, p. 22.

16. Taylor, *March of Conquest*, p. 196; Bauer, *Panzerkrieg*, 1: 68.

17. Taylor, *March of Conquest*, pp. 191 ff.; "Armeeoberkommando 18, Abt. Ia," May 12, 1940, T-354/610/000047.

18. *Kriegstagebuch Nr. 1, Art. Abt. LSSAH*, entry for May 14, 1940, T-354/610/000451. Most of Leibstandarte's war diaries dealing with the campaign in the West were badly

damaged by a fire which swept the Heeresarchiv Potsdam on
February 27–28, 1942.

19. Taylor, *March of Conquest*, p. 199.

20. Ibid.; Guderian, *Erinnerungen*, pp. 91–95.

21. Cajus Bekker, *The Luftwaffe War Diaries*, p. 100.

22. Ibid.; Taylor, *March of Conquest*, p. 201.

23. "Vorbefehl für den Angriff der LSSAH am 14.5,"
T-354/610/000052.

24. Taylor, *March of Conquest*, pp. 203–4.

25. Ibid.; Meyer, *Grenadiere*, p. 25.

26. "Tagebuchaufzeichnungen," Bock, entry for May 15,
1940, in Jacobsen, *Dokumente*, p. 34.

27. II Bataillon LSSAH, "Marschbefehl für den 16.5.40,"
T-354/212/3876244; II Bataillon, "Vorbefehl für den Weiter-
marsch der LSSAH am 17.5.40," ibid., 3876243.

28. Ninth Panzer Division to Leibstandarte, May 19, 1940,
T-354/610/000060; II Bataillon, LSSAH, "Bataillonsbefehl
für den Vormarsch am 20.5.1940," T-354/212/3876240.

29. Guderian, *Erinnerungen*, p. 101.

30. Lionel F. Ellis, *The War in France and Flanders 1939–
1940*, pp. 87 ff; Taylor, *March of Conquest*, pp. 236–37;
Guderian, *Erinnerungen*, p. 102.

31. George Stein, *The Waffen-SS*, p. 69; "Tagebuchaufzeichnungen," Bock, entry for May 23, 1940, in Jacobsen,
Dokumente, pp. 72–73.

32. Guderian, *Erinnerungen*, p. 102; F. W. von Mellenthin, *Panzer Battles*, p. 18.

33. "Marschbefehl für den 24.5.1940," T-354/610/
000547.

34. Guderian, *Erinnerungen*, p. 104.

35. XIX A.K., "Korpsbefehl Nr. 13 25.5.40" in *1. Pz.
Div. Ia Anlagen zum KTB, Nr. 3*, U.S. National Archives
Microfilm Publication, "Records of German Field Com-
mands—Divisions," T-315/15/000048–50.

36. See various entries for May 24, 1940, in Jacobsen,
Dokumente, pp. 73 f.

37. Dietrich issued the order at 0900 on May 25, 1940.
"Aufträge für die Leibstandarte am 25.5.40." T-354/610/
000548.

38. Guderian, *Erinnerungen*, p. 105.

39. "Regimentsbefehl," May 25, 1940, T-354/610/000549–51.

40. Guderian, *Erinnerungen*, p. 106. Cf. Meyer, *Grenadiere*, pp. 29–30.

41. Bauer, *Panzerkrieg*, 1: 86; various entries for this date in Jacobsen, *Dokumente*, pp. 82 f.

42. 20. Division, "Divisionsbefehl für den Angriff am 27.5.40," T-354/610/000552–55.

43. Ibid.; "Regimentsbefehl für den Angriff am 27.5.40," T-354/610/000556–57; Meyer, *Grenadiere*, p. 30.

44. Most of the French Army's mechanized formations, however, had already been destroyed.

45. Generalkommando XIX A.K. "Korpsbefehl Nr. 15," May 28, 1940, reproduced in Guderian, *Erinnerungen*, p. 454; "Vorbefehl für den Angriff auf Dünkirchen," May 30, 1940, T-354/610/000104; "Marschbefehl für den 1.6.1940," T-354/617/000351.

46. Bauer, *Panzerkrieg*, 1:89.

47. Ibid., p. 90.

48. "AOK 6, Abteilung Ia/op.," June 6, 1940," T-354/160/000132.

49. "Marschbefehl für den 7.6.1940," T-354/610/000142; Gen Kdo. XVI A.K. "Korpsbefehl für den 7.6.40," T-354/610/000139–40.

50. Gen. Kdo. XVI A.K., "Korpsbefehl für den Angriff am 8.6.40," T-354/610/000148.

51. "Kriegstagebuch," Halder, entry for June 6, 1940, in Jacobsen, *Dokumente*, p. 177; Taylor, *March of Conquest* p. 292.

52. 3. Pz. Div., "Divisionsbefehl für den Angriff am 8.6.40," T-354/610/000152–57.

53. 3. Pz. Div., "Divisionsbefehl für die Herstellung der Abwehrbereitschaft," June 8, 1940, T-354/610/000161–62; "Kriegstagebuch," Halder, entry for June 8, 1940, in Jacobsen, *Dokumente*, p. 180.

54. 3. Pz. Div., "Divisionsbefehl für die Herauslösung der Leibstandarte Adolf Hitler," June 8, 1940, T-354/610/000163; Heeresgruppe B to Leibstandarte Adolf Hitler, 9.6.40, T-354/610/000164.

55. Generalkommando XXXXIV A.K., "Korpsbefehl für die Fortsetzung des Angriffs am 10.6.1940," T-354/610/

000168; LSSAH, "Angriffsbefehl für den 10.6.1940," T-354/610/000169.

56. 72. Inf.-Division to Leibstandarte, 12.6.1940, T-354/610/000119; Meyer, *Grenadiere*, p. 33.

57. "Tagebuchaufzeichnungen," Bock, entry for June 10, 1940, in Jacobsen, *Dokumente*, p. 199; ibid., entry for June 12, p. 210.

58. LSSAH, "Marschbefehl für den 13.6.1940," T-354/610/000193; Gruppe v. Kleist, "Gruppenbefehl Nr. 30 für den 14.6.1940," T-354/610/000197–98; "Tagebuchaufzeichnungen," Bock, entry for June 14, 1940, in Jacobsen, *Dokumente*, p. 217.

59. "Anlage II zum Gruppenbefehl Nr. 30 vom 13.6.40," T-354/610/000195.

60. Stein, *Waffen-SS*, pp. 83 ff.; "Tagebuchauzeichnungen," Bock, entry for June 20, 1940, in Jacobsen, *Dokumente*, p. 233.

61. LSSAH, "Marschbefehl für den 17. Juni 1940," T-354/610/000203; "Funkspruch Nr. 4," 9. Pz. Div. to Leibstandarte, 17.6.40, T-354/610/000204; Gruppe v. Kleist to LSSAH, 17.6.40, T-354/610/000206; cf. Stein, *Waffen-SS*, p. 85; "Regimentsbefehl," June 20, 1940, T-354/610/000221.

62. "Tätigkeitsbericht der 12. Batterie vom 19.-22.6.1940," T-354/610/000616.

63. "Regimentsbefehl für den 21.6.1940," T-354/610/000227.

64. Bauer, *Panzerkrieg*, 1:103–4.

65. Taylor, *March of Conquest*, pp. 305–9

66. XVI A.K., "Korpsbefehl für den J-Tag," T-354/610/000233–35; XVI A.K., "Korpsbefehl für den 24.6.40," T-354/610/000239–40; XVI A.K., "Korpsbefehl für den 25.6.40," T-354/610/000241–42.

67. Throughout the campaign, the Oberkommando der Wehrmacht gave scant credit to the Waffen-SS. Stein, *Waffen-SS*, p. 89. See Bock's victory statement to his troops in Jacobsen, *Dokumente*, pp. 243–44.

68. "Regimentsbefehl," June 25, 1940, T-354/610/000247.

69. BDC/12; Roger J. Bender and Hugh P. Taylor, *Uniforms, Organization and History of the Waffen-SS*, 4 vols.

(Mountain View, Calif.: James Bender Publishing, 1971), 2:64.

70. Albert Speer, *Inside the Third Reich*, p. 172.

71. "Ausbildungsweisung für die SS-Leibstandarte Adolf Hitler," August 14, 1940, T-354/614/000058–59; Gen. Kdo. XXXXI A.K., "Merkblatt für die Verladung motorisierter Truppen auf Seedampfern," August 16, 1940, T-354/621/000529 ff.

72. Kommando der Waffen-SS, "Verstärkung der LSSAH," August 13, 1940, T-175/106/2629693–97; *Kriegstagebuch des Oberkommandos der Wehrmacht*, ed. Hans-Adolf Jacobsen, 1:24 (hereafter cited as *KTB/OKW*); "Sonderbefehl betr. die Verstärkung der Leibstandarte SS Adolf Hitler," August 19, 1940, T-354/614/000055–57; K. G. Klietmann, *Die Waffen-SS, eine Dokumentation*, p. 72. See also Walter Warlimont, *Inside Hitler's Headquarters 1939–45*, p. 104.

73. Kommando der Waffen-SS, Ia/Tgb., Nr. 85/40 g. Kdos., August 13, 1940, T-175/106-2629693–97; "Sonderbefehl betr. die Verstärkung der Leibstandarte SS Adolf Hitler," T-354/614/000055–57.

74. "Sonderbefehl betr. die Verstärkung der Leibstandarte SS Adolf Hitler," T-354/614/000055–57; Kommando der Waffen-SS, "Verstärkung der LSSAH," August 19, 1940, T-175/106/2629689.

75. "Leibstandarte SS Adolf Hitler, Abt.Ic Nr. 12/41 g. Kdos.," January 6, 1941, T-354/614/000293.

76. "Befehl für die Verladung des Vorkommandos der LSSAH," January 11, 1941, T-354/614/000296; Anlagen AOK 12, Ia, "Zuführung SS-Adolf Hilter," January 31, 1941, T-312/424/8001900.

77. Fernschreiben, OKH to Oberkommando der Truppen des Deutschen Heeres in Rumaenian, March 1, 1941, T-312/424/8001904.

6 MARITA

1. Hans-Adolf Jacobsen, ed., *Der Zweite Weltkrieg, Grundzüge der Politik und Strategie in Dokumenten*, pp. 107–8; Kurt von Tippelskirch, "Der Deutsche Balkenfeldzug 1941," *Wehrwissenschaftliche Rundschau* 5 (February 1955), 50.

2. Tippelskirch, "Deutsche Balkenfeldzug," p. 50; Eddy Bauer, *Der Panzerkrieg*, 1: 109; *KTB/OKW*, 1: 224.

3. "Abschrift aus dem Kriegstagebuch Nr. 3 des III/ LSSAH über den Einsatz im Südosten," T-354/622/000002; "Marschbefehl Nr. 3 für den Abmarsch der LSSAH aus Rumänien," March 20, 1941, T-354/614/000930–31; K. G. Klietmann, *Die Waffen-SS, eine Dokumentation*, p. 76.

4. Leo Hepp, "Die 12. Armee im Balkenfeldzug 1941," *Wehrwissenschaftliche Rundschau* 5 (May 1955), 204; Bauer, *Panzerkrieg*, 1: 109; 12. Armee, "Armeebefehl Nr. 4," April 2, 1941, p. 1, T-312/424/8002740.

5. 9. Pz. Div., "Divisionsbefehl Nr. 11," April 4, 1941, T-315/529/000514–18; "Gefechtsbericht der LSSAH für die Zeit vom 6.4.41-24.4.41," p. 1, T-354/609/001154.

6. "Gefechtsbericht der LSSAH," p. 1, T-354/609/ 001154.

7. Ibid.

8. Ibid., pp. 2–3, T-354/609/001155–56.

9. Ian S. O. Playfair, *The Mediterranean and Middle East*, 2:86.

10. "Gefechtsbericht der LSSAH," pp. 3–4, T-354/609/ 001156–57; Playfair, *Mediterranean and Middle East*, 2: 86–87.

11. "Gefechtsbericht der LSSAH," p. 9, T-354/609/ 001162.

12. Playfair, *Mediterranean and Middle East*, 2: 86–87; "Standarten-Befehl für den 11. April 1941," T-354/620/ 000835.

13. Playfair, *Mediterranean and Middle East*, 2: 88.

14. "Gefechtsbericht der LSSAH," pp. 6 ff., T-354/609/ 001159 ff.; Gavin Long, *Greece, Crete and Syria*, pp. 53 ff.

15. "Gefechtsbericht der LSSAH," pp. 16–18. T-354/609/ 001169–71.

16. Ibid., pp. 18 ff., T-354/609/001171 ff.

17. Ibid., pp. 23–24, T-354/609/001176–77; Playfair, *Mediterranean and Middle East*, 2: 88.

18. "Gefechtsbericht der LSSAH," pp. 24–25, T-354/ 609/001177–78; Long, *Greece, Crete and Syria*, p. 71.

19. "Tagesbefehl," April 27, 1941, T-354/617/000758; "Verleihung von Auszeichnungen," April 16, 1941, T-354/

619/00326 ff.; Witt had already earned the Knight's Cross for his exploits in France.

20. "Gefechtsbericht der LSSAH," p. 26, T-354/609/001179.

21. Ibid., pp. 27–28, T-354/609/001180–81.

22. Ibid., pp. 29–31, T-354/609/001182–84; Alexander Papagos, *The Battle of Greece, 1940–1941*, p. 375.

23. "Gefechtsbericht der LSSAH," pp. 31–34, T-354/609/001184–87; Long, *Greece, Crete and Syria*, p. 93; Papagos, *Battle of Greece*, p. 378. For a dramatic account, see Kurt Meyer, *Grenadiere*, pp. 59–67.

24. "Tagesbefehl Nr. 61," June 11, 1941, T-354/617/000662.

25. Gen. Kdo. (Mot.) XXXX A. K., "Korpsbefehl für den 16.4.41," T-315/529/000571–73; Playfair, *Mediterranean and Middle East*, 2: 90.

26. "Gefechtsbericht der LSSAH," p. 34, T-354/609/001187.

27. James R. M. Butler, *Grand Strategy*, 2: 456; Playfair, *Mediterranean and Middle East*, 2: 90.

28. "Gefechtsbericht der LSSAH," p. 35, T-354/609/001188; Hepp, "Die 12. Armee," p. 208.

29. "Gefechtsbericht der LSSAH," pp. 35–36, T-354/609/001188–89; LSSAH, II Bataillon, "Gefechtsbericht," pp. 2–3, T-354/620/000740–41.

30. Ehrengard Schram-von Thadden, *Griechenland und die Grossmächte im Zeiten Weltkreig*, p. 196.

31. Ibid., pp. 221 ff.

32. Walter Warlimont, *Inside Hitler's Headquarters*, p. 131.

33. Thadden, *Griechenland*, pp. 199–201, 224–25. A copy of the revised surrender instrument, predated to April 20, is to be found in T-354/620/000871.

34. II. LSSAH, "Zusammenfasste Abend-und Morgenmeldung v. 20.–28.4.41," T-354/620/000889–91. Hepp, "Die 12. Armee," p. 208.

35. Long, *Greece, Crete and Syria*, p. 143.

36. Butler, *Grand Strategy*, 2:457.

37. AOK 12, "Abendmeldung vom 25.4.41," T-312/424/8001423–24; AOK 12, "Abendmeldung vom 26.4.41." T-312/424/8001427–28.

38. Playfair, *Mediterranean and Middle East*, 2: 103; Long, *Greece, Crete and Syria*, pp. 183–84.

39. Daleuge to Dietrich, May 8, 1941, BDC/116–17.

40. "Tagesbefehl," May 25, 1941, T-354/624/000498–99; SS-Führungshauptamt, Org. Tgb. Nr. 2043/41 geh., May 30, 1941, T-175/108/2632336–37.

41. SS-Führungshauptamt, T-175/108/2632336–37.

42. See George Stein, *The Waffen-SS*, pp. 99 ff.

43. Der Chef des Hauptamtes Haushalt und Bauten, "Neubau Leibstandarte SS Adolf Hilter," October 6, 1941, T-175/83/2609429–31.

44. *The Goebbels Diaries 1942–1943*, p. 288.

7 BARBAROSSA

1. Eddy Bauer, *Der Panzerkrieg*, 1:117.

2. "Zusatzbefehl zum Befehl für den Abmarsch der LSSAH aus dem Unterkunftsraum um Brünn," June 23, 1941, T-354/614/000324–26; Kurt Meyer, *Grenadiere*, p. 77.

3. Alfred Philippi and Ferdinand Heim, *Der Feldzug gegen Sowjetrussland*, p. 46.

4. Ibid.; Paul Karl Schmidt [Paul Carell], *Hitler Moves East, 1941–1943*, p. 20.

5. "Fernschreiben, von Kleist Ia an III A.K.," June 22, 1941, T-314/183/000047; Der Oberbefehlshaber der Heeresgruppe Süd, June 28, 1941, T-314/183/000169.

6. "Fernschreiben Nr. 158, Pz. Gr. 1 Ia an III A.K.," July 1, 1941, T-314/183/000233-34.

7. Panzergruppe 1, "Gruppenbefehl Nr. 9," July 4, 1941, T-314/183/000320-23; Eberhard von Mackensen, *Vom Bug zum Kaukasus*, p. 12.

8. "Fernspruch, Panzergruppe 1 Ia an III A.K. Ia," July 7, 1941, T-314/183/000378.

9. Panzergruppe 1 Ia an III A.K., July 7, 1941, T-314/183/000392; Der Befehlshaber der Panzergruppe 1, July 9, 1941, T-314/183/000409; Mackensen, *Vom Bug zum Kaukasus*, p. 14.

10. Philippi and Heim, *Der Feldzug*, p. 62.

11. Meyer, *Grenadiere*, pp. 88 ff.; Mackensen, *Vom Bug zum Kaukasus*, p. 16 and map opposite: "Leibstandarte an LI A.K.," July 14, 1941, T-354/610/001134–35.

12. *Kriegstagebuch Nr. 1 der Abt. Ib/LSSAH*, entry for July 16, 1941, T-354/611/000766.

13. Bauer, *Panzerkrieg*, 1: 128; Mackensen, *Vom Bug zum Kaukasus*, p. 19; Philippi and Heim, *Der Feldzug*, p. 63.

14. *KTB Nr. 1 Abt. Ib/LSSAH*, entry for July 24, 1941, T-354/611/000767; *Generalkommando III Pz.-Korps Ia, Kriegstagebuch vom 24.7-15.12.41*, p. 3, T-314/183/000709; Mackensen, *Vom Bug zum Kaukasus*, p. 19.

15. Schmidt, *Hitler Moves East*, pp. 119–20.

16. Gen. Kdo. XXXXVIII A.K. (mot.), Der Kommandierende General to Leibstandarte SS Adolf Hitler, August 8, 1941, T-354/213/3877863.

17. *KTB Nr. 1, Abt. Ib/LSSAH*, entry for August 3–4, 1941, T-354/611/000770.

18. Ibid., entry for August 19, 1941, T-354/611/000773; K. G. Klietmann, *Die Waffen-SS, eine Dokumentation*, p. 77.

19. Meyer, *Grenadiere*, p. 104.

20. Leibstandarte SS Adolf Hitler, Abt. Ic, "11. Bericht über den Einsatz der LSSAH vom 22.8–22.9.41," T-354/213/3877870.

21. Bauer, *Panzerkrieg*, 1:129; Philippi and Heim, *Der Feldzug*, pp. 70–71; Walter Warlimont, *Inside Hitler's Headquarters*, p. 190.

22. Philippi and Heim, *Der Feldzug*, p. 75.

23. Ibid., p. 78.

24. Schmidt, *Hitler Moves East*, p. 127; *KTB Nr. 1, Abt. Ib/LSSAH*, entry for September 3, 1941, T-354/611/000775.

25. "11. Bericht über den Einsatz der LSSAH," T-354/213/3877871 f.; Leibstandarte SS Adolf Hitler, Abt. Ic, "12. Bericht über den Einsatz der LSSAH vom 22.9.–18.10.1941," T-175/108/2632263.

26. Philippi and Heim, *Der Feldzug*, p. 88; Schmidt, *Hitler Moves East*, p. 281.

27. "12. Bericht über den Einsatz der LSSAH," T-175/108/2632264.

28. Philippi and Heim, *Der Feldzug*, p. 89; Der Oberbefehlshaber der Heeresgruppe Süd, "Weiterführung der Operationen," September 21, 1941, T-311/292/000665-68; "Heeresgruppe Süd Ia an Pz. Gr. 1,"September 30, 1941, T-311/292/000689.

29. Meyer, *Grenadiere*, p. 139; cf. "12. Bericht über den Einsatz der LSSAH," T-175/108/2632265.

30. Schmidt, *Hitler Moves East*, p. 283.

31. "Fernschreiben OKH an Herresgruppe Süd," September 28, 1941, T-311/292/000604–5.

32. "Korpsbefehl für die Verfolgung auf Rostow," October 8, 1941, T-314/185/000862–65; "12. Bericht über den Einsatz der LSSAH," T-175/108/2632266; Mackensen, *Vom Bug zum Kaukasus*, p. 36.

33. "Fernschreiben Heeresgruppe Süd an 1. Pz. Armee," October 11, 1941, T-311/292/000996.

34. Mackensen, *Vom Bug zum Kaukasus*, p. 38; Meyer, *Grendaiere*, p. 145.

35. Mackensen, *Vom Bug zum Kaukasus*, p. 38; "Korpsbefehl für die Fortsetzung der Verfolgung auf Rostow," October 11, 1941, T-314/185/000931–33.

36. 1. Panzerarmee, "Morgenmeldung," October 15, 1941, T-314/185/001013.

37. "Korpsbefehl," October 16, 1941, T-314/185/001044; Meyer, *Grenadiere*, p. 145.

38. "Panzerarmee—Befehl," n.d., T-311/292/001177; Meyer, *Grenadiere*, p. 145; Mackensen, *Vom Bug zum Kaukasus*, p. 38.

39. Dietrich to Himmler, October 13, 1941, T-175/108/2632281–82.

40. "Tagesmeldung," October 28, 1941, T-314/185/001242; "Zwischenmeldung," October 29, 1941, T-314/185/001246; Mackensen, *Vom Bug zum Kaukasus*, p. 39.

41. "Fernschreiben an 1. Panzerarmee, Chef," October 31, 1941, T-314/185/001264.

42. Ibid.

43. Philippi and Heim, *Der Feldzug*, p. 29.

44. Mackensen, *Vom Bug zum Kaukasus*, p. 41.

45. "Korpsbefehl für 6.11.," T-314/185/001321; Mackensen, *Vom Bug zum Kaukasus*, p. 41.

46. Mackensen, *Vom Bug zum Kaukasus*, p. 41; "Kampfführung des III. Panzerkorps ab 14.11.41," T-314/185/001380–82.

47. Mackensen, *Vom Bug zum Kaukasus*, p. 42; "Tagesmeldung," November 11, 1941, T-314/186/000033; "Auf-

träge für 19.11," T-314/186/000044; "Zwischenmeldung," November 11, 1941, T-354/186/000050.

48. "Zwischenmeldung," November 21, 1941, T-314/186/000112.

49. "Sondermeldung 22. November 1941," T-314/186/000112.

50. "III. Panzerkorps an die Kommandeure der 14. Pz. Div., 60. (mot.) Div., Leibstandarte," November 21, 1941, T-314/186/000105-8; "Panzer Armeebefehl Nr. 31," November 22, 1941, T-314/186/000110.

51. "Fernspruch, Pz. AOK 1 an III. A.K.," November 23, 1941, T-314/186/000134-35.

52. "Fernspruch, Pz. AOK 1 an III A.K." T-314/186/000169-70; III Panzerkorps Abt. Ia, November 25, 1941, T-314/186/000167-68.

53. "Beurteilung der Lage," November 27, 1941, T-314/186/000204-5; Mackensen, *Vom Bug zum Kaukasus*, p. 46.

54. *Kriegstagebuch 7, Gen. Kdo. III. Pz. Korps, Ia*, entry for November 27, 1941, T-314/183/000998 ff.; ibid., entry for November 28, 1941, T-314/183/001004 ff.; Meyer, *Grenadiere*, p. 152; "Panzerarmee Befehl Nr. 38," November 28, 1941, T-314/186/000222-27.

55. "Panzerarmee Befehl Nr. 40," November 30, 1941, T-314/186/000261-64; Mackensen, *Vom Bug zum Kaukasus*, p. 47.

56. Walimont, *Hitler's Headquarters*, p. 194; Keitel, *The Memoirs of Field-Marshal Keitel*, p. 161.

57. *KTB 7, III. Pz. Korps, Ia*, entry for December 1, 1941, T-314/183/001018-28; "SS A.H. an Führerhauptquartier," December 1, 1941, T-314/186/000294.

58. Keitel, *Memoirs*, p. 161.

59. Warlimont, *Hilter's Headquarters*, pp. 212, 222-23.

60. "Eichenlaub für Sepp Dietrich," BDC/130.

61. *Hitler's Secret Conversations*, pp. 178-79.

62. Ulrich von Hassell, *Vom Andern Deutschland*, pp. 218-19.

63. *Goebbels Diaries*, pp. 51-52.

64. Gottlob Berger to Heinrich Himmler, January 22, 1942. T-175/108/2631503-4; Richard Hildebrandt to Heinrich Himmler, May ?, 1942, T-175/108/2631498.

65. SS-Führungshauptamt, "Aufstellung einer Panzer Abteilung für die LSSAH," January 30, 1942, T-175/108/2631615-17.

66. Reichsjugendführung, Hauptamt I, "Nachwuchs für die Leibstandarte SS Adolf Hitler," November 18, 1941, T-175/108/2632300.

67. SS-Führungshauptamt, "Gliederung der LSSAH," February 21, 1942, T-175/108/2631569 ff.: Meyer, *Grenadiere*, p. 159.

68. Albert Speer, *Inside the Third Reich*, pp. 189 ff.

69. *SS-Panzer Grenadier Division Leibstandarte Adolf Hitler, Kreigstagebuch Nr. 5 Ia vom 16.12.1941-16.7.1942*, T-354/611/000502; Mackensen, *Vom Bug zum Kaukasus*, pp. 55–56.

70. Leibstandarte SS Adolf Hitler, Abt. IVa, Tätigkeitsbericht als Beilage zum Kriegstagebuch der Abt. Ib/LSSAH, "Ostfeldzug vom 1. Juli 1941–31 Dezember 1941," p. 9, T-354/611/000829; Dozent Dr. E. G. Schenk, "Ein Jahr Osteinsatz bei der Leibstandarte SS Adolf Hitler," pp. 20 ff., T-354/612/000110 ff.

71. Mackensen, *Vom Bug zum Kaukasus*, p. 158.

72. Meyer, *Grenadiere*, p. 159; *LSSAH, KTB Nr. 5 Ia*, entry for June 9, 1942. T-354/611/000634.

73. SS-Führungshauptamt, "Aufstellung des VII./LSSAH," February 14, 1942, T-175/108/2631605–6; SS-Führungshauptamt, Tgb. Nr. 8141/42 geh., December 4, 1942, T-175/108/2631427; Klietmann, *Die Waffen-SS*, p. 441.

74. *Kriegstagebuch Nr. 1, V./Leibstandarte SS Adolf Hitler, 21 Februar 1942-10 Juni 1942*, pp. 2, 14, T-354/610/000626, 000639.

75. Ibid., p. 6, T-354/610/000630.

76. Ibid, p. 48, T-354/610/000673.

77. Warlimont, *Hitler's Headquarters*, p. 247.

78. Ibid.; *LSSAH, KTB Nr. 5 Ia*, entry for July 11, 1942, T-354/611/000648.

79. *Kriegstagebuch Nr. 6, Leibstandarte SS Adolf Hilter, 16.7.1942–9.1.1943*, entry for July 29, 1942, T-354/611/000699.

80. Dietrich to Himmler, Dec. 17, 1941, BDC/121. *LSSAH, KTB Nr. 6 Ia*, entry for October 21, 1942, T-354/611/000699.

81. *SS-Leitheft* 9 (January 1943), 20.

82. Klietmann, *Die Waffen-SS*, pp. 59, 81, 92, 112: *LSSAH, KTB Nr. 6 Ia*, cover sheet, T-354/611/000659.

83. Ibid., T-354/611/000674 ff.

84. Ibid., entry for October 9, 1942, T-354/611/000691; OB West to SS-Gen. Kdo. (Pz.), October 2, 1942, T-354/116/3750378.

85. *LSSAH, KTB Nr. 6 Ia*, entry for October 22, 1942, T-354/611/000699; George Stein, *The Waffen-SS*, pp. 202–3.

86. *Kriegstagebuch SS-Generalkommandos (Pz.), 2. Teil*, entry for October 28, 1942, T-354/116/3750230; SS-Führungshauptamt, ''Aufstellung einer schweren Panzer-Kompanie für das SS-Panzer-Regiment der SS-Div. LSSAH,'' November 13, 1942, T-175/108/2631551–52; Heinz Guderian, *Erinnerungen eines Soldaten*, p. 254.

87. Klietmann, *Die Waffen-SS*, p. 79.

88. Philippi and Heim, *Der Feldzug*, p. 181.

89. *KTB Nr. 3, Gen. Kdo. SS Pz. Krops*, entry for December 30, 1942, T-354/117/3751122.

8 KHARKOV AND KURSK

1. SS Panzer Corps had been initially earmarked for a last desperate attempt to rescue Paulus' army. See Alfred Philippi and Ferdinand Heim, *Der Feldzug gegen Sowjetrussland*, p. 204.

2. Ibid., pp. 201 ff; F. W. von Mellenthin, *Panzer Battles*, p. 206.

3. *KTB Nr. 4, Gen. Kdo, SS-Pz. Korps*, T-354/118/3751478; K. G. Klietmann, *Die Waffen-SS, eine Dokumentation*, p. 114.

4. Fernschreiben, Hr. Gr. B to SS Pz. Korps, February 2, 1943, T-354/118/3751502.

5. Armee Abt. Lanz to Gen. Kdo. SS Pz. Korps, February 14, 1943, T-354/118/3751658; Gen. Kdo. SS Pz. Korps to SS-Führungshauptamt, February 19, 1943, T-354/118/3751719; Eric von Manstein, *Verlorene Siege*, p. 453.

6. Philippi and Heim, *Der Feldzug*, p. 204.

7. Otto Kumm, ''Die Dritte Schlacht um Charkow,'' *Der Freiwillige* 14 (May 1968), 11/12; Eddy Bauer, *Der Panzerkrieg*, 1:242.

8. Bauer, *Panzerkrieg*, 1:242.

9. *Gen. Kdo.* SS Pz. Korps to Reichsführer-SS, February 26, 1943, T-354/118/3751886.

10. Mellenthin, *Panzer Battles*, p. 208. An index of the ferocity of combat is Leibstandarte's claim to have killed six hundred Russians during February while having taken five prisoners. Leibstandarte to Gen. Kdo. SS Pz. Korps, March 2, 1943, T-354/118/3752046–47.

11. Kumm, "Die Dritte Schlacht," p. 15; Gen. Kdo. SS Pz. Korps, "Korpsbefehl Nr. 8," T-354/118/3752256.

12. Kumm, "Die Dritte Schlacht," p. 15.

13. "Ia-Tagesmeldung," March 11, 1943, T-354/118/3752293.

14. LSSAH to Gen. Kdo. SS Pz. Korps, March 12, 1943, T-354/118/3752308; Kumm, "Die Dritte Schlacht," p. 15.

15. "Sondermeldung aus dem Führerhauptquartier," March 14, 1943, T-354/118/3752364.

16. Bauer, *Panzerkrieg*, 1:242.

17. SS-Pz.-Korps to Leibstandarte, "Auftrag für 13.3," T-354/118/3752314.

18. *Goebbels Diaries*, p. 300.

19. "Die Schwerter für Obergruppenführer Sepp Dietrich. Wie die Leibstandarte Charkow eroberte," BDC/13 ff.

20. Gen. Kdo. I. SS Pz. Korps, "Tätigkeitsbericht der Abteilung IIa für die Zeit vom 1.4/30.4.43," p. 4, T-354/603/000056.

21. Milton Shulman, *Defeat in the West*, p. 104.

22. George Stein, *The Waffen-SS*, p. 205; cf. Klietmann, *Die Waffen-SS*, p. 181.

23. Kurt Meyer, *Grenadiere*, pp. 204–8; BDC/16; Klietmann, *Die Waffen-SS*, p. 59.

24. Himmler to Dietrich, June 22, 1943, BDC/171.

25. Himmler to Dietrich, June 23, 1943, BDC/173.

26. See biographical sketch of Kraemer in "I SS Panzer Corns in the West," NAMS C-048.

27. *Kriegstagebuch nr. 1, Gen. Kdo. I. SS-Pz. Korps "Leibstandarte SS Adolf Hitler,"* entry for July 27, 1943, T-354/603/000528.

28. *Kriegstagebuch Nr. 5, Generalkommando I. SS-Pz. Kps.*, entries for the period March 27–April 6, 1943, T-354/603/000003–5.

29. Ibid., entry for March 27.

30. Paul Karl Schmidt [Paul Carell], *Scorched Earth: The Russian-German War, 1943–1944*, p. 199.

31. *KTB Nr. 5, Gen. Kdo. I SS-Pz. Kps.*, entry for April 16, 1943, T-354/603/000011.

32. Gen Kdo. SS Pz. Kps., "Personelle Vorratstaktik," April 12, 1943, T-354/603/000248; "II./2. Pz. Gren. Rgt. an der Einheitsführer," April 18, 1943, T-354/624/000743.

33. *KTB Nr. 5, Gen. Kdo. I SS-Pz. Kps.*, entry for April 16, 1943, T-354/603/000011 and Gen. Kdo. SS-Panzer Korps, "Zusammenstellung der Ist-, Verpflegungs- und Gefechts-stärken mit Stand vom 21.4.43," T-354/603/000088.

34. Philippi and Heim. *Der Feldzug*, pp. 208–10.

35. "Unternehmen 'Zitadelle' (Vorbereitung)," T-354/603/000094 ff.; Earl F. Ziemke, *Stalingrad to Berlin*, pp. 124–33; Philippi and Heim, *Der Feldzug*, pp. 210–11; Gotthard Heinrici and Friedrich Wilhelm Hauck, "Zitadelle (II)," *Wehrwissenschaftliche Rundschau* 15 (September 1965), 529-31, 537.

36. Heinrici and Hauck, "Zitadelle," pp. 542–43; Schmidt, *Scorched Earth*, p. 24.

37. Generalkommando SS-Panzer-Krops, "Personelle Vorratstaktik," April 12, 1943, T-354/603/000248–49.

38. Ziemke, *Stalingrad to Berlin*, pp. 133–35; Mellenthin, *Panzer Battles*, p. 217.

39. *LSSAH, Kriegstagebuch der Abteilung Ib, 1.4.1943–10.6.1943*, entry for July 5, 1943, T-354/612/000016.

40. Ibid., entry for July 6, 1943, T-354/612/000017; Schmidt, *Scorced Earth*, p. 66.

41. *KTB, Abt. Ib*, entires for July 8–9, 1943, T-354/612/000019–20.

42. Ibid., entry for July 10, 1943, T-354/612/000021.

43. Ibid., entry for July 12, 1943, T-354/612/000023.

44. Schmidt, *Scorched Earth*, p. 79.

45. *KTB, Abt. Ib*, entry for July 14, 1943, T-354/612/000025; Ziemke, *Stalingrad to Berlin*, p. 136; Bauer, *Panzerkrieg*, 2:20–21; Manstein, *Verlorene Siege*, p. 504.

46. Manstein, *Verlorene Siege*, pp. 501–2.

47. *Chronology of the Second World War* (London: Royal Institute of International Affairs, 1945), pp. 193–94.

48. Walter Warlimont, *Inside Hitler's Headquarters*, p. 319.

49. *KTB, Abt Ib*, entires for July 21–28, T-354/612/ 000032–39; *Kriegstagebuch Nr. 11, Pz. AOK 1, Ia*, entry for July 18, 1943, U. S. National Archives Microfilm Publication, "Records of German Field Commands—Panzer Armies," T-313/58/793622 f.; Manstein, *Verlorene Siege*, p. 503; Philippi and Heim, *Der Feldzug*, p. 212; Schmidt, *Scorched Earth*, p. 93; Klietmann, *Die Waffen-SS*, p. 93.

50. "Besprechung des Führers mit Feldmarschall von Kluge am 26. Juli 1943," *Hitlers Lagebesprechungen*, pp. 379–80; Warlimont, *Hitler's Headquarters*, pp. 356–57; Paul Hausser, *Soldaten wie andere auch*, p. 111; Klietmann, *Die Waffen-SS*, p. 61.

51. *Kriegstagebuch Nr. 1, Gen. Kdo. I. SS-Pz. Korps, "Leibstandarte SS Adolf Hitler,"* entry for July 27, 1943, T-354/603/000528; Klietmann, *Die Waffen-SS*, p. 85.

52. Himmler to Dietrich, August 30, 1943, BDC/176. See Shulman, *Defeat in the West*, p. 63.

53. Gilbert A. Shepperd, *The Italian Campaign, 1943–45* (London: Barker 1968), pp. 63–65; Heeres Gruppe B, Ic, "Beurteilung der Lage," July 30, 1943, T-311/276/000007–8.

54. Hr. Gr. B, Ic, "Anlage zum Tätigkeitsbericht der Abt. Ic," August 11, 1943, T-311/276/000021; *KTB Nr. 1, Gen. Kdo. I. SS Pz. Kps. "Leibstandarte,"* entry for August 17, 1943, T-354/603/000530.

55. Hr. Gr. B, Ic, "Anlage zum Tätigkeitsbericht der Abt. Ic," August 25, 1943, T-311/276/000033–34.

56. Enno von Rintelen, *Mussolini als Bundgenosse*, p. 242; F. W. Deakin, *The Brutal Friendship*, pp. 512–13.

57. Hr. Gr. B, "Anlage zum Tätigkeitsbericht der Abt. Ic, Abschlussbericht der Entwaffnungsaktion in Nord Italien," September 19, 1943, T-311/276/000065–67; "Besonderes Feindnachrichtenblatt," September 22, 1943, T-311/276/000084–86; Stellungnahme des Einheitsführer," n.d., T-354/624/0000363; Klietmann, *Die Waffen-SS*, p. 80.

58. *KTB Nr. 1, Gen. Kdo. I. SS Pz. Kps. "Leibstandarte."* entry for October 20, 1943, T-354/603/000536.

9 CRISES ON THE DNIEPER

1. Earl F. Ziemke, *Stalingrad to Berlin*. pp. 151–73; Alfred Philippe and Ferdinand Heim, *Der Feldzug gegen Sowjet-*

russland, pp. 212 ff; F. W. von Mellenthin, *Panzer Battles*, pp. 235–41.

2. Eric von Manstein, *Verlorene Siege*, pp. 541–45.

3. Ziemke, *Stalingrad to Berlin*, p. 181; Manstein, *Verlorene Siege*, p. 549.

4. *KTB Nr. 1, Gen. Kdo. I. SS Pz. Kps. "Leibstandarte,"* entry for October 28, 1943, November 4, 1943, T-354/603/000538; Ziemke, *Stalingrad to Berlin*, p. 182.

5. *KTB Nr. 1, Gen. Kdo. I. SS Pz. Kps. "Leibstandarte,"* entry for October 28, 1943, T-354/603/000536; ibid., entry for November 11, 1943, T-354/603/000540.

6. Ibid., entry for December 11, 1943, T-354/603/000544; Gen. Kdo. I. SS-Panzer Korps "Leibstandarte SS Adolf Hitler," "Korpsbefehl," December 24, 1943, T-354/603/000559–60; K. G. Klietmann, *Die Waffen-SS, eine Dokumentation*, p. 166.

7. Engagement list of 1. SS-Pz. Div. "Liebstandarte-SS Adolf Hilter," p. 2, T-354/623/000096.

8. Eddy Bauer, *Der Panzerkrieg*, 2:33; Manstein, *Verlorene Siege*, p. 550.

9. Manstein, *Verlorene Siege*, pp. 551–52.

10. Ziemke, *Stalingrad to Berlin*, pp. 184–85.

11. Manstein, *Verlorene Siege*, p. 555.

12. Ziemke, *Stalingrad to Berlin*, p. 186.

13. Mellenthin, *Panzer Battles*, pp. 253 ff.

14. Bauer, *Panzerkrieg*, 2:36.

15. Mellenthin, *Panzer Battles*, pp. 255–56.

16. Ibid., p. 256.

17. *German Defense Tactics* (Washington, 1951), pp. 15–19; Mellenthin, *Panzer Battles*, p. 261.

18. Ziemke, *Stalingrad to Berlin*, p. 188.

19. Ibid., p. 189; Mellenthin, *Panzer Battles*, p. 261.

20. Ziemke, *Stalingrad to Berlin*, p. 189.

21. Mellenthin, *Panzer Battles*, p. 263.

22. Philippi and Heim, *Der Feldzug*, p. 230; Manstein, *Verlorene Siege*, pp. 565 ff.; Bauer, *Panzerkrieg*, 2:41.

23. Manstein, *Verlorene Siege*, pp. 567 f.

24. Ziemke, *Stalingrad to Berlin*, pp. 224 ff.

25. Otto Weidinger, *Kameraden bis zum End*, p. 231.

26. Ziemke, *Stalingrad to Berlin*, p. 226.

27. Paul Karl Schmidt [Paul Carell], *Scorched Earth*, pp.

299 ff.; Bauer, *Panzerkrieg*, 2:45; Ziemke, *Stalingrad to Berlin*, p. 228.

28. Manstein, *Verlorene Siege*, pp. 582–86; Schmidt, *Scorched Earth*, pp. 399–433. For a vivid description of SS-Brigade Wallonien at Cherkassy, see Leon Degrelle, *Die verlorene Legion* (Stuttgart: Veritas Verlag, 1952), pp. 225–322.

29. "II/2. Panzer-Grenadier Regiment an 2. Pz. Gr. Rgt. LSSAH," March 4, 1944, T-354/623/000073.

30. Schmidt, *Scorched Earth*, p. 436; Ziemke, *Stalingrad to Berlin*, p. 273.

31. Ziemke, *Stalingrad to Berlin*, p. 276.

32. "Funksprüche aus dem Abwehrkampf der Leibstandarte·SS Adolf Hitler u. der 7. Panz. Division," p. 4, T-354/623/000010.

33. Ibid., pp. 6 ff., T-354/623/000012 ff.

34. Manstein, *Verlorene Siege*, pp. 610–13; Klietmann, *Die Waffen-SS*, p. 80.

35. Bauer, *Panzerkrieg*, 2:58; Schmidt, *Scorched Earth*, p. 454.

36. Walter Warlimont, *Inside Hitler's Headquarters*, p. 419; Manstein, *Verlorene Siege*, pp 615–16.

10 INVASION FRONT

1. Fritz Kraemer, "I. SS Panzer Corps in the West in 1944," NAMS, C-024, p. 4.

2. The most critical shortages were of commissioned and noncommissioned officers. See *Heeres Gruppe D (Ob. West), Anlagen zum Kriegstagebuch Ia*, May 1–15, 1944, "Stand der Neuaufstellungen," p. 11, T-311/24/7028288; Walter Warlimont, *Inside Hitler's Headquarters*, p. 414.

3. *Heeres Gruppe D, Kriegstagebuch Ia*, May 1–31, 1944, entry for May 3, 1944, T-311/24/7028083; Leibstandarte SS Adolf Hilter, "Divisionssonderbefehl," April 22, 1944, T-354/622/001084–86.

4. *Heeresgruppe D, Kriegstagebuch Ia*, June 1–5, 1944, entry for June 4, 1944, T-311/24/7029030; ibid., June 6–30, 1944, entry for June 6, 1944, T-311/24/7029187.

5. Ibid., T-311/24/7029190; II./Panzer Gren. Rgt. 2, LAH, Alarmplan!," T-354/622/001130.

6. Chester Wilmot, *The Struggle for Europe*, p. 196n2; p. 274n1.

7. *KTB, Hr. Gr. D*, June 6–30, entry for June 7, T-311/24/7029194.

8. Ibid., T-311/24/7029195.

9. Lionel F. Ellis, *Victory in the West*, I: 228–29; Wilmot, *Struggle for Europe*, pp. 296–97.

10. *KTB, Hr. Gr. D*, entry for June 7, 1944, T-311/24/7029195.

11. Ibid., entry for June 8, 1944, T-311/24/7029199; Wilmot, *Struggle for Europe*, p. 299.

12. See, for example, the statement of Lieutenant-General Bodo Zimmermann, Chief of Operations, OB West, in *OB West. A Study in Command*, 1:98–99.

13. *KTB, Hr. Gr. D*, entry for June 8, 1944, T-311/24/7029201; Otto Weidinger, *Kameraden bis zum Ende*, pp. 277 ff.

14. Panzergruppe West was organized on June 8 and given responsibility for the sector of the front between the Dives and Tilly. Friedrich Hayn, *Die Invasion*, p. 44. See also: *Kriegstagebuch Panzer-Armeeoberkommando 5 (Panzergruppe West) Ia, 1. Teil*, entry for June 10, 1944, T-313/420/8713531; Hans Speidel, *Invasion 1944*, p. 88; Wilmot, *Struggle for Europe*, p. 303.

15. *KTB, Hr. Gr. D*, entry for June 11, 1944, T-311/24/7029215, 7029217.

16. E. Belfield and H. Essame, *The Battle for Normandy*, pp. 46 ff.

17. Ibid., p. 87; Hayn, *Die Invasion*, p. 51.

18. *KTB, Hr. Gr. D*, entry for June 12, 1944, T-311/24/7029221; Wilmot, *Struggle for Europe*, p. 308.

19. Paul Karl Schmidt [Paul Carell], *Invasion—They're Coming!*, pp. 168–73; Wilmot, *Struggle for Europe*, p. 310; Ellis, *Victory in the West*, 1:256. "Ein kühner Tigerprüfung," *SS-Leitheft* 10, no. 11, p. 6.

20. Kraemer, NAMS, C-024, p. 38; *SS-Leitheft* 10 (October 1944), 7–8; K. G. Klietmann, *Die Waffen-SS, eine Dokumentation*, p. 185.

21. *KTB, Hr. Gr. D*, entry for June 13, 1944, T-311/24/7029228.

22. Wilmot, *Struggle for Europe*, p. 319.

23. Belfield and Essame, *Battle for Normandy*, pp. 91 ff.

24. Wilmot, *Struggle for Europe*, pp. 333, 335n/; cf. Speidel, *Invasion 1944*, pp. 93 ff.

25. "Befehl für die Ausladung und Versammlung der Division." June 19, 1944, T-354/622/001117.

26. OB West to Panzergruppe West, June 21, 1944, T-313/420/8713755.

27. Pz. AOK 5, "Besprechung am 24.6.44 Montmerrey," T-313/420/8713758 f.

28. George Stein, *The Waffen-SS*, pp. 277–78.

29. "Der schwere Kampf der SS-Panzer Division 'Hitler Jugend,'" *SS Leitheft* 10 (October 1944), 9–10.

30. *KTB, Pz. AOK 5*, entries for June 22 and June 26, 1944, T-313/420/8713533-34; Wilmot, *Struggle for Europe*, p. 342.

31. *KTB, Pz. AOK 5*, entry for June 28, 1944, T-313/420/8713534.

32. Ibid., entry for June 29, 1944, T-313/420/8713535-36.

33. Ibid.

34. Ibid.; cf. Hayn, *Die Invasion*, p. 70.

35. *KTB, Pz. AOK 5*, entry for June 29, 1944, T-313/420/8713535-36.

36. Ibid., entries for June 29–30, T-313/420/8713536-37.

37. *KTB, Hr. Gr. D*, entry for June 30, 1944, T-311/24/7029313; *KTB, Pz. AOK 5*, entry for June 30, 1944, T-313/420/8713537.

38. *KTB*/OKW IV, 322; Warlimont, *Hitler's Headquarters*, p. 435.

39. Wilmot, *Struggle for Europe*, p. 350.

40. *KTB, Pz. AOK 5*, entry for July 1, 1944, T-313/420/8713537-38.

41. Belfield and Essame, *Battle for Noramndy*, p. 115.

42. *KTB, Pz. AOK 5*, entry for July 2, 1944, T-313/420/8713538.

43. Ibid., entires for July 4–5, 1944, T-313/420/8713540-41.

44. Ibid., entry for July 6, 1944, T-313/420/8713541; Wilmot, *Struggle for Europe*, p. 351.

45. *KTB*/OKW, IV, 322, *KTB, Pz. AOK 5*, entry for July 8, 1944, T-313/420/8713542-43; "Ferngespräch Feld-

marschall v. Kluge mit Gen. d. Inf. Blumentritt,'' July 9, 1944, *KTB, Hr. Gr. D, Anlagen,* T-311/28/7034343-44.

46. Situation Report, July 11, 1944, *KTB, Hr. Gr. D, Anlagen,* T-311/28/7034369 f.; Situation Report, n.d., ibid., T-311/28/7034404 ff.

47. ''Bericht; über die Frontfahrt des Gen. Feldm. v. Kluge am 14.7.44 zur Panzergruppe West u. I. SS-Pz. Korps,'' ibid., T-311/28/7034537 ff.

48. Ibid., T-311/28/7034540; *KTB, Pz. AOK 5,* entry for July 11, 1944, T-313/420/8713546; *KTB/OKW,* IV, 326.

49. Speidel, *Invasion 1944,* pp. 102-3; Wilmot, *Struggle for Europe,* p. 351.

50. Panzer Lehr and 2nd SS Panzer Division ''Das Reich'' had already been moved to Bradley's front. *KTB/OKW,* IV, 324. See also: Ellis, *Victory in the West,* 1: 327-28; Belfield and Essame, *Battle for Normandy,* pp. 133-34.

51. *KTB, Pz. AOK 5,* entry for July 16, 1944, T-313/420/8713549; *KTB/OKW* IV, 325.

52. *KTB, Pz. AOK 5,* entry for July 16, 1944, T-313/420/8713550; Wilmot, *Struggle for Europe,* p. 357.

53. *KTB, Pz. AOK 5,* entry for July 17, 1944, T-313/420/8713550.

54. ''Ferngespräch Feldmarschall v. Kluge—Gen. Speidel, Zeit 21.00 bis 21.15 Uhr,'' July 17, 1944, *KTB, Hr. Gr. D, Anlagen,* T-311/28/7034560-62.

55. ''Der Oberbefehlshaber West an OKW/Wehrmachtführungsstab,'' July 17, 1944, *KTB, Hr. Gr. D, Anlagen,* T-311/28/7034586 ff.; *KTB, Pz. AOK 5,* entry for July 18, 1944, T-313/420/8713551.

56. *KTB, Pz. AOK 5,* entry for July 18, 1944 T-313/420/8713552; Wilmot, *Struggle for Europe,* pp. 358-60.

57. *KTB, Pz. AOK 5,* entry for July 19, 1944, T-313/420/8713552-53.

58. Ibid.; *KTB, Panzergruppe West,* ''Anlage 177,'' July 24, 1944, T-313/420/8713994; Belfield and Essame, *Battle for Normandy,* pp. 145-46.

59. Kraemer, NAMS, C-024, Appendix 2, p. 40.

60. Idib.; *KTB/OKW* IV, 326.

61. *KTB, Pz. AOK 5,* entry for July 19, 1944, T-313/420/8713553; ''Fernschreiben, Ob. West an OKW/WFSt/Op. (H)/

West,'' July 23, 1944, *KTB, Hr. Gr. D, Analgen*, T-311/28/
7034761 ff.

62. "Ferngespräch Feldmarschall v. Kluge—Gen. Eberbach, Zeit 18.00 bis 18.30 Uhr,'' *KTB, Hr. Gr. D. Anlagen*,
T-311/28/7034764 ff.

63. Gen. Kdo. I. SS-Panzerkorps "Leibstandarte SS Adolf
Hitler,'' "Tagesbefehl,'' July 24, 1944, T-354/604/000370.

64. Kraemer, NAMS, C-024, Appendix 2, p. 40.

65. "Divisions-Sonderbefehl,'' April 22, 1944, p. 2,
T-354/622/001084–86.

66. Hedwig Maier, "Die SS und der 20. Juli 1944,'' *Vierteljahrshefte für Zeitgeschichte 14* (July 1966), 305.

67. An Interview with Obstgrf. "Sepp'' Dietrich, 8–9
Aug. 1945, NAMS, ETHINT 15, pp. 5–6.

68. *KTB, Pz. AOK 5*, entry for July 25, 1944, T-313/420/
8713559.

69. "Fernschreiben, Ob. West an OKW/WFSt/Op.(H)/
West,'' July 26, 1944, *KTB, Hr. Gr. D, Anlagen*, T-311/28/
7034811 ff.; Martin Blumenson, *Breakout and Pursuit*, p. 195.

70. "Ferngespräch Feldmarschall v. Kluge—Gen. d. Inf.
Blumentritt Zeit: 10.23 bis 10.28 Uhr,'' July 31, 1944,
T-311/28/7034950–51.

71. "KR-Blitz, OKW/WFSt/Op.(H) West Nr. 772701/
44,'' August 3, 1944, *KTB, Hr. Gr. D, Anlagen*, T-311/28/
7035065–66.

72. *KTB, Pz. AOK 5*, entry for August 3, 1944, T-313/
420/871358 f.

73. "Anruf OKW/WFSt/Gen. Major Frh. v. Buttlar,''
August 3, 1944, *KTB, Hr. Gr. D, Anlagen*, T-311/28/7035089.

74. Theodor Wisch, "Attitude to the Questionnaire Con-
cerning the Commitment of LAH in August 1944,'' NAMS,
B-358, p. 2; "15.25 Uhr Anruf Gen. Oberst Jodl bei Chef
des Gen. St. Ob. West,'' August 6, 1944, *KTB, Hr. Gr. D,
Anlagen*, T-311/28/7035204 ff.; "Fernschreiben, Ob. West an
OKW/WFSt/Op.(H)/West,'' August 7, 1944, *KTB, Hr. Gr.
D, Anlagen*, T-311/28/7035214 ff.; Blumenson, *Breakout and
Pursuit*, p. 462; Hayn, *Die Invasion*, p. 100.

75. Hayn, *Die Invasion*, p. 101; "Fernschreiben, Ob. West
an OKW/WFSt/Op.(H)/West,'' August 8, 1944, *KTB, Hr.
Gr. D, Anlagen*, T-311/28/7035262 ff.

76. *KTB/OKW IV*, 339.

77. Ibid., p. 440; Blumenson, *Breakout and Pursuit*, p. 464.

78. BDC/228.

79. Wilmot, *Struggle for Europe*, pp. 412–13.

80. *KTB, Pz. AOK 5*, entry for August 8, 1944, T-313/ 420/8713599.

81. Quoted in Belfield and Essame, *Battle for Normandy*, p. 201.

82. *KTB, Pz. AOK 5*, entries for August 8, 1944, T-313/ 420/8713601, 8713605.

83. Ibid., entry for August 8, 1944, T-313/420/8713602–4; Wilmot, *Struggle for Europe*, p. 412.

84. Belfield and Essame, *Battle for Normandy*, p. 202; *KTB, Pz. AOK 5, Teil II*, entry for August 9, 1944, T-313/ 420/8713616.

85. Blumenson, *Breakout and Pursuit*, p. 481.

86. Ibid.; pp. 483–84.

87. *KTB/OKW*, IV, 340

88. Ibid., p. 341.

89. Blumenson, *Breakout and Pursuit*, pp. 503–5.

90. Ibid.

91. Quoted in ibid, p. 505.

92. *KTB, Pz. AOK 5, II*, entry for August 13, 1944, T-313/420/8713621.

93. *KTB/OKW* IV, 343–44.

94. Quoted in Wilmot, *Struggle for Europe*, p.417.

95. Blumenson, *Breakout and Pursuit*, pp. 506–9.

96. Belfield and Essame, *Battle for Normandy*, p.211.

97. *KTB, Pz. AOK 5, II*, entry for August 14, 1944, T-313/420/8713622–24.

98. Ibid., entry for August 15, 1944, T-313/420/8713625.

99. Ibid., entries for August 15–16, 1944, T-313/420/ 8713626–27.

100. Ibid., entry for August 17, 1944, T-313/420/8713629; Wilmot, *Struggle for Europe*, p. 419; Hayn, *Die Invasion*, p. 111; Schmidt, *Invasion*, p. 292.

101. Blumenson, *Breakout and Pursuit*, p. 518; Hayn, *Die Invasion*, p. 111.

102. *KTB, Pz. AOK 5, II*, entries for August 17–18, 1944, T-313/420/8713630–32; *KTB/OKW* IV, 346–47.

103. *KTB, Pz. AOK 5, II*, entry for August 18, 1944,

T-313/420/8713631–32; Blumenson, *Breakout and Pursuit*, p. 523.

104. Hayn, *Die Invasion*, p. 120; Blumenson, *Breakout and Pursuit*, p. 549.

105. Blumenson, *Breakout and Pursuit*, pp. 573–74.

106. *KTB, Pz. AOK 5, II*, entry for August 20, 1944, T-313/420/8713634.

107. Schmidt, *Invasion*, p. 297.

108. Blumenson, *Breakout and Pursuit*, pp. 576–77; *KTB/ OKW IV*, 358.

109. *KTB, Pz. AOK 5, II*, entries for August 21, 1944, T-313/420/8713634–36.

110. Ibid., T-313/420/8713636–37; *KTB/OKW, IV*, 359.

111. *KTB, Pz. AOK 5*, "Anlage 44," SS-Standartenführer Wilhelm Mohnke to Dietrich, August 24, 1944, T-313/420/ 8714224–25; Generalkommando I. SS-Panzer-Korps "Leibstandarte," Ia, Tgb. Nr. 1236/44 g. Kdos., August 24, 1944, T-354/604/000180–81.

112. *KTB, Pz. AOK 5, II*, entry for August 23, 1944, T-313/420/8713640–41.

113. Ibid., T-313/420/8713642; *Anlage 44*, T-313/420/ 8714224–25.

114. The war diary of 5th Panzer Army claims that 25,000 vehicles were ferried to safety, but this is probably an exaggeration. *KTB, Pz. AOK 5, II*, entry for August 25, 1944, T-313/420/8713646.

115. Ibid., T-313/420/8713645.

116. Quoted in Wilmot, *Struggle for Europe*, p. 434.

117. *KTB, Pz. AOK 5, II*, entry for August 25, 1944, T-313/420/8713645–46.

118. Ibid., entry for August 28, 1944, T-313/420/8713650; "Anlage 50," n.d., T-313/420/8714231.

119. *KTB, Pz. AOK 5, II*, entry for August 28, 1944, T-313/420/8713650; "Anlage 57," Panzer-Armeeoberkommando 5 Abt. Ia Nr. 1054/44 g. Kdos., T-313/420/8714239.

120. *KTB/OKW IV*, 363; *KTB, Pz. AOK 5*, "Anlage 67," n.d., T-313/420/8714251; *KTB, Pz. AOK 5*, entry for August 31, 1944, T-313/420/8713654.

121. *KTB, Pz. AOK 5*, "Anlage 80," Model to Pz. AOK 5, September 4, 1944, T-313/420/8714264–65; Blumenson,

Breakout and Pursuit, p. 678; Walimont, *Hitler's Headquarters*, pp. 475–76.

122. *KTB, Pz. AOK 5*, "Anlage 79," Obkdo. H. Gr. B to Pz. AOK 5, September 4, 1944, T-313/420/8714263; *KTB, Pz. AOK 5, Teil III*, entry for September 11, 1944, T-313/420/8713663.

11 ARDENNES

1. *KTB/OKW IV*, 345; Walter Warlimont, *Inside Hitler's Headquarters*, p. 476; K. G. Klietmann, *Die Waffen-SS, eine Dokumentation*, p. 55.

2. Charles B. MacDonald, *The Siegfried Line Campaign*, pp. 300, 301, 304.

3. An Interview with Obstgrf. "Sepp" Dietrich, 10 July, 1945, NAMS, ETHINT 16, p. 1; An Interview with Genmaj. (W-SS) Fritz Kraemer, 14–15 August, 1945, NAMS, ETHINT 21, p. 1; *KTB/OKW IV*, 385.

4. "Mittagslage vom 12 Dezember, 1942," *Hitlers Lagebesprechungen*, p. 97.

5. Georg Keppler, NAMS, B-623, p. 25.

6. Klietmann, *Die Waffen-SS*, p. 85.

7. Fritz Kraemer, "Commitment of 6 Panzer Army," NAMS, A-924, p. 5.

8. General der Panzertruppen West, "Notiz über Besprechungen in Berlin," October 14, 1944, T-311/18/7020017.

9. Fritz Kraemer, "I SS Panzer Corps in the West," NAMS, C-048, p. 17.

10. See personnel records of SS Pz. Gren. Rgt. 2, T-354/622/000762 ff.

11. 1.SS Pz. Div. Leibstandarte, "Ausbildungsplan für die Zeit vom 23.10–20.11.44," pp. 1–2, T-354/615/000811–18; "Keiner dünke sich besser," *Politische Wochenschau, Informationsdienst der Abt. VI, LSSAH*, November 29, 1944, pp. 1–2, T-354/624/000588–89.

12. "Warum sind sie uns nicht gewachsen?," *Politische Wochenschau*, December 6, 1944, T-354/625/000145–46; "So haust der Feind," *Politische Wochenschau*, November 29, 1944, T-354/624/000590.

13. Mohnke would be promoted to the rank of SS-Oberführer on November 4, 1944. *Dienstaltersliste der Schutzstaffel der NSDAP. SS-Oberst Gruppenführer—SS-*

Standartenführer, Stand vom 9. November, 1944 (Berlin, 1944), P. 31.

14. 1. SS Panser Division LSSAH, "Der Kommandeur, an alle Kompanien," October 18, 1944 [two documents]. T-354/615/000808-10. T-354/625/000218-20.

15. Kraemer, NAMS, A-924, p. 6; Rudolf Lehmann, "Ardennes," NAMS, B-577, p. 2.

16. Lehmann, "Ardennes," NAMS B-577, pp. 6-7.

17. General der Panzertruppen West, "Notiz über Besprechungen in Berlin," October 14, 1944, T-311/17/7020017.

18. Kraemer, NAMS, A-924, enclosure 2; Rodolf Lehmann, "The I. SS Panzer Corps during the Ardennes Offensive," NAMS, B-779, pp. 13-14.

19. Hugh M. Cole, *The Ardennes*, pp. 1-2.

20. "Befehl für den Aufmarsch und die Bereitstellungen zum Angriff," OKH, Nr. 31/44 g. K. Chefs. St. WFST/Op. (H), November 10, 1944, P. 1, T-311/18/7020270-79.

21. Ibid., pp. 1-2.

22. Ibid., pp. 2, 4.

23. Ibid., pp. 2-3, 6, 7.

24. "Planspiel des I./SS-Pz. Gren. Rgt. 2 'LSSAH' am 22.10.," T-354/624/000523-25; "Lage zum Planspiel am 26. October 1944," T-354/624/000514; "Lösungsvorschlag zu Teil II zum Planspiel des I./SS Panz. Rgt. 2 am 29.10.1944," T-354/624/000530-31; "Lösungsvorschlag für Beurteilung der lage, Planspiel am 2.11.1944," T-354/624/000503-4.

25. An Interview with Obstgrf. "Sepp" Dietrich, NAMS, ETHINT 15, p. 5.

26. Kraemer, NAMS, A-924, p. 8; NAMS, ETHINT 21, pp. 1, 3.

27. Cole, *The Ardennes*, p. 31.

28. NAMS, ETHINT 16, pp. 2-3.

29. OKW to OB West, December 12, 1944, T-311/18/7020693-95; Cole, *The Ardennes*, P. 69; cf. Jacques Nobecourt, *Hitler's Last Gamble*, p. 122: NAMS, ETHINT 16, p. 3.

30. Kraemer, NAMS, A-924, pp. 1-2.

31. OKW to OB West, December 11, 1944, T-311/18/7020583-85.

32. Kraemer, NAMS, A-924, pp. 16-18.

33. The most recent study is that of John Eisenhower, *The Bitter Woods*.
34. NAMS, ETHINT 15, p.22.
35. Kraemer, NAMS, A-924, p. 52.
36. *Dienstaltersliste der Schutzstaffel der NSDAP. Stand vom 1. Dezember 1938 (Berlin, 1938), p. 441; Führerlist der LSSAH*, November 20, 1936, T-354/201/3861602–5; Charles Whiting, *Massacre at Malmedy*, pp. 16–19.
37. *Congressional Record*, 81st Cong., 1st sess., 1949, 95, pt. 11: 145123. George Stein, *The Waffen-SS*. pp. 375–76; Roger J. Bender and Hugh P. Taylor, *Uniforms, Organization and History of the Waffen-SS*, 4 vols. (Mountain View, Calif.: James Bender Publishing, 1971), 2: 67.
38. Eisenhower's discussion of Peiper's preparations is based on the latter's postwar statements while in American captivity. Eisenhower, *Bitter Woods*, pp. 218–19.
39. Ibid., pp. 219–20; Cole, *The Ardennes*, pp. 260–61.
40. *Congressional Record*, 81st Cong., 1st sess., 1949, 95, pt. 11: 145123; Eisenhower, *Bitter Woods*, p. 220.
41. *Congressional Record*, 81st Cong., 1st sess., 1949, 95, pt. 11: 145123; Cole, *The Ardennes*, p. 261.
42. For an account favorable to Peiper, see Dietrich Ziemssen, *The Malmedy Trial*, pp. 16–17. SS-Obersturmführer Dietrich Ziemssen was Leibstandarte's divisional chief of staff at the end of the war. A more recent but equally tendentious account is to be found in Lothar Greil, *Die Wahrheit über Malmedy* (Munich, 1958), pp. 11–18.
43. The name of such an officer appears in *Dienstaltersliste der Schutzstaffel der NSDAP. Stand vom 1. Dezember 1938* (Berlin, 1938), p. 444.
44. See U.S. Senate Committee on Armed Forces, *Malmedy Massacre Investigation Hearings* (Washiangton, D.C., 1949), p. 1199. The complete trial transcript is available at the U.S. National Archives.
45. U.S. Senate Committee, *Malmedy Massacre*, p. 1199; Cole, *The Ardennes*, p. 261.
46. See statements of Kenneth F. Ahrens and Virgil P. Lary, in U.S. Senate Committee, *Malmedy Massacre*, pp. 102–12, 1030–31, 1041.
47. Ibid., p. 417; Cole, *The Ardennes*, p. 262.

48. Ziemssen, *Malmedy Trial*, pp. 16–17; U.S. Senate Committee, *Malmedy Massacre*, pp. 1033–34.

49. Nobecourt, *Hitler's Last Gamble*, p. 126.

50. Cole, *The Ardennes*, p. 262. When apprised of reports of the incident, Dietrich ordered Kraemer to conduct an investigation which, he later claimed, produced no evidence of a massacre. NAMS, ETHINT 15, p. 26.

51. *Congressional Record*, 81st Cong. 1st sess., 1949, 95, pt. 11: 145123; Eisenhower, *Bitter Woods*, p. 271.

52. See U.S. Senate Committee, *Malmedy Massacre*, pp. 1199 ff; affidavit of Father Louis Blokian, ibid., pp. 401–2; testimony of Lt. Col. John S. Dwinell, ibid., p. 435.

53. George Stein, *The Waffen-SS*, p. 133.

54. *Hitlers Lagebesprechungen*, p. 460n1. *The Trial of German Major War Criminals*, 22: 352. Bohuslav Etcher, *The Lessons of the Kharkov Trial* (London, 1944), p. 6, gives thirty thousand as the total figure of those slaughtered at Kharkov.

55. *Kriegstagebuch Nr. 5, Generalkommando I. SS-Panzer-Korps*, entries for March 27–April 6, 1943, T-354/603/000003–5.

56. This statement is based on an examination of *SS-Leithefte* and other ideological literature.

57. See Cole, *The Ardennes*, pp. 368–77.

58. Basil Lidell-Hart, *The Other Side of the Hill* (London: Cassell, 1948), p. 360; Warlimont, *Hitler's Headquarters*, p. 490.

59. Kraemer, NAMS, A-924, pp. 51–54.

60. Ibid.

61. Robert S. Allen, *Lucky Forward: The History of Patton's Third U.S. Army* (New York Vanguard Press, 1947), p. 246.

62. NAMS, ETHINT 15, p. 20; Cole, *The Ardennes*, pp. 623 ff.

63. KTB/OKW IV, 1353.

64. Kraemer, NAMS, A-924, p. 56.

65. Ibid., p. 57; NAMS, ETHINT 15, p. 27.

66. See, for example, Eisenhower, *Bitter Woods*, p. 144; Robert E. Merriam, *The Battle of the Bulge* (New York: Ballantine, n.d.), pp. 17–18 (originally published by Ziff Davis in 1947 as *Dark December*).

67. Rundstedt judged Dietrich to be "decent but stupid." Milton Shulman, *Defeat in the West*, p. 104.

68. Günther Reichhelm, "Commentary on Kraemer's Report of Oct. 1945, Commitment of the Sixth Pz. Army in the Ardennes 1944/45 (MS A-924)," NAMS, B-676, pp. 4, 6–7.

69. *Hitlers Lagebesprechungen*, pp. 781–82.

70. Alfred Philippi and Ferdinand Heim, *Der Feldzug gegen Sowjetrussland*, p. 274.

12 THE LAST ACT

1. Earl F. Ziemke, *Stalingrad to Berlin*, pp. 416–17.

2. Heinz Guderian, *Erinnerungen eines Soldaten*, p. 352.

3. *KTB/OKW* IV, 1354; cf. "Oberkommando SS-Pz. AOK 6 an Gen. Kdo. I. SS Pz. Korps, Gen. Kdo. II. SS Pz. Korps," January 21, 1945 (National Archives photostatic copy).

4. Ziemke, *Stalingrad to Berlin*, p. 422; Guderian, *Erinnerungen*, p. 357.

5. Kraemer, NAMS, A-924, pp. 56–57; An Interview with Obstgrf. "Sepp" Dietrich. NAMS, ETHINT 15, p. 22; *KTB/OKW* IV, 1358–59.

6. Guderian, *Erinnerungen*, p. 375.

7. *Dienstaltersliste der Schutzstaffel der NSDAP. Stand vom 1. Dezember 1938* (Berlin, 1938), p. 437; *Dienstaltersliste der Schutzstaffel der NSDAP. SS-Oberst-Gruppenführer— SS-Standartenführer, Stand vom 9. November 1944* (Berlin, 1944), p. 23; Otto Kumm, "Gefechstberichte aus der Zeit vom 6.6.44–8.5.45," NAMS, B-168, p. 1.

8. Ziemke, *Stalingrad to Berlin*, p. 448.

9. *KTB/OKW* IV, 1104.

10. Ibid., p. 1125; Ziemke, *Stalingrad to Berlin*, pp. 448–49; "Fernschreiben der 6. SS-Panzer Armee von 3.3 1945 an SS-Gruppenführer Fegelein" (U.S. National Archives photostatic opy).

11. Eddy Bauer, *Der Panzerkrieg*, 2:277; Alfred Philippi and Ferdinand Heim, *Der Feldzug gegen Sowjetrussland*, p. 282; Ziemke, *Stalingrad to Berlin*, p. 450.

12. *KTB/OKW* IV, 1148; Bauer, *Panzerkrieg*, 2:278.

13. Erich Kern, *Die letzte Schlacht—Ungarn 1944–45*, p. 244.

14. *KTB/OKW* IV, 1171; Bauer, *Panzerkrieg*, 2:278.

15. *KTB/OKW* IV, 1179; Philippi and Heim, *Der Feldzug*, p. 282; Ziemke, *Stalingrad to Berlin*, p. 452.

16. Ziemke, *Stalingrad to Berlin*, pp. 454–55.

17. *Hitlers Lagebesprechungen*, p. 926.

18. Guderian, *Erinnerungen*, p. 381; *Hitlers Lagebesprechungen*, p. 907n1; Milton Shulman, *Defeat in the West*, p. 316.

19. Shulman *Defeat in the West*, pp. 316–17.

20. Kern, *Die letzte Schlacht*, p. 289.

21. *KTB/OKW* IV, 1212.

22. Ibid., p. 1222.

23. Ibid., pp. 1227–38; Philippe and Heim, *Der Feldzug*, p. 288.

24. K. G. Klietmann, *Die Waffen-SS, eine Dokumentation*, p. 55.

25. Ziemke, *Stalingrad to Berlin*, p. 456; Philippi and Heim, *Der Feldzug*, p. 288; George Patton, *War as I Knew It* (Boston: Houghton Mifflin, 1947), p. 318.

26. *KTB/OKW* IV, 1441–42; Klietmann, *Die Waffen-SS*, p. 96.

27. *Dienstaltersliste der Schutzstaffel der NSDAP. SS-Oberst-Gruppenführer—SS-Standartenführer, Stand vom 9. November 1944* (Berlin, 1944), p. 21; see "Ustuf. Schultz an LSSAH Stab," June 25, 1936, T-354/220/3887042.

28. Wilhelm Willemer, "The German Defense of Berlin," NAMS, P-136, p. 58.

29. Ibid., p. 45.

30. Ibid., p. 21; Erich Kuby, *The Russians and Berlin, 1945*, p. 123; Vasili I. Chuikov, *The Fall of Berlin* (New York: Holt, Rinehart & Winston, 1968), pp. 204 ff.

31. Andrew Tully, *Berlin: Story of a Battle* (New York: Simon & Schuster, 1963), p. 273; Kuby, *The Russians and Berlin*, p. 200.

32. Philippi and Heim, *Der Feldzug*, p. 288; cf. Marlis Steinert, *Capitulation 1945: The Story of the Dönitz Regime*, trans. Richard Barry (London: Constable, 1969), pp. 176, 180.

13 TOWARD A HISTORICAL PERSPECTIVE

1. Robert G. L. Waite, *Vanguard of Nazism: The Free Corps Movement in Postwar Germany 1918-1923* (New York: Norton, 1969), pp. 23–27.

2. Klemens von Klemperer, *Germany's New Conservatism: Its History and Dilemma in the Twentieth Century* (Princeton, 1957), p. 183. Reprinted by permission of Princeton University Press.

3. Joachim C. Fest, *The Face of the Third Reich*, trans. Michael Bullock (New York, 1970), pp. 142–43. Reprinted by permission of Pantheon Books, a division of Random House, Inc.

4. Heinz Höhne, *Der Orden unter dem Totenkopf*, p. 31.

5. Hans Klöcker, "Künstler und Soldat," *SS-Leitheft 9* (January 1943), 11.

SELECTED BIBLIOGRAPHY

UNPUBLISHED RECORDS, STUDIES, AND INTERVIEWS

Berlin Document Center, SS Biographical Records, Dietrich File.

U.S. National Archives Foreign Military Studies Collection. Manuscript No. A-924. Fritz Kraemer. "Commitment of 6 Panzer Army."

U.S. National Archives Foreign Military Studies Collection. Manuscript No. B-168. Otto Kumm. "Gefechtsberichte aus der Zeit vom 6.6.44–8.5.45."

U.S. National Archives Foreign Military Studies Collection. Manuscript No. B-577. Rudolf Lehmann. "Ardennes."

U.S. National Archives Foreign Military Studies Collection. Manuscript No. B-676. Gunther Reichhelm. "Commentary on Kraemer's Report of Oct. 1945, 'Commitment of the Sixth Pz. Army in the Ardennes 1944/45' (MS #A-924)."

U.S. National Archives Foreign Military Studies Collection. Manuscript No. B-779. Rudolf Lehmann. "The I. SS Panzer Corps during the Ardennes Offensive."

U.S. National Archives Foreign Military Studies Collection. Manuscript No. C-024. Fritz Kraemer. "I. SS Panzer Corps in the West in 1944."

U.S. National Archives Foreign Military Studies Collection. Manuscript No. ETHINT 15. An Interview with Obstgrf. "Sepp" Dietrich.

U.S. National Archives Foreign Military Studies Collection. Manuscript No. ETHINT 16. An Interview with Obstgrf. "Sepp" Dietrich, 10 July 1945.

U.S. National Archives Foreign Military Studies Collection. Manuscript No. ETHINT 21. An Interview with Genmaj. (W-SS) Fritz Kraemer, 14–15 August 1945.

U.S. National Archives Foreign Military Studies Collection.

Manuscript No. ETHINT 24. Interview with Fritz Kraemer, CoS, I. SS Pz. Korps.

U.S. National Archives Foreign Military Studies Collection. Manuscript No. P-136. Wilhelm Willemer. ''The German Defense of Berlin.''

U.S. National Archives Microfilm Publication. Microcopy No. T-78. Records of Headquarters, German Army High Command *(Oberkommando des Heeres)*.

U.S. National Archives Microfilm Publication. Microcopy No. T-175. Records of the Reich Leader of the SS and Chief of the German Police.

U.S. National Archives Microfilm Publication. Microcopy No. T-311. Records of German Field Commands—Army Groups.

U.S. National Archives Microfilm Publication. Microcopy No. T-312. Records of German Field Commands—Armies.

U.S. National Archives Microfilm Publication. Microcopy No. T-313. Records of German Field Commands—Panzer Armies.

U.S. National Archives Microfilm Publication. Microcopy No. T-314, Records of German Field Commands—Corps.

U.S. National Archives Microfilm Publication. Microcopy No. T-315. Records of German Field Commands—Divisions.

U.S. National Archives Microfilm Publication. Microcopy No. T-354. Miscellaneous SS Records: Einwandererzentralstelle, Waffen-SS, and SS-Oberabschnitte.

U.S. National Archives Microfilm Publication. Microcopy No. T-611. Non-Biographic Material Filmed at the Berlin Document Center by the University of Nebraska.

BOOKS AND ARTICLES

Bauer, Eddy. *Der Panzerkrieg: Die wichtigsten Panzeroperationen des zweiten Weltkrieges in Europa und Afrika.* 2 vols. Bonn: Verlag Offene Worte, 1965.

Bekker, Cajus. *The Luftwaffe War Diaries.* Translated by Frank Ziegler. London: Macdonald & Co., 1967.

Belfield, E., and Essame. H. *The Battle for Normandy.* Philadelphia: Dufour, 1965.

Blumenson, Martin. *Breakout and Pursuit.* United States Army in World War II. The European Theater of Operations, no. 6. Washington, D.C.: Department of the Army, 1961.

Buchheim, Hans. "Die SS in der Verfassung des Dritten Reiches." *Vierteljahrshefte für Zeitgeschichte* 3 (April 1955), 127–57.

Buchheim, Hans. et al. *Anatomie des SS Staates.* 2 vols. Munich: Deutscher Taschenbuch Verlag, 1967.

Bullock, Alan. *Hitler: A Study in Tyranny.* New York: Harper Torchbook. 1964.

Butler, James R. M. *Grand Strategy.* 6 vols. History of the Second World War. United Kingdom Military Series. London: H. M. Stationery Office, 1957.

Cole, Hugh M. *The Ardennes: Battle of the Bulge.* United States Army in World War II. The European Theater of Operations, no. 8. Washington, D.C.: Department of the Army, 1965.

Deakin, F. W. *The Brutal Friendship: Mussolini, Hitler and the Fall of Italian Fascism.* New York: Harper & Row, 1962.

Eisenhower, John. *The Bitter Woods.* New York: Putnam, 1969.

Ellis, Lionel F. *Victory in the West.* Vol. 1, *The Battle of Normandy.* History of the Second World War. United Kingdom Military Series. London: H. M. Stationery Office, 1962.

——. *The War in France and Flanders, 1939–1940.* History of the Second World War. United Kingdom Military Series. London: H. M. Stationery Office, 1962.

The Goebbels Diaries, 1942–1943. Edited and translated by Louis Lochner. Garden City: Doubleday, 1948.

Guderian, Heinz. *Erinnerungen eines Soldaten.* Heidelberg: Kurt Vowinckel, 1951.

Hassell, Ulrich von. *Vom Andern Deutschland.* Frankfurt am Main: Fischer Bücherei, 1964.

Hausser, Paul. *Soldaten wie andere auch.* Osnabrück: Munin Verlag, 1966.

——. *Waffen-SS im Einsatz.* Göttingen: Plesse Verlag, 1953.

Hayn, Friedrich. *Die Invasion. Von Cotentin bis Falaise.* Die Wehrmacht im Kampf, no. 2. Heidelberg: Kurt Vowinckel, 1954.

Heinrici, Gotthard, and Hauck, Friedrich. "Zitadelle (II)." *Wehrwissenschaftliche Rundschau* 15 (September 1965), 529-44.

Hepp, Leo. "Die 12. Armee im Balkanfeldzug 1941." *Wehrwissenschaftliche Rundschau* 5 (May 1955), 199-216.

Hitlers Lagebesprechungen: Die Protokollfragmente seiner militärischen Konferenzen, 1942-1945. Edited by Helmut Heiber. Stuttgart: Deutsche Verlags-Anstalt, 1962.

Hitler's Secret Conversations, 1941–1944. Translated by Norman Cameron and R. H. Stevens. New York: New American Library, Signet Books. 1961.

Höhne, Heinz. *Der Orden unter dem Totenkopf. Die Geschichte der SS.* Gütersloh: Sigbert Mohn Verlag, 1967.

Jacobsen, Hans-Adolf, ed. *Dokumente zum Westfeldzug, 1940.* Göttingen: Musterschmidt Verlag, 1960.

———. *Der Zweite Weltkrieg: Grundzüge der Politik und Strategie in Dokumenten.* Frankfurt am Main: Fischer Bücherei, 1965.

Keitel, Wilhelm. *The Memoirs of Field-Marshal Keitel.* Translated by David Irving. New York: Stein and Day, 1966.

Kern, Erich. *Die letzte Schlacht-Ungarn 1944-45.* Göttingen: Verlag K. W. Schütz, 1960.

Klietmann, K. G. *Die Waffen-SS, eine Dokumentation.* Osnabrück: Verlag "Der Freiwillige," 1965.

Kramarz, Joachim. *Stauffenberg, The Architect of the Famous July 20th Conspiracy to Assassinate Hitler.* Translated by R. H. Barry. New York: Macmillan, 1967.

Kriegstagebuch des Oberkommandos der Wehrmacht (Wehrmachtführungsstab), 1940–1945. 5 vols. Edited by Hans-Adolf Jacobsen, et al. Frankfurt am Main: Bernard & Graefe Verlag für Wehrwesen, 1961-63.

Kuby, Erich. *The Russians and Berlin, 1945.* London: Heinemann, 1968.

Kumm, Otto. "Die Dritte Schlacht um Charkow." *Der Freiwillige* 14 (May 1968).

Long, Gavin. *Greece, Crete and Syria.* Canberra: Australian War Memorial, 1962.

MacDonald, Charles B. *The Siegfried Line Campaign.* United States Army in World War II. The European Theater of Operations, no. 7. Washington, D.C.: Department of the Army, 1963.

Mackensen, Eberhard von. *Vom Bug zum Kaukasus.* Die

Wehrmacht im Kampf, no. 47. Neckargemund: Kurt Vo-winckel Verlag, 1967.

Maier, Hedwig. "Die SS und der 20. Juli 1944." *Vierteljahrshefte für Zeitgeschichte* 14 (July 1966), 299–316.

Manstein, Eric von. *Verlorne Siege*. Bonn: Athenäum, 1955.

Manvell, Roger, and Fraenkel, Heinrich. *Himmler*. New York: G. P. Putnam's Sons, 1965.

Mau, Hermann. "Die Zweite Revolution—Der 30. Juni 1934." *Vierteljahrshefte für Zeitgeschichte* 2 (January 1953), 119–23.

Mellenthin, F. W. von. *Panzer Battles*. Norman: University of Oklahoma Press, 1956.

Meyer, Kurt. *Grenadiere*. Munich: Schild Verlag, 1957.

Nobécourt, Jacques. *Hitler's Last Gamble: The Battle of the Bulge*. New York: Schocken Books, 1967.

O'Neill, Robert J. *The German Army and the Nazi Party, 1933–1939*. New York: James H. Heinemann, 1966.

Papagos, Alexander. *The Battle of Greece, 1940–1941*. Athens: The Hellenic Publishing Co., 1949.

Philippi, Alfred, and Heim, Ferdinand. *Der Feldzug gegen Sowjetrussland*. Stuttgart: W. Kohlhammer Verlag, 1962.

Playfair, Ian S. O. *The Mediterranean and Middle East*. 4 vols. History of the Second World War, United Kingdom Military Series. London: H. M. Stationery Office, 1956.

Reichsführer! . . . Briefe an und von Himmler. Edited by Helmut Heiber. Stuttgart: Deutsche Verlag-Anstalt, 1968.

Rintelen, Enno von. *Mussolini als Bundgenosse: Erinnerungen des deutschen Militärattaches in Rom, 1936–1943*. Tübingen: R. Wunderlich, 1951.

Schmidt, Paul Karl [Paul Carell]. *Hitler Moves East, 1941-1943*. Boston: Little, Brown, 1965.

——— .*Invasion—They're Coming!* New York: Bantam, 1964.

——— .*Scorched Earth. The Russian-German War, 1943-1944*. Translated by Ewald Osers. Boston: Little, Brown, 1970.

Schramm-von Thadden, Ehrengard. *Griechenland und die Grossmächte im zweiten Weltkrieg*. Wiesbaden: Franz Steiner Verlag, 1955.

Shepperd, Gilbert A. *The Italian Campaign, 1943–45*. London: Barker, 1968.

Shulman, Milton. *Defeat in the West*. New York: E. P. Dutton, 1948.

Speer, Albert. *Inside the Third Reich*. Translated by Richard and Clara Winston. New York: Macmillan, 1970.

Speidel, Hans, *Invasion 1944*. Chicago: Regnery, 1950.

Stein, George. *The Waffen SS. Hitler's Elite Guard at War, 1939–1945*. Ithaca: Syracuse University Press, 1966.

Taylor, Telford. *The March of Conquest: The German Victories in Western Europe, 1940*. New York: Simon and Schuster, 1958.

Tippelskirch, Kurt von. "Der Deutsche Balkanfeldzug 1941." *Wehrwissenschaftliche Rundschau* 5 (February 1955), 49–56.

The Trial of German Major War Criminals: Proceedings of the International Military Tribunal Sitting at Nuremberg, Germany. 23 vols. London: H. M. Stationery Office. 1949–55.

United States Senate Committee on Armed Forces. *Malmedy Massacre Investigation Hearings, 1949*. Washington, D.C.: U.S. Government Printing Office, 1949.

Vormann, Nikolaus von. *Der Feldzug 1939 in Polen; die Operationen des Heeres*. Weissenburg: Prinz Eugen Verlag, 1958.

Warlimont, Walter. *Inside Hitler's Headquarters 1939–1945*. Translated by R. H. Barry. New York: Praeger, 1964.

Weidinger, Otto. *Division Das Reich. Der Weg der 2. SS-Panzer-Division "Das Reich."* 3 vols. Osnabrück: Munin Verlag, 1967–73.

——— . *Kameraden bis zum Ende*. Göttingen: Plesse Verlag, 1962.

Weingartner, James J. "Sepp Dietrich, Heinrich Himmler, and the Leibstandarte SS Adolf Hitler, 1933–1938." *Central European History* 1 (September 1968), 264–84.

——— . "The SS Race and Settlement Main Office: Toward an *Orden* of Blood and Soil." *The Historian* 33 (November 1971), 62–77.

Whiting, Charles. *Massacre at Malmedy*. New York: Stein and Day, 1971.

Wilmot, Chester. *The Struggle for Europe*. New York: Harper & Row, 1952.

Ziemke, Earl F. *Stalingrad to Berlin: The German Defeat in the East*. Army Historical Series. Washington, D.C.: Office of the Chief of Military History, U.S. Army, 1968.

Ziemssen, Dietrich, *The Malmedy Trial*. Munich: Joseph Deschler, 1952.

Zimmerman, Bodo. *OB West. A Study in Command*, 3 vols. Department of the Army, German Report Series. Allendorf, Germany, 1946.

INDEX